*For Roshan, the light of our lives*

'We are here, because you were there.'
Ambalavaner Sivanandan

PART ONE
BENGAL

# Prologue

Chompa wrinkled her nose as her mother ran the wooden comb firmly through her ever-knotted mass of hair, and dipped her toes into the river to distract herself. Ammi teased at a particularly large knot, and Chompa let out a little grumbling snort.

'If you looked after it, Chompa, we would not have to do this every morning.'

But her hands became gentler while the comb and pins hovered like hummingbirds.

Eventually, Ammi rested her chin upon her daughter's head, and they gazed into the river at each other's faces, one propped on top of the other. The sounds of the jungle became muted around them, and the water stilled, as if the world was holding its breath. It was Chompa's favourite moment of the daily ritual.

It wouldn't last, of course. Soon everything would spring

back to busy life, and her hair would quickly follow. It was wild, stubborn, and twice the thickness of any other girl's hair in the village. It was why, Chompa thought, the village children disliked her so much.

That and the fact that she and her mother were witches.

# Chapter One

O r rather Ammi was a witch. Chompa was *trying* to be one.

Chompa had always known she could do magic. She knew she could move and transform things, little things, if she focused hard enough and channelled that focus through her index finger. But whenever she raised that finger to show her mother what she could do, Ammi would fold her hand round her daughter's and gently forbid it.

'You mustn't, Chompa. It's dangerous, and it's not real power,' she would say, pushing Chompa's book towards her. 'Please, learn your Farsi letters so you can help me write these charms.'

Letters. Why did she have to learn them when her finger-magic was so much faster, so much stronger? But Ammi insisted; and it was Ammi's writing-magic that put food on their table. And so Chompa sat in the shade of the mango tree, grimacing and grunting as she bent over her book to make sense of the words in front of her.

On the left were the neat blocks of Bangla, all hanging from straight lines, with little curved tails underneath, and umbrella loops over them. Their meaning came clear and fast to her.

On the other side of the page, though, was the slanting, looping lace of Farsi. It flowed like the river they lived by, carrying the meaning of the letters away from her before she could catch it.

She blew air from her cheeks in frustration.

'You just need patience, Chompa. It will come,' Ammi called from the cooking hut. 'Just as I need patience with this stove forever going out!'

Chompa heard Ammi click her teeth in frustration, smelled the bitter smoke of burning straw as her mother relit the fire.

Chompa crossed her arms. 'Why do we have to use Farsi to do writing-magic, anyway? Why can't we just use Bangla? No one even speaks Farsi here. No one speaks Farsi for about a thousand miles! It doesn't make any sense.'

Ammi laughed as she came back out of the hut with a brass bowl tucked in the crook of her arm. She placed a palm upon her daughter's head, smoothing the wild hairs down.

'Seven ancient languages alone have the power to speak with djinn. You know that. Farsi is the closest one we have, and people did use to speak it here, centuries ago. You could try one of the others? Let me see, there's Kikuyu, Ge'ez, Hebrew, Middle Chinese, Norse, and Ancient Egyptian. But the grammar formation of Ancient Egyptian is a bit tricky, and the Elder Futhark characters in Norse have multiple meanings, so they take years to even begin to interpret correctly.'

Chompa's head swam. She sighed. Farsi it was.

'I don't think I'll ever get the hang of it,' she grumbled, staring down miserably at the page.

Ammi stroked her daughter's shoulder. 'Achaa, achaa, not today, then. What about your English studies?'

Chompa scrunched up her nose as if there was a bad smell. Every day, Ammi would go on at her: Farsi, English, Farsi, English. If anything, English was even worse. It didn't even make any sense. And it sounded horrible.

'No one speaks it in the village, so why do I? What's the point?' Chompa sighed. 'I know, I know, we're *different*. "Each of the five fingers of a hand is not identical".' Chompa waggled her fingers and rolled her eyes.

Ammi laughed. 'Clearly I have to come up with some new sayings. Fine. Make yourself useful and peel these onions.'

Chompa took the bowl filled with little pearl and purple-coloured bulbs from her mother. Ammi padded back to the cooking hut, a rickety bundle of bamboo sticks with a straw-thatched roof that was attached to their main room by a roughly cut doorway in the clay wall. A soft hiss came from inside as she threw spices into the hot pan to temper. The green scent of cardamom mingled with the warmth of cinnamon and bay, all wrapped in the buttery scent of frying ghee. Chompa's jaw ached with the anticipation of her favourite smell: the sweet, mellow scent of the onions frying with slivers of garlic.

She kept peeling and staring out beyond the courtyard,

towards the river, edged by swaying fronds of rice paddy, wondering, as she always did, what marvels might lie at its end: in Dacca, the great city. But that was something Ammi never liked to talk about.

The sound of a cough made her swivel her head back to the tangle of forest that stood like a dark wall between their home and the village.

A small, thin woman with silver hoops in her ears was standing there. Jamila, Chompa thought her name was. She twisted the loose end of her ragged sari between her fingers, like a protective charm.

'Is your mother home?' she mumbled into her sari veil.

Chompa couldn't count the number of times she'd heard that question. Always mumbled in an attempt to conceal the desperation beneath. She nodded and got to her feet, padding over to the cooking hut.

'Ammi. Someone.'

That was all she needed to say for her mother to wipe her hands on her sari end and get to her feet, because no one came to see them – ever – unless they needed magic. Not for tea, not for gossip. Just magic.

As Ammi came back into the room, Chompa seized her chance.

'Let me help her, Ammi. Your charms take so long, but my finger-magic could change things straight away –'

Her mother pushed Chompa's hand down hard, her eyes serious and her voice firm. 'No, Chompa. Be a good daughter – make some tea and bring it through. You may stay and watch, and learn.'

Ears burning with indignation, Chompa stirred the tea to urge it on, the dark leaves swirling in the pale milk. Her finger twitched. Magic never worked with tea, Ammi said, because it was too subtle an art, though Chompa was sorely tempted to try.

All of a sudden, the little bubbles swelled into a thick cinnamon foam. She sploshed the tea into two tin cups, slammed them on to a tray, and hurried back into the main hut.

Jamila was weeping quietly, perched on their bed next to Ammi. She narrowed her eyes at Chompa.

Ammi waved a hand at her daughter. 'Sister, do not worry. My daughter has no magic. She will tell no one of our meeting. You've come for my help, and only I will help you.'

Chompa darted a scowl at her mother as she settled herself down in the corner.

'Achaa, sister, tell me: what's the matter?' Ammi asked in a low, warm voice, placing her palm gently upon Jamila's wrist.

Jamila shook off Ammi's hand as if it had burned her. Chompa hissed inwardly, but, as if nothing had happened, Ammi pushed the tin cup towards Jamila. 'Drink, and be calm.'

The woman hesitated, then picked her cup up, sipped tentatively at first, and then gulped, as if it was cool lime water, and she'd been walking in the summer sun for days. Chompa's rage deflated a little as she wondered when Jamila had last tasted sugar.

Finally, Jamila lowered the mug, her shoulders slumping.

'My husband . . . if he knew I was here . . .'

Ammi nodded lightly. 'I won't tell, sister.'

Jamila clutched her empty mug. 'We – we're running out of food. Last season, we were persuaded to turn our rice fields over to indigo – but I fear we were tricked. Men came to harvest the crops, but we've been paid nothing. We cannot buy food, and we cannot eat indigo. Now my husband wants to switch back to rice, but nothing at all will grow in our soil.'

Ammi opened her tattered spellbook and flicked through the pages. Then she reached for a small silver box. From it, she removed a tiny scroll of fine cream paper and her silver rule, quill, and inkwell. Using the rule, she drew a rectangle, and then a diamond shape within it. She murmured questions to Jamila about the placement of the fields and the birthdates of her family, and, as Jamila responded, Ammi wrote on various parts of the diagram in tiny, looping Farsi script.

Chompa's brain fizzed with questions. She knew some of the characters, but couldn't decipher the meaning of the words yet. She wondered what the shapes meant, why they were placed exactly so. Why had Ammi drawn a rectangle and a diamond where sometimes she drew circles, or eyes, or palms? Chompa knew she had to learn her Farsi before Ammi would explain. If only it wasn't so boring, so hard, so slow.

Ammi finished the tiny diagram, sliced the rectangle out of the paper carefully with a sharp sliver of a knife and began to roll the paper between her finger and thumb. Then she reached into the box again and took out a cylindrical silver locket the size of Chompa's finger joint. A taviz. Crafted by Ammi's own hands.

Ammi snapped it open, tucked the little scroll into it. Then she closed it again and handed the capsule to Jamila.

'Sister, you need to make a hole in the earth in the field and place this taviz by the indigo roots. Can you do this?'

Jamila nodded.

'It will take a season. After monsoon. Have faith.'

Chompa gasped. A season! That would be one hundred and fifty whole days! Chompa's magic was so quick – and here Ammi was, asking a starving family to wait an age when Chompa knew she could help them straight away. Why had Ammi lied about her magic? She seethed and bristled.

Jamila pushed a bundle of coins towards Ammi, but Ammi pushed them gently back. 'Sister, I could teach you letters if you like, and then you could write the charms yourself? No charge,' she said, waving a hand at the silver box and pen.

Jamila frowned, shook her head once, and then darted from the house like a fleeing mongoose.

Chompa rounded on her mother. 'Ammi! How could you? You told her I didn't have magic, but I could have helped! My finger-magic is so much faster than your charms – you know it is! Jamila will have to wait a whole season! They could die! I could do something much quicker –'

Ammi grabbed Chompa's wrist so hard that Chompa gasped.

'You mustn't, Chompa. Whatever happens, you mustn't use your finger-magic. Promise me.' She spoke in a hoarse whisper.

Chompa's rage wavered. 'Why? Why can't I use it?' she asked uncertainly.

Ammi's grip tightened. 'Promise.'

Chompa was almost frightened for a moment. She nodded.

Ammi released Chompa's wrist and rose. She turned away, and Chompa felt the rage surge again.

'You didn't answer me! Why mustn't I use it?'

'You're not ready,' Ammi said softly.

It was the answer she always gave, and it wasn't enough any more.

Chompa scrambled to her feet. 'When will I be ready? When?'

Ammi didn't reply.

Chompa raised her finger in one sharp movement. Ammi's spellbook flew into the air and swirled round the room before slamming to the floor at Ammi's feet.

Ammi swung round at the sound, her eyes flashing with anger.

'Chompa, the magic at your fingers is too quick and easy, and that makes it dangerous. And finger-magic always leaves a trace, and always comes with a price. I fear what that price might be.'

She picked up the spellbook and carefully dusted off its edges as she spoke. 'Writing-magic is powerful in a way you cannot appreciate now, but you will. It's careful, thoughtful. It requires us to consider what is needed, and why: and ultimately it doesn't change things; it only asks for them to be changed for us. Jamila will plant that taviz, and next season the crops will not fail, and her children will not starve. That's what we're here to do. To listen, ask, and wait.'

'I don't want to wait! I don't have to! How do I even know that what you're saying is true? Maybe you're just scared that my power's stronger than yours! You don't even know what I could do if I put my mind to it!'

Ammi looked surprised for a moment, and then tired.

'Chompa, I've asked you before to trust me, and be patient. Now, please – I have much to do. Either return to your studies or go outside and play.'

Chompa stomped sullenly out of the house, turning her resentments over in her mind. Ammi didn't have any faith in her magic. The little things Chompa had done before were silly – making leaves into butterflies, summoning ripe guavas from the highest branches down into her palm. But if she did something useful, something *big*, then Ammi would see for herself.

The cooking hut door was ajar. There was the feeble flame – already going out again. They had to spend so long gathering straw for the stove. It went out all the time, and there was so much smoke. And now monsoon was coming it would be nothing but trouble.

An idea came rushing to her.

She stepped inside, closing the door behind her quietly.

# Chapter Two

Chompa gazed at the tiny glowing embers, pale little red lights among the black ash. She raised her finger and pointed at them. She wasn't sure what would happen. When she'd done her silly pieces of magic – before Ammi had forbidden her – all she'd had to do was look at something and think hard about what she wanted. Now she wanted the red lights to grow, become stronger, and stay like that forever.

So she kept pointing and urging the red sparks on.

*Grow, grow.*

And they did. The flickers of pale red started to grow brighter, bigger, like flowers blooming in the ashes. Chompa almost gasped with joy, but knew she had to stay focused.

*Grow. Grow.*

Now sparks spread to the coals, turning them to red glowing jewels.

She had done it! The fire would never go out, not even in monsoon!

Chompa turned round to fetch Ammi. But Ammi was already in the doorway, with her eyebrows raised. Getting her daughter into the cooking hut was usually a very difficult business.

'Look, Ammi!' Chompa stuck her hands on her hips and lifted her chin in triumph.

Ammi peered over Chompa's shoulder.

'Chompa, what did you do?' she said, her voice trembling.

'I enchanted the flames! Now they won't ever go out!'

'Get out of the way. *Now!*'

It was then that Chompa noticed the beads of sweat prickling on her skin. She swung round and gasped.

It wasn't just the coals now. The clay stove itself was glowing a pale scarlet, too, and the heat from it was immense. The red light was spreading up the walls of the hut, making it glow like a hurricane lamp. Then the light reached the thatched roof, and in a moment it was alight.

Ammi shoved Chompa out of the hut, and they staggered backwards. And Chompa saw that the red light was spreading further still – across the earth, towards the trees. Towards the village.

Suddenly there was a cry. 'Hai Allah! Badruddin Saheb!'

Chompa's stomach sank as the villagers called for the chief. She could see a cluster of figures standing on the riverbank, pointing towards their cooking hut, now a column of pure, blazing red. Among them, Chompa noticed with a scowl, was Jamila, looking down at her feet.

Ammi grabbed the pail of milk from the side of the hut and threw it at the wooden planks. The glowing wood consumed the liquid, the fire not even dimming for a second.

Chompa shrieked with horror. Ammi stood absolutely still.

'It's enchanted flame. It needs to be cancelled out by a stronger enchantment.'

'But there's no time! We can't get the paper or the quills!'

Ammi's mouth set grimly. 'No, charms won't work. I have to do this. I have to. There isn't another way.' She seemed to be talking to herself more than to Chompa.

And Ammi raised her finger.

Chompa's eyes widened. She'd never seen her mother do finger-magic before, only writing-charms. She didn't even know Ammi *had* the same kind of magic she did, and her heart raced with a confused excitement.

She felt the strangest sensation of heavy, thick coldness on her face, pushing away the heat from the flames. She looked up and saw clouds clustering together above them into a thick, flat blanket.

Ammi's eyes and finger focused on it.

Suddenly heavy rain thundered from the cloud-quilt. Ammi drove the rain harder. Within seconds, Chompa was drenched to the skin, rain in her eyes, her ears, her mouth. She felt like she was drowning.

But the downpour was dimming the light, too. The scarlet flame began to blacken at the edges. Her finger still trained on the cloud, Ammi walked steadily towards the hut, and drove the rain down hard upon it. Chompa saw the glowing lights in the coals shrinking, getting smaller and smaller, until there were just tiny dots blinking out one by one like eyes, and then . . .

And then it was just raining.

Chompa shivered uncontrollably.

Ammi raised her finger again, and the cloud and the rain shrivelled to nothing. The water spilled away from the remains of the hut, darkening the scorched earth beyond.

Chompa's stomach lurched as she surveyed the devastation she'd caused. The hut was gone, burned to nothing, just a few fragments of scorched wood remaining. The dug-out hole in the earth that used to hold the stove was now a pitiful pool of water and mud.

And yet her heart felt full.

Ammi had the same kind of magic as Chompa, after all.

She'd always thought that writing-magic was Ammi's skill, and finger-magic was hers. Every time she'd asked about finger-magic, Ammi had changed the subject, or told her she would explain when Chompa was old enough. And always: '*You mustn't use your magic.*' Mustn't. Mustn't. Mustn't.

Ammi had collapsed on the verandah, her sari sodden, her hair in dripping tendrils. She looked at Chompa, and Chompa was silenced even before she could speak, before she could even demand an explanation.

Ammi was trembling, her eyes heavy with fear.

Then she rose, turned away from her daughter, and walked slowly into the house without uttering a single word.

Chompa finally understood why her mother had stopped her from using finger-magic all this time. The fear in Ammi's eyes said it all.

It wasn't the magic that was dangerous.

It was Chompa.

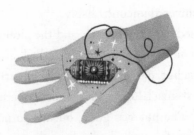

# Chapter Three

The next morning, Chompa woke to find her mother gone from their bed. She heard ringing, clattering sounds, and smelled acrid smoke as waves of hot air billowed in through the window. Chompa went out to the shack next to the riverbank where Ammi did her silverwork.

'Shona! It's ready. Come here – asho, asho.'

There was a small fire burning. The logs glowed white in its intense heat. Ammi was crouched on her haunches, using a small hammer to tap a piece of silver flat. She was pale, but she beckoned eagerly, and Chompa shuffled over, relieved that Ammi seemed to have forgiven her, even if it wasn't deserved. She'd even called her 'shona', her golden one, which she *never* did when Chompa was in trouble.

Ammi worked the softened hot silver deftly, rolling and shaping it into a slender tube. Then she picked up her tongs and plunged the tube into the river. The water hissed like an angry snake, steam rising as it had from the cooking hut.

Ammi pulled the tongs out and turned to a low table, her

back to Chompa. Finally, she wheeled round with a too-bright smile on her face.

'Look – it's your very own!'

There in the centre of her earth-brown palm, criss-crossed with dark lines like paths, lay the little silver locket, just like the one Ammi had given to Jamila, and like Ammi always wore herself. The thread that would tie it round Chompa's wrist or neck lay curved by its side, like a fine purple stream.

'A – a taviz?'

Ammi nodded eagerly. 'Look, I have one too, to match!' She pulled down the folds of the sari covering her collarbone. A silver locket, threaded on purple cotton, danced at her throat. It was new.

Ammi grasped Chompa's wrist. Her brightness faded for a moment. 'You must wear this, shona. Promise me that you'll wear it.'

Chompa chewed her lip as she made out the cream edge of the paper peeking out from the locket. Ammi noticed it, too, and hastily clicked open the taviz and set it right. Chompa raised an eyebrow.

'What is the spell inside for?'

'It's to protect you.'

'From what?'

Ammi's gaze darkened.

'Oh.'

Chompa understood. Ammi had made these charms to shield them both: from Chompa.

Chompa felt a little fire of resistance flickering inside her.

The taviz would stop her from doing any more finger-magic – she knew that. But, after yesterday, perhaps that was for the best. With great effort, she nodded, her heart heavy with resignation. She had no choice but to focus on her letters now.

She lifted her hair from her nape to allow Ammi to loop the thread round it. It felt heavy for such a light, thin piece of cotton thread, and Chompa realized Ammi's hands were shaking.

'Once I've tied this, go and wash in the river. There's a letter I need to write.'

'A letter? Who to?' Chompa couldn't help asking, twisting her head round.

Their world was the two of them: there'd never been anyone else. Chompa's father had died when she was a baby, after a fever had raced through the village. Neither he nor Ammi had any living family. So who could Ammi possibly be writing to?

'A friend,' said Ammi curtly. Then, rubbing her temples, she snapped, 'Arré, Chompa, for once, just do as I say. Stop wriggling. I'm not feeling well.'

Chompa pursed her lips and stared down at the ground. Ammi looked so tired, and Chompa knew it was all her fault.

And then it was done. The taviz was tied.

Ammi exhaled deeply as she drew her hands away. She smoothed Chompa's hair down over her shoulders, her fingers lingering for a moment upon her daughter's cheeks.

They had stopped shaking.

Chompa lay awake, staring at the bright white disc of the moon. She couldn't get used to the feeling of the taviz round her neck, even though it had been three days since Ammi had tied it.

She had been woken by Ammi talking in her sleep – no, pleading in her sleep, hands clenched together – in . . . English. English! Her words were fast, the sounds hard and cold. The only thing she'd been able to make out was her own name: *Chompa, Chompa, Chompa*.

Chompa smoothed her hand across her mother's damp forehead, like Ammi did when Chompa had a fever. It seemed to calm her, and Chompa sat watching her mother's chest rise and dip with her breath, too troubled to sleep.

She tugged at the taviz. With a flicker of guilt, she touched the thread with her finger, and tried to cut it using her magic. But her finger made no mark on the knot.

She sighed, running her hands across the silvery patterns of the trelliswork the moonlight cast upon the quilt. There was a heavy cloak of silence over the world. But, beneath, a myriad of insect and bird and animal lives scurried and flittered and called. Those sounds were as much a part of the landscape as the shadows of the trees and the ever-dancing rice paddy. Chompa lost herself in them for a time, imagining the creatures busy in the darkness.

Then there was a cracking, crunching sound – so wrong that it seemed to rip the landscape.

Chompa held her breath.

*Thud.*

*Crunch.*

*Thud.*

*Crunch.*

The sounds were slow and deliberate, and getting louder. Feet on twigs.

Coming towards them.

*For* them.

Chompa pressed her mouth to her mother's ear. Her heart was thumping, her hands slick with sweat.

'Ammi, someone's out there,' she breathed.

Her mother sat up, straight-backed and now alert. She put a finger to her lips and whispered very softly in Chompa's ear.

'My shona, whatever happens, you must stay hidden. I've asked you to promise before. But now you really must. Promise me that you won't come out once I've hidden you. No matter what. And if – if something happens to me, take my spellbook and study it well. And do not – *do not* remove your taviz unless you're safe, and with someone you can trust.'

Chompa opened her mouth to ask why, but Ammi placed her finger on Chompa's lips.

'Shh – I'm sorry. I should have explained everything before, but there's no time now – just promise.'

Her mother's eyes were wide with terror, and Chompa found she couldn't breathe. She nodded.

Ammi pushed Chompa under the bed. It was a very low frame, and she could barely squeeze beneath it. Ammi pushed boxes and tins after her, concealing her daughter. Chompa watched her silently through a gap in the boxes.

Ammi grabbed the small, bent blade of their kitchen knife.

Then a tall, broad shadow was blocking the door frame and the light. Chompa could see huge, wide feet in shining brown leather boots. Ammi pressed herself flat to the side of the door, clutching the little knife.

As the ribbons that hung in the doorway parted, Ammi sprang, jabbing with the blade.

There was a deep, hacking laugh – a big man's laugh.

As Chompa saw the plate-sized hand in a dark blue sleeve enclose Ammi's wrist and force the knife out, so that it clattered on to the floor, she bit hard on her fist so as not to scream. Ammi scrabbled madly as the man's arms wrapped round her slight body. She was biting, scratching, spitting out words in the same cold language she had spoken in her dreams.

Everything in Chompa wanted to push the boxes away and launch herself at the intruder with her nails, teeth, her fear, and her fury. She couldn't just lie there, in the dark, while her mother was attacked. But she had promised, promised. And the last time she'd broken a promise everything had gone wrong. She had to trust her mother now.

She heard brutal male laughter as her mother was dragged through the door, feet flailing.

'*Ammi! Ammi!*' she mouthed as she leaped from her hiding place towards the door. She crouched behind it and raised her finger. Then she remembered the taviz, that dead silver weight round her neck, and she screamed silently in frustration. She scrabbled at her neck, all the while peering through the ribbons, as her mother was carried further and further from her. Other men, all pale in the moonlight, joined the huge brute in tying Ammi's wrists and ankles, in holding her head down.

Chompa noticed flickering lights in the distant darkness. For a moment she thought help was coming. But then she realized the villagers were holding up their lamps to watch the witch being taken away. Among them, she glimpsed Jamila's frightened face, washed pale by her hurricane lamp. Chompa seethed. Betrayal. *That* was the price for Ammi's help.

Chompa ran after the men and crouched in the paddy by the river. She watched them clamp iron cuffs on Ammi's wrists and drag her on to a dark blue boat bobbing on the water; she watched as it glided across the water, until it turned down the bend in the river and disappeared.

She could barely breathe.

Blackness flooded her vision.

# Chapter Four

She woke in the half-light of dawn.

The events of the night came back to her in a series of awful dark pictures. Chompa raced outside and looked across the river, hoping that something might have stopped the boat on its way. But the broad grey river rippled and flexed lazily, nothing but a few brown ducks bobbing along it in the distance. The villagers had all returned to their beds.

The reality was cold and unrelenting: Ammi was gone, and Chompa didn't know where her mother was, or why she'd been taken, or how to get her back.

And the men! How pale they'd been! Even the lightest-skinned grey-eyed girl in the village still had a hint of yellow cream to her skin. Those men had the pallor of the spiders who lived in the deepest jungle, who'd never seen the sun.

Chompa fell to the soft silt beneath her, sobbing uncontrollably as wave after wave of grief and shock overcame her. Eventually, there was nothing left, her body like a well run dry. She listened to her own shuddering breaths. Calmer, she suddenly felt the presence of something within her, a fine thread that still connected her to Ammi, as fine as the cotton that Ammi had tied round Chompa's neck. Somehow she knew that if her mother was dead it would snap, and she'd know she was alone.

This steeled her. She picked herself up off the sand and turned back towards home.

*Home.*

Her stomach lurched with sickness at the word. It meant nothing without Ammi.

Chompa whispered in the direction of the breeze.

'Hold on, Ammi. Don't give up. Magic or no magic, I'll find you. I promise.'

She packed Ammi's spellbook and bag of coins, the silver box of taviz-making equipment, two sets of salwar kameez, a piece of soap wrapped in wax paper, a blanket, and – after a moment's pause – the comb for her unruly hair. Remembering Ammi's nightmare, and not being able to understand it, she reluctantly picked up her English and Farsi books, too.

Her bag nearly filled, Chompa paused. Her stomach was twisting with pain, and, surprised, she realized she was hungry. She scrabbled around in the cupboards, finding half a packet of sweet biscuits: they would have to sustain her on the journey ahead.

She was so engrossed that she didn't hear someone approaching.

'Hello? Hello?'

Chompa stopped. A man's voice, breathless from running, calling out in a refined accent different from village Bangla. Her hand tugged at her silver taviz automatically. Then she grabbed the stiff jharu, the broom barely more than a bundle of sticks tied together. But it might give her time to run, and it was the only weapon she had.

'Amina, are you there?' Then quieter, to himself, 'Maybe I got it wrong – maybe this isn't the place.'

*Amina.*

He had called her mother's name. Not *witch*, not *hag*, but her name. How did he know her name? What did he want? The fine hairs on Chompa's arms twitched with a thrill of terror, confusion, and curiosity.

And . . . just a touch of hope.

She peeked out through the ribbons.

The man was tall and slim. He dropped his bag to the ground as he fumbled in his pocket for something – spectacles. Putting them on, the man frowned at an envelope. He wore a rumpled green woven kurta. He had scruffy reddish-brown hair, which flopped into his eyes as he read. His eyes matched his kurta: not brown or hazel, or even grey, but a deep, sparkling green.

'This has to be the place . . . Amina?' This man knew her mother. Chompa couldn't let him leave. She gripped the broom firmly in both hands and took a deep breath. She parted the ribbons and crept outside.

The man took a step backwards, eyebrows raised in surprise. He pushed his glasses up the bridge of his nose, blinked at Chompa, and blinked again. Then he gave the

27

tiniest nod. 'Hello? Is this Amina Begum's house?' He spoke gently, as if to a feral cat.

Chompa clutched the broom harder, wary of the smooth, deep voice. It didn't matter if he was handsome or refined: he could still be dangerous.

The man looked around with a frown on his face.

'I received a letter from Amina saying she was in danger. That she needed help. So I came right away. My name is Mohsin. Are you . . . Chompa?'

The letter! This must be the friend Ammi had been writing to! Chompa felt relief surge through her and let the broom clatter to the ground.

Mohsin grinned.

'Jharus are greatly underappreciated as weapons, I find,' he said. Then he frowned and looked around again. 'But where is Amina?'

Chompa's restraint came crashing down. 'You're too late! They took her – those terrible men!' she cried. 'They came in the night and took her! They put her on a boat and sailed away! And I don't know where to start, how to find her again! I can't sit about like this – I need to follow and find her – but I just don't know how!'

She darted back inside to continue packing. She had wasted too much time already. Mohsin followed her.

'Chompa, I'm so sorry – I came as quickly as I could. What happened? What did they look like? Which direction did they go?'

Chompa kept stuffing things into her bag, but looked up quickly. 'Did she mention anything in her letter?

I just don't know where to begin!'

Mohsin shook his head sadly and handed Chompa the envelope he had been holding. Chompa opened it and pulled out the letter. She read slowly, a knot of guilt and despair growing in her stomach with every word.

*My friend,*

*What I feared most has taken place. I had to use finger-magic, and now I don't have many days left before they find me.*

*Please come – the address is on the other side of the envelope – and keep Chompa safe for me. Teach her what I should have a long time ago.*

*I know I don't have the right to ask, after all these years, but you're the only one I can turn to.*

*Amina*

Chompa bit her lip to stop herself from crying as she put the letter back into the envelope with a shaking hand. Carefully, she placed it in her pocket.

'It's my fault. I have to get her back. But – the men . . . their hands were so large, their skin so pale. I've never seen anyone like them! I think they might have been demons. How can I defeat demons?'

Mohsin looked up, excited. 'They were pale?'

She nodded, and Mohsin clapped his hands together.

'Then I think I know something about the men who took your ammi, Chompa. I think they were British.'

# Chapter Five

Chompa blinked.

'British?'

Mohsin took a stick and drew a circle on the ground in front of him. Within it, he sketched out one small shape that looked like an anxious rabbit peering over its shoulder, and then another much larger one, like a proud bull kicking its back legs across the earth.

'Britain is a country thousands of miles away. If this is the world, then Britain is this small shape, while we are this bigger one, with all these countries –' he sketched shapes between the rabbit and the bull – 'and seven seas and thirteen rivers in between, as they say. I'm certain that those pale men you saw come from there, where they're almost all coloured that way. There, they speak English, a language they're wanting to establish here too.'

Chompa clapped her hands together as pieces of a puzzle clicked together in her mind.

'English! I heard Ammi speaking English in her sleep! But

what are they doing here? What do they want with Ammi?'

Mohsin's mouth was set in a grim line. 'For many years, the British have been very interested in the riches that India has to offer – so interested that I'm afraid they have taken many of these riches for themselves, and often by violent means. Jewels, silk, tea, indigo, spices. Already they've stolen so much. And . . .' He hesitated. 'And perhaps this now includes India's magic. There are rumours of traders capturing magical people, and it seems they now know how to trace them, too. That's very worrying.'

Chompa looked at him. 'So . . . so you know that Ammi has magic?'

Mohsin's grave face broke into a warm smile. 'Oh, Chompa – I do indeed know she has magic. A most wise and talented witch.'

Chompa had never heard anyone speak about Ammi that way. She recalled the wary faces of the villagers, the insults she and her mother would hear being spat across the river. She felt a pride and longing for Ammi burn inside her. 'So they've – they've taken her to Britain? Thousands of miles away?'

How would she get there when she hadn't even heard of the place until a few minutes ago?

Mohsin stroked his beard thoughtfully.

'A riverboat would be too small to undertake the journey. No – I would imagine they're taking her to Dacca, to change to a bigger ship there.'

Chompa breathed a sigh of relief. She could get to Dacca! She could still catch up with them if she started out soon. She stood up, suddenly impatient to be on her way.

'I'm sorry, Mohsin Saheb –'

'Uncle – call me Uncle.'

'Uncle –' Chompa's cheeks flushed with awkwardness – 'I – I have to go after that boat. I don't really have time to spare.'

Mohsin blinked. 'What do you mean, *go after that boat*?'

Chompa looked over her shoulder at the river. 'I need to rescue Ammi.'

Mohsin started to pace, agitated. 'But, Chompa – your mother asked me to keep you *safe*. You're suggesting the very opposite! I can't let you follow those men and fall into their clutches, too! No, we should stay here and wait. She may be able to escape.'

Chompa stuck her chin out. 'It was *my* fault they took her. And *I* have to get her back.'

She swung her bag over her shoulder and started to walk away.

'Chompa – *Chompa*. Amina is my oldest childhood friend,' Mohsin spluttered desperately. 'She's entrusted me to look after you.'

'I'm sorry, but you don't understand,' Chompa said as she marched on.

'I understand more than you realize. Please, STOP!' he cried.

Chompa halted, fists bunched in frustration.

'Please, Chompa: just look.'

Mohsin's voice was soft, different to before. Curious, she looked down.

By her feet, there was another rabbit outlined in the earth. She frowned. When had he drawn it?

Then the rabbit raised an ear, and jumped.

Chompa dropped her bag. She swung round to look at Mohsin. He had his index finger raised.

Then she looked behind her once more, at the rabbit. She gasped as it hopped round her feet, and then across the earth, and back to Mohsin. She followed it, until she was standing in front of Mohsin, staring unblinking at his finger.

'Yes, Chompa. Like your mother – and like you, I think – I also have magic.'

He had used magic. Finger-magic.

*Her* magic.

Mohsin was watching her carefully. 'Your ammi asked me to teach you about magic. Does that mean . . . that she hadn't yet started to show you what you can do?'

Chompa pursed her lips, and Mohsin nodded slowly.

'Raw finger-magic is a force of great power. It requires immense control and focus to be wielded without danger. Your ammi favoured the old traditions – writing-magic, the use of charms – for her own practice. I imagine she told you it was safer; am I right? Well, it's true. But I am a scientist, and I've studied magic of all kinds for many years. I've developed methods that help magic people like us to control our powers, but still make change happen in the world. With the right understanding, we can do incredible things. And we must, Chompa. Otherwise, why do we have these gifts?'

Chompa found herself nodding hard. Mohsin was voicing thoughts she herself had had so many times.

'Your mother chose not to use finger-magic because of the risks, but she does have tremendous natural power, as well as her writing-magic skill. That's why those men took her.' His brows creased together in thought.

Chompa's mouth went dry. 'It – it was me. I did the magic.'

Mohsin looked at her. 'You did?'

Chompa stared at her feet, utterly miserable.

'It was all my fault. She forbade me from doing finger-magic, but I did it, anyway. And then the villagers betrayed us because of what I did. That's why I have to find her, to make it right.'

Mohsin walked over to her and kneeled down to look directly into Chompa's eyes.

'It's not your fault. You aren't the first magical child to have experimented with her powers. I did as a child. Amina was the same. You weren't to know this would happen.'

His voice was kind, but Chompa only felt worse. She needed to find Ammi. She was wasting precious time.

Then a flicker of handwriting flashed in her memory. And an idea came to her.

She pulled Ammi's letter from her pocket and tapped the front excitedly.

'The address on this says Dacca College.'

Mohsin blinked in confusion. 'That's right. That's where I live and work.'

'Dacca. Where they're taking Ammi! Let's go!'

She ran to retrieve her bag, then picked up Mohsin's too, bundling it into his arms.

'Go – go where? I don't understand, Chompa.'

'Ammi wanted you to keep me safe. Well, I'm not safe here, not with those traitors right over there. So I'll come and stay with you! You can teach me about our magic, and we can look for Ammi together! In Dacca.'

PART TWO
DACCA

# Chapter Six

She'd asked Ammi about it so many times.

'*Where is Dacca, Ammi? Can we go there?*'

'*For the hundredth time, Chompa, it's far away. It's a big place, and in big places bad things happen.*'

But it sounded so different to the village, which Chompa had never once left, and was so small, and where nothing happened and nothing changed, that Chompa had dreamed of it nevertheless. And now she was here.

She and Mohsin walked down the rickety gangplank and on to the Buriganga River's sandy shore. Mohsin had managed to get them passage on a little fishing boat bringing its catch to the city, and, just five hours later, here they were. Chompa darted a look around for the large, gleaming, dark blue boat that had taken Ammi, heart pounding. Vessels jostled for space, but she could see they were all simple river craft with woven jute canopies.

'Uncle – that boat isn't here!' she cried in dismay.

Mohsin scanned the dock himself, looking crestfallen.

'We came here directly, Chompa; it may be that it's making stops and is still on its way.'

'Well, we'll just have to wait.' Chompa sat down on a rock and fixed her gaze on the river.

'But it could be days before it arrives.'

Chompa set her jaw and crossed her arms. 'I'm not moving until it's here.'

Mohsin gave a sigh, took off his spectacles and cleaned them on his kurta.

'Wait. I have an idea.' He flagged down the fisherman whose boat they had just stepped off. 'Bhai! My brother! We're searching for a boat, a blue one. Manned by Britishers.'

The fisherman looked uneasy.

'It's very important!' cried Chompa.

The fisherman backed away, startled. Mohsin rummaged in his kurta pocket and offered him some notes.

'Please, bhai – will you send word to me when it comes in? There's twice this for you when you do. Dacca College, ask one of the guards for me, Dr Kabir. And jaldi – as quickly as you can.'

The fisherman nodded, gazing at the notes in his fist.

Mohsin placed a gentle hand on Chompa's shoulder. 'Come now, you must be tired. It's been a long journey. We'll return the moment he sends word.'

Mohsin hailed a rickshaw, and they were soon bowling through the narrow alley-streets.

Chompa allowed herself to drink in the sights of the city. There were more people than she had ever seen in her life. They were lining the roads, selling things from wheeled carts, or buying things before they embarked upon journeys: pickled limes to stop river sickness, puffed rice, green coconuts cut open on request. The place smelled of fish and river silt. Chompa craned her neck to take in every tiny detail: the signs on the shops, the things they sold, each face, and each story they might have.

Mohsin chuckled and placed a gentle arm on her shoulder to pull her back into the seat.

'Please allow me to host you in Dacca for at least one day, Chompa, before you break your neck! I tell you what – we'll take the long route through the city so you can see all you wish.'

The rickshaw bobbed through the narrow streets and their stacked, slim buildings. The air was red with dust kicked up from the ground: Mohsin showed Chompa how to cover her mouth with the end of her scarf. They wheeled through an area that smelled of wood and chemicals.

'Dacca's organized in its own peculiar way, almost like books in a library, by subject. In fact, this is the Library Quarter, where books are printed and sold. For some reason, it's wedged between the areas dedicated to mynah birds and wheels.'

Sure enough, the bookshops started to give way to small warehouses with circular wooden frames hanging from every inch of wall space. Gradually, the roads became wider, cleaner, smoother, and the buildings were more spaced out and grander in scale, with domes, pillars and arches, and lines of neat green palm trees in front.

'What are these buildings for?' Chompa asked, puzzled.

Mohsin smiled.

'A good question, Chompa. They've all been built by the British, our wonderful new *rulers*,' he said, scorn dripping from his voice, 'within the last twenty years. The city is changing; the whole country is changing. These buildings are the law courts, police headquarters, a sanitation department, an office of taxation. The British argue they're bringing us into the modern age . . . but they have a very specific idea of what that is, and who should be in charge.' Mohsin's eyes darkened.

Suddenly Chompa heard voices shouting in unison, getting louder, behind the rickshaw. In the other direction, a column of people advanced, also shouting. The rickshaw-wallah looked around, agitated.

'What's going on, bhai?' asked Mohsin.

'Arré, trouble – that's what's going on,' the driver muttered. Both columns had advanced towards one another, and they were bang in the middle. 'Writing-charms – everyone's talking about them now.'

Chompa's eyes widened. Charms!

The driver continued grumbling. 'These Britishers should have left well alone. Before they arrived, *that lot* knew their place, and kept to themselves. Now that there's talk of a charm ban, they're everywhere, shouting about stuff that shouldn't be spoken of.'

The driver spat betel juice on the ground, making his feelings about *that lot* very clear. Mohsin frowned, and Chompa's hand went up to her neck to make sure her scarf was covering her taviz.

Suddenly someone tugged at Chompa's arm, and she

sprang back, every nerve alive like a cat under attack. The hand was pulled away, dragged by the force of the crowd, but not before it pressed a pamphlet into her hand.

Chompa looked down at it.

DEFEND OUR CHARM-WRITING TRADITIONS! it said. And below there was an image of a taviz.

But before she could ask Mohsin more, the rickshaw swerved suddenly on to the other side of the road, cycling head first into the oncoming traffic. Chompa was almost tipped out, and the piece of paper danced away on the air.

'Hold tight!' yelled Mohsin as they headed straight towards a massive bullock cart.

Chompa closed her eyes and grabbed the rickshaw hood for dear life. The rickshaw swerved again, just missing the huge beasts with their lethal-looking horns, before making its way back to the right side of the road.

Behind them were the sounds of whistles, yells, and cries as the two crowds made contact.

'Eesh,' breathed Mohsin in relief.

'Life in the city is certainly dramatic, huh?' said Chompa, heart rate finally calming down.

The rickshaw slowed by a set of beautiful red stone buildings, with domes and pillars like the village mosque, and tall arched windows. Behind it stretched long, tidy green squares, where neatly dressed young men hurried or lounged, books tucked under their arms.

'This is Dacca College. Most of the college is dedicated to producing the bright young men who will work in the buildings you saw. Cogs in the British machine.'

Mohsin waved a hand at the grand buildings with a look of distaste. Then he directed the rickshaw driver down a scruffier road. They stopped at some small buildings, in the same pretty red brick, and got out of the rickshaw.

'This, Chompa, is my home. And yours for the time being. It's not much, I'm afraid. My work means I'm not high on the university's pecking order.'

'They let you do magic as a *job*?' Chompa breathed, mesmerized.

Mohsin chuckled. 'Not quite, no. I call myself a scientist of the elements. The university just doesn't know the kind of elements I research. Or *how* I research them.' He raised his index finger and gave her a smile. 'You heard our friend back there. Just like in your village, Chompa, there are many people in Dacca who fear and distrust all forms of magic – and that includes Britishers *and* Indians. I'd be escorted off campus rather quickly if they knew the truth. So we must be careful and practise magic only where we won't be seen.'

Chompa nodded.

They walked into a cool hallway decorated with black and white mosaic tiles. Several doors led off it, and a slim curved staircase wound upward.

'The stairs lead up to my room and the guest room, where you'll be staying. Come, let me take your bag. I'll show you. It's very small, and the furniture's a bit old, but I hope it will do. After all, you'll only be here for a short time, while we find Amina.'

Chompa climbed the stairs after Mohsin. He opened a door.

Light streamed into the dim corridor from the airy interior. Chompa gawped. There was a high, large bed with four pillars and light muslin drapes hung about it, a table with a mirror, and a faded green chair in the corner of the room. Even though the furnishings were worn and a bit musty-smelling, it was still finer than anything she'd ever owned. Chompa snorted with triumph, wishing the villagers could see her now. Then came a pang that took her breath away — all this space was just for her. She and Ammi had shared one room, much smaller than this.

'I'll leave you to change and rest.'

Once he'd gone, Chompa sat down on the bed, which squished under her, soft like a bale of spring hay. She slipped the chappals off her feet and lay back, allowing the bed to envelop her.

There was a sudden metallic crash outside the door, and a loud, cackling female voice cursed in Bangla.

Chompa leaped to her feet and pushed the door open. Squatting on the floor, her back to Chompa, was a plump female form dressed in a simple purple cotton sari.

'These stupid things — so slippery and cold they are! Tsk, why would you use these when you can eat with your hand like a civilized person?' the girl muttered grumpily, scooping up a bunch of long, slim silver implements from where they had scattered on the floor and flinging them into a tray with discernible distaste.

Chompa coughed to announce her presence.

The girl jumped up, banging her head on the door handle. She cursed as she turned round, rubbing her head and

43

narrowing her eyes at Chompa. Chompa's cheeks flushed under the gaze of the older girl.

'Hello. I'm Chompa. Sorry – is this your room?'

The girl threw her head back and gave a rough cackle.

'O-ho! The new little memsaheb thinks this is my room!'

Chompa was very confused. 'So . . . it's not?'

The girl gave a knowing look. She was a little taller than Chompa, with round cheeks and a small mouth red from chewing betel leaves.

'Leeza. I'm here to look after the master, and now I'll be looking after you. I'll be sleeping on the floor in here and will be attending to your every need.'

Chompa was speechless. Leeza was not.

'Arré, are you not hungry and thirsty? Come sit!'

Leeza dumped the tray with a clatter on the table and started to pour the chai.

Chompa did as she was told. The chai was hot and black, infused with cinnamon. There were crisp, just-fried samosas, an omelette wrapped in a flaky paratha, slices of cake studded with crystallized melon, and spiced biscuits.

Leeza chattered as Chompa ate.

'My father worked here as a porter, but he was killed in an accident – one of those Britishers going too fast in a carriage.' She spat the word *Britishers* with venom. 'Saheb took me on, even though the university kept sending my mother away when she came to ask for help. When Ma got sick, he did all he could to help her. Paid for a good hospital, the funeral, everything.'

Chompa tried to reach out to pat Leeza's arm to comfort her, but Leeza shrugged her off.

'It's God's will. What I'm saying is that Saheb is kind, *too kind* sometimes. People take advantage.' Leeza narrowed her eyes at Chompa as if warning her.

'Are you magic, too? Is that why he helped you?' Chompa asked between flaky mouthfuls.

Leeza clucked her tongue. 'My mother would have had a fit if I was. Even when my abba died, and we ran out of food and money, she wouldn't go to a charm-writer to help us. It was me who did, and that's how I got this job. Saheb turned up the very next day.'

She pulled out a taviz from under her blouse, tied with green thread.

Chompa smiled and showed Leeza her own round her neck. She pushed the plate of cake over to Leeza, who took a slice and ate it much more daintily than Chompa had.

After tea, Chompa hurried down to Mohsin's study, refusing Leeza's instruction to rest. She had so many questions for him, after all, and napping would only delay things. She knocked, and the door opened.

Chompa stepped into the room and gave a cry. An actual, villager-like 'Baap ré!', in fact.

The room was dominated by tall cabinets full of brass spheres and bowls, polished to the most impossible shine, glowing like buttery glass. Instruments ticked and hummed on small plinths while crisp paper scrolls wrapped with burgundy velvet ribbon lay stacked on dark wooden racks.

Her eyes came to rest almost immediately on a set of long tables towards the back of the room. Little clay contraptions and glass beakers and vials sat alongside – most incongruously – rows and rows of little plant pots.

Mohsin was sitting at a small, crumbling desk, scribbling on pieces of thick paper and stuffing them into envelopes. He looked up and smiled, clapping his hands together in delight.

'Ah, Chompa! It's been a while since I've heard a good baap ré! Please, sit. I'm nearly finished.'

He pointed to a rickety chair on the opposite side of the table while he wrote a couple more lines, folded the paper and stuffed it in an envelope, placing it on top of a small, teetering tower of identical ones. There was a knock on the door, and a boy in a burgundy uniform hurried in. Mohsin handed him the letters, along with a silver coin.

Once the boy had left, Mohsin pushed the pen away and flexed his hand.

'I'm not used to doing much writing – it's actually painful, isn't it? But needs must. I'm sending word out to anyone I know who might be able to help us find Amina – magical scholars, journalists, and so on. I hope we'll know more very soon.'

'I hope so.'

'And how are you feeling, Chompa? Have you rested enough? Is the room all right?' Mohsin's brow furrowed in concern.

'I'm fine, I'm fine. Everything's fine,' said Chompa gruffly, with an impatient wave.

'Good, good. Now. Let's get down to business. I've been thinking. You were learning English, I believe? Did you bring your books?'

'Yes.' Chompa grimaced.

'Usually, I'm not one for books, for reading, writing. I prefer more practical ways of learning. However, if you can grow more confident in English, I think it will help your investigations. What do you think?'

'If it helps me find Ammi, I'll have to.'

Mohsin grinned. 'That's about as much enthusiasm for the language as I had. I assume your ammi was also teaching you writing-magic?'

Chompa flushed. 'I was learning my Farsi letters, but . . . it wasn't going in.'

'Yes, I understand,' said Mohsin, nodding. 'I'm sure Amina would want me to teach you those, too, but much as I admire writing-charms, and people like your mother who practise them, I'm just no good at them.' He rubbed at a patch of his hair with a rueful smile. 'In fact, even Amina lost patience with trying to teach me once. She threw a textbook at my head! In her defence, I was a *terrible* student.' He grinned at Chompa.

Chompa felt relief rush through her. It wasn't just her. Mohsin – bright, clever Mohsin – found it difficult, too!

'So let me show you what I *can* teach you.'

Mohsin got to his feet. He raised his finger, his eyes focused on one of the small plants on the table between them.

Slowly, spear-shaped violet flowers began to bud and bloom from long stems.

It was only the third time in her life that Chompa had seen another person do finger-magic. She couldn't tear her eyes away.

Finally, when the plant was covered in violet petals, Mohsin lowered his finger and wiped a single bead of sweat from his brow.

'See? It is possible to use our magic safely. *If* we practise control and focus.'

Chompa nodded eagerly, but then her hands flew up to the taviz round her neck. She flushed with frustration. There was surely no point in learning it while she was wearing a taviz that stopped her doing magic. She tugged it so hard that her neck reddened.

Mohsin's brow knitted together, and he leaned across the table.

'Chompa, are you all right? Is there a problem?'

She wondered for a moment whether she should tell him. But she didn't know where else to turn, or how else to get her magic back. Mohsin had studied many forms of magic and was bound to know how to help her.

'Yes, Uncle. There is a problem.' She allowed the taviz to drop from her fist on to her throat. 'It's – it's a charm. My ammi made it for me, to protect me, she said. It stops me doing my magic. There's no point in teaching me because I can't do anything, and it won't come off. I've tried and tried!'

Mohsin walked round the table and leaned in close to her. He lifted the taviz and examined it carefully. 'Ah, ingenious.

Amina charmed the knot so that only magic might release it. A taviz to prevent magic, only to be released with magic.' Mohsin's voice was full of admiration, and Chompa's heart swelled with pride for Ammi.

'Your mother made this for you to keep you safe. But I can't believe she wanted you to stop doing magic altogether. Her letter asked me to teach you, after all. It may be a concealing charm to make sure the trace of your magic stays hidden, rather than your magic. *Your* belief that the taviz stops you doing magic might actually be what's blocking your power.'

'What's a trace?' Chompa asked, head tipped to one side. Ammi had mentioned this word, too, she remembered.

'We leave a mark on the world when we do finger-magic – like a fingerprint, in fact – which a particular device, called a trace-box, can detect. If you removed the taviz and did magic, and the men who took Amina realized they'd missed you – well, they might come looking for you, too. I suggest we keep it on for now. If you really can't use magic, I'll search for a way to remove it.'

Chompa chewed her lip, reluctant. But she saw Mohsin's mouth was firm, and that he would not be dissuaded. Finally, she nodded.

Mohsin sighed. 'Writing charms takes so much skill and time. It's sometimes a little frustrating, but truly an art to admire.'

'Uncle – what's the difference between the two magics? Where do they come from? There's so much I don't know – don't understand. Ammi never told me anything. If I had

49

better control of my magic, I could have stopped them taking her! I have to find her. I have to learn, learn it all –' The words tumbled from her, full of a hunger she thought might never be satisfied, now that someone finally wanted to teach her.

'Be calm, Chompa – calm yourself. I promise I'll help you. But it will require patience and focus. We shall begin our lessons tomorrow.'

'Can't we start now? There's just no time to waste!' Chompa cried.

Mohsin nodded.

'Very well, Chompa. Let us begin.'

# Chapter Seven

They walked towards a tall building with long arched windows and rows and rows of door-height shelves filled with books. It made Chompa feel a little ill.

They headed to a section cordoned off by a red velvet rope. There was no one else here, yet Chompa thought that Mohsin stepped quietly, as if he didn't want to draw attention to them.

Mohsin pulled out a huge book and rested it on a latticed wooden stand on one of the dark wooden tables. The pages were browned with age, the cover patchy, but the drawings inside were dazzlingly coloured and so finely detailed that Chompa couldn't make them out at first. She found herself holding her breath in case the fragile pages disintegrated to powder in front of her.

'So, Chompa: the foundations of magic. We won't do much book study in our lessons – I have little patience for it, and I sense you're the same. But I thought this picture might help us begin. What do you see?'

Chompa's heart flipped within her. She felt she'd been waiting so long for this moment – perhaps her whole life. Yet the picture looked like one from her storybooks – pretty, unreal – and she wasn't sure how it would explain anything.

A black line divided the page in two. On one side were noble-looking warriors dressed in white and sitting on horseback. They wielded torches of yellow-orange flames, clouds of grey smoke tendrilling round them.

On the other side were figures with barrel chests, massive glowing yellow eyes, and skin in a rainbow of impossible shades: red, blue, black. Chompa knew what they were from Ammi's stories.

The figures held their palms upward. When Chompa realized what they were holding, her bare arms ran cold. Flames, delicately tinted scarlet – flames without smoke. She snapped her head round to Mohsin. 'Uncle! I don't understand. How –'

'Chompa, for now, just tell me what you see. It will become clear.'

She gazed back at the page, at the incredible creatures and their impossible fire. 'I see . . . I see djinn.'

'Yes, Chompa. Djinn, or what the Britishers call "genies". *They* think djinn are the stuff of fairy tales, but *we* know different. We know they live alongside us, in trees, in ponds, in ruins, waiting to possess the weaker-minded among us.

'Of course, we cannot see djinn. Over time, we've given them certain familiar visual characterizations, which have been handed down in stories. But there are two elements of this picture that are true. One is the line, and the other is the fire.

'Djinn are beings made from the strange smokeless fire that they also wield. Humans are made from more substantial – and vulnerable – stuff: bone, matter, blood. Blood and fire. Fire and blood. We and djinn live parallel lives on earth, almost side by side, but divided from each other by this thin, thin line, which means we cannot see them, and only certain rare people can even hear or sense them.'

'The fire – what is it made from?' Chompa asked hesitantly.

'It's hard to say. I think we are only now, through recent scientific advancements – such as those happening here at the university – truly coming to understand it. A poetic word for it might be essence. A scientific one would be energy.'

Chompa took a deep breath. 'I – I made flames that looked like those. That pale red colour, with no smoke. What am I?' She could barely utter the question for fear of the answer.

'Chompa, the line that exists between us was not always there. Centuries ago, there was a great war between djinn and humans. Humans won. Suleiman, a human sorcerer of great power, charmed the line into being, and djinn were banished beyond it. Before that, it didn't exist.'

He stared intently at her. 'There was once no line. Chompa, think. What would that mean?'

'That . . . that we could see and hear the djinn? That they lived – here? With us?'

Each of her answers was a question, raised at the end – because, well, surely that could not be?

'Yes. Precisely. And we fought, and were enemies, often, as powerful races can be with one another sometimes. Eventually, enmity won out. But before it did there were other things, too. Friendship. Love.'

'Between djinn and humans?' Chompa exclaimed.

Mohsin nodded gently. 'And those loves sometimes bore children. Part-djinn, part-human children.'

Mohsin turned the page. Chompa found herself holding her breath as he placed a finger on the image there. A flame-spirit on the left, a man on the right. And, in the middle, a smaller figure: a child, with a doll in one hand and a ball of flame in the other.

'When the line was brought down, these half-beings had to choose which side to live on. Many chose to go with the djinn. Only a few elected to remain and live short human lives on this side.

'Those half-beings had some djinn powers, but they were diminished by their humanness. Many were hunted and executed in a surge of desire for purity. A few centuries ago, a magician used Suleiman's writings to develop the instrument I mentioned to you earlier: one crafted from silver that could detect a magical trace. The tragedy was, she invented it in order to find other djinnborn like her and bring them together. But she was captured, and it fell into the wrong hands, and then locating magical people became brutally simple. After that, very few remained to live full human lives, to have families themselves.

'But some did, and generations and generations passed. With each one, the djinn blood – and powers – were further diluted. But they have always remained, the part-djinn, hidden among us. Some never even know who they are. Their powers lie quiet, unused within them.

'There are some, though, who find they can hear the voices of djinn caught and bound inside some natural element like a tree, a flower, even a grain of sand – they can speak with them, and work with their energy. We call them djinnspeakers. Their powers tend to be weak, and limited to certain skills or areas, such as the weather.

'And a very small number, maybe no more than a few hundred across the world, find they can summon djinn-magic themselves, and change things as djinn once did, using this.' Mohsin raised his index finger, but kept looking straight at Chompa. 'We call them djinnborn.'

'Djinnborn,' Chompa repeated. 'Djinnborn.'

Suddenly she understood. It was as if she was walking out of dawn mist into daylight. Everything was brighter, crisper. Clearer.

'I'm – I'm djinnborn? I'm not fully human?'

'Well, I prefer to think of it as being *more than* human, Chompa. Apart from magic, we function just as other humans do. But we can do things they can't.'

'Terrible things!' Chompa cried out.

Mohsin smiled gently. 'If left uncontrolled, yes. But I believe that, with understanding and practice, we can do extraordinary things. Wonderful things. Djinnborn are very special – very rare now.'

'So Ammi is djinnborn, too? And you?'

'Yes.'

'Are there more of us? Do you know anyone else like us?'

'I'm searching for others like us, but, no, I haven't come across anyone else for many years.'

'So are you and Ammi related? Is that how you know each other?' Chompa looked Mohsin up and down, for similarities. But his green eyes and cream-coloured skin were nothing like Ammi's and Chompa's.

Mohsin shrugged. 'Possibly distantly. It's hard to know. The records that we have left don't go back very far. Our families were close once, as you'd expect of two djinnborn families in the same city. But then our fathers had a disagreement, and Amina moved away.'

Chompa felt dizzy and warm.

'But she never told me – she never told me any of this! I never knew why I could do these things, and I didn't even know Ammi could until that day in the cooking hut!'

'Amina feared people knowing of our magic, and really she was right to, Chompa. Because we're the most powerful, the least limited in our abilities, djinnborn have always been most preyed upon. Either to exploit us, or to eliminate us.'

Chompa shuddered. 'The people who took Ammi . . . do they want to do the first or the second, Uncle?' she said, eyes wide with fear.

Mohsin placed a hand upon hers, looking grave. 'The first, I'm sure of it. If they wanted to do the second, I think they wouldn't have made the effort to take her away on the boat.'

Chompa swallowed, reading between the lines Mohsin

couldn't bring himself to say. As in, *They would have killed her there and then.*

'Chompa, I think we'll move on to some more practical learning now. Something, I feel, we both might prefer. If you're ready?'

'I'm readier than I've ever been,' said Chompa, gritting her teeth as she sprang to her feet.

She had to get a grip on herself. Ammi needed her.

# Chapter Eight

They entered a shabby, plant-filled glasshouse on the edge of the college campus. 'This is where I do most of my experiments,' said Mohsin, smiling apologetically as he dusted earth from a rickety wooden table.

Chompa's attention was drawn to a large machine on wheels, partly hidden by thick foliage. It looked like a farming tool from the village, except that it was made of clay, not wood, and had a long clay pipe connected to a circular pot. She ran her fingers over its cool, smooth surface.

'What's this for, Uncle?' she said, fizzing with curiosity.

'Ah, I'm trying to develop some machines that might help our farmers water crops during droughts, but it's a very early prototype. I've not been able to get it to work yet.'

He patted the machine like it was an old friend and then placed a plant pot on the table. In it was a plant that looked closer to death than life, its leaves half brown and shrivelled. Chompa raised an eyebrow. She hadn't imagined that her magical lessons would be about *gardening*, something she disliked almost as much as languages.

'To our lesson. This is how I make a plant come back to life, Chompa: I hold a specific word, which I call an intention word, in my mind, and I point to the plant at the very same time. The intention word I'm using now is "thrive".'

Chompa watched avidly as Mohsin focused. Within seconds, the fraying yellow-brown edges of the leaves turned to a plump, glossy green, and the stems began to pull themselves up.

'Now you try.' Mohsin directed her to another ailing specimen.

Chompa did her best to copy him, but her magic still didn't come. Her hands went up to her throat, and suddenly the taviz felt like it was choking her.

'It's no good, Uncle. There is something there stopping me. I can feel it. It's not just in my mind. Uncle Mohsin, please could you remove it?'

Mohsin looked doubtful. 'Chompa – your mother placed it there for a reason. I really think that –'

'Please!' she pleaded, looking directly into Mohsin's eyes. 'I can't do anything to help Ammi while I'm wearing it!'

Mohsin nodded, his brows knotting together in a line.

'If you're sure, then very well.'

Mohsin tapped the knot once with his index finger, the same right index finger Chompa had used for her magic.

Nothing happened, and Mohsin frowned.

Chompa turned her head round to look at him.

'What is it? Can't you remove it?' Panic made her voice high and tight.

59

'Calm, Chompa, calm. I need to think . . . Amina wanted to protect *you* from using your magic impulsively. So she must have enchanted it . . . to resist *your* magic. But perhaps . . . she also feared that someone might *force* you to use magic. That is, after all, what we believe the Britishers are doing: capturing magical people and forcing them to use their magic, for the Britishers' own gain. So maybe she would also have enchanted the taviz to resist other people trying to remove it.'

Chompa felt her shoulders sagging with despair.

'Yes . . . yes. It makes sense,' Mohsin muttered softly, almost to himself. 'Chompa, I wish to try something. I want us both to place our right index fingers on the knot at the same time.'

Chompa leaned back in surprise. Then she nodded, pulling the knot to the front of her throat and holding up the thread.

'On three, then. One, two . . . three.'

They each pressed a finger to the knot. Chompa held her breath.

The knot came undone, and the dense little silver locket tumbled from Chompa's neck into her palm as if it had been eager to be free all this time. She looked at it, so small and insignificant, and could hardly believe it had felt so heavy round her throat. She dropped it into her pocket and breathed a sigh of impossible relief.

'Amina wanted to make sure it would only unravel if you worked together with someone else,' Mohsin said quietly. 'Fascinating.'

'Of course!' Chompa slapped her hand against her

forehead. 'I forgot – that's what she said! "*Only remove it with someone you trust*." She meant you, but I didn't know who you were then! Uncle, tell me – when was the last time you and Ammi met? Because we've lived in the village for as long as I can remember –'

'Chompa, Chompa – we must focus. I promise I'll answer your questions later. But that's the past, and we have Amina's future to think about at the minute. Right now, we need to see whether removing your taviz worked, surely?'

Chompa scrunched her mouth up in frustration, and then sighed. Of course he was right. And she *was* itching to do magic again.

She raised her finger and focused on the plant in front of her. She reached out with her mind to the vibrant greenness of it. She began to lose consciousness of the world around her, focusing only on the green. It was moving, it was alive, like her. She shifted her thought to 'be more, more, more' and felt the green pulsing more intensely each time her mind called to it.

'All right, Chompa, come back now.'

She blinked, and looked in front of her.

There were three identical plants in pots where there had been one before.

'It worked!' she cried, delighted, clapping her hands together. 'It *was* the taviz! I can do magic now!' She felt the glow of pride rush through her.

Mohsin smiled. 'Well, Chompa, you were right. And, yes, you've done well. But I asked you to make the plant larger, not to make more of them.'

Chompa gave a little snort of indignation before she could help herself.

'Larger, more – what's the difference? I made it *change*, and nothing bad happened! I can control my powers now!' She stuck her chin out in triumph.

Mohsin sighed, took off his glasses and polished them. The weary expression on his face was a mirror of the one Ammi used to wear when teaching Chompa Farsi.

'Out of interest, what was the thought you channelled towards the plant? Your intention word?'

'I was thinking "more".'

'Ah, yes. A good thought to begin with, but not quite specific enough. Our magic requires intense precision. That's why I view it as a science, and myself as a scientist. Your "more" thought grew the *number* of plants, but not the plant itself. But if you had chosen "grow", or "enlarge", or "become taller" as your thought, would you have had different results? Each of those thoughts produces a slightly different spell. Let's try each one and see what happens.'

And, sure enough, each had a slightly different outcome: 'grow' produced a lusher plant with more leaves, while 'enlarge' made the whole plant bigger, including the pot itself, and 'become taller' made the plant stretch its leaves higher, but didn't make the plant any lusher or its leaves more plentiful.

Chompa looked at them all, a little deflated. 'I thought my magic was simpler than Ammi's charms, Uncle, but it looks like this is just as complicated in its own way.'

Mohsin laughed. 'They both require discipline and care,

it's true. But charms are slow, and for all the effort they require they aren't even guaranteed to work, while finger-magic is immediate and powerful.'

Chompa nodded. 'And that's what I need to get Ammi back. I won't have time for second chances.'

The next morning, Chompa returned to the glasshouse and, to her surprise, found Mohsin standing behind a small trough of water.

'Now, Chompa, we shall seek your affinity. As we are made partly of djinn-fire, working with fire comes naturally to all of us djinnborn, but alongside that power we each have another gift: a substance that we are most skilled at manipulating. It's sometimes passed down through families. The substance can be earth, water, wood, sand, or other natural materials. When you are weak, or when a material resists changing into another, you may wish to change it to your skill-element first. A substance in its purest form is easiest to transform: for example, sand is easier to transform than glass. Never metals, however; we cannot change or manipulate these.'

'Why not?' asked Chompa.

'Suleiman, the sorcerer I told you about yesterday, banished the djinn using a golden ring. To prevent djinn from destroying the enchantment, he knitted the molecules of metals together to create a barrier to magic at the most minute level. That is why metal has always been used to contain magic. If you bind a djinn to metal, you will cause them great pain, and they'll be easy to control. Perhaps you've heard the old story about Al-a-deen and his brass lamp, Chompa? While just a story, there is some truth behind it.'

'Is that why taviz are made from silver?' Chompa asked eagerly.

Mohsin nodded. 'That's correct. Silver, like other metals, can contain and store magic. But, Chompa, remember that we're focusing on finger-magic now, not charms. Please do not become distracted. We haven't even begun to search for your magical affinity, and that's your most powerful magical weapon.'

Chompa flushed and nodded. 'So what's your affinity, Uncle?' she asked.

'Mine is earth. A humble affinity, I know, but why I spend so much time doing experiments with crops and clay! And your mother's is water,' Mohsin told Chompa. He smiled. 'A strange quirk for beings who are essentially made of fire, no?'

Chompa remembered Ammi putting the fire out in the cooking hut, how quickly the water-magic had come to her. It seemed an age ago.

Mohsin nodded at the trough. 'So I thought we'd try water first. If it is your affinity, you should barely have to focus on it; it'll yield to your will almost immediately. Please raise a ball of water into the air and keep it aloft for a minute.'

Chompa channelled all her concentration on the water, on the clarity of it, the lights dancing upon it. She barely had to think of the idea of 'split' before the water separated into droplets, then, flicking her finger, she lifted them up out of the trough, like rain in reverse. She circled with her finger, and the droplets gathered together smoothly into a ball. Once she had thought 'remain', she took her attention away from the sphere, and grinned at Mohsin.

'That wasn't difficult at all! I'm just like Ammi!'

Mohsin smiled. 'I hope so. But would you say that it was easier than changing the plant?'

Chompa frowned. Both had been equally easy for her.

Mohsin led Chompa to another table on which there was a neat row of glass beakers, each filled with different things: sand, earth, salt, honey, and more. Chompa tried the same spell with each, and all yielded easily enough for her to control without feeling at all tired.

Mohsin looked both impressed and baffled.

'That's extraordinary, Chompa. I've never seen anyone able to change *every* material so effortlessly. It's . . . well, it's highly unusual. And it doesn't point to one of these things being your affinity.' He ruffled his hair, brow creased in thought.

'Perhaps I don't have an affinity,' she said, flumping down into a chair. She felt strangely sad rather than proud. She would have liked to share Ammi's affinity: it would have made her feel closer to her mother to be like her in magic. She rubbed her temples. Her scalp twinged from all the concentration, and a few loose strands of hair wafted to the floor around her.

She shoved her hand in her pocket and felt the cool

smoothness of the taviz Ammi had made for her soothe her fingers. Even though Chompa had hated wearing it, now she wanted to keep it close to her. It seemed to radiate a little of Ammi's serenity.

Mohsin ran his fingers through his beard. 'It is strange. These are all the common affinities. But no matter, Chompa, we will find yours eventually.

'Now to spells. Ideally, I would have liked to start from the basics and build up, but I want to arm you with some in particular, especially since we don't know your affinity. Spells we might need in an emergency.' Mohsin's eyes darkened.

Chompa sat up straight in her chair, fully focused.

Mohsin set one of his wooden instruments in front of her. He pressed a lever, and various cogs and dials began to tick and spin.

'First, we have to work on the spell for stillness. It's very useful, but you need to fix your attention very specifically. If you let your mind wander, you can end up stilling a lot more than you intended!'

Chompa remembered how Ammi would still the water of the pond and grinned. 'Ammi used to do this through a writing-charm! I think I even remember the letters!'

Mohsin's genial face suddenly changed. He looked sternly over his glasses at Chompa.

'Chompa, we have much to learn. It's imperative that you learn to control and use the magic you were born with. We can't afford for you to get your magic all mixed up with charms. Set Amina's taviz and learning charm-writing aside for now. You must focus, and *only* on this form. Your thoughts must be completely clear for you to master your magic, and yourself. Rescuing your ammi depends on it.'

Chompa was taken aback at his seriousness. But he was right. She did need to focus.

'I promise,' she said in a small voice.

She looked at her finger. She had one niggling doubt left.

'Uncle ... Ammi said that every act of finger-magic comes with a price. Is she right? I feel fine!'

But before Mohsin could answer there was a knock on the laboratory door, and Leeza came in.

'Saheb, there's a man at the door. He says the boat has come in.'

They dropped everything.

# Chapter Nine

minutes later, Mohsin had hailed a rickshaw, and they were speeding back towards the Buriganga River, and the same dock they had arrived at the previous day. When they arrived, it was blazing red from the setting sun.

Mohsin hurried off towards a group of fishermen. Chompa started to follow and then stopped.

There it was.

The sleek fishing boat, gleaming midnight blue.

The one that had taken Ammi.

Suddenly she was plunged back into that terrible night. Her lungs felt as though they'd stopped working – she couldn't get breaths in or out, and the blood pulsed hard in her head.

Chompa looked up to see Mohsin some distance away still talking to the fishermen. Before she could catch up with him, the cabin door opened, and Chompa knew she had to hide. She ducked down behind a crate, peering over towards the boat. She almost cried out – the men pouring out of the door were pale! Just like the men who'd taken Ammi, they had brown boots and dark blue uniforms, but these ones had weapons, too – big, palm-thick muskets with a blade on the end. Chompa shivered. They seemed more like soldiers than sailors.

She felt sick with terror, but she forced herself to think. If Ammi was still on the boat, they had to rescue her. But how, with just the two of them, and all these armed men?

She looked around. There were some raggedy children stitching fishing nets nearby.

'*Pssh*,' she hissed.

One of the children looked up.

'Come over here – quietly. I need you to do something for me.'

The child looked at her shrewdly. Chompa thought fast.

'I need you to cause a disturbance. I have a feeling you and your friends will be experienced in these matters. And I know you'll want something in return. I'm a witch – look.'

Chompa directed her finger towards the net the child was holding, training her eye on the thread, pulling it from the needle and up and down through the netting. The stitches sewed themselves, without her touching the net.

The little girl's mouth hung open.

'If you help me, I'll do some more magic for you.'

The child nodded eagerly.

'Do you kids have a signal?'

The girl nodded again. She opened her mouth and made a 'kaak' noise, just like the city crows. Chompa copied her.

'When I crow five times, OK? That's the signal to start.'

Grinning, the little girl raced off.

It was getting darker. Chompa ducked her head above the crate and saw Mohsin in the distance looking harried, searching for her with panicked eyes, wringing his hands. She aimed a small pebble at him and flicked with her magical finger. The pebble nicked his ear. He rubbed at it. But Chompa kept her finger trained on the pebble, keeping it a few inches off the ground – and then his eyes focused on it, too. She drew the pebble towards her, and Mohsin followed.

He breathed out heavily as he sank against the crate.

'Chompa . . . I thought they'd taken you! I told you not to wander off!'

Chompa put a finger on her lips. 'Uncle, I have a plan.'

'What do you mean, a plan?' Mohsin whispered through gritted teeth. 'There's only two of us – and they're armed! We can't possibly do anything right now! We should wait – go back –'

'There's no time, Uncle. They will have smuggled her off by the time we get back. Don't worry. I've enlisted some help.'

She nodded towards the ragtag group of children who were taking up a range of positions behind crates and nets. Chompa noticed they had rounded objects bulging in their pockets and rocks in their hands. She looked around and put a handful of rocks and shells in her pocket, too. *Just in case.*

Then Chompa cupped her hands round her mouth and let out a series of five screeches.

Two older children climbed like monkeys up ropes on to the deck of the boat, while the younger ones started to throw things at it. A horrible smell reached Chompa's nose, and

yellow splats dribbled down the previously gleaming hull.
Rotten eggs.

The soldiers started to stream out of the cabin, bellowing
indignantly. They set their muskets down and jumped right
off the boat to chase away the assailants. Now that they were
scattered and angry (and a few had even been hit by eggs,
Chompa saw with satisfaction), she realized they were only
human, and not demons as she'd thought back in the village.
She sighed with relief – she could fight humans. Even if they
did have muskets.

A few men stayed onboard, yelling and waving their
arms. The two children on the deck then launched their
attack, grabbing a small crate and making over the side with
it. Most of the remaining men gave chase. The other workers
in the port simply crossed their arms, smirking. Chompa
noted this: these pale men weren't liked.

'It's our turn now, Uncle,' Chompa whispered. 'We have
to get Ammi out.'

Mohsin nodded, and together they crept from their hiding
place towards the boat. Mohsin lifted Chompa on to the deck
and climbed up after her. They crouched in the shadows,
unseen by the three remaining soldiers.

'Where shall we look?' Mohsin whispered.

Chompa shook her head. 'There's no sign of her up here.
Below deck, maybe?' She nodded at a doorway and a staircase
leading down.

They crept forward. They had almost made it to the door
when one of the soldiers shouted, 'Hey! There's two more!'

Mohsin stood up, concealing Chompa behind him.

'Focus on the planks underneath them, ready with "move", Chompa. I'll move the plank the other is standing on at the same time. Overboard.' He stretched a hand out behind him, and she clasped it, tucking her head to one side to focus on the soldier's form.

They raised their index fingers. Chompa felt a whirring through her palm.

'Magic strengthens when two djinnborn touch,' Mohsin whispered. 'But only when we focus. On my count. Three, two, one – now.'

They cast their spells. The planks, and the soldiers standing on them, rose into the air, hovered for a second, and then fell into the river with a massive splash.

'Two down, one to go. You get to the hull, Chompa. I'll be right behind you once he's been removed.'

Chompa nodded and darted towards the door. She ducked down the steps into the belly of the boat. It was dark, and for a moment she considered trying to create a light with her magic, but then she remembered how swiftly she'd lost control of her fire and decided against it. Instead, she rubbed her eyes and started to grope around, listening hard.

And then she heard it. A scrabbling, like rats. And heavy, desperate breathing. Not like rats.

'Ammi! Ammi, I'm here! I came for you! Don't be afraid!'

But as her eyes became accustomed to the darkness, she saw the shapes of bodies – small bodies. Pairs of eyes shimmered from the shadows.

Children.

All children.

Chompa felt her heart plummet into her belly. Ammi wasn't there. But what she was seeing was almost worse. Dozens of children, dirty and terrified, huddled together in the darkness. She had to help them. She knew that's what Ammi would have wanted.

'Don't worry!' she called softly. 'I'll get you all out of here! Just stay quiet!'

She took one child's wrists and saw that there were dull metal cuffs round them, and a metal thimble on her index finger. Chompa's eyes widened. She was djinnborn, like her.

Chompa knew metals were unchangeable, but she tried, anyway. And failed.

'Iron,' whispered a little voice. 'Because some of us can enchant rope, but none of us can change iron.'

Chompa looked down at the child. 'Who are you? You have magic?'

'All of us do. I'm Layli. The ghost men took me from my house a couple of nights ago and put me on this ship. I live up in the Steel Quarter; I could just run there from here! My abba and amma must be sick with worry.' Layli paused. 'You seem so familiar . . . just like . . .'

Chompa's heart raced.

'Just like who? A woman? She looks a bit like me, and she's djinnborn, too. That's my mother. My ammi.'

'Please hurry up!' begged a boy.

Layli nodded. 'She's your mother? She was so kind to us. They brought her onboard, and we travelled together for a night. But then we stopped this morning, and one of the ghost men came, and he started to drag her out, and we all screamed and screamed. He could speak Bangla, and he laughed and said she was lucky because she was being taken off the *Albion* to be put on a new ship, going to a place called Larnden, which he said was much better than here. I don't know where that is, sorry.'

'Come on, please!' hissed a girl. 'They'll find you soon!'

Chompa's heart hammered in her chest. She looked around desperately, then remembered the river stones in her pocket. She pulled one out and bashed it on Layli's chain until a link broke.

Chompa pushed the little girl up the stairs. 'Hurry. I'll free the others and be right behind you.'

Layli was halfway up the steps when the hull went completely black.

'Hey!' a man's voice shouted down, his body blocking the light. 'Who's there?'

Layli squealed in terror and shrank back into the shadows. Chompa gritted her teeth and clambered upward, finger pointed.

She aimed at the man and flicked. He fell backwards, his head slamming against the deck with a thud. She raced up the rest of the stairs, dodging the groaning man and dragging Layli behind her, to see Mohsin backed into a corner, index finger raised, as two soldiers advanced from different directions, wielding their dull metal blades. She saw his eyes flicking between them, working out which soldier looked faster, and which he should attack first.

'Jump!' whispered Chompa to Layli, pointing to the shallow water of the river. 'Run home to your family, and then leave Dacca, move. Don't let them find you again!'

Layli nodded, squeezed Chompa's hand, and jumped.

Chompa crept up behind the men, raising a finger to her lips as Mohsin saw her and opened his mouth. She knitted her brows together in concentration. She couldn't move just one plank because the other man would still be there, blade in hand, and she hadn't tried moving two things at the same time yet. It was no use. She had to find another way to incapacitate them both at the same time.

Instinctively, her hand went to the taviz in her pocket.

She looked round the deck quickly – sure enough, there was a coil of rope nearby. Carefully, she snaked it between the men and, with a loop of her finger, wrapped it quickly, tightly, round their ankles. The men fell hard on to their backsides, yelling with confusion and rage. They tried to pull free. But the ropes wouldn't yield, and they had turned a strange colour – glinting coldly like the moonlight. The same colour as Chompa's taviz.

Silver.

Chompa had turned the rope to silver.

She rushed over to Mohsin and helped him up. His hair was dishevelled, and he was breathing hard. 'Where is Amina, Chompa? Did you find her?'

'Uncle, it wasn't Ammi! It's children – magical children like me! One of them said Ammi was on here, but they took her off – and she's being taken to . . . to Larnden!'

Mohsin sank to the deck, his face in his hands. 'London . . . It's the capital city of England, part of Britain,' he repeated faintly. 'It is as we feared, Chompa.'

Chompa felt her stomach clench in panic. She gritted her teeth, forced herself to focus. 'We need to rescue the other children, Uncle. There are more of them, so many more. And we have to capture one of the pale men, question him!'

But, as she spoke, a dozen men jumped back on deck, muskets raised. A sharp bang seemed to rend the air as one of them fired in their direction, only missing them because of an egg missile hitting him in the face.

'Chompa, we must leave,' hissed Mohsin. 'Now.'

'But the other children on the boat! They're trapped!'

Now more of the men started firing, and Mohsin's arm became firm on Chompa's shoulder.

'I'm sorry, Chompa. As it is, we've come too close to being captured. We'll have to find another way to rescue them all.'

They jumped off the boat, and ran, crouching, towards the rickshaw waiting for them. Before they could get to it, a cluster of fishing-net children shoved themselves in front of Chompa. They had sharp clamshells in their hands, an expectant gleam in their eyes.

Chompa's stomach lurched. The bangs from the guns were getting louder and more frequent. What could she give these children for holding up their end of the deal? She dug around in her pocket, but she had no sweets or coins – just her taviz and the river rocks and shells.

Her taviz.

Quickly, she placed a shell in each child's palm. Then, tucking her left hand in her pocket and grasping the taviz, she trained her right index finger on each shell, turning them all to solid, gleaming silver.

As the children scarpered with their loot, Chompa and Mohsin jumped into the rickshaw. Tapping on the hood, Mohsin urged the driver to go as fast as he could. Looking behind them, Chompa saw the armed men getting into a large horse-drawn truck.

'Uncle – surely horses are faster than a rickshaw? We need to get off and hide before they catch up with us!'

'Through the alleys, bhai!' shouted Mohsin to the driver, who nodded and swerved off the main road, down a maze of narrow streets barely wide enough for the rickshaw.

'They won't be able to follow us down these streets,' Mohsin breathed, sinking back into the cushioned seat. 'Only Daccaiyas know how to get through them. We've lost them for now.'

Then he blinked and turned to stare at Chompa, as if he'd never seen her before.

'Chompa, did I see what I thought I saw back then? That you changed the shells to silver? And before that – the rope?'

Chompa shrugged. 'It might not be common, but surely some djinnborn can do it? It was easy.'

'Easy? Don't you remember what I said earlier? Metals are not materials djinnborn are able to change. Metals resist us. I think it must be unprecedented – I've certainly never heard of it. I believe we've found your affinity, Chompa, and it's an extraordinary one. Extraordinary.'

But Chompa didn't feel extraordinary.

She felt strange, confused, and very alone.

✳

Back in Mohsin's study, Leeza poured them cups of soothing cardamom chai as Chompa relayed what Layli had told her. Chompa found that her hands were still shaking as she gripped the cup. Even as she spoke, her thoughts raced from Ammi, imprisoned halfway across the ocean, to the huddle of children she had found locked in the dark. Had left locked in the dark.

Mohsin sat deep in thought, too.

'They must have transferred Amina to another larger vessel, one suited to crossing the ocean. Perhaps the children are going to be kept in Dacca, or perhaps they'll be transported to Europe at a later date. Either way, Amina's abduction isn't a one-off. They *are* targeting magical people, Chompa. I don't know who's behind it, but one thing is certain: we're all in grave danger.'

Chompa took a gulp of hot tea, but felt chilled from within.

Mohsin looked directly at Chompa, his green eyes deep and sombre. 'There are guards at the gates of this campus, so I feel confident when you're here. But, Chompa, I entreat you: please do not leave the campus without me to protect you. I wasn't able to save your ammi from being taken – if you're lost, too, well, I won't be able to live with myself.' He breathed out shakily. 'Will you promise?'

Chompa nodded absently. Her mind was on something else.

'Uncle . . . that boat had a name. The girl, Layli – she said it. It was called . . .' She thought back through the hurried conversation. 'The *Alb* . . . the *Albi-on*.'

Mohsin sat up abruptly. 'Chompa! If we know the name, we can find out –'

'Who owns it,' Chompa finished.

Mohsin hurriedly put down his teacup and got to his feet. 'There are shipping registers I can consult at the Custom House. It's late, but I think I can persuade the guards to grant me access.'

It was midnight before he returned, covered in pink dust, his eyes glowing emerald with triumph. Chompa was still wide awake, full of fidgety energy.

'I discovered where the ship is registered to, Chompa. It's registered to the Lalbagh Fort, right here in Dacca. At first, that made no sense to me. The Lalbagh Fort has been empty for as long as anyone can remember. It was built by Dacca's ruler at the time for his daughter, but she died before it was finished. He believed the palace to be cursed and abandoned it. Legends grew up that it was haunted, and now no one goes near the place.

'So I took a trip to the fort. And it's not empty any more. In fact, quite the opposite. It's been spruced up, and there's someone living there: Sir Clive Devaynes. An Englishman. I've heard of him – he's been in the newspapers a lot recently. He has just been appointed by the British government as their Adviser on Indian Affairs. He owns a business called the Eastern Merchant Company, but it's so powerful people just refer to it as the Company.'

'The Company,' repeated Chompa. She felt a little chill down her spine.

Mohsin looked worried. 'Do you remember that I told you the British have taken a great deal from India, Chompa, using whatever means they deem necessary? Silk, tea, spices, indigo? Well, the Company has possibly taken more than any other organization. They have ripped through towns and villages, seizing goods and razing crops like locusts.' Mohsin's face was pale and drawn. 'And Sir Clive Devaynes, like his Company, is extremely powerful. He would be a dangerous adversary to have, Chompa. If the Company has begun abducting magical people – well, that changes everything. We're in even greater peril than I thought. We're going to have to tread very carefully, very carefully indeed. I need to make further enquiries.'

He placed a hand on Chompa's shoulder.

'We're getting closer to finding your ammi, I promise. For now, let's focus on what happened earlier. Silver, Chompa. Silver! All on your own!'

Chompa smiled tightly. She didn't think Mohsin would approve if she told him about the taviz she'd held in her pocket – the one she was supposed to have set aside. Had the charm helped her turn that rope to silver, or would she have been able to do it, anyway? Had Ammi known anything about it when she'd first given it to Chompa? She had to read Ammi's spellbook, see if she'd written anything about it in there. With a prick of guilt, Chompa remembered that Ammi had urged her to read the spellbook just before she'd been dragged away.

She was distracted by these thoughts, and yet everything Mohsin placed in front of her she turned effortlessly to silver:

a skein of thread, strips of paper, leaves and feathers. Other metals, though – a brass bowl, a steel cup – were not as easy. They took energy, concentration, and didn't do exactly what she wanted them to. And iron – iron was impossible, a solid wall of refusal, just as she'd felt in the hull with Layli's cuffs.

Mohsin noticed her flagging. 'Chompa, get some sleep, please. I'm sorry. I was just so fascinated, I got carried away. Your power is extraordinary. But it has its limits, just as mine does. Please forgive me. I will have Leeza come up with a cup of warm milk.'

She nodded and went to her room, but she didn't lie down to rest. Instead, she drew Ammi's spellbook from her bag. Just holding the book brought memories back, sharp and vivid like the prick of a needle. Ammi had always passed Chompa her Farsi textbook when she got her own book down for spellwork. She had come to resent the spellbook for that, but now, holding it in her hands, she felt strangely comforted by it.

The deep burgundy silk cover was fraying and unweaving itself in places. It was fastened together with a silver clasp that had been stitched into place. The pages were made of wood pulp so coarse that, here and there, bits of bark and leaf and plant matter could be seen poking through the words on the pages. It was drawn in, scrawled over, had pieces of paper tucked in it, symbols and diagrams spilling from the margins on to the printed words themselves.

Chompa ran her fingers over the spellbook. She tried to sound out a word slowly, then blinked. It was just a jumble of characters and didn't make any sense. She had to be reading it wrong. She rummaged in the bag for her textbook to check she'd got the characters right.

She opened the textbook and tried to match character to character. But when she turned back to the spellbook, the characters in Ammi's spellbook had *changed*. At first, Chompa thought she'd jumbled them up. But then she wrote out the letters carefully above the word in Ammi's book, checked her textbook, and glanced back again. The word below her handwriting was now completely different. The letters were *moving* and *changing* when she looked away.

An enchantment to stop anyone reading the book.

She snapped it shut in despair. Ammi had asked her to study her spellbook – but Chompa couldn't even read the letters! And she couldn't ask Mohsin for help when he had asked her to focus only on her finger-magic. He'd looked so stern when he'd said that.

*Think*, she urged herself. There had to be something there she needed to see. Ammi had been so insistent that she read the spellbook. It had to be important.

No – not *read*, she hadn't said *read*.

*Study.*

Chompa looked through the spellbook again, her brow furrowed with concentration.

At the bottom corner of the final page was a little green ink stamp. *The Writing-Magic Press*, *Old Dacca Chowk Bazaar* it read in crisp, satisfying blocks of legible type.

Something clicked.

# Chapter Ten

**B**ut it had to wait.

'Come, the saheb wants to see you after breakfast,' said Leeza the following morning. She clucked at Chompa's hair, hands on hips. 'I did your plaits last night. How are they already undone? And is that a . . . shell? Feral, feral . . .' she muttered, attacking Chompa's head with her comb, with none of the gentle dancing movements that Ammi used, but a ferocious jabbing style all her own.

Twenty minutes later, Chompa entered the study, her scalp twinging from the tightness of her new plaits. Mohsin sat at his desk, his expression grave.

'Come in, Chompa, and sit down. I made some enquiries into Clive Devaynes. I'm afraid – well, it's not looking promising.

'Devaynes is even wealthier than I thought. He's one of the richest men alive today, I'm told. He's made a massive fortune from shipping indigo. We call it "nil": blue. He has a huge fleet of ships, all painted that colour, taking indigo to Europe.'

Chompa thought of the deep inky blue of the *Albion*. 'Blue? As in a colour?' How could you grow rich on a *colour*?

Mohsin shrugged. 'In Britain, they call indigo "blue gold". It's a blue dye made from the indigo plant. Britishers so love to wear clothes in this particular shade that they are willing to pay handsomely for it. Indigo is hard to cultivate, and it leaves any ground it grows in infertile for other crops. But Devaynes has found a way to make it thrive here and has grown rich on it.'

*Indigo*. Something about this seemed familiar to Chompa. Then she had it, and her eyes grew wide. Jamila – the woman who had come for Ammi's help – had said that her family had been persuaded to turn all their rice crops over to indigo. But Chompa hadn't known what it meant at the time, and hadn't thought it interesting enough to ask about it, either. She could have kicked herself.

'But now it seems he's turning his attention from indigo to the magical people of India, Chompa. We already knew he's a favourite of the British government. Given how the Britishers are involving themselves in things in India, that doesn't bode well. *And* he has his own private militia. Those were the men guarding his boat yesterday. This is who we're up against! I simply don't know what to do!'

Chompa grabbed the edge of the table. 'We have to do something – we can't just give up!'

Mohsin looked tired. 'Honestly, I'm utterly out of my depth. What do we have to negotiate with? I doubt my tricks with plants will be of any value to him.' He waved a hand dismissively at the instruments on his desk with a bitter laugh.

Chompa frowned. 'You said he's wealthy, Uncle?'

'Unfortunately, yes; wealthier than I expect a humble scientist or a young witch could even imagine. And yet seemingly eager to grow richer and richer, no matter the cost to our people, our land.'

Chompa's fingers gripped the taviz in her pocket.

'But I could offer that to him. Couldn't I? With my affinity? Silver? I could turn a whole lot of worthless stuff to silver – like I did with those shells!' Her head was spinning, the plan taking shape in her mind only as she spoke. 'And, in return, I can ask him to take us to England.'

Mohsin looked astonished for a moment, and then shook his head.

'Absolutely not, Chompa. I utterly forbid it. It is far, far too dangerous! You want to work for – *with* – the man who might have been responsible for kidnapping Amina? You want to travel on one of his ships – maybe even the same ship that took her? It's out of the question. I will save up for our passage – it will take some time . . .'

Chompa jumped up, banging her hand on the desk.

'WE DON'T HAVE TIME, Uncle! It's my ammi at stake. I'll do whatever I have to do to get her back. Pretending I'm working with him is the only way I'll be able to get to England fast, the only way I'll find out where Ammi is. If you don't agree to help me, then – well, you said I could always go my own way whenever I wanted to. You've risked so much for me and Ammi already. Thank you for everything. I can take it from here.'

Mohsin sat back in his chair, looking stunned.

'Chompa – I – no. No. If anything happens to you, Amina will have my head.'

Chompa decided to take another tack. Tilting her head to one side, she softened her voice. 'If I go on my own, anything could happen to me. I'll be safer if you help me.'

Mohsin nodded hesitantly, running shaky fingers through his hair. 'Very well. I'll send him a note, introducing us and our . . . *proposition*. Something to do with your unusual skills might get his attention.' He shivered.

Chompa smiled. 'I have to get to England, Uncle. And no price I can pay will be too high. No price.'

Mohsin looked at her. 'Yes, Chompa. And that's exactly what I'm afraid of.'

An answer came with the university messenger just three hours later, on smooth ivory paper sealed with a blue wax stamp.

Mohsin read it and looked astonished. 'He's invited us to a dinner party! Tonight, at the Lalbagh Fort!'

It was Chompa's turn to look astonished. 'Dinner?'

'Yes. We have to wear "evening dress". We're to be among his guests, Chompa. I thought he might allow us ten minutes in his study, not this!' Mohsin looked despairing.

But Chompa brightened. 'If we're part of a group, it'll be easier to sneak off and do some exploring! This is much better than just meeting him on his own!'

Mohsin tugged worriedly at his beard. 'What if it's a trap? What's to stop him from simply capturing us?'

Chompa nodded slowly. 'It is possible, Uncle. But . . . I see no other way. No other way to reach Ammi. We have to take this chance.'

✳

'You've been sent this.'

Leeza bustled into Chompa's room later that afternoon, almost invisible under a dark blue oblong box that she then proceeded to dump on the bed.

Chompa opened it warily to reveal a cloud of cream fabric. Leeza hung it up and then slouched against a wall, watching Chompa, her mouth twitching with amusement.

Chompa frowned. The material was pretty – a fine muslin embroidered with delicate violet and green sprigs of flowers. In shape, it almost looked like her usual kameez tops – only it was longer, tighter at the waist, and flowing out more widely in pleats from there. But it had short sleeves, and a deep neck, and no scarf, or – or –

'Where are the salwar trousers?' she asked.

Leeza guffawed, and Chompa found herself getting cross. She hadn't had a maid before, but she wasn't sure this was at all how they were supposed to behave.

'What's so funny?' she demanded, scowling.

'Where did Saheb even pick you up? You really are just freshly plucked from the village, aren't you? This, my junglee, is a ferock. FER-OCK.'

'I see,' Chompa said, not seeing at all. 'But where are the salwar and the orna?'

Leeza started to giggle, but saw the displeasure growing on Chompa's face.

'There aren't any,' she replied quickly. She opened the wardrobe and thrust a bundle of white cotton skirts at Chompa. 'No trousers, no scarves. There are these petticoats that go underneath, but the pale ladies don't cover themselves like us. It's brazen, ungodly, but there you are.'

Leeza made a show of tucking her own scarf piously about her ears and raised an eyebrow at Chompa's wild, uncovered hair.

'Pale ladies?' Chompa's blood ran cold.

'Britisher memsahebs. Swanning all over the city with their husbands as if they own the place.' Leeza clucked her tongue. 'Now try it on. I need to see if it fits. If it doesn't, I'll have to fix it myself, I suppose. Tsk, the stitching is so fine. If I go blind like a muslin weaver, I'll have you to thank!'

Chompa looked the ferock – FER-OCK – up and down. She steeled herself and approached it as if it was a wild animal that needed tackling quickly. They were due to leave for Devaynes' home in just a few hours, and she had no time to dither about a *ferock*.

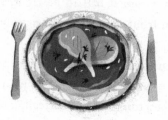

# Chapter Eleven

L eeza came huffing and puffing into Chompa's bedroom, bearing the adjusted ferock in her arms a couple of hours later. Chompa took a deep breath and advanced towards it.

Leeza made a scoffing sound. 'I stitched the pockets in as you wanted,' she said, pointing to little tucks on the sides.

'That's something at least.' Chompa transferred her taviz carefully from her kameez pocket.

She descended the stairs awkwardly and saw that Mohsin, too, was dressed differently, in a stiff-looking jacket rather than his usual fluid woven kurta.

'Why am I wearing this – this FER-OCK?' She pronounced the word carefully, just as Leeza had.

'Ah, that is a perfect rendition of Leeza's Old Dacca accent, Chompa! Fer-rock!' Mohsin laughed, and Chompa felt oddly put out.

Mohsin stopped laughing at once. 'I'm sorry. It's a frock. FR-OCK. Leeza pronounces it the way she does because she's, well, she's not familiar with English.'

'Oh.' Leeza had said the word with such solemnity that Chompa was sure it had to be right. And now she'd looked stupid in front of Mohsin. She ground her teeth in indignation.

'Devaynes sent it as a gift, as everyone there will be in English clothes, even the Indians. I know it's uncomfortable – I hate these clothes, too. But I have a feeling if we dress as we usually do, they won't even let us through the gate.'

Chompa felt like she took up far more space in the rickshaw than she had the previous day, all flounce and frill. Mohsin kept tugging uncomfortably at his collar. They didn't speak as they travelled to the Lalbagh Fort and walked up the pink path by a long rectangular pool that reflected the fort in its dark waters. The fort itself was a veritable dessert of a building, built of the same pretty pink stone as the path, topped with greened copper domes that looked like pistachio-cream swirls. Chompa's stomach rumbled somewhat inappropriately.

'Ready?' Mohsin asked, looking pale.

'Ready as we'll ever be, Uncle.'

They were ushered into a grand reception room. While the pink stone fort was crumbling outside, everything within had been painted white and blue and gleamed with a bright newness. There were men and women, mostly pale, but a few who were Indian, dressed in European finery, milling around with glasses. Chompa gulped. This was a completely different world. Mohsin put his hand on her shoulder, and she felt a bit more solid.

'Professor Mohsin Kabir, Dacca College, and Miss Chompa Begum, his ward.'

Chompa started at her name and swivelled round to see a servant reading loudly from a piece of paper. At the announcement of their names, all the guests in the room turned round to gaze at them. Chompa flushed, but then raised her head high. Let them stare: she was here for a reason.

And that reason was walking towards them, smiling.

As he approached, Sir Clive Devaynes reminded Chompa of a jungle animal lurking in the shadows before pouncing on its prey. He looked as if he'd once been broad and powerful, but his body had begun to sag at the seams, as though his wealth was accumulating in his bones. He appraised Mohsin and Chompa with cloudy grey eyes, a faintly amused expression playing about his pink lips. He gave a little bow, and Mohsin bowed back.

'Ah, Professor. Your letter this morning certainly piqued my interest! I am so very glad you and Miss Begum were able to attend my little . . . gathering.' He extended his hand in a lazy wave towards the guests. 'It is my pleasure to welcome you to my humble home.'

Chompa stood dumbstruck. The man was speaking Bangla, albeit with a glass-sharp accent. She frowned, unable to understand why he was talking about things as if they were small or humble when they were anything but.

Mohsin gave a thin smile. 'We were honoured,' he replied

smoothly. 'I've always wanted to visit the fort, despite all the rumours.'

Devaynes bent his head towards Chompa.

'And, Miss Begum, is everything to your taste?' His eyes twinkled in a way that made her uncomfortable, as if he was mocking her.

'It's l-lovely,' she stammered.

Mohsin leaned in towards Devaynes and spoke in a lower voice.

'Sir, while this is very pleasant, we do have something particular we wish to discuss with you. In my letter, you may recall I mentioned a very unusual skill that –'

Devaynes waved his hand. 'Later, later, my dears! I always like to acquaint myself socially with those who wish to conduct business with me. We shall continue our conversation after dinner.'

And with that he left to greet new guests at the door.

Once he was out of earshot, Mohsin gave a groan of frustration. 'What do we do now?'

Chompa thought. 'Let's listen to him talking to his guests. We need to find out everything we can about him.'

Mohsin nodded, and they shuffled closer to the ring of guests round Devaynes.

'India is serving you well, it seems, Sir Clive, with this indigo business,' gushed a red-faced man in a too-tight dinner suit.

Devaynes gave a little chuckle and a small bow. 'Yes, it's going as well as I could hope. But, Edward, I have a new project, and I shall need your legal eye over the next few days. The government back home has tasked me with passing a law that will ban the magical-charm trade.'

Next to Mohsin, Chompa gasped. So *he* was behind that too! He wasn't just kidnapping djinnborn. He was banning charm-writing at the same time.

She remembered the chaos of the protests. The pamphlet, reading *Defend our charm-writing traditions*. He was threatening everything. She swallowed a cry and stood absolutely still, listening avidly.

A thin woman shook her head and wrinkled her nose. 'These natives are still in the Dark Ages! Believing in charms and magic like children! You'll have to drag them kicking and screaming into the modern age. This country is lucky to have us.'

Devaynes gave another little bow. 'I rather hope it won't come to dragging. But certainly rooting out the fraudsters manipulating this country's poorest people is essential. The charm-writers have exploited them long enough.'

*Exploited*. Chompa's blood rushed to her ears. Despite her own impatience with charm-writing, she bristled at Devaynes calling Ammi's careful work *fraud*, as if it was simply a way to cheat poor people out of money. She thought of all the times Ammi's charms had helped the villagers back home. Her mother had never once accepted payment, or used magic for her own gain. Secretly, Chompa vowed to get better at writing-magic herself, as a kind of revenge – even though Mohsin had asked her to concentrate solely on finger-magic.

'But is there any basis in the rumours, Clive? That a certain form of magic *is* real?' said the red-faced man.

The slim woman snorted in disgust, but Devaynes' grey eyes twinkled.

'Ah, Edward, that would be telling, would it not?'

Devaynes bowed and turned away, and Chompa felt Mohsin grip her arm tightly.

When she looked down, she realized that she had raised her index finger, and that it was pointed directly at Clive Devaynes' back.

After drinks, they were ushered into a very long, grand room containing a long, grand table surrounded by chairs. Chompa was conspicuous as the only child in the room. Her feet couldn't reach the floor, and her chin nearly touched the table itself. Mohsin sat to her right, the man called Edward on her left. He peered at her in puzzlement once before turning to speak to the man on his other side.

Chompa muttered, 'When the time's right, I'll ask for directions to the bathroom, and get myself lost. Then I'll have a snoop around.'

'I don't know if that's a good idea, Chompa,' whispered Mohsin. 'He must have a large staff all around the fort.'

'I have to try, Uncle. We heard him talking about magic – and we know it was his boat that Ammi was on. There must be clues here as to what he wants with her and where she is.'

Mohsin looked nervous and ran a hand through his hair, but nodded.

Dinner was brought out by serving staff on bright white china plates with silver domed lids.

The first dish was delicate lamb chops, and Chompa's mouth watered when her plate was set before her. Lamb chops made by Ammi were one of Chompa's favourites. Ammi would cook them directly on a silver skewer over the fire, and they would be crisp and charred at the edges, tender in the middle, zinging with their chilli-lime-yoghurt marinade. With her fingers, Chompa could wolf down a dozen in five minutes.

Her fingers itched to put down the silly blunt knife and cumbersome fork and pick up the chops by the bones (what else were they there for if not to act as handles?). But she watched, and saw all the other guests around the table delicately slicing into the tiny cutlets, some with brows furrowed in effort and concentration. Inwardly, Chompa shook her head at the absurdity and, with resignation, clutched her cutlery again.

After sawing through the edge of a chop, Chompa put a chunk of pale brown lamb in her mouth and started to chew.

And chewed some more.

And she kept chewing, the piece of meat becoming more leathery and flavourless the harder she tried to break it down with her teeth. She wanted to spit it out, but something told her that would be even less acceptable than eating with one's fingers.

She forced herself to swallow the lump with a hasty gulp of water. Clearly, the chef had made some kind of mistake, at least with hers. He had entirely forgotten to spice the lamb. There was a vague saltiness, a hint of something like turmeric, but that was it. No garlic, no ginger, and absolutely no chilli.

Chompa peered around carefully to see if anyone else had noticed. But every plate looked exactly like hers, and all the guests round the table were making complimentary noises, even the brown-skinned ones. She looked up and down the table for a bowl of green chillies, but there were none. She seized upon the salt and pepper as though they were life rafts and shook them so enthusiastically over the chops that Mohsin began to chuckle.

'Welcome to British cuisine, Chompa!' he whispered conspiratorially.

Chompa's moment to slip away came during dessert, and she was half sorry that it did when she saw the little pot of rice pudding decorated with slivers of pistachio and pomegranate seeds.

Chompa ducked out from behind her chair, backed away through one of the doors and whispered to a servant that she was looking for the bathroom. The servant gave a sleepy wave in one direction, and she hurried on. Her heart thumped hard in her chest – how would she find what she didn't know she was looking for?

# Chapter Twelve

Chompa walked down the corridor as fast as she dared. The floors were paved with pink and green mosaics, the golden-brown wooden doors gleaming with fresh polish. She dipped her head into each room, searching for one that looked like Mohsin's study, a place Devaynes might spend most of his working hours. She thought quickly as she walked: Mohsin's office was at the front of the building so that people arriving for meetings didn't come into his personal rooms. She made her way round to what she felt, rather than knew, to be the front of the fort, looking over her shoulder from time to time.

Suddenly she heard voices, and her heart stopped. She pressed herself against the wall, squeezing her eyes shut, even though that wouldn't prevent her from being discovered. She squeezed the taviz hard in her pocket for luck.

'Arré, Laurie, just shine the shoes, yaar,' came a voice – a high, chirpy voice. A boy's voice.

'Tipu, we are not boot boys. We're magical. Honestly, it's

an insult to our profession to be used this way.' It was another boy, but his voice was a lower, languid drawl.

*Magical!* Chompa took a sharp breath.

'Laurie, we've got to keep our jobs. No one else wants to hire us, remember? So just shine them, please. It's not magic, but it is work.'

'Work we don't get *paid* for. Unlike the white servants,' the drawling boy grumbled.

'But we've got a roof over our heads, and I don't know about you, but I'm actually enjoying getting two meals every day rather than having to scavenge from rubbish heaps. Anyway, once the Big Saheb's new ship is ready, we'll be back to working magic and be on our way to London. If we last that long without getting thrown out on to the street.'

Chompa gasped. *London!* They were going to London, and they had magic! She was so taken aback she didn't hear the door opening.

Chompa froze as one of the boys came out and stood right in front of her. He was around her age, small and skinny. He was dressed in a neat white kurta shirt and trousers, but his hair was big and very messy.

'Are you lost, miss? Shall we show you back to the dining room?' he asked her, glancing at her frock. From his voice, she realized he was the one called Tipu.

Chompa flushed. She pulled the boy by the hand back into the room he'd stepped out of and closed the door firmly behind her. She looked around her quickly. There was a long table in the centre of the room covered with a cloth, and simple shelves lined the walls, stacked with shoe polish, brushes, and cloths. A whole room just for shining shoes. She shook her head in disbelief.

The boy called Laurie uttered an objection, and Chompa looked at him sharply. He was taller and sturdier than Tipu, darker-skinned, and his hair was a mass of soft curls where Tipu's stuck up in straight chunks.

'You two have magic?' she whispered.

The boys frowned and nodded.

'So do I,' said Chompa, chin raised.

'We're djinnspeakers,' Tipu said.

'I'm . . . I'm djinnborn,' she replied, trying to get used to the word.

Laurie snorted in disbelief.

Chompa glared at him. 'I am!'

She jabbed a finger at him, her other hand holding the taviz in her pocket. The fancy brown brogues in the boy's hands turned to silver.

His face fell. 'Hey! These are Saheb's shoes – if he finds them ruined, we'll be out on our ear! Again!'

She smiled in satisfaction, released the taviz and flicked her finger in a reverse motion. The shoes darkened to brown leather again. Laurie scowled, but she thought a look of admiration passed across the other boy's face.

'Listen, I know I have no right to ask you two, but I need your help. I have to find the place your saheb keeps his work things.'

Tipu nodded and stepped towards the door, but Laurie grabbed his arm and didn't let go. 'We can't help you, even if we did want to.' He turned to Tipu. 'We've got a few months left of our five years. We're going to be free, in *London*, to make our fortunes. We can't risk it,' he hissed, plonking the shoes down.

'This man, your *Big Saheb*, kidnapped my mother – I'm sure he did. He got men to come in the night and take her. He's kidnapping magical children, and adults, and taking them to England. I just don't know *why*.'

The other boy, Tipu, wrinkled his nose. 'That doesn't make sense – *we're* magical children. We've not been kidnapped. All right, we're not *paid*,' he admitted, seeing Chompa's raised eyebrow. 'But we're fed, and have a place to live. If he was abducting magical children, wouldn't we have been kidnapped, too?'

Chompa pursed her lips. They were right. It didn't make sense.

'I don't know . . . but he's definitely up to something. You have to help me. Please. Just show me the way and keep an eye out. If I get caught, I promise I won't give you away. To anyone.'

Tipu nodded once more, but Laurie elbowed him. 'So much for keeping our jobs, Tipu. Suddenly a pretty face comes along and –'

Chompa saw Tipu's ears go red. He shoved Laurie into the corner and spoke between his teeth. 'She's got magic – not quite like ours, no, but we have to stick together, right?

Look – I'll help her. You can stay here. Then you won't get in trouble.'

Laurie rolled his eyes. 'And what use is a weather diviner on his own, huh?'

Tipu turned back to Chompa. 'We'll help you. It's his study you're after. That's where he works, and people come for meetings, and we have to show them the way there if no one else is around. There are books and drawers of stuff there.'

'But she can't tell anyone about us helping her, OK? *Anyone*,' Laurie said, craning over Tipu's shoulder.

'I won't,' said Chompa, just as firmly. 'And I'm not *she*. My name's Chompa.'

Tipu and Laurie led the way to a corridor at the front of the building, and an ornate wooden door with a golden lion's head for a knocker. Tipu tried it with a glance back at Laurie and Chompa as he did so. Chompa bit her lip nervously. What if it was locked? All three breathed out simultaneously when the brass handle turned, and the door to Devaynes' study opened.

Facing Chompa in the airy room was a grand desk of pale wood. She crept in and shut the door behind her, leaving the boys to stand guard outside, one at either end of the corridor. Chompa knew she'd spent too long persuading them to help her – she had to be quick now.

She ran to the desk and tugged at a drawer – it stayed

firmly shut. She groaned in frustration. Thinking fast, she pulled out one of her wooden hairpins and pushed it into the lock. She placed her index finger on it, turned it to silver, and then thought 'fill'. The silver pin flowed into the hollow of the lock. Chompa had made herself a key.

She twisted it and opened the drawer, searching for something connected to Ammi. There were unusual objects in there: a dagger in the form of a tiger claw, a silver ring with a huge green stone, a hexagonal box that Chompa thought might be made from pure gold, a small silver globe . . .

And then she opened a second drawer.

Taviz.

So many taviz.

She sifted through the tangle of threads, in a rainbow of colours, each unique to the writer of the charms. Then her eyes spied it, and she nearly cried out. A taviz with a deep purple thread, a taviz she'd have known anywhere: the twin to her own. Ammi's.

Finally. She had *proof*. A weight – uncertainty – left her shoulders. She bunched up her fists, Ammi's taviz digging into her palm.

She knew what she had to do.

Suddenly she could hear clapping. Some kind of speech was starting. Chompa knew she only had a few minutes left before someone at the meal would realize she was missing.

She took a shaky breath and crept out of the door, whispering a quick 'Thank you!' to the boys, and darted back to the dining room, dropping Ammi's taviz into her pocket as she ran and hearing it clink against her own. Slipping quietly back into her seat, her absence utterly unnoticed, she looked at Devaynes, leaning back and basking in his easy power like a venomous lizard.

She shivered.

She was about to make a deal with a monster.

After the meal, some of the guests trailed out, all shaking Devaynes' hand. Others remained, chortling and ambling around the grounds.

In a corner, Chompa took Ammi's taviz out of her pocket and showed it to Mohsin.

'It's Ammi's. The thread is dark purple, like mine,' she whispered.

His face lost its colour, but he nodded.

They waited for Devaynes to say his farewells to the departing guests, and then approached. Mohsin had an easy smile on his face, but Chompa could feel his hand trembling on her shoulder.

'Such wonderful hospitality, Sir Clive. I wonder if we may further impose upon your kindness now?'

Devaynes bowed and ushered them towards his study, his eyes twinkling with amusement. Chompa's cheeks burned with rage. A nervous-looking young Indian man entered behind them with a clipboard and took his place at Devaynes' elbow.

Chompa and Mohsin sat down opposite the desk Chompa

had searched just minutes ago. Her throat tightened. Would Devaynes notice anything out of place? But he just eased himself into his chair, and leaned back, his speckled fingers steepled.

'Yes – let's talk, Professor Kabir. I must confess, your letter intrigued me! A business opportunity, you say; something to do with your ward?'

Mohsin didn't seem to know where to begin: his green eyes clouded and darted this way and that. Chompa took a deep breath.

'Actually, Sir Devaynes, I've come to ask for your help. I know you have ships that travel from here to London. The *fastest* ships. And I need to get there as soon as I can.'

Devaynes' face remained immobile apart from one reddish eyebrow, which arched slightly. 'I see,' he said coolly. 'Well, passage on my ships can be booked at the Eastern Merchant Company offices. My manager, Ismail, will provide you with directions.'

Ismail nodded eagerly and started scribbling on his clipboard.

Chompa's cheeks grew hot. She raised her palm to refuse the piece of paper.

'I haven't got enough money for that.'

Devaynes smiled pityingly. 'My dear, I am not in the business of charity. I'm terribly sorry, but if I allowed free passage on my ships, well, I would not be where I am now.'

Chompa forced herself to smile sweetly, her eyes wide and innocent.

'I know I'm asking a great deal of you. But we really need

a way to get to England quickly. I don't have much to offer in return, but I do have this.'

Chompa pulled over a little vase that stood on the table. She curled her fingers round the two taviz in her pocket, Ammi's pressing next to her own, making her feel bolder, more powerful. She concentrated on the pale pink rose in the vase. The stem of the flower turned silvery at its base, and then the pale, shimmery colour spread up the stem to the leaves and petals.

Chompa lowered her finger and lifted the silver rose out. Devaynes looked at it in Chompa's hands almost hungrily.

'Uncle tells me my power is unique. I can turn anything you want to silver. It's easy for me. I could even turn this fort to silver if you wished. That would be worth a fortune — much more than passage on your ship.'

Chompa paused and offered the rose to Devaynes. He reached out for it, but she held it firm.

'But only in return for getting us to London.'

Devaynes raised his eyes to hers, and nodded, just once, and she released the rose.

'You have a most extraordinary gift,' Devaynes murmured as he turned the rose over and over in his hands. 'I cannot deny . . . this changes things. It changes things significantly. As it happens, my new ship is about to start its maiden voyage — faster than anything you'll have ever seen before. I wasn't planning on accompanying it, but, yes, I see it might be better if I did. Very well, my child.

'Ismail, make arrangements for our journey.'

# Chapter Thirteen

Chompa smiled sweetly at Leeza over lunch the next day. Too sweetly.

'What is it that you want, hnnh?' asked Leeza immediately, eyes narrowed in suspicion.

Chompa had woken that morning with a plan buzzing in her head. Mohsin was busy tying up his university work while they waited for news about the journey to England, and she knew she had to act while she could. 'Leeza, I need to go somewhere, without Uncle knowing. Can you take me? I'll pay you.'

'Coins! You think I'm so cheap and low that a few poisha would tempt me to lose my job, huh?' Leeza cried indignantly, placing her hands on her hips.

'All right, all right,' said Chompa hastily. She pulled Ammi's spellbook out and showed the stamp to Leeza. 'Look at this. My mother bought this book from that shop, right here in this city. I need to find this place, Leeza – I need to find out more about Ammi, about her life and her magic, and she bought her books from there.'

Leeza screwed her eyes up over the book. Then she turned red and backed away. Chompa watched her carefully.

'Can you read it?' she ventured.

Leeza looked angry for a second, and then seemed to deflate. She shook her head miserably.

Chompa reached a hand out to her. 'I could teach you! I could teach you to read!'

Leeza put her nose in the air. 'And what use has a girl like me for your book learning, hnnh?'

Chompa hesitated. She herself had never liked reading much. But then she caught sight of a newspaper lining the base of the wardrobe. She pulled it out.

'Look here – on the middle pages. There are recipes, stories – and,' she said, tapping an etching of a group of women in fancy saris and jewellery, 'gossip columns.'

Leeza pursed her lips, clearly wavering.

'And how will I show you, huh, without losing my job? How would we even get past the guards at the campus gates?' she asked, head tilted enquiringly.

Chompa smiled. 'Trust me – I've got a plan. No one will know.'

Twenty minutes later, bedecked in a ragged cotton sari, the loose end draped modestly across her face, Chompa danced about her room, pulling this pose and that, as Leeza twitched and fidgeted with nerves. Then, as Chompa inspected herself in the mirror, she stilled, overcome by a memory.

The last time she'd dressed in a sari, she had been much younger, and it had been half of one of Ammi's that she'd stitched into a miniature version. They had had so much fun pretending to be old village crones together. The memory was a thread that pulled her out of time, and Chompa's heart bloomed suddenly with a longing that she thought might burst it. She shook herself and focused, bundling Ammi's bag of coins into the waist pleats of the sari, as she'd seen Ammi do on the rare occasions they went to market.

'Come on – let's go before it gets too late,' said Leeza, chewing nervously on the loose end of her sari.

Chompa squeezed Leeza's arm to calm her, but found that her own hand was shaking as they approached the gate. But the guard idly puffed at his bidi and scarcely glanced at them as they slipped through it. Maidservants like them were not worth any attention.

As soon as they were away from the university, people, noise, and smells seemed to spring up everywhere. Being back in the city after a couple of days in the neat, contained campus or the luxury of Lalbagh Fort was like seeing jungle after a manicured garden: it was so thrillingly alive. Chompa breathed in deeply, a cramp fading from her limbs. Used to roaming the river and the jungle, she realized just how caged she had been feeling.

She raised her hand and, for the first time in her life, hailed a rickshaw. A cyclist slowed and raised his head in enquiry.

'Old Dacca Chowk Bazaar,' she said haughtily, with a deeply satisfying rush of grown-upness.

The breeze blew playfully through Chompa's hair as the rickshaw wheeled along the wide streets, darting and weaving between the lumbering horse-drawn carriages like a little silver fish. Leeza grabbed Chompa's waist tightly as she waved her hand through the air.

'You should hold the edge of the hood. Any bump and you'll go flying into the street – and how will we explain your injuries, huh?'

'Chup-chup, Leeza, I'm fine. I won't fall!'

Chompa pulled herself up to standing, both hands reaching to the sky. The rickshaw-wallah muttered in rough, accented Bangla to Leeza.

'He's agreeing with me – sit down. He thinks you might be mad. I know you are.'

Soon the streets started to narrow, and the buildings became disordered, tumbling structures of tiles, brick, aluminium – anything that was spare, cheap, and would hold off heavy monsoon rains. And people – suddenly there were people *everywhere*. It didn't seem possible, but the noise seemed to grow louder as they approached a slightly more uniform set of buildings packed into a tight grid. The rickshaw slowed to a stop.

Chompa jumped out and paid the driver. Her nerves thrilled with excitement.

'Look – talking mynah birds. Do you want one, Leeza? I'll buy you one.'

Leeza looked surprised and then a little mollified. She shook her head.

'I have no need of a pet. I've enough looking-after to do with you. But – I am a bit hungry . . .'

She arched an eyebrow at a stall with five giant black cauldrons at the front. In them boiled thick, clear sugar syrup, and a range of different sweetmeats. Into the one right in the centre, a thin man in a dirty apron poured batter in a blur of movement. Chompa looked down into it, and her stomach rumbled, too, and she reached for her coins.

The pair searched the market for the bookstall, munching on sweet, crisp spirals of amber-coloured jalebi from a banana-leaf packet. It was chaos here, but as with the rest of the city it was of an ordered kind. One row of stalls was for vegetable sellers, the air heavy with the heady green scent of coriander, then came a row of butchers' stalls, where flies buzzed about hung carcasses enthusiastically, and blood ran in rivulets across the earth. Each row was teeming with customers, but Chompa was looking for only one particular place.

At the very edge of the market, they found it.

The last row had a single dusty dark stall with not a single customer. It was run by a wizened old woman, her entire face concealed by the end of her black sari. Chompa walked slowly in silence as she browsed the items on show: bottles of various shapes in vivid colours; cooking equipment and trinkets; bowls and grinding stones made from old discoloured brass; little carved boxes; ceramic dishes of silver necklaces and bracelets. The wares varied in age, beauty, and quality, but all of them were completely covered in Farsi writing.

On the final table lay neat stacks of crisp, unblemished books, all with familiar sari-silk covers and silver clasps. Chompa's heart leaped with excitement. She might meet the person who had sold Ammi her book.

'Excuse me, Auntie-ji, but can you tell me who makes these books, please?'

The woman raised her head sharply in Chompa's direction, her crooked, ancient back suddenly snapping straight. The end of the sari flapped away from her face for a moment, and Chompa had the briefest impression of an unlined face surrounded by incongruously short curls.

'Why do you ask?' she growled in a deep, low, strong voice as she tucked the sari end back behind her ear tightly.

'I – I've just seen one before.'

The woman turned away, muttering. 'It's of no business to a nosy little child like you – this is not a toyshop. Go find another place to spend your coins.'

Chompa snapped. 'I am not a nosy child, thank you. I'm here to find out about my mother. Her name was Amina Begum, and she bought books from this stall.'

The woman gasped and then stumbled, clutching the table. Chompa looked over her shoulder, confused, thinking that something must have frightened the old woman. But the alley was empty, Leeza clearly having traipsed off to friendlier stalls. Chompa turned back and jumped to find the stallholder right in front of her, pulling at the sari end, unveiling herself.

She was young, perhaps in her early thirties. She raised her gloved hands to Chompa's face and cupped it gently.

'Mash'Allah,' the woman breathed. 'It's like a young mirror. As if Amina never left.'

*Left?*

'Did you know my mother?' Chompa spluttered.

The woman looked around her, behind her, uneasy.

'We cannot speak here. There's going to be another demonstration, so I was about to close up, anyway. My name is Farhana. Follow me.'

Chompa found Leeza at the jewellery stalls, and they hurried after the woman, wheeling her wares away on a trolley. The dusty, sweet smell of books even overpowered the open drains, and the air was filled with clanging and clattering from the presses, which peeked from half-open doors along the street. Book reading might be quiet, but book making was a noisy, dirty business.

One hut was hung with a faded red sari in place of a door. The woman and the trolley disappeared through it. A little nervously, Chompa followed, pulling Leeza after her.

Setting the cart to one side, the woman ducked behind a curtained area.

On edge, Chompa looked about the hut to gather clues about this strange woman. The room was dominated by the carved wooden body of a machine that looked like a gigantic bed, hollowed out and filled with levers and two large, square metal plates. Every remaining area of space was covered with books, scrolls, and stacks of pamphlets. The air smelled of freshly cut wood and chemicals.

Farhana returned with lime sherbet in tin cups and a plate of salty little cumin-studded biscuits.

'Sit, sit,' she said, gesturing impatiently at some tattered cushions round a low wicker table. 'Amina will be cross if I don't feed you. Where is she?'

Chompa was startled at the hospitality. Was Farhana someone she could trust? She decided to be cautious. 'My name's Chompa. This is Leeza. How did you know my mother?'

'She was my friend. We lived here in Dacca together.'

Friends! Ammi had more friends in the city – first Mohsin, and now Farhana! And – Ammi had *lived* in the city herself. Why, then, had Chompa and her mother eked out such a lonely existence in so backward a place?

Ammi's accent wasn't quite the same as the villagers', but that was because they lived on the edge, and Ammi had immersed herself in writing rather than in village life – or so Chompa had always thought. She'd never once considered the possibility that Ammi was from Dacca, particularly because Ammi had always been so reluctant to answer Chompa's questions about it. Chompa's mind buzzed and whirred, but she knew she had to focus, to ask the right questions.

'How did you meet her? When? Where?'

Farhana's brow furrowed. 'Where have you been living? Why isn't she here with you?'

Chompa looked down at her palms.

'If Ammi bought her books from you, does it mean I can trust you?' she asked, almost speaking to herself.

Farhana held out her wrist. 'Look.'

Chompa took Farhana's slim wrist in her hands. It jangled with dozens of silver bracelets and a dozen or so taviz on dark green thread but tucked among them was the familiar purple thread of her ammi's taviz. Chompa ran her finger over the scrollwork, and put her hand in her pocket, searching out the two taviz that lay entwined there together.

'Amina didn't buy books from me, Chompa. We wrote and we printed them together. This was our printing press.'

# Chapter Fourteen

Chompa started in surprise. 'I thought she was just a village witch!'

Farhana looked astonished. 'Amina! A village witch? She was the leader of our circle!'

'What circle?' Chompa asked.

'There were fifteen of us at one point. We wanted to spread knowledge of magic to all. To make magic something that every single person could learn, could better their lives with – not just the djinnborn. *Everyone*.' Farhana's eyes looked bright as she spoke. 'It was her idea to print books to teach writing-magic. But . . . Was. Was. Why do you speak of her in the past tense? What's happened to her?'

Chompa hated telling the story. The images came back thick and fast, the same feelings of terror and failure. She didn't know where to begin.

'She was taken. And then someone came –'

Farhana grabbed Chompa's wrist in shock. 'When? Who took her?'

Chompa forced herself to explain the events of that terrible night. By the time she was describing the sight of the blue boat sailing away, Farhana had risen and was pacing, agitated, her fingers twisting through her curls, muttering to herself.

'She always feared this would happen. I wrote to her, telling her to come and live back here where we could protect you at least. But she wouldn't listen.'

'Is the rest of the circle still here?'

Farhana looked at Chompa. Her mouth was drawn into a line of sadness, and her eyes seemed even wearier.

'Until last week, there were four of us. But Shahrin, Nita, and Taanvi were arrested after the last writing-magic demonstration. The British plan to execute them. No trial. So there's just me here now.'

The room seemed to shift for Chompa. She felt like she couldn't breathe. So many disparate little pieces of information all rending apart her own knowledge of Ammi's life until now. She clasped the two entwined taviz in her fist, her stomach a knot of guilt.

'You said she was afraid this would happen. Did she have any idea who was going to be after her?'

Farhana shook her head. 'She didn't say. She said I was better off not knowing – safer, even. She was always trying to protect everyone. Everyone but herself,' she muttered bitterly.

Chompa felt a surge of pride for Ammi and remembered what the little girl on the boat had said – that Ammi had tried to take care of them all, even when she was in danger herself.

'It's happened this way for centuries – hunting down

djinnborn and forcing them to do magic for the hunters' own gain. It half makes me glad I'm not,' Farhana went on.

Chompa's eyes widened. 'You're not djinnborn?'

'No, I'm not.'

Leeza leaped in. 'But then why are you doing all this? What's the point if you don't have magic?' She waved her hand towards the press and the books.

Farhana raised her finger mockingly. 'I *have* magic. Just not that kind. You can't learn djinn-magic – you're either born with it or you're not – but *anyone* can learn writing-magic. With the right instruction, the right books –' here Farhana gestured at the printing press – 'it's available to anyone. Doesn't that seem a better way? Not that everyone agrees. Our new rulers, the British, for example.' Farhana's tone was bitter.

Chompa frowned, unsure. Even though she'd promised herself she'd start taking writing-magic more seriously, it was so *slow*. But then she turned, saw that Leeza was staring at Farhana, transfixed, and she finally understood.

When she had offered to teach Leeza to read and write, she hadn't even realized that would mean Leeza would be able to learn writing-magic, too. And writing-magic could give Leeza a way out of the life she chafed against, just as Ammi had offered Jamila a way out.

It could give *anyone* a way out.

Suddenly Chompa felt dizzy – dizzy at the possibility, at the power of her mother's charms. And they were under threat. From the same person who was kidnapping djinnborn and djinnspeakers.

'There's this British man – he's called Devaynes –'

Farhana exhaled with disgust. 'I know the name. Yes, he's behind the ban. It's his thugs who are trying to clamp down on writing-magic.'

Men's voices outside silenced Farhana. She darted to the red sari and peered out, then turned back, flushed, eyes wide.

'Speaking of thugs . . . You need to leave – now.'

Chompa began to object and then saw the unconcealed fear in Farhana's eyes.

'Chompa, I told you that writing-magic is being outlawed. My friends are going to pay the ultimate price. The British are our rulers now – and they want to stop anyone practising it. They're coming. They're coming for all this.' Farhana pulled Chompa and Leeza up off their cushions and pushed them towards the sari. 'If writing charms is to have any chance of surviving, I can't be caught. What are you waiting for? Go!'

'How will I find you?'

Farhana just pointed to her wrist of bangles and bracelets.

'Chompa, your taviz –'

But they could hear the men's voices more clearly now, and Chompa and Leeza found themselves pushed out into the street before Farhana could finish. The voices had become more like beats of a drum: measured, rhythmic, and getting louder. Chompa looked around wildly, grasping Leeza by the hand. They ran down an alley into the main street, and Chompa pulled Leeza into a bookshop. They crept under a shelf, only to hear rickshaw bells and shouts as a throng of Indian men marched towards them, carrying sticks with squares of cloth stretched across, with red, angry words painted in big, bold characters. They could hear the chant clearly now: the beat of it slow, intent, violent.

'*Burn out writing-magic. Burn it out. Tear it, rip it, burn it out.*'

The men funnelled down the alley, coming to a halt outside Farhana's sari door.

'Chompa, we've got to go!' hissed Leeza.

Chompa set her mouth in an obstinate line. 'I need to make sure she's OK. I've still got so much to ask her!'

They watched from behind a bookshelf as the men entered the press. They heard loud crashing and breaking sounds coming from inside and instinctively clutched each other's hands, their palms slick with sweat. Eventually, the noises died down, and the men marched on. Chompa peeped over the bookshelf. Farhana wasn't with them.

'She must have got away,' she whispered in relief.

'We need to go,' Leeza hissed again, tugging at Chompa's wrist.

Chompa shook her head. 'I have to see if she's left me a message, a way to find her.'

With a heavy feeling of dread, Chompa pushed through the red-sari curtain. The sheer scale of the devastation left her open-mouthed.

'Ai-hai!' cried Leeza in horror.

The printing press was turned over on its side. Levers had been wrenched and snapped off, leaving pale wounds of raw, splintered wood. Outside, other printing machines clacked on as if nothing had happened. Only Farhana's magical press had been targeted.

Chompa sagged to the floor. It was too much to bear.

'I should have stayed with her . . . I shouldn't have let anything stop me . . .' she whispered.

Leeza patted Chompa's shoulder. 'Let's have a look around. Maybe we'll find that message.'

The girls picked their way carefully through the chaos in the hut. There was torn, shredded paper everywhere, fibres even floating in the air, making them cough. The floor was carpeted with the empty covers of books that had had their pages brutally ripped from them, and little metal cubes with digits and characters on them were scattered everywhere.

Leeza gathered up heaps of paper, sorting them into colours. Chompa tried to piece bits together. But the paper had been shredded and crushed, and there was so much of it, it was impossible. Chompa felt tired and lost in the face of some huge, violent danger that just kept taking things away from her, for no reason she could fathom. Devaynes.

'There's nothing here,' said Leeza, tugging at Chompa's arm. 'Let's go – it's not safe.'

But Chompa didn't move, just stared at the piles of paper. She thought that some had been posters, others the pages of spellbooks ready to be stitched together. 'This was Ammi's work. I can't just leave it like this.'

Her fingers closed round the pair of taviz in her pocket. The cool touch of the etched silver, made by her mother's hands, seemed to awaken her. She snapped her eyes open.

Paper was made from trees, and trees had been alive once. There were fibres still streaming all around, and Chompa could almost sense the pulsing pain of the dying books within them. There was energy in the pages, in the fibres dancing in the light.

She could work with energy.

She trained her eyes on one of the shreds, and ran her fingers through the soft, feathery heaps around her. She unwove the knotted fibres in her mind, focusing on the idea of healing. She didn't know if the spell would return the fibres to paper or tree form, but she had to try.

Paper began to swirl like leaves during monsoon round Chompa's still form, until she was almost completely concealed by a greyish-white swarm.

Leeza stopped her browsing of the paper and watched, mesmerized.

Chompa brought her hands together.

Leeza's eyes grew huge in the half-light as the pieces of paper looked, actually *looked*, for their sister selves – there was no other way to describe it. They flurried and turned away from some, and moved towards others, gradually drawing together in the air in little clouds.

Then Chompa unlaced her fingers, straightened her hands into flat palms, and laid one on top of the other. The clouds trembled and unravelled, winding themselves into flat, almost perfect pieces of paper.

Leeza clapped her hands together and cackled with glee, making Chompa snap back into focus. Together, they watched the pages waft gently to the ground, settling themselves into neat little piles as they did so.

Leeza picked up one of the cushions and removed its cover.

'We should leave soon – it's getting dark. Let's put one of each pile in here and go.'

Chompa took a little stack of each pamphlet. Glancing at one, she saw an image of a taviz and above it the words DEFEND OUR CHARM-WRITING TRADITIONS! She started. She'd seen it before. And then she remembered – someone had pushed a leaflet into her hands when she was in the rickshaw, arriving in Dacca. To think, now, that it might even have been Farhana!

Chompa turned the pamphlet over and over in her hands, stunned. All these connections, and yet she'd had no idea.

As they prepared to leave, Chompa stopped and looked back at the printing room.

'My mother was here once, making these books. She never told me about it, about so many things. And Farhana could have told me, and now she's gone, too.'

Leeza put her hand on Chompa's shoulder.

'Do you think Farhana's all right?' Chompa asked, even though she knew Leeza wouldn't know. She suddenly felt very young, and her voice trembled as she clutched Leeza's hand, pleading for a scrap of hope.

Leeza's mouth twitched in an attempt at a hopeful smile. 'She seemed like someone who could take care of herself.'

'I hope so.'

Later, they laid out the sheaves of paper across the floor of Chompa's room, munching on spicy puffed rice and peanuts as they looked at them.

Chompa picked up the pamphlet to read aloud the smaller print under the headline.

'The British want to ban our writing-magic, claiming we are cheats. But they want to ban it because they wish to control us.

'Anyone can learn it. Anyone can practise it. Anyone can improve their life with it. This is what the British fear.

'That is what the Writing-Magic Press was set up for, to help get magic to those who need it most. But now we all need it. Now we are all under threat.

'We must rise. We must stop this. The British may be starting with magic, but what comes next? Our freedom. We must unite and fight.'

She let it flutter back to the ground. 'Ammi and Farhana wanted to spread writing-magic,' she murmured. 'They believed everyone should learn it. That's why they made textbooks and spellbooks, to help people. I never realized. I never realized it was important.'

She turned to Leeza. 'What I said before – I mean it. I will teach you letters, and *then* I'll teach you charms, once I've got the hang of them myself. That way I'll be helping Ammi and Farhana, too.'

For the first time, she pulled out her textbooks with something like excitement.

An hour later, they were still engrossed in their studies and both jumped when there was a knock on the door, quiet but urgent. Chompa tucked the textbooks away hurriedly, and Leeza started folding the quilt on the bed.

Chompa opened the door to reveal Mohsin standing there with a letter in his hand. He looked pale.

'Uncle, what is it? Is it Ammi?'

Mohsin swallowed. Chompa noticed his hand was shaking.

'It's from Sir Clive, Chompa. It just arrived. He says passage has been arranged for the three of us on his brand-new ship's maiden voyage to England. But it's sooner than I thought. We leave Dacca tomorrow.'

Chompa slept badly that night, as if she was in a fever, tossing and turning, reliving the terror of Ammi's abduction. The rest of the evening had been spent packing and preparing, and practising some new English phrases Mohsin had taught her. Speaking the language made her feel like a traitor, but she knew she'd need it. Would Ammi be proud of her? she'd wondered. She didn't know. The two of them had always lived in the present, and Ammi had never shared her hopes for Chompa with her. Ahead was a new, uncertain future, of which she snatched only glimpses.

Exhausted, nerves jangling, she had climbed into her bed – for the last time, she thought. All she'd wanted was to get one step closer to Ammi, and now she was about to take that step – but Farhana, her mother's friend, was missing, and the printing press they had built together destroyed. Chompa had no time now to find Farhana again. And what if Ammi wasn't in England, after all, or they couldn't find her there? What if Devaynes ended up imprisoning Chompa – and Mohsin, too?

Chompa didn't know when she'd fallen asleep, but asleep she must have been for she woke abruptly, heart hammering, sheets twisted and damp, in the half-light.

*Mohsin! Mohsin! Mohsin!*

The words seemed to ring so loud that she wondered why others weren't stirring, too. The silence and the stillness about her seemed unnatural. She held her breath, waiting for the voice again. Nothing. Only the hum of crickets and Leeza breathing in and out.

The voice rang once more in Chompa's ears, a sharp pinch of memory. It slowly dawned on her that it had only been heard by her in her sleep.

Ammi's voice, crying out for Mohsin, over and over and over.

# Chapter Fifteen

Tipu scaled the trunk of the tree without effort, making for the nest of splayed, tender palm leaves – his favourite place to watch all the goings-on that accompanied imminent departure. As he munched on the salty yellow cheese Laurie had 'procured' for them from the galley – the one item of Company rations he was actually getting used to – his eyes were drawn downwards towards the pair walking onboard.

'Look, it's that magical girl, Laurie – the one from Big Saheb's house!' called Tipu to his friend down on deck. 'She's with someone, and they're boarding!'

'Arré, what are they doing here?'

Tipu shrugged and kept watching.

It was different seeing the girl from up in the tree. She seemed less bossy, less full of herself than she had at the fort. She was small, slight, and dark like him, with a shock of hair that almost out-shocked his own. Her skin had a warm copper tone while his was more yellow.

Tipu leaned into the papery leaves, trailing his fingers

through the sliced ribbon edges, and whispered in Farsi.

'That girl over there is called Chompa. She can do magic like us! But guess what? She can change metals! Silver, at least. How can that be? Djinn hate metals, right?'

The palm leaves bristled under his fingers like the fur of an angry cat. Tipu stroked them placatingly.

'Calm yourself, Aaliya. She does magic; we do magic. I'm just curious, on a professional level.'

The tree arched one of her branches back very taut, and then released it, smacking Tipu hard in the face.

'I am not lying!' Tipu exclaimed with the hot indignation of one caught out, as he rubbed his stinging cheek.

The leaves folded in on themselves in a haughty fashion. Tipu was tempted to roll his eyes, but it was too close to casting off, and he and the djinn needed to work together.

'Come, Aaliya, I'm sorry. I know we haven't known each other long, but let's focus, both of us, or Farook Miah will have my hide, and he'll put that iron clamp round you again. I know that's painful for you. I'll polish your leaves,' he wheedled, knowing the djinn was vain about the appearance of her tree.

It was a funny thing to be vain when you were invisible, but Tipu supposed the tree was as close to having a body as the djinn could get, and she had been bound to it since it was a seedling.

The leaves unfurled, and one of the branches curved round expectantly, just as a holler came from the top deck.

'Later, I promise. But we must get the ship moving now. The anchor's been pulled up. This is our first and only shot at getting this right. You're a powerful being, Aaliya. I know this is small fry for you.'

It was Aaliya who – if she chose to cooperate – would propel the ship forward using the roots of her tree, the deepest of which were woven among the timbers of the vessel. She would use her branches, in place of a sail, to steer. Tipu held his breath, fearful that she'd refuse. It had taken him months to gain the trust of the little fishing boat's djinn when he and Laurie had worked the Buriganga River, and he'd only been put on the *Kohinoor* last week – the biggest ship he'd ever seen, let alone worked on. It still seemed unbelievable that he, an ordinary, unwanted boy from a tiny village in Gujarat, should be able to persuade anyone to do his bidding, let alone this powerful tree-djinn.

The *Kohinoor* began to move. Actually, it began to rock from side to side. Tipu was flung out of his nest, and found himself dangling over the water, grabbing on to a branch for dear life. Cries came from the crew below.

'I knew this was bad luck!'

'We're doomed, and we haven't even left port!'

Tipu blocked out the voices and whispered a flurry of encouraging words to Aaliya. 'Focus on the tips of your roots, on where you make contact with the water. Focus on pushing forward first. Don't worry – we'll steer after. Focus, focus.'

The ship gradually righted itself, and then lurched forward, causing water to splash on to the decks. Another lurch and the *Kohinoor* moved smoothly in a straight line.

Tipu felt a heady rush of relief. Swinging himself back

into the nest, he shook his head to regain clarity, and then spoke directions, relayed to him from below by Laurie, to Aaliya to guide the ship out of the tricky, crowded port. Tipu could see the sailors in the smaller fishing boats craning their necks to take in the impossible sight: no masts, no sails, not even a wheel to steer the huge ship. Just a massive, straight-trunked date tree sprouting upward from the deck into a fountain of green palms, a tiny brown boy balanced among them. Tipu watched the fishermen shake their heads in awe, muttering prayers to ward off bad luck.

Tipu and Aaliya nudged the helm past the little boats, and then they were out into open water. They plunged forward, and the waves foamed about the *Kohinoor* as they set sail for England.

Double-checking with Laurie, Tipu fixed the direction with Aaliya, who angled her branches appropriately, and then started looking for the girl again. Chompa. He saw her pacing the deck, her back to him. He scaled down the trunk, jumping lightly on to the roof of the cabin. He gripped a metal pipe on the side, ready to jump on deck.

'As one of Sir Clive Devaynes' esteemed guests, I could have you flogged for following me.'

Her voice was cold and crisp. Tipu lost his grip on the metal pipe and landed heavily on the deck.

'Smooth.'

Tipu felt deflated. But then Chompa grinned, and helped him up, and he grinned back.

'Why are you dressed like those Britishers?' he asked. 'You

were wearing something like that at the fort, too. Isn't it uncomfortable?'

She crossed her arms about herself, uneasy.

'My uncle said it would help the other passengers treat us better. It doesn't mean I'm one of them.'

'No.'

'I'm not!'

He was bewildered by her ferocity.

'Your magic,' he said, changing the subject, 'that's some seriously unusual, powerful stuff.'

She narrowed her brown-black eyes dangerously. 'Yes. Everyone keeps telling me that.' But then she softened. 'Thank you for helping me find the study, back at the fort. It was brave of you. And your friend – Laurie, was it? You're Tipu, right?'

Tipu puffed his chest out.

'All in a day's work. Us magical folk, we must stick together. I've been promoted. Used to work on these little fishing boats taking indigo up and down the river. Now look. Look at this ship. I'm entirely responsible for us being afloat, you know.'

'How?' asked Chompa, curious. 'How are we not sinking? We don't have any sails, and the tree's got to weigh a lot.'

'Ah,' said Tipu. 'Well, see that circle there cut in the deck? It's filled with earth all the way down to the bottom of the hull – it's just a massive pipe. Usually, date palms have very shallow roots, but I commanded my djinn to grow some of her roots all the way down, and wrap themselves round the timbers. Some of the timbers are made from her branches, so she's connected to them, and can control them. And I, of course, control her.'

Tipu glanced uneasily at the tree, hoping the djinn hadn't heard, and Chompa raised a dubious eyebrow. He decided to change tack.

'Anyway, it's so nice to not be in a straggly, spiky rattan tree like before – oof, it was so uncomfortable!' Tipu rubbed comically at his back, hoping to get a laugh out of her. He didn't.

Tipu coughed uncomfortably. 'Are you going to England, then? Is that where your mother is?'

Chompa hesitated, looking around. Two English passengers were strolling on deck.

Tipu lowered his voice. 'Let's speak up in the tree. No one can hear us there. This palm gives date sap – you've honestly never tasted anything like it. It's so sweet, with a burnt-sugar taste, but refreshing, too –'

She looked up at the tree, and Tipu could see that she was clearly tempted.

A few minutes later, Tipu was clutching his sides, guffawing.

'There's nothing to hold on to!' Chompa hissed down to him, as she clung desperately to the tree's trunk, about two inches off the ground.

Tipu stopped laughing, and tried to guide her, but after managing about a foot she lost the remaining strength in her arms and painfully scraped down the trunk and into the damp earth.

He landed lightly beside her, incredulous. 'Are you seriously telling me that you lived in a village, with trees all around, and you can't climb? However did you pick mangoes or guavas?'

'I'm a witch. If I wanted a mango, I just used this.' She waggled her index finger. 'I never needed to climb anything like a stupid monkey.'

Tipu chuckled to himself very quietly. She was already really angry, and he didn't want to risk her storming off and never coming back. In Farsi, he asked Aaliya to put out some of her branchlings for Chompa to climb up with. But the tree remained stubbornly still and unsprouted. Tipu rolled his eyes in exasperation and finally, after much pleading, convinced her.

'You speak Farsi? How did you learn?' Chompa said once they were settled at the top of the tree.

Tipu shrugged. 'My father taught me. I guess you were taught it, too, right? So you could talk to djinn?' Tipu felt gladdened that they had something in common.

Chompa shook her head slowly. 'I'm learning. But I don't need to talk to djinn.'

Tipu's eyes widened. 'What do you mean?'

'I mean, I don't have to ask a djinn to do magic for me. I'm not a djinnspeaker, like I told you before. I'm djinnborn. I just focus on something I want to change, think of the right words, and then I change it, using my finger. My uncle's the same, and so's my ammi, even if she never uses it.'

Tipu looked at her long and hard. 'That's odd. I always thought you had to summon the spirits you can speak to and ask them to help you. That's what me and Laurie do, anyway. But for me it only works with tree-djinn. And he can only use his sandbox to ask about the weather. I definitely couldn't just point my finger and . . . do stuff.'

She arched an eyebrow. 'Have you tried?'

'Well – no.'

'Then how do you know you can't?'

Tipu raised his index finger and tried to focus. Aaliya made rude noises, using the wind through the leaves.

'Shh just for a second. We're trying something,' Tipu whispered.

She rustled angrily, but then became still, curious.

He kept his eyes screwed shut. He tried to silence all the thoughts and sounds and the huge presence that was Aaliya in his mind, but one kept tumbling over the other even as it subsided, like rolling waves.

He opened one eye a little. 'Nothing's happening. No – it's you. You're different.' He looked at her sideways, half resentful, half impressed. 'Special.'

'We have different amounts of djinn blood in us. I just have more.' But Chompa didn't look at him when she said it.

He puffed out his cheeks and exhaled. 'Shame. Krishna knows there's plenty I'd change if I could.'

'What would you do if you could change things?' Her head was cocked to one side, eyes focused on Tipu, interested.

Tipu thought long and hard. There had always been someone in control of his life: first his father, then his stepmother, then Farook Miah, the man who had bought him from her. Even Laurie made most of his decisions for him now, Tipu thought with a pang of unease. He wondered what it would be like to take charge of his own life, to be *free*. It felt like a precipice – one that made his stomach tip, but which also called to him to jump, even though he had no idea what lay below.

Yet he was poor, and wouldn't become less so working for nothing. And, like the fishermen who muttered protective prayers at the sight of him, most people in India wouldn't employ kids with magic as far as they could throw them. He and Laurie were tainted goods, and they'd never be free.

'Everything,' he said quietly. He dug his hands into the branches, feeling the bark pressing painfully into his skin.

Chompa looked down at his gripped pale fists and nudged one gently.

'I know. There are things that magic on its own can't change.'

Laurie pulled his sleepy form up through the tree hole. 'Good morning, madam,' he said theatrically, in English, with a bow so deep he nearly tipped over.

Chompa scowled.

Tipu produced a branch of dates for the three of them. It looked like a pale golden ear jewel, the dates like little amber stones cascading from it. They were round and plump and fragranced like brown sugar. Laurie put his palm out flat, expectantly, as he fixed his gaze on Chompa.

'So, Madam Witch Princess, why don't you show us a bit more of what you can do, huh? Or is it only shoes you can turn to silver? Not that that isn't a useful skill to have, of course.'

Chompa narrowed her eyes dangerously. Tipu flicked a date stone at Laurie with a stern glare. Laurie rubbed his elbow and blithely ignored him.

'And what is it *you* do?' Chompa growled through clamped teeth.

Laurie flourished his hands towards the sandbox down on the deck.

'I read the weather, or rather the djinn in the box does, at my command. And then I navigate us away from storms, safely to our destination. Rather invaluable for a ship.'

'Read the weather? Can't you just look around you?' Chompa scoffed.

Laurie sighed wearily. 'A subtle art would, of course, be lost on someone who prefers a *flashier* style. I *divine* the weather that will come. Tipu and I come as a package. Observe.' He slipped down the trunk and jumped lightly on to the deck. Curious, Chompa followed him down in a series of bumps and slithers, scowling when she got to the bottom. The dates were not worth the indignity, she decided, as she dusted herself off.

Laurie settled into a cross-legged position, his face solemn, and opened a drawer on the sandbox to reveal a small pink shell.

'My djinn, Muyaka, is bound to this.'

He placed it on the sand. Then he used his index finger to scratch out a series of symbols – a long zigzagged line, an outline that looked like a spoon, which Laurie filled with dots, and a squat rounded shape with spiked lines round the edge.

Chompa leaned over the box, fascinated. 'That's not Farsi,' she said.

Laurie clicked his tongue. 'Farsi isn't the only magical language. This is Kikuyu. *Watch.*'

The etchings in the sand began to move, just like Mohsin's rabbit sketch had. Chompa couldn't make out what most meant, but one she could – an arrow.

Laurie pulled out a compass and placed it next to the arrow.

'Tell Aaliya we need to be headed twelve degrees east,' he hollered through cupped hands.

Tipu nodded, and spoke in quiet Farsi. Chompa felt the ship start to shift to the right.

They were a perfect team.

Tipu landed on the deck seconds later, with a grin.

'Are you brothers?' Chompa asked curiously. The boys didn't look related.

'No. My father was a djinnspeaker, like me,' said Tipu, 'but my stepmother hated it. When he died, she sold me to the Company – well, Farook Miah, who'd picked Laurie up a few months before.'

'I'm Siddi – our ancestors were originally from Zanzibar. My parents worked as weather diviners in a village not far from Tipu. They got malaria and . . . well, they didn't recover. Farook Miah bought me from the landowner two days after. We've been working together on the indigo ships since we were about seven. Five *lonnng* years almost.' Laurie gave a weary sigh.

'Having magic should make our lives better,' said Chompa quietly. 'I never realized it could mean the opposite.'

'But in London – in *London* – we'll be able to be anything!' said Laurie dreamily. 'In London, no one will know us or what we can do. We'll be safe.'

'I'm not looking forward to seeing so many pale people everywhere.' She shivered, remembering the plate-sized hands in the jungle, the snooty looks from the Britishers on deck. 'Some of them took my mother. I can't seem to shake the idea that they all had something to do with it somehow.

'But the one thing I do know is that it's definitely Devaynes' doing. I need to find out everything I can about him to work out where he might be keeping her.' She looked meaningfully at Tipu and Laurie.

'We can divvy up the ship and explore different sections between the two of us, and report back,' Tipu said eagerly. 'We've been exploring while the ship's been in dock. There are places in the hull where you can even listen in to the upper-deck rooms, through the gaps in the timber. Don't worry – we'll get to the bottom of it all together.'

Laurie didn't look convinced.

'Please, Laurie,' said Chompa, placing a hand on his arm. 'I need to find my mother. I don't have anyone else.'

Laurie sighed and rolled his eyes. Tipu clambered up a little higher, tapped the tree for sap and trickled it into three coconut-shell cups.

They knocked the cups together and took long sips of the cool, honey-sweet sap, and started planning.

✳

In the evening, after an hour of furious huffing and arm-crossing otherwise known as a reading lesson, Chompa brought Leeza back with her to the tree. She looked around, but Tipu was nowhere to be seen.

'Laurie, this is Leeza – my *friend*. Leeza, this is Laurie – also my friend.' Chompa felt her cheeks grow warm. She'd never had a friend beyond Ammi, and now she had three. 'Where's Tipu?'

'He went snooping for you, Madam Witch Princess.' Laurie shrugged as he idly made marks in the sandbox, barely looking at it. Leeza's eyes became huge as the marks shifted.

'How is that sand moving on its own? There isn't a . . . snake in it, is there?' she asked, backing away slightly.

'That's the sand-djinn replying,' said Laurie. 'Of course, reading its signs is a very complex business –'

'*Ksst!*'

The three of them sat up, alert.

'*Ksst!*' came the sound again.

They calmed a little when they realized it was Tipu's voice, but exchanged puzzled glances – Tipu himself was nowhere to be seen.

'I'm down here, below deck,' whispered Tipu urgently. 'I managed to find Devaynes' cabin! Chalo, come on – down the steps, through to the back of the galley and there's a gap past the jaggery sacks. Sounds like he's saying something important.'

✳

In the hull, it was dark and musty. There was a sickly-sweet smell coming from the sacks of jaggery, which Laurie had begun to 'inspect' for holes.

A scuffling sound made Leeza start. 'What's that?'

'Ship rats,' answered Laurie, with a little too much glee, as he chewed on a chunk of jaggery. 'Much bigger than land ones.'

Leeza slapped a hand over her mouth, horrified.

'*Shh*,' said Chompa, impatiently. She peered up through the cracks in the timbers, but she couldn't see anything.

But they could hear *everything*.

'And how are the finances looking, Ismail?' came Devaynes' smooth, oiled voice.

There was a shaky, nervy sigh. 'Saheb, they're not so healthy. Father Saltsworth has purchased the boat and leased some of our warehouses for his East London church mission, to help him spread the word of God around the Godless waterways, apparently. That provides us with a certain amount of revenue. But our investors are uneasy about the rumours of a new direction. And, I confess, I don't know how to reassure them. Some, Lady Inglis especially, have been querying how we can be banning magic with one breath and using *this* ship with another.'

'So little imagination,' said Devaynes, a hint of steel in his voice. 'She cannot see the possibilities. Eliminating writing-magic will increase the value of djinn-magic. But we must make an impression when we get to England. Rolling into the East India Dock in the *Kohinoor* will be a start among the lower orders, but we'll need something – something *big* – to convince the Miranda Inglises of this world. Something using the girl.'

It was like cold well water had been poured down Chompa's back. He was talking about *her*.

'Yes, yes. The *girl*. Ah, she could not have turned up at a better time.' Devaynes' voice had died down to a dreamy murmur.

'Saheb?' said Ismail, his voice uncertain.

'I will deal with it. You are dismissed,' Devaynes snapped. A door closed, and there was silence, save for a pen scratching away.

Leeza tugged at Chompa's sleeve. 'Chompa, we've been gone ages – Mohsin Saheb will be looking for us,' she hissed.

Chompa nodded absently as she went over Devaynes' words and what they could possibly mean. What had she got herself into? She was still in a daze when they were back on deck and arranging to meet the next day.

'Don't worry, Madam Witch Princess – I'll keep listening in,' said Laurie, chewing on a hunk of date sugar, and passing some to each of the others from bulging pockets. 'It's more interesting than staring at sand day in, day out, that's for sure.'

'Are you certain it's not because the jaggery is kept down here?' said Leeza suspiciously, waving her hand to refuse the sugar. Laurie grinned and pocketed her piece with a shrug.

But Tipu looked solemn. 'Chompa, are you sure you know what you're doing?' he asked. 'He doesn't seem like the kind of man you want as an enemy.'

Chompa gritted her teeth. 'He is my enemy, whether I want it or not. He just can't know it.'

# Chapter Sixteen

Tipu was awoken from his branch bed the next night by a sudden rocking and lurching of the tree, nearly throwing him off. He grabbed the branch, wrapping his arms tightly round it. Immediately, he sensed the djinn's panic.

'It's just a few rough waves. We have Laurie, remember? It's his job to warn us about the big storms so we change direction.'

As he spoke, fists of driving rain hit his face, causing him to gasp with the cold. The tree – their tree – started to creak as the ship bucked on the steep waves. His stomach tipped and queased. Aaliya screamed silently in his ears, and the blood gushed like the waves round his brain, making it impossible for him to think.

Aaliya lashed stems about Tipu's wrists and ankles to prevent him from being tipped on to the deck, or into the sea, and Tipu felt grateful. But he dreaded what would happen to both him and the djinn if they weren't able to keep the tree upright, the ship afloat. Their fortunes were tied.

He heard shouts and cries as the men woke each other up, realizing something was wrong. Passengers poked terrified heads out of their cabin windows.

'I say, Clive, what's going on?' cried Lady Inglis as Devaynes came hurrying across the deck. Devaynes turned and flashed a smile that didn't reach his eyes.

'Nothing whatsoever, Miranda. Just the wild oceans in this part of the world! But do sit tight and keep the porthole closed. I wouldn't want your silk frock to be ruined by the spray!'

The porthole slammed shut.

Devaynes' face turned purple as he glared up the tree. 'You! Where's the weather boy?' he roared at Tipu. 'Both of you can think again about your five years being up! That's IF we get through this alive!'

The floor of the cabin lurched so sharply to one side that Chompa found herself flung out of her downy bed on to the hard floor. Then there was a massive dip, as if they were falling down a crevasse. Her stomach gave way within her, and she thought she'd be sick. She stayed pressed against the floor, terrified.

Then Mohsin's voice yelled from the other side of the door. 'Chompa, the ship's in danger! They need our help! Hurry!'

When Chompa had wrestled the door open, she saw Mohsin was dressed in a blue jacket and boots, his hair soaked. He handed her a big yellow coat.

He spoke into Chompa's ear as they hauled themselves up the steps to the top deck. 'If the storm doesn't die down, the tree will split from its roots and die. If the tree dies, the djinn will, too. If that happens, the *Kohinoor* will sink.'

The roar around them was replaced in Chompa's ears with a yawning terror. They would die, and she'd never see Ammi again.

'I need to use djinn-fire on the waves. It demands absolute precision, otherwise the ship will be set alight.'

Chompa nodded with a lurch of her stomach.

'So you must help the boy keep the tree intact. Focus on the roots. If the tree leans over too far, its roots will split from the timbers, and the djinn will lose control of the ship. Keep pulling the roots downwards to keep the tree in place.'

Mohsin draped a coil of thick rope over Chompa's shoulder. He brought his face close to hers.

'Lash yourselves to the deck, but with enough room to move if the tree comes down. But it won't. I have faith in you, Chompa.'

With that, he strode towards the helm of the ship. Chompa cried out as a wave towered over Mohsin, about to engulf him. He flung an arm at it, and a jet of red light hit the wave, fizzling it to steam.

Chompa dragged the rope towards the tree, struggling forward against the force of the wind. The salt spray whipped at her face, making it almost impossible to see. Her hair worked its way out of the knot she'd hastily tied, and it streamed into her eyes and mouth.

When she collided with something soft, she thought it might be a sandbag. With a shock, she realized who it was.

'Laurie!'

He didn't hear her. He was quivering with shock and cold. Dropping the rope, she reached out and took his face in her hands, wrenching it to face hers. 'Laurie, can you fix this?'

His eyes were huge with panic, and he shook his head wildly.

'I – I can't change the weather. I only read it, and we change course to avoid it. I missed it! I missed this! I was listening in to Devaynes for you when I should have been *here*! I'm dead, Chompa!' he wailed, clutching at his hair in despair.

Chompa felt her stomach clench with guilt, but there was no time for that now. 'Don't be dramatic. If someone has to rescue you, you'll put them in danger, too. Go below deck. NOW.'

Her voice surprised her, and Laurie, too. He nodded and dragged his sandbox towards the steps.

'Chompa!' Tipu's voice could barely be heard over the roar of the waves and the wind. He was clinging to the trunk, precariously high as the tree swayed and swung.

Chompa put her hands round her mouth and yelled as loudly as she could, 'Tipu! You need to come down!'

Tipu carefully climbed down as the tree bucked back and forth like a wild, crazed animal. He was breathless when he landed on the deck next to her.

'I can't get her to focus – she's panicking too much. She

just wants to be freed before the tree hits the water, but I don't know the words.'

Chompa nodded grimly. Tipu looked at her again, registering her presence as if for the first time. 'What are you doing here? It's not safe!'

Chompa threw the rope at Tipu. 'I'm here to help.'

In the distance, they could make out the straight-backed form of Mohsin at the very tip of the bow. If the ship dipped too quickly, he would be plunged into the ocean. He stood strong, fierce, his arm outstretched as if it could stop the walls of rain, the roaring wind, the awful massive clouds.

'What's he doing?' Tipu asked. 'The waves are too huge; he can't hold them back!'

And he didn't. He evaporated them.

But the sea was a monster with limbs that kept reproducing, and, as Mohsin evaporated one, another wave came rolling towards them. Tipu put his hands over his ears as the djinn's screams, in his head only, became increasingly distraught.

'Can you expose one of the tree roots?' Chompa asked Tipu.

He looked confused, but nodded and scrabbled in the earth with his bare hands until the pale fingers of roots could be seen.

'Try to calm Aaliya, see if she can stop the trunk bending so much in the wind,' Chompa yelled.

They stood side by side, leaning against each other. Somehow it made everything seem more solid around them. They clasped palms firmly as one looked at the trunk and the other at the roots.

Tipu began to mutter in slow, calming Farsi. He could feel Aaliya's energy fluttering within her tree cage like a panicked, desperate bird. Part of him wanted to free her. It was cruel to keep her like this, he thought with a start. Instead, he soothed her and pleaded with her.

'Aaliya, we're friends, no? Then don't let me drown. Don't let us drown. Be strong. Be still. Keep that trunk high in the sky. Brave, Aaliya. Be brave. It'll be fine. I promise I'll stay with you. If we survive – I promise I'll be the one to set you free. It might not be today, or even tomorrow, but I promise I will.'

Tipu kept on speaking as Aaliya twisted and squirmed and wailed. He realized that he didn't really have magic, just words – but, in the right situations, words were enough.

The tree stopped swaying.

Chompa exhaled. If the tree was still, it would be easier. She raised her finger. What word to choose? Spread? Strengthen? Grow? Precision, Chompa remembered. And so she chose 'anchor'. She hoped it would be enough.

She urged the pale roots deeper and outwards with her finger. They grew longer, wider, curling, burrowing, winding themselves round the timbers. The trunk of the tree began to straighten up, pulled back into place by the djinn. With it, the ship, too, regained balance, tilting itself gently so it was level on the water.

They both breathed a sigh of relief, and then Tipu started to instruct Aaliya to guide the ship forward, over the settling waves.

Chompa was soaked through, but suddenly she became aware that the rain had stopped. She looked up, and saw Mohsin standing at the bow still, darting jets of djinn-fire at the heavy grey clouds until she could see a glimmer of clear, dry sky. Then he collapsed on to the deck.

Chompa dragged herself over to him, her limbs heavy with exhaustion.

'Uncle! Uncle! You did it! You saved us.'

Mohsin's eyes opened. 'We did it, Chompa. We did it.'

# Chapter Seventeen

Devaynes bowed to Chompa and Mohsin at the entrance to the ballroom the following evening. He was wearing a sleek black suit with a white shirt and a dark blue-green tie. He reminded Chompa of a magpie, ready to swoop and steal away anything that took his fancy.

'Professor Kabir, Miss Begum. Welcome to the *Kohinoor*'s first ball! I cannot thank you enough for your exertions yesterday. I do hope you are recovered?'

Mohsin bowed stiffly, his expression cold. But Devaynes didn't seem to notice, smiling blandly as he spoke into Chompa's ear.

'Miss Begum, I wondered if you'd care to give a demonstration of your magic for my guests this evening?'

Chompa opened her mouth in outrage. She was not a performing monkey!

'As part of our *agreement*?' said Devaynes meaningfully.

Chompa considered grudgingly. It *could* help her to find out what the guests already knew about Devaynes' magical plans. She clamped her back teeth together and nodded.

Devaynes beamed and patted Chompa's shoulder. 'Very good, very good.' Then he turned to greet the next guests, and Chompa and Mohsin found themselves moved to one side of the room.

Lady Inglis, wearing a gigantic maroon frock, sailed towards them. 'Do direct me to my table, boy,' she drawled, barely looking at Mohsin.

Chompa saw Mohsin's jaw tighten. He gave a quick, cursory bow, and then smiled. 'I'm afraid you are mistaken, Lady Inglis. I'm not staff. My ward and I are guests of Sir Clive, just like you.'

Lady Inglis turned and looked Mohsin and Chompa up and down very slowly. She wrinkled her nose. 'Ah, yes. You two. I cannot for the life of me understand why Sir Clive would invite natives as guests. Well, you may not be staff, but I assure you, you're definitely nothing at all like me.'

Only when she turned away did Mohsin's jaw loosen. Chompa frowned.

'Why does she think she's so much better than us?'

'Who knows, Chompa?' Mohsin sighed. 'Who knows why they believe they have the right to hold dominion over the rest of us?'

Chompa and Mohsin found their table. Devaynes was last to be seated, hovering between tables, paying all his guests lavish attention, laughing at jokes, charming ladies with compliments on their outfits. Chompa watched to see who he might sit with – who was closest to him. There were a few tables with empty chairs. But there was one chair empty on their table, too. Surely not . . .

Devaynes came over and sat down with them. Chompa was astonished, as were the other guests, especially Lady Inglis.

Mohsin looked nervous and took off his glasses to polish them.

'Sir Clive, you do us a great honour,' he said.

Devaynes waved a hand airily. 'No, no, I do believe you honour me. This is the table with the greatest amount of *talent*, I believe.'

Chompa smiled with her lips pressed tightly together. Mohsin kept polishing his glasses and coughed before speaking.

'On the subject of talent, Sir Clive, the boys who are working on the ship have magic. Forgive me, but I must ask. Are you paying them fairly?'

One of the English guests appeared to choke on their flavourless prawn salad. Chompa's eyes widened, and she held her breath, waiting for Devaynes' answer.

Devaynes merely chuckled. 'Not at all, Professor Kabir. I'm happy to say that I pay them the going rate.'

Chompa seethed. A blatant lie! He wasn't paying them at all. And now Tipu and Laurie were looking at years more in unpaid servitude, since Devaynes had blamed them for the storm.

'The going rate for Asian crewmen, perhaps. Not magical navigators.'

'That is true, but if I start to raise wages then I'll have a war with the rest of the shipping trade on my hands! They will both be given an extra sum, discreetly, once we've made our return journey safely. I need to keep those young ragamuffins on their toes. After all, we don't want a repeat of yesterday's shenanigans!'

He chuckled again, but Chompa remembered the fury in his eyes as he'd roared at Tipu.

A waiter came up to him and whispered something, and Devaynes excused himself. Chompa looked admiringly at Mohsin. Mohsin smiled, his green eyes twinkling. 'You are inspiring me to be bolder, it seems.'

Devaynes was now in the centre of the circle of tables, a glass in his hand.

'My esteemed guests, thank you all for having the nerve of the most audacious pioneers, for firstly investing in my boldest venture, and secondly for joining me on its maiden voyage. I have been trialling coastal fishing boats using this . . . *unusual* form of power, but never before with a ship of this size or a journey of this scale. Ladies and gentlemen, I know that some of you may still have some uncertainties, some doubts, about magic. Whether it is right and proper that we harness its power. Whether it is real at all. Let me be clear: it's as real as the shoes on my feet! And it's about to change the world as we know it.

'The journey from India to London generally takes months. I estimate that ours will be a matter of ten days. Consider what this means! The possibilities for trade, for managing our dominions, spreading our influence across the world! There are eyes in high places watching us with

155

great interest. And not just back home. We shall be the talk of the globe. And that globe will henceforth be much smaller – at least for those who sail on the *Kohinoor* and her future sisters.

'You have all witnessed the skills these unusual children possess. Yet the two steering this ship are nothing in comparison to my dear young friend here, Miss Chompa Begum. Already her magic has steered us through a storm that would have sunk a lesser ship. Her skills promise a whole new world of opportunity – and you are privileged to be the first to witness a taste of them this evening. Ladies and gentlemen, please welcome Miss Begum.'

There was a smattering of uncertain applause. Chompa froze at the sound of her name, but found herself rising from her chair nevertheless. She swallowed and focused on putting one foot in front of the other, and not on the fact that every guest's gaze was now fixed on her.

A waiter rushed into the centre of the circle and placed a little table in front of Chompa, with a large bouquet of pale pink roses, just like the one in Devaynes' study.

She didn't dare breathe lest she lose concentration. She placed her hand in her pocket, and curled her fingers round the two taviz. She focused on the centre of one flower and raised her index finger.

One by one, each flower lost its colour, its velvety softness replaced by a hard, silken sheen. Each leaf turned from glossy green to a gleaming cool white. When the last stem had turned to metal, Chompa lowered her finger and blinked. There was still silence in the room. Then, all of a sudden, Devaynes clapped his hands together in a slow rhythm.

'Bravo, bravo!' he bellowed. Others joined in until the ballroom was filled with the roar of applause.

Chompa looked in the direction of Lady Inglis, raised her chin, and smiled. Lady Inglis sniffed and turned away.

# Chapter Eighteen

The air was becoming cooler, and a fine pale mist blanketed the deck in the mornings. Laurie was lying low, afraid to run into Devaynes, and the tree was still in poor shape after the storm. Tipu had never had to fix a tree before, and Aaliya had to guide him as to what to do. He went about the exposed roots, sprinkling earth and water on them. Mohsin enchanted a nourishing compost that Tipu packed round the base of the tree.

When he wasn't watching anxiously for any sign of improvement, Tipu caught himself looking out towards the sea for hours, not saying a word. When England appeared on the horizon, how would he know?

'*Psst.*'

Tipu nearly fell out of his tree. Only one person would whisper that loudly. Within seconds, Tipu had jumped down on to the deck and grasped his friend in a rough, quick hug. But Laurie was hopping with impatience.

'Devaynes is having a meeting. Sounds important. We've got to get Chompa and Leeza. Come on.'

✳

After a few strategically pinged date stones at their porthole, Leeza and Chompa joined the two boys, and they all hurried through the dark nooks and crannies below deck. They could hear two male voices rumbling in discussion, getting louder as they scrambled on.

Suddenly Devaynes' drawl was as clear as if they were in the same room.

'Tell me how things look, Ismail.'

'Saheb, because the ship is – er, *injured*, we are proceeding more slowly than we had expected.'

'Tell me how it is plainly.' Devaynes was no longer drawling.

'We will incur a week's delay. I have told the guests it is a result of slow winds. But . . . but it means the shipment will arrive before us.'

Chompa froze. What shipment? Were they talking about indigo? More children? Or . . . Ammi?

'But you have no doubt sent a message to our final port to ensure it's moved immediately to the secure location, Ismail.'

'I have. But it's risky. We only have a skeleton guard at hand in London.'

*A guard*, thought Chompa, mind racing. That had to be for Ammi and the other magical people. *Please say where*, she thought desperately.

'Then hire *more*,' snarled Devaynes.

'There's a little problem with the finances currently, Saheb. So much has gone into the new project.' Ismail sounded terrified.

'So sell five more of the fleet. We can buy them back later.'

'As you wish, Saheb. But, if I may be allowed an impertinence, the risk of bankruptcy is great . . .' He wavered, his voice a tremor.

'If my only goal was money, I'd have stuck with indigo,' snapped Devaynes. 'But it is not. This is the route to *power*. Anyone can grow indigo. But no one else has access to this. And you're right: it was an impertinence. You may leave me now, Ismail.'

The next day, Tipu, Laurie, Leeza, and Chompa sat in a hunched circle round the trunk of the palm.

'Bhai, we *have* to plan jumping ship when we arrive. We don't have a choice any more, not since the storm. Who knows how many years Farook Miah will add to our time?' mumbled Laurie, spraying crumbs everywhere.

Leeza dusted off her shoulder, clucking in disgust. 'If you both just work hard, you can make it up to Farook Miah. How else are you going to get home? Surely this isn't that bad a job?'

Laurie shook his head. 'It's not a job if you're trapped in it for the rest of your life. And this man Devaynes – we can't work for him. Chompa was right. He's up to all kinds of things. Nah, nah, we've got to go.'

But the closer they drew to London, the uneasier Tipu became. It had been different when it had just been a vague idea, something they'd dreamed about while lolling in the branches of the tree, sleepy after a date feast. But now it was real, and Tipu had doubts. Lots of them.

'We won't know anyone there. In all those white faces, we're going to stick out like two brown thumbs. We don't have any money, or anywhere to stay. It's just too dangerous, Laurie.'

'Don't worry, my chicklet chokro – I'll look after you in London.' Laurie patted Tipu's shoulder.

Tipu bristled. 'I don't need looking after.'

Laurie, Leeza, and Chompa shared a sceptical glance. Tipu gritted his teeth.

'And there's Aaliya to think of, for a start.'

Laurie waved his hand dismissively. 'They'll find someone else to talk to her. I can't stay. And you won't be able to hack it on your own on this ship. So it's settled. We're jumping.'

'I can't cope on my own?'

Laurie grinned. 'You know you can't.' He started counting on his fingers. 'First, unlike me, your parents never primed you for a life on the sea. Second, despite all our time working for a Britisher, you've still not got the hang of this Ingrezi language of theirs –'

'Ei! I can speak a bit!'

Laurie raised a sceptical eyebrow. ' "Get out the way, you little lascar varmint" isn't going to get you very far, is it?' Tipu closed his mouth. 'Where was I? Ah, and *third*, let's face it, you're lovely, Tipu, but you're a bit soft.'

Laurie saw that Tipu was getting angry. He raised his hands placatingly. 'It doesn't matter – that's why we make such a good team.'

But the bristling within Tipu didn't settle. Stiffly, he told Laurie he'd think about it.

Tipu retreated up the tree and looked portwards. The water was quiet, little waves rippling and dancing upon the flat grey surface. Tipu couldn't visualize it, this place they were gliding their way towards. London. *Lunn-dunn.* He sounded the name out over and over in his head.

'Tell me, Aaliya, should I go with Laurie?' Tipu dangled his legs over the edge of the palm's fan-shaped leaves.

Aaliya had grown to like this boy more than all the others before him combined. He was sweet and polite. She'd waited for his head to swell with the power, but it never had.

If she was a true djinn, she'd possess him right now. He was unfocused, dreamy – the perfect host. But possession lasted a few fleeting moments before the bodies gave way, and then there would be the burn and torment of the iron shackles that would be put round the tree by Farook Miah. The leaves shivered. Besides that, she'd grown to love these frail, flawed beings, barely alive for longer than a butterfly. And this one the most.

And that meant letting him go.

So she told him what she knew of djinnspeakers like him. She told him what had happened to the boy before Tipu – Aadam – back when her tree was on one of Devaynes' local 'country ships'. She told him about the boy before Aadam. She told him about all five of them that had spoken to her so far in this tree. Each young, sweet, or not-so-sweet child who had learned her language, laughed with her, and been worked to death, drowned in the rivers, or lost to fever or dysentery.

By the time she'd finished, Tipu had to clutch at the branches to keep himself steady. His chest felt like it was being crushed.

He was still in a daze when Chompa walked towards the tree with a new bag of enchanted compost from Mohsin.

After he had scaled down the trunk and told her, Chompa looked pensive. 'What will you do in London? It's not home.'

'Where's home for us, really? Me and Laurie – we don't have family; we don't have houses; we just go from place to place. All we have is each other.'

Chompa ran her fingers through the mix of compost and earth, quiet for some time.

'Find me some date stones – I'll turn them silver for you.'

She poured the silver seeds into a handkerchief, tied it up and tucked it into Tipu's kurta pocket. 'Keep them safe.'

They practised some English exchanges he might have, but the words were always like water to him – they flowed out quicker than they flowed in. 'Devaynes' address in London is Malplaquet House, Mile End. I don't know where we'll be staying yet, so leave a message for me there – but write it in Farsi.'

Tipu nodded, storing the name away.

They looked out towards the rising sun. England was a dark blurred shape on the horizon.

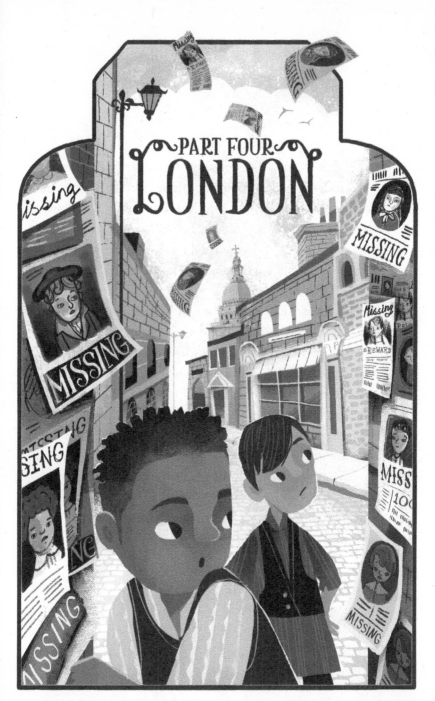

PART FOUR

LONDON

The boy fished the doll from the waste pile where he had hidden it. It was a crude thing that he'd made from Thames riverbed clay, and it reeked. But it was his. Wiping his nose with his ragged sleeve, he placed it on the ground carefully. He stood back a bit and focused, training his right index finger on it. Then he raised his left hand slowly. The doll's left hand lifted up, too, a tiny, slightly muddier mirror. The boy lowered his hand. The doll did the same.

The boy smiled. The street was quiet – it was that brief window after the last drunkards had gone to their beds or inns, and before the market traders were up. He began to walk backwards, towards the row of shops. The clay doll mimicked his movements exactly. The boy became absorbed in his elegant piece of magic, and had stopped looking about to see if anyone was watching.

And so it was too late when a hand clapped a cloth over his mouth, stoppering a scream that never came.

He fell to the ground. The doll crumpled in exactly the same shape, a broken five-pointed star.

# Chapter Nineteen

The East India Dock could barely be seen through the thick white fog that bleached London of all colour. The boys stood on the edge of the deck, their packs strapped tightly to their chests, their thin cotton uniforms flapping in the wind. Tipu stared down into the black water and gulped. He could tell it was freezing just from looking at it.

'Arré, this dock makes Dacca seem like a toy,' said Laurie in a hushed, awed tone, craning his neck to look at the black cranes reaching high into the dense white air.

'Ready for our next adventure, bhai? Time to make our fortunes!' Laurie flashed a too-bright smile, patting his pocket where Tipu knew a small pink shell was tucked away safely, Muyaka inside.

Tipu couldn't speak, just nodded. He turned round for one last glance at the tree, at Aaliya, even though he couldn't really see her. But he could sense her bravely nudging him along. Leaving her made his heart squeeze tight with regret so that he could hardly breathe, in a way that leaving the rattan-djinn hadn't. But Tipu didn't know the words to free her, and he could hardly saw the tree down and take it with him. He forced himself to look ahead at the docks, to leave Aaliya behind, trapped with her sadness, his broken promise to her a sour, bitter taste in his dry mouth.

Laurie nudged him. 'Chalo – let's go. We need to move. Before –'

But Laurie never finished the sentence.

'*Hai-ré!*' roared a familiar nasal voice. Farook Miah's wizened face appeared out of the cabin, pointing his long finger in the boys' direction. 'Ship-jumpers!'

Tipu turned to hear a splash – Laurie had already jumped. Tipu glanced over the edge, but the mist made it impossible to spot him.

'I'm here! Follow my voice!' yelled Laurie, but Tipu couldn't see him. He looked around wildly, waiting for Laurie to shout again, to get his bearings.

But nothing. Laurie didn't shout again. And then other yells took over as the members of the *Kohinoor* crew advanced towards Tipu.

When a hand gripped his shoulder, Tipu knew he couldn't wait. He pulled free and threw himself over the railings and into the dark water.

Tipu's body plunged down. The water was so cold that his breath stopped in shock. His head felt like it was going to explode from the pressure of the water, his chest from the lack of air. He tried to scramble upward, but his pack dragged him down further. He scrabbled free of it, and pushed up desperately. Back home, warm golden light would have told him when he was reaching the surface, but this water was black, black, black. He didn't know how much further he could go, how much further he had to go. The water began to feel like dough. Maybe, maybe he shouldn't fight it . . .

And then he was at the surface, gasping, body shuddering, teeth chattering. He pulled himself up on to the dock and looked around for Laurie. But there was no time. The dark blurred outlines of men had started coming towards him, getting crisper as they drew closer – there was a handsome reward for recaptured ship-jumpers. Tipu forced his worry down – Laurie was a strong swimmer, and he'd already have come up to the surface before Tipu had jumped. He must have fled. And now Tipu had to do the same, before he was caught.

Leaving a trail of wet footprints behind, Tipu ran.

The fog muffled sounds, just as it had Laurie's voice, yet, as it moved, deep ringing noises of metal or a loud, clipped shout would suddenly force itself through. Tipu was dizzy, disorientated. The city felt like a secret he wasn't supposed to know.

His bare feet were bruised with cold. He kept to the dark edges of the streets, not wishing to draw attention to himself. He'd stolen some rags from a cart and was at least dry, and less conspicuous than he was in his blue-and-white uniform. But the thin shirt and trousers were more hole than cloth, and no match for the wind that took his breath away, that seemed to claw at his skin.

He kept to the shadows for some time, afraid of being identified and hauled back. But soon he realized that no one was looking at him. No one was looking at anything.

The English crew on the *Kohinoor* had a swagger that came from knowing they were higher up on some tree. But that swagger was nowhere in evidence here. Instead, there was ragged poverty; sewage pouring from ramshackle, creaking buildings; thin, resentful, tired faces. Tipu shook his head in wonder. It was just like Dacca.

Tipu searched the streets for a friendly Indian face. Or even an unfriendly Indian face. If he found someone he could speak to in Gujarati – or even any of its sibling languages he had picked up easily in the docks, Hindustani, Bangla, or Urdu – then he could persuade them to help him and ask if they'd seen Laurie. But he saw only pale faces, and the English phrases he knew had twisted into indistinct noises in his head.

His stomach churned with hunger, and the cold started to sap his energy. In desperation, he pulled out Chompa's silver date seeds. But how could he make any trades with them without Laurie to negotiate? He sighed and put them back in his pocket.

He missed them all: Laurie, Chompa, Leeza, and especially Aaliya. If she was here somehow – did dates even grow in this city? he wondered – London would be a different story. Tipu felt his resolve dissolving into misery. Then he shook his mop of hair. *Enough*. Laurie, Chompa, and Leeza had thought he couldn't survive alone here. Tipu needed to prove that he could.

He passed a row of stalls and carts along the roadside, manned by men and women, their cheeks burned red with cold, yelling their wares. Men in flat caps and rough clothes handed over coins with reluctant fingers as they grabbed crescent pastries or breads and shoved them into their mouths as they walked on.

But other stalls weren't selling food. At one, a Chinese man was sitting at a table, carefully painting red symbols on to a strip of yellow paper for a woman who was weeping. At another sat a woman with dark hair and pale skin, her head wrapped ornately in layered and braided scarves. She was surrounded by jars and pieces of parchment, writing carefully on to the upturned palm of an old man.

*Magic*, Tipu realized. So many different types of magic!

He started forward eagerly to chat to them, to show them what he could do. Then, with a jolt, he fell back. They had magic, but he didn't – not really, not without Aaliya. He moved on before the wistfulness got too strong, focusing instead on the twisting of his stomach instead of his heart.

He sniffed at the air. Among the smells, of which many were not appetizing, there was a sweet, spiced scent that made Tipu's jaw and stomach ache. He followed the scent to a cart manned by an especially loud and stout woman, with hair like flames and cheeks to match. She sold squares of something that looked like bread, but softer, from stacks of rusty steel tins.

'Puden!' she yelled in a sing-song voice, chatting to her

customers in a rough, cackling banter that brought a smile or laugh to the faces of the men. Whether it was the food or her cheer, or both, it was a popular cart, keeping her constantly busy, too busy to even scrape out the almost empty tins that she threw on the ground in a pile. The edges of these discarded tins, Tipu noticed, were thick with burnt batter.

He was dark and small, and for once this was to his advantage. If he crept, if he was careful . . . He watched a little more and then moved under the cart itself. Crouched tight, he was the very same size as the wheels of the cart. Carefully, he pulled one of the tins towards him, and began to pick at the blackened batter, stuffing it into his mouth. It was dry and bitter, and he didn't even know if he could get it all down, or if it would stay in his stomach. But it had to do.

A sharp kick made him drop the tin with a clatter.

'Oi. You stealin' from Ma Sheeran?'

A firm, rough hand pulled him out from under the cart by the scruff of his neck.

'Oi, you little devil, did Old Rubes send yer to try and steal me tins?'

Tipu shook his head desperately. She peered down at him more closely, then used one blackened fingernail to scrape at his skin and held it up to her eyes. She scraped him again, harder, and then examined her fingernail again.

''Ang on . . . You en't filthy. You're a bleedin' lascar! I didn't even know they made 'em so small!'

*Lascar.* The word never sounded anything but accusatory. White sailors on the ship had used it scornfully for all the Asian crew: as if they didn't have names, as if they weren't worth names. He was nothing here in London – just like everywhere else, magic or no.

Tipu tried to wriggle out of her grip, but it was strong.

'Eh, Sam!'

A stocky boy with a cap at a jaunty angle was leaning casually back on a doorstep. He was flanked by smaller children and carried an air that signalled he was their leader.

'Wot, Ma?'

'Take this kid to your Auntie Sal. She'll know what to do with 'im. And search 'im first in case 'e does a runner.'

Tipu's mind raced in panic, even from the snatches he'd understood. Who was Auntie Sal, and *what* would she know to do with him? Before he could wrench free, the children closed round him in a tight circle. The stocky boy wrestled Tipu to the ground and searched his pockets. Triumphantly, he shook the handkerchief bundle in front of Tipu's nose.

Tipu's heart sank. '*Keep them safe*,' Chompa had told him. He'd failed at that, too.

'Wot's these, then?' Sam crowed as he unknotted it. 'Cor, Ma, they look pricey.'

His mother peered down into the handkerchief. 'Ooh, nice,' she cooed. 'Give 'em 'ere an' off with yer.'

She poured half into her palm, pocketed them, and bundled up the rest and gave them back to the boy. He protested a little, and his mother cuffed him, but affectionately, and popped a coin in his pocket.

'Up yer get,' he said, nudging Tipu roughly. 'We're going to see me Auntie Sal.'

"E's a lascar, innit, guv. Might not know what you're sayin',' said one of the small, snotty boys.

'Oh yeah. Well then.' The red-haired boy coughed theatrically. 'Oot jow,' he said slowly. 'Gadha,' he added with considerable relish, to a chorus of titters from the children, for whom trading insults in a foreign tongue was truly delicious.

Tipu's eyes grew enormous with surprise. The boy had just called him a *donkey*, but he'd felt as overjoyed as if he'd called him a prince, just to hear Hindi again. But, as he got to his feet, two of the group clamped grubby hands round his arms and moved him along behind the red-haired leader.

'Chop-chop,' said the boy. 'Jaldi, jaldi,' he translated as if talking to a very young child.

Wooden shopfronts lined the streets, but the green or burgundy paint was faded and scuffed, and many signs had been hastily painted over, their previous incarnations still showing through. Tipu recognized the round, squat shapes of English, but also, intriguingly, angular blocks of vertical lines of script that looked almost like pictures.

They scooted from the main thoroughfare down a dull, bricked, nondescript little lane of houses. At the far end of the alley was an inn with dark wood and smoky patterned glass of the type found on each street corner. A crooked old sign dangled above the door from one rusty nail. Tipu noticed there was Hindi script under the English. It said The Pickled Egg. Tipu shook his head. The English sailors had complained about the smell of spiced food in the lascar galley, but *pickled eggs* sounded truly disgusting.

At Tipu's movement, the children at his sides clamped their arms firmly about his thighs and the other children silently went back into the crescent formation behind him. Though they were at a standstill again, they'd left him nowhere to run. It was all very slick, Tipu thought with dismay and a degree of admiration.

The boy knocked hard on the splintery surface of the door they were standing in front of. A gravelly voice grumbled and muttered. The door creaked open, and then fell off one rusty hinge.

Holding the collapsing door up with one broad hip was another red-haired, ruddy-faced woman. As with all the people he'd seen and walked past, Tipu couldn't make out if she was kind or cruel – here people kept their expressions closed.

The boy poured the silver seeds into the woman's hand, and then waited expectantly, hand extended. She raised an eyebrow, then rolled her eyes and put a few back into his hand, and he grinned and stepped aside dramatically.

Tipu hunched his shoulders, hoping he might disappear entirely if he just made himself small enough.

As she looked him up and down, there was a gleam in the woman's eyes, a hint of a smile at her mouth. Her large pink hands hauled Tipu over the threshold into the dim interior of the tavern, lifting him right off his feet.

# Chapter Twenty

She dropped him down on a seat in a wooden booth.
'Mera naam hai Sal.'

Tipu's eyes became great orbs in his face, and his mouth opened in a large 'O' shape, no sounds emanating from it. He couldn't quite believe what he was hearing from this ruddy red-haired woman, just as he hadn't when the boy had sworn at him. To hear that tongue here, among a sea of white faces, in London, completely disorientated Tipu.

She seemed used to this response.

'Achaa, achaa,' she continued in fluent but strangely accented Hindustani. 'I get it. I'm a white woman, so wot the baakvaas am I doin' speakin' like this? Well, young man, the folks around these parts call me Lascar Sal.'

She nodded her head behind her, to a single daguerreotype photograph up on the wall. It was faded, ragged about the edges, but it was possible to make out two figures in it: a slender pale woman with a bunch of flowers in her hand, and a darker man, lean and straight-backed, his arm interlocked with hers.

'That's me old man. Nasir. Died five years back. But I'm still known as Lascar Sal. Be known as it till I get carted off to me final place, too.'

She ran her hand across and down her chest and then turned away from Tipu. She made her way through a doorway, and he followed her with his eyes, shaking his head slightly in an effort to absorb what he'd heard. He didn't know what she might want with him, but it was better here than staying out on the streets.

London kept on surprising him, and strangely – as hard and painful and cold as it was – it made him want to stay.

Tipu looked about the room. It was dusty and faded, but not dirty. In fact, the dark wood, which lined the bar and the walls up to Tipu's head height, gleamed with polish, even though the burgundy paint above his head was chipped and flaking. A few glasses glinted from hooks above the bar, and a couple of dark green bottles gleamed upon the shelves.

He could hear clinking and banging sounds and muttering coming from the doorway and then, suddenly, the most unexpected of smells hit Tipu's nose, transporting him back immediately to the warm fug of the galley, to the smoky cooking hut of his sot-ma, to memories, so many memories. It wasn't so much a scent as something solid that seized his body, wound itself inside him, and took him home.

Tipu sniffed, his eyes closed, and unpicked the layers of the scent. Spices. Cumin. Coriander. Frying onions. It was the garlic that was always his undoing, and his mouth watered so intensely his jaw ached.

A few minutes later, Sal bustled out, and firmly placed a metal plate down in front of him. Shreds of egg and potato cubes, golden with turmeric, prickling with chilli and spice, dotted with mustard seeds. Tipu had never seen anything so beautiful, or smelled anything as delicious, in his life.

His stomach was yawning like a monster, and his fingers itched to attack the plate, but he knew better, and he looked up at Sal to check it really was for him.

'My, en't yer a timid one, eh?' she chuckled, and she ruffled her hand through his hair. 'D'you see anyone else in 'ere it could be for? Nah? Then eat, eat.'

Sal left him to it, and Tipu ate slowly, making it last. A lifetime of small portions and clouts to the head made him wary, unlike Laurie, of ever asking for a second helping. Tipu felt a sharp pain within him. Laurie. What was he doing? Was he being fed, or dragged back to the ship? The thought of the ship brought another pang. Who was tending to Aaliya?

The muffled sounds of two voices started to get clearer through the doorway. A rasping Indian man's voice, along with Sal's, high with irritation, both rattling away in Hindustani.

'Achaa, achaa, I know it en't your job. But we en't had a young un for years, an' darned if I've got the time. An' – you owe me years of lodgin's, if you've forgotten.'

'How could I forget!' cried the man's voice, getting louder as they approached the tavern room. 'You remind me twenty times a day!'

'Funny how those reminders don't bring those owings down, though, en't it?' Sal chuckled. 'You're a leech, Yasser, an' yer know it.' Yet there was no venom in her sounding of the Hindi for leech, 'jonk', unlike the way in which Tipu's sot-ma used to spit out the Gujarati equivalent at him.

'So I'm just your dog, achaa, performing tricks for you?'

'Glad we understand one another,' Sal chortled as they finally made their way into the bar.

A short, wizened figure shuffled out from behind Sal. He looked a little like the man in the photograph, but was thin and his body crooked from having lost an arm. He had a nose that curved nobly, like an emperor's, and his long face ended in the point of a fine greying beard. He looked Tipu up and down, as if assessing a good cut of meat.

'Boy – what's your name?' Sal asked.

'T-Tipu.'

To his bewilderment, this elicited hoots of laughter from the man. He stretched out a thin, shrivelled palm towards Tipu.

'This? This mouse of a boy is named after our bravest warrior king? Hahaha!' The man bent over in laughter. Tipu found his ears burning.

Sal hauled Yasser up by the collar. 'Enough, Yasser. Tipu, ignore me wonderful brother-in-law. He promised my Nasir on his deathbed to protect an' provide for me, though it's turned out more the other way round, en't it, Yasser?' She jabbed him in the ribs, but her eyes twinkled.

She turned round to Tipu again. 'Little Rajput, do you know any English? Eeng-rish?' She said it slowly as if Tipu was stupid.

'Thora. Little,' said Tipu meekly.

Sal sighed, raising her eyes to the ceiling. 'They jump

without even thinkin'. You'll 'ave to teach 'im, Yasser. No use to us otherwise, is 'e? Else we'll 'ave to give 'im back to the ship. We'd get the finder's fee then.'

Yasser sat himself down opposite Tipu, unpeeling him with those sharp, shrewd eyes. He put his one hand into his pocket, drawing out an improbably long stick with a hook on the end. He raised the stick in the air with a glinting smile, and then the entire thing, stick and hook, disappeared down the back of Yasser's heavy wool coat. His arm moved mechanically up and down, crooked over his head, and his eyes were closed in pleasure.

'Aaah. The worst thing about this country, boy, is the dryness. Idiot back – itches all day.'

He pulled out the hook from his coat with a flourish and placed it on the table in between the two of them. The hook was dusty-looking now, Tipu observed, feeling a bit sick.

'Are you sharp, boy? Because I've better things to do than repeat myself. I hope you'll catch on quick.' He goggled his eyes at the stick meaningfully and then hooted like an owl at his little hook-related pun.

Tipu swallowed, weighing up his options. He could bolt, right now, belly somewhere near full. He was sure this frail old man wouldn't be able to catch him. Or he could stay. The man was gross, and possibly cruel, but Tipu needed to learn English, and there might be more food. He decided to nod and keep his eyes down.

'Achaa. So let us begin.' Yasser tapped the long talons of his one hand on the table.

'English. English is not like our languages. It lacks the

poetry of Urdu, but is too straight-backed to be earthy like Punjabi. English is like a cat – every rule that is set down it also breaks. So pay attention.' He rapped Tipu's head with the stick. 'The English are obsessed with niceties. They can spend half a conversation saying nothing at all. Repeat after me. Good morning. How do you do? Lovely weather for ducks.'

After his lesson, which had resulted in only two or three dusty taps on Tipu's head, Yasser had beckoned him behind the bar and through the doorway and along a corridor. It was dimly lit and narrow – two fully grown men could not have walked down it comfortably.

'It stops the fights. Not enough room to pull the arm back.' Yasser acted out the gesture with his hook, pulling it backwards until it tapped on the wall behind him. He sighed. 'This country is full of brutes.'

They walked past a flight of stairs, and through to a lighter room, which turned out to be the kitchen where Sal had made Tipu's eggs. The smell of spices still lingered in the air.

Yasser pointed at the sink, the cast-iron pots hanging from hooks on the wall, the raised cooking stove, not on the floor like his sot-ma's, but level with Tipu's chest like the one onboard the *Kohinoor*. Everything, just as in the tavern room, was tidy, neat, and clean, even if the pots were blackened and the paint chipped.

'You've been on a ship, nah? Well, my behn Sal likes this place run shipshape, achaa? Dishes, cleaning – your job now, lad.'

Yasser hauled himself up the stairs with his one good hand, uttering hmmphs and aahhhs to demonstrate to Tipu that he was going to considerable trouble to give him this tour. When they reached the first-floor landing, Tipu realized that the shabby frontage, in fact, concealed a very sizeable three-storey property, with at least eight rooms on the first floor alone.

'Lodgings,' muttered Yasser. 'You'll clean 'em when there's lads coming.'

The second set of stairs was steeper, a tight spiral that Yasser stumbled up, breathing heavily. The doors weren't as tall as the ones on the floor below, but there were still six of them. Tipu was impressed.

'These is Sal's own rooms.' He jabbed his hook at one door, which had a little glass evil eye hanging from the knocker. 'My room. No go. Achaa?'

Tipu visualized a room full of heaps of skin flakes accumulated through years of hook-scratchings. He had absolutely no desire to enter.

Yasser stood in front of his own door, and pointed his stick towards the ricketiest door, at the furthest end of the narrow corridor. 'Your room, little Rajput. You must earn your keep, mind, or we'll give you back to the ship. If we have a full house, you sleep in the kitchen, achaa? But otherwise she says you can stay.'

Yasser closed his door behind him. Tipu walked along the corridor and opened the creaky door to his own room.

It was sparely furnished with bare timber boards and thin cotton curtains hanging at the little square window. The ceiling sloped steeply overhead, making the small room seem even smaller. The furniture looked like it had been in a fight: a set of wooden drawers were missing two, while a wooden wardrobe boasted only one splintery door.

But there, stuffed into the room, were three narrow, rusty iron bedsteads, each with a mattress on it and a blanket at the foot.

A bed. For the first time in his life, Tipu would sleep on a bed.

He decided not to give it a go right away, wanting to savour the experience later, in the dark, with no disturbances. But he couldn't resist giving the blanket a quick pat – it was bobbly with use, but clean and soft – before he left his room. His own room.

In the evening, he made Sal, Yasser, and himself fried spiced potatoes and chapattis, and even Yasser admitted they were good. Then he cleaned until the kitchen was gleaming, Sal watching with what Tipu thought was an approving look as she sipped at a tin mug. Then she told him he could go up to bed because he'd be wanted at dawn the next day.

Rolling out the mattress over the criss-cross of ropes that made up the bedframe, he looked fondly at his new bed. It was funny how things turned out sometimes. That morning, he'd been freezing wet, on the streets. The night before, he'd been in the tree. He winced as he thought of Aaliya. Leeza. Chompa. Laurie.

Laurie had said he wouldn't survive. But here, for the first time in his life, Tipu had a bed – and all to himself. A warm glow filled his belly. He wasn't just surviving. He was on his way. He hoped that wherever Laurie was, he was on his way, too. Tomorrow he'd start looking for him.

Blowing out his candle, Tipu took a deep breath and clambered into bed, stretching his arms out and then bringing his hands together under his head. He sighed happily.

And then he clutched the headrest, bewildered.

It felt to him like he was at sea again. The web of ropes sagged under his body, and his stomach dipped as if they were falling over the crest of a wave. Through the thin, lumpy mattress, he could feel each and every knot, like a row of little fists digging into his back.

He turned on his side. The bedstead creaked and rocked as if he was a massive weight upon it, and now the knots were pushing up into the softest part of his belly. He shifted on to his back again, which was accompanied by further complaints from the bedframe. All the while, he felt a seasickness he had never experienced on deck, in the fresh air, in his nest of twigs and leaves in the branches of the date palm.

Aaliya. He wondered how she was, if she'd fully recovered from the storm.

Eventually, Tipu gave up. He took the blanket from the bed and laid it on the floor. He rolled himself into a tiny ball on one half and used the other half to cover himself.

He was learning English and the ways of London. But he doubted he'd ever get the hang of these soft, squishy, and surprisingly uncomfortable things called beds.

# Chapter Twenty-one

The next day, Tipu worked to clean the tavern from top to toe. In the afternoon, after an enormous nap, Yasser went walking with Tipu and pointed out things he needed to know: which handcart sellers would fleece you and which gave a good deal, which groups of children carried blades and which preferred their fists.

Tipu had scratched out a rough image of Laurie on a scrap of newspaper, and asked Yasser the English words for 'have you seen this boy?' He waved the paper in people's faces, but they just shook their heads.

Tipu returned to the inn despondent, but Sal pointed him to a massive mound of dough and a thin wooden rolling pin. 'Get rollin'. We're going to need rotis – an' plenty of 'em.'

He rolled and rolled until his arms cramped and his palms chafed on the spindly rolling pin, while Sal hauled out massive ship-sized pots and started cooking vegetable, potato, meat curries, enough to feed a boatload of hungry stomachs.

✳

That evening, they came.

Tipu returned from buying groceries to hear a clamour of male voices – Indian voices – coming from inside the public room. He pushed open the door.

It was like the galley at rations time, there were so many lean brown men crowded into the room. But while things were hushed on deck, here it was raucous with laughter and banter and singing, the men hugging each other, patting one another on the back. They weren't dressed as he was, in the flimsy dhoti trousers and tunic that sailors wore, but in the thick dark suits that were worn by English people. Cases and sacks were scattered about the floor by the chairs. Were these men different to those he'd known on the ship, Tipu wondered, or was it the ship that made them so different? He had a feeling, which he couldn't fully explain, that it was the latter.

Some of the men were swilling from tall glasses of beer. Others had cups of tea in front of them. Some engaged in games like chess or ludo, while others read, or simply stretched back in their chairs, talking. Sal was right in the middle, sitting, Tipu realized with a fierce blush, on the lap of one young man with slicked-back, shining black hair, his arm tight about her waist. She was laughing, a light in her eyes he hadn't seen before as another fellow pulled her off the man's lap and jigged her about the room.

It was rough, it was disrespectful, and it was one of the warmest sights Tipu had ever seen.

'Arré, what is this, Sal? You've gone and got yourself a baccha?' cried one of the sailors as he noticed Tipu standing in the doorway. At this, others began to turn round towards Tipu with interest and amusement.

'Miss us all too much when we're gone, eh? Want to grow your own?' bellowed a voice at the back of the room, to much hilarity.

Tipu felt awkward, and he picked up the shopping bag to make his way quickly through to the kitchen.

'Aw, leave off, lads. 'E's a soft un, but a good un. Eh, nipper –' Sal beckoned to Tipu – 'come and meet my pedlars.'

He shuffled into the centre of the room, keeping his eyes on the ground. A dozen intent gazes focused on him.

'Where you from, boy?' one asked in rough Hindustani.

Another voice interjected. 'Gujju – just look at how square that face is. Got to be Gujju.'

The first voice coughed, spat, and then, in mock-polite Gujarati, asked Tipu again.

'Surat. Village near Surat,' Tipu mumbled, and there was a smattering of sarcastic hand-claps.

The man who could speak Gujarati continued smoothly. 'I'm Ali. You jumped ship?'

Tipu nodded.

'How many voyages?'

'Just – one.'

'O-ho. Couldn't you handle it?'

'No – no. It was fine. I just –'

'Hai, hai, it's fine. We all jumped – at some point. You're young to start on the ships, mind.'

Tipu puffed himself up. 'I'm sixteen,' he lied.

Ali didn't even blink. 'Yes, and I'm the Queen of Egypt. You're thirteen, if that. Which ship did you come on?'

'The *Kohinoor*.'

'That new ship? The one all the sailors are cussing?' Ali whistled. 'Now it really makes sense. You must be one of the magical kids. We've got our sources, and word gets around.'

Tipu could feel Sal suddenly looking at him keenly, and his cheeks grew hot.

'So show us your magic?' said Ali, giving him a nudge.

Tipu shook his head miserably.

'Djinn – trees. I can't do anything – show you anything here.'

Ali scruffed up Tipu's hair in consolation.

'Arré. I had a cousin who could speak to djinns. Fig tree, it was. Lost his mind in the end. At least you're with Sal now. Sal'll sort you out.'

But Sal had left the party and was speaking quietly to Yasser behind the bar.

The hum of activity and idle talk grew louder again. But Tipu could barely hear it, for the man's words were reverberating in his head. Would Aaliya have destroyed his sanity in the end? Was that why she'd told him to go? Tipu felt a rush of gratitude, and then guilt. She'd put him first – and he'd abandoned her.

Then he couldn't think any more: it was time to serve dinner. Tipu carried four plates of food and rotis on each arm at a time. The men ate with a hunger that he couldn't seem to sate.

'Arré, baccha,' one slurred in Bangla, 'asho with those chapattis.'

Tipu put them down in front of the men, who just grunted a kind of acknowledgement between mouthfuls. Eventually, the frenzied eating gave way to something more peaceful. Tipu cleared glasses and began to wipe the tables and the bar. He wondered if any of these men might have come across his friends: Chompa. Leeza. Laurie.

One man had pulled a wooden flute from his pack and was playing the wistful, evocative songs of a village left far behind. Some of them had been drinking since they'd arrived and were now swaying dangerously or mumbling along with the melody as they listened. A few were clustered about a carrom board, flicking at the counters.

Sal had high colour in her cheeks, and her eyes sparkled as she stood, proudly, behind her bar. Yasser was now seated at a central table and tapped his hook loudly on the table. 'Time to hand over those earnings, boys,' he announced, pointing impatiently at the huge, battered red ledger that sat in front of him.

'Oof, it's not so easy now in the north, yaar. Housewives in Newcastle and South Shields are getting wise to the prices. Then we have to go further out, to the villages, and in those places they don't always like our brown skin.' A neat, turbaned man whom Tipu had heard addressed as Gurdeep rubbed at his forehead where there was the shadow of a bruise still visible. 'It's risky, bhai.'

Ali nodded. 'And now there are all these others coming from India because of the Britishers changing food crops to that weird blue dye, so there're food shortages and price rises. Dead-eyed, starved poor fools coming straight off the boat, willing to do anything for a pittance. Those damned Britishers want to steal everything from us, even the food from our mouths, the earth under our feet.'

He spat on the floor, and Sal cuffed him round the ear, but Ali continued.

'Things are bad back home, Yasser bhai. And when things get bad at home, things get bad here, too.'

Yasser's face darkened. 'Yes, yes. Nothing we can do about it, though, is there? Just tell me the numbers.'

The men began to get out their wallets and notebooks, and soon the parts of the table that were not taken up by the ledger were covered instead by piles of dull copper and brass coins.

The next day was Saturday, and a cranky Sal with a sore head ushered them all out for a bit of hush. Tipu and Yasser went for a walk round the recently opened Victoria Park, pedlar crew in tow. Some of the English strollers clutched protectively at their pockets at the sight of them, causing Yasser to bow and grin at them in sarcastic mock-humility.

Tipu paused by each of the trees in the park, straining to listen for the presence of a djinn. He found himself being slapped roughly on the back and jumped to find Yasser cackling and wheezing.

'Poor little kuttah. You en't going to find a spirit around these parts, nah? You were special only there – here, you're just like the rest of us: poor, brown, and out of place.'

Tipu stared at the ground, feeling wretched.

'Sal told me what Ali said. You came on the magic ship, eh? It's a shame, I can't deny. If you had any other powers, we could do such things.' Yasser sucked air through his teeth.

Tipu thought back to Aaliya, still trapped on the moored *Kohinoor*. Guilt gnawed at his insides.

Yasser sucked on his bidi thoughtfully as they promenaded. 'I remember the tree-djinn from my village. He made a man drown in the river. Poor beggar, he'd heard someone saying his goats had got in there. We found his body in the morning, on the riverbank.

'I used to get a chill whenever I walked near that tree, but I never heard anything. Still, not just to hear them but to speak to them, control them, and not to be dead –' He flicked an admiring eye at Tipu. 'Well, you must have a real gift . . . Yes, it's a shame indeed if it could only be used on the ship.'

His eyes suddenly gleamed. 'Can't you summon the djinn out of the tree?'

Tipu looked up at the trees. 'She has to be bound to a tree to cross over into this world from the djinn-world. She can be unbound once she's on our side, yes – but only if I say the right words. And unbinding a tree-djinn is dangerous. Once she's free, she could possess people, start djinn-fires, create havoc. And what about the ship? If we free her, it'll sink and all the lascars will be stranded here with no way to get home to their families. And no pay to feed them when they get back, either.'

Yasser was nodding impatiently. 'Yes, yes. But it can be done? These words –'

'I don't know them. And if she says them herself, she'll be extinguished. If we were in India, I could try to find out what they are. But not here.'

'What do you mean, if you were in India?'

Tipu frowned. 'We need a scholar, someone who's studied Farsi and djinnspeaker magic. There are charm-writers on Brick Lane, but no djinnspeakers.'

Yasser scoffed and slapped Tipu on the back.

'Arré, kuttah, this is London. Everything you have in India, in the world, you can find here. Most of it, they've stolen. But we can find a djinnspeaker scholar if a djinnspeaker scholar is what you need.'

Yasser disappeared from the lodging house for a couple of days. It wasn't that unusual, Sal explained, particularly after the earnings had come in, so everything went on as normal, just with Tipu doing more work. But when he got back, Yasser clapped Tipu on the back with such ferocity that Tipu leaped a good few inches into the air.

'Aha, chokro! You think Yasser is just a lazy old fool?' He leaned in and tapped his nose as he spoke in a loaded whisper. 'I have found something. Tonight, tonight we go. But now, now I must sleep.'

He stumbled up the stairs, singing as he went, leaving Tipu to stew in his curiosity.

# Chapter Twenty-two

Yasser and Tipu walked through the docks towards the spot where the *Kohinoor* was moored. Yasser gabbled delightedly on the way, waving his hook wildly in the air. It was dusk, and a damp grey blanket was falling over the silhouettes of the ship masts in the dock, and the incongruous palm tree among them.

As Tipu got closer, he could sense Aaliya's presence, but it was fainter than it had been. Her leaves, usually a proud fountain of green, were drooping, and tinged brown at the edges. He felt himself walking quicker. The crew hadn't been looking after her at all.

They stopped on the quay, right in front of the glossy blue hull of the ship.

'Yasser . . . I absconded from this ship. I shouldn't be here,' whispered Tipu, darting worried looks about him.

'Arré, all lascars look the same to them,' scoffed Yasser. 'And now there's no one about except them, anyway. All the white Company men have gone home to their families. It's only us who have to stay chained to the ships. Come, stop fretting. They are our people. We'll be welcome.'

They clambered up the ladder, one by one, Yasser, despite having only one arm, with surprising agility. Like so many of the Indians in their part of London, he'd been a lascar once, too.

Yasser knocked on the door to the galley. Aaliya's flickering, flame-like presence grew louder in Tipu's mind.

The door opened, and a lascar who Tipu remembered was called Iqbal stepped out, looking wary. To Tipu's surprise and relief, his face brightened when he saw Yasser, and the two embraced like brothers and started chattering in a stream of rapid Hindustani. Iqbal looked down at Tipu, and frowned at first, but Yasser put his hand on Iqbal's shoulder.

'Paanch minute, bhai, achaa? Five minutes.'

Iqbal looked at the top deck. There was no one there. He nodded. Tipu and Yasser made their way to the tree mast, Aaliya suddenly shrill in Tipu's ears.

*You lead-brained single-humped camel – I told you not to come back!*

Djinn-language was rude in a surprisingly creative way, Tipu discovered. His pained expression made Yasser smirk.

'The djinn is making you pay for abandoning it, hnnh?'

'I don't understand, Yasser bhai. Why are we here? I told you, I can't release her.'

'You can, and you will.' Yasser's voice had a cold edge, like a knife.

Tipu gulped. He now understood why Yasser had been so happy of late. He saw Tipu as another money-making opportunity, just like the pedlars. 'She's – she's bound to the tree.'

'Then she just needs to be bound to something else.'

Tipu shook his head. 'She needs a date tree, bhai, and they don't grow here in London!'

'Tsk. I was thinking of those stories we heard as children about djinn, nah? Thinking of Al-a-deen, that story? He finds a djinn in a lamp. And it gave me an idea. Whoever thought fairy tales could be useful, hah!'

He stuffed his hand in his pocket and, with the flourish of an illusionist, brought out a tiny cork-stoppered green glass bottle wound with twine.

'Bhai –' Tipu began again uncertainly.

'Wait, wait. That is not the genius. The genius,' interrupted Yasser, 'is this.'

More rifling in pockets while the bottle dangled from his hooked stick, and then a final triumphant waggle of his fingers, with something small, long, and grooved in between them. Tipu peered closely to make it out, but Yasser's fingers were dancing, and it was a little brown blur of a thing between them.

'See – a tree. A tree in its smallest living form!' Yasser stretched his hand towards Tipu, and he finally realized what it was.

It was a stone. A sprouting date stone.

'I checked it out with an Indian witch. Wasn't difficult to find, not for Yasser – and not in London. Wherever there are people whose spirits and dreams are being broken, there's a market for magic. We have Jewish magicians, Chinese,

Indian. This one just arrived in London last week, as a stowaway, carting books and all sorts on this very ship, very hush-hush like. My friend here –' Yasser nudged Iqbal with affection – 'is very useful. They should be here any minute.' Yasser made himself comfortable on deck. Iqbal and some of the other lascars brought out a hookah pipe and chai and they began talking adda, the long, slow art of idle conversation, Yasser keeping one eye on Tipu the whole time.

A magician, on their own ship? For a hopeful moment, Tipu was sure it had to be Chompa's uncle – and that maybe Chompa would be coming with him. Then he turned to see a youngish Indian woman with short black-and-steel-coloured curls marching towards them. Tipu felt surprise, and then a little disappointment.

The woman strode over and shook Tipu's hand. Her clasp was so firm Tipu's hand twinged.

'Dr Farhana Rahim. I hear you wish to transfer a djinn? It's a risky business, one that I would not normally be willing to support. However –' she looked up at the hull and scowled – 'this is a Company ship. If you're the enemy of my enemy, that's good enough reason for me. How have you persuaded the djinn to do this?' Her voice was as brisk as her handshake.

Tipu flushed. 'I haven't had a chance to talk it over with her. If she refuses, well, I'll have to respect that.'

'I'm glad you're not a tyrant, at least. Well, jaldi, then. I haven't got all day.'

Tipu dared not climb the tree. Instead, he rested his face

against the bark, allowing Aaliya's cries to fill his ears, feeling Yasser's eyes boring into his back.

'I'm sorry, I'm sorry,' he whispered in Farsi. 'I can't free you, not yet. But do you want to remain fixed in this tree? Or do you want to come with me? You've always complained about being bored. Neither of us will be bored in London. And don't you want revenge on those who bound you to the task in the first place? Wouldn't leaving this ship be the best start?'

Aaliya's wails settled. There was a final bristling of leaves, but then the tree was still.

Tipu breathed in relief, and then nodded to Dr Rahim, who was watching avidly with a shrewd, thoughtful expression on her face.

'Your relationship is an interesting one,' she said. 'If I had time, I'd do some research to see if there's a precedent.' Then she straightened up, looking businesslike again. 'But I do not, so let us begin. This process will require you to first hold the ship so that it doesn't sink, then unbind your djinn from the tree, and bind her to this seedling. Shame that our sailors are onboard – I'd rather sink it. But it won't be the fastest ship on the sea any more – more like the slowest. And no one will be any the wiser until they find a new djinnspeaker.' Her eyes gleamed with satisfaction.

Dr Rahim pulled one of the green-threaded taviz from her wrist and tied it to Tipu's. 'Whether this works or not depends on you and if you can do the two pieces of magic at the same time. I'm a charm-writer; you have the connection to the djinn. I've placed a little written magic in the locket with the full binding spell, so that you can unbind her and rebind her quickly after you've persuaded her to keep the ship afloat. This means you'll be able to bind and unbind her in the future. But to extricate her without sinking the ship will be difficult. Her instinct will be to destroy her prison.'

Yasser leaned over and passed Tipu the date seed and the bottle.

'You'll need to touch the taviz and say these words in Farsi: "*The flame of your spirit I permit now to roam*", to unbind her. Then to rebind her: "*The flame of your spirit I return to this home.*"'

Tipu breathed in deeply, focused, and said the first line.

'*The flame of your spirit I permit now to roam.*'

Immediately, he felt Aaliya's energy bloom hungrily, like oil catching fire, as a plume of pale red flame spiralled from the top of the tree. For a second, he forgot himself – aware for the first time of her power, her scale – her non-humanness. For a second, he was afraid. But then he sensed her joy at being free, the expansiveness of her spirit stretching out, spinning, swirling, rejoicing in the ability to move as she chose for once. Tipu felt his chest contract – how could he imprison her again? She who had chosen imprisonment so that he could be free?

*I'm sorry, I'm sorry.* He spoke to her in his mind. *But I need you. I can't make it in London without you. I will set you free, I promise. But right now I need your help.*

As he explained, he saw Aaliya's form grow limp, the darting scarlet plume of flame clustering together into tear shapes.

*I know. I'll let you out whenever I can if you promise to return.*

*And the other promise, to set you free for good one day, still stands. It does.*

Then he spoke the second.

'*The flame of your spirit I return to this home.*'

The flame-tears came together once more and spiralled round Tipu, before howling, a sound of pure pain only he could hear, and then diving into the bottle.

'Thank you,' he whispered. 'Thank you, Aaliya.'

Tipu stoppered the bottle, coming back to himself a little with the physical act. He could see the seed pinging against the sides as Aaliya fought the spell and herself at the same time. Watching the seed's desperate dance, he also felt something tighten round his heart. Almost reluctantly, he looked around, half-expecting the ship to be filling with water already.

It was still afloat.

'Thank you, thank you,' he exclaimed breathlessly to Aaliya. How would he ever repay her?

'Shabbash!' roared Yasser in triumph, clapping his hands together.

Tipu turned to Dr Rahim to thank her for her help, but she was already hurrying away from the quay. Yasser and Iqbal and the other sailors clustered around the bottle, fascinated.

Then a figure bounded out of the shadows and straight into Tipu's stomach. Tipu fell back on to the deck in alarm, scrabbling to make sure the bottle hadn't broken, while fending off the sturdy brown body that appeared to be attacking him.

'Arré, arré – stop!' he pleaded.

The boy stopped pummelling him and then, most unexpectedly, pounced upon him again in a hug. Tipu exclaimed in hearty Gujarati slang as he realized who it was.

'Laurie!'

Seeing his face again made Tipu's shoulders feel light as relief flooded him. He hugged his friend.

'Where've you been? How's London been treating you?' Tipu asked with concern in his voice.

Laurie shrugged casually. 'Fine. Some church ladies fed me a few times, all for being lectured about the "right path". It's not been too bad.'

Laurie leaned in closer and spoke in a low voice. 'Bhai, we need to be careful. There's talk of children going missing – kids with magic.'

Tipu's eyes grew wide. 'Here, too?'

Laurie nodded gravely.

'Devaynes,' they whispered at the same time.

'Chompa was right,' said Laurie. 'That's why I've been hiding out here. It's not safe further into the city, especially not at night. I don't know what I'll do when the ship heads out again.'

Tipu put a hand on his friend's shoulder. 'I do. You're coming with me.'

Tipu felt a bit taller as they walked away from the tree, the djinn-bottle in his pocket, his friend at his side.

'And who's this?' Yasser shoved Tipu with his hook before the boy could answer. 'Does he have magic too?' he said, coins practically shining in his pupils.

Tipu nodded, then quickly introduced them to one another.

'If you're a jumper, you can't stay here, my boy,' said Yasser, putting his arm round Laurie. 'Any magical friend of Tipu's is a magical friend of ours. Our home is your home. Come, come.'

As they made their way back to Brick Lane, Yasser hummed dreamily to himself.

'Now you two magical geniuses are reunited, let's go have some fun, nah!' Yasser said, grinning.

Tipu looked uneasy. 'Exactly what kind of fun are you talking about, bhai?'

'The earning kind. Chalo. And jaldi.'

An hour later, Yasser, Tipu and Laurie were feasting on butter cakes. Yasser's scheme, once Tipu had finally got Aaliya to cooperate, had been to get Laurie to predict the weather for the wealthy people who liked to tour the East End of an evening, embellishing wild tales of woe and misery on the ships and streets, while Tipu whispered commands to Aaliya to lift out their purses, and bring them to him. After emptying a few coins – not too many, nothing that would change the weight discernibly – Tipu persuaded the djinn to put the purse back. She grumbled that she could feel the metal through the leather, but had done it all the same. After each theft, Tipu let Aaliya twist and wind through the air, before uncorking the bottle and thinking the reversal words.

'Serves them right for coming to gawp at us like we're zoo animals,' reasoned Yasser, taking a bite from his butter cake.

They made their way back to Sal's, giddy with magic, money, and food, entirely unaware of a small boy in a neat grey cap following them, watching their every move.

Sal was very pleased to have another djinnspeaker to add to her troupe, especially as Tipu now had Aaliya, too. It put her in the best of moods, and she welcomed Laurie in with one of her rough hugs.

She slapped Yasser on the back triumphantly. 'Shabbash! Well done, Yasser. You're beginnin' to earn your keep. If your keep had been for a week an' not a decade, that is!' She chuckled and shoved him affectionately. 'An' you boys – empty out those pockets of yours. I may not 'ave magic like you, but I can smell money on yer both.'

Her green eyes flashed with expectation. Laurie and Tipu slowly stacked their coins on the table somewhat reluctantly.

'An' the rest, you,' said Sal, tapping her foot and looking pointedly at Laurie.

'Are you sure you don't have magic, Sal?' Laurie groaned as he pulled a fistful of coins from inside his shirt. 'Arré, these East End types – nothing gets past them. And, believe me, I've tried.'

'Too right.' Sal nodded, satisfied. 'Good work, boys. But this is just the beginnin'. I see the two of yer work nicely together. Yer can start earnin' your keep an' all from now on.

Get some kip, lads,' she said, clapping her rough hands together with glee. 'You'll be out there workin' those pockets tomorrow bright and early.'

She pushed one small stack of coins back towards Tipu and Laurie, winking as she turned away, singing a merry Punjabi folk tune.

# Chapter Twenty-three

Chompa stood on the gangplank, looking dubiously at the England before her. Then she heard an almighty splash. And then another. She tried to peer into the water to see if Tipu and Laurie had made it safely on to land, but the fog clung to the water like mould.

Behind her, Farook Miah was now screaming, waving a furious fist at the water. She smiled to herself and willed Tipu and Laurie to be safely on their way, and then hurried after Leeza and Mohsin. Gingerly, as if she might explode on contact, she placed one foot, and then the other, on British soil. Nothing happened. It was no different – no *better*.

She glowered. Devaynes and Lady Inglis might think Indian soil was owned by the British now, but it never would be to her.

An Indian crew member set their bags down in front of them, bowed, and left.

Mohsin took off his glasses. He tried to wave down one of

the many drivers milling about, but they were all occupied with trying to get the business of the English passengers. Chompa blew enraged air out of her nostrils and was alarmed to see it come out as a puff of smoke.

Then a glossy dark blue carriage pulled up in front of them.

'Do get in, Professor Kabir, Miss Begum,' came the oil-smooth voice of Devaynes as the carriage door opened. 'Your maidservant will travel with your luggage and my housekeeper, Mrs Illsley.'

'Actually, Sir Clive, we plan to make our own way from here. I've looked up some lodging houses in the newspaper –' began Mohsin, but a tall, stern-looking woman in a frilly cap suddenly appeared at Chompa's elbow and grabbed Leeza, pulling her away.

'Hai!' cried Leeza, eyes wide in alarm.

'No!' yelled Chompa as she tried to pull Leeza back towards her. But the woman was too strong, and Leeza disappeared into the fog.

Chompa grabbed Mohsin's hand. 'Uncle, we need to leave!' Turning to the carriage, she shouted, 'Where are you taking her? Bring Leeza back!'

Terror started to rise in Chompa's chest. Not again. *Not again.*

She and Mohsin looked around wildly. There were men in dark blue uniforms busy on the dock, inadvertently, or deliberately, blocking them in. And they were armed.

'I don't think we have a choice, Chompa,' whispered Mohsin. 'We have to go with him. He has Leeza.'

'It's better this way, Uncle. We still haven't worked out where he's keeping Ammi. If we go with him, we have a better chance of finding her,' she muttered through gritted teeth. She would not let Devaynes have the satisfaction of feeling like he'd tricked her. She pulled the carriage door open, and forced herself to shrug dismissively as she climbed in.

Devaynes smiled and leaned back against the plush leather seats.

'Of course you're staying with *me*,' he said with a smile that didn't reach his eyes. 'I can't have the two of you getting lost in London – *anything* could happen to you.'

Mohsin's face coloured. 'Sir, you're very kind, but –'

'I will not take no for an answer,' interrupted Devaynes coolly. 'Might I remind you, Miss Begum, that I have held up my part of the deal, and you are yet to deliver on *yours*? It would be so easy for you to disappear in London, and then I'd look like quite the fool.' He rapped his knuckles on the door and the carriage started moving.

Hot fury seethed through Chompa, and she had to clutch at the handrail to stop herself losing her temper. Devaynes, leaning back with that self-satisfied smile on his face. Leeza, travelling with the *luggage*. Chompa's stomach twisted at the thought: Leeza had no English and would feel so exposed and frightened.

Chompa looked out of the windows at London, forcing herself to become acquainted with this cold country. When she found Ammi, she would need to be able to find her way to the docks to get them all back home. But the streets were strange: fancy, cake-like buildings stood right next to crumbling shacks. While the rich and poor, the new and older parts of Dacca, were neatly partitioned off from one another, in London, poverty lived cheek by jowl with the grand buildings of the rich. Some things were the same, though: the beggars here were as filthy and desperate as the ones at home – only here they looked colder. So this was the land of Lady Inglis, of the men who thought they were so much better than Indians. Chompa felt resentment surge through her and clutched at her and Ammi's entwined taviz fiercely. Once she'd got Ammi back, she wanted nothing more to do with these hypocrites and their cold grey land.

The journey was not a long one: soon the carriage came to a stop on a broad, busy thoroughfare. Wedged between a shabby shop and a coffee house was an incongruous, elegant, red-bricked house tucked behind tall trees. Two black railed gates kept the riff-raff at bay, each gate topped with a black iron lion.

'Welcome to Malplaquet House, my home here in London.'

Chompa followed Mohsin up the stone steps. The English doorman opened the great door and, while doing so, bowed at Devaynes, then at Mohsin, and then at Chompa.

Another servant hurried to greet them and take their coats. Chompa stared, and then shivered. The house was as grand within as it was outside, but something about the grandeur was also very sinister, even a little crazed. Every surface, every table and wall was stuffed or covered with things: hangings, paintings, masks, animal skulls. She instinctively knew that they all came from India: the paintings were of plants Chompa recognized; the hangings were of nakshi kantha embroidery of the type Chompa and Amina had on their quilt at home, but in shimmering silk rather than cotton. Everything was gleaming with new polish, but Chompa couldn't breathe for looking at it all. She felt sorry for the servants who had to keep all this in order. She thought about how Leeza would feel to be presented with such a task.

Turning to Devaynes, Chompa stamped her foot. 'Where is she? Where's Leeza?'

Devaynes smiled. 'Your maidservant will be unpacking your luggage in your room, I expect. Miss Begum, Professor Kabir – London is dangerous for those not acquainted with its ways and language. With notice, Professor, you will be free to use my carriages, but you must at all times be accompanied by Ismail – for your own protection, you understand. For the same reason, the exterior doors will remain locked and will only be opened by my staff, to prevent Miss Begum from – shall we say – *adventuring*.'

Chompa stifled a gasp. She was a prisoner.

'Now, the London air is filthy. I imagine both of you wish to wash, change, and rest. Please, my house is yours.'

Devaynes waved a hand at one of the servants, who bowed and guided Mohsin and Chompa upstairs.

Chompa trudged after the servant, stomach like a lead anchor. How would she find Ammi, locked in this house? Only the sight of Leeza, sitting cross-legged on the plush rug in Chompa's room, chewing a rolled paan, a classic scowl on her face, lifted her spirits.

'Leeza!' cried Chompa, throwing her arms round her. 'You're here! I was so worried!'

Leeza rolled her eyes as she peeled Chompa off, but looked secretly pleased.

'O-ho – the drivers are careful with the English saheb's carriage, and go slowly, but not so with luggage and maids! Who cares if we fall and get smashed to pieces!' She gave a little snort of disgust. 'And so cold!'

Chompa nodded and leaned in. 'Leeza – we're prisoners. The doors are locked! What are we going to do? How will I ever find Ammi?'

Leeza patted Chompa's arm. 'Locks have keys, and keys are kept by servants. We'll find a way. But just look at this place!'

The carpet was patterned with tigers, the eiderdown on the four-poster bed embroidered with elephants, and the golden fireplace was patterned with peacocks.

'Eesh, it's more Indian than India,' scoffed Leeza, rolling her eyes at Chompa again. Chompa smiled back, but couldn't get rid of her feeling of unease.

✳

After a fitful night's sleep, in which Chompa kept dreaming she was running down corridors in the Lalbagh Fort only to find her way blocked by tall brick walls, she was presented with a pale yellow rice dish with flaked fish and a slice of lemon at breakfast.

'Kedgeree,' said Devaynes with a smile. 'A British twist on your native khichri, or, as I think you'd know it, *khichuri*, rice and lentil dish. Something nourishing before we visit the project I have in mind for you as way of payment for your passage here, Miss Begum.'

By now, Chompa was prepared for any kind of bland mulch that passed for British cooking. She knew this 'kedgeree' could be nothing like the bright yellow khichuri she loved, the way the mashed lentils and rice melted together so creamily. She and Ammi always had it during the monsoon, large steaming clay bowls of it, with a big dollop of melted buttery ghee on top, while they listened to the warm, fat raindrops splashing on the thatched roof of their hut. The memory hurt almost physically.

Devaynes, though, seemed interested in her verdict, so she took a mouthful. An overwhelmingly salty fishiness filled her mouth. She swallowed quickly, and with a smile that was more of a grimace said, 'You don't even need to add salt!'

'Ah, excellent! I knew you'd appreciate how we've refined the peasant dish.'

Honestly, these Britishers thought they were so superior. Chompa glowered. They even had to meddle with something as simple and delicious as khichuri.

As Devaynes left the breakfast table, Mohsin leaned in and whispered in Chompa's ear, 'Whatever it is that Devaynes asks of you today, I want you to pace yourself with the magic, Chompa. As soon as you feel tired, you must stop.' His green eyes were serious, worried.

Chompa raised her chin. 'I can handle it, Uncle. I'm strong enough.'

But Mohsin didn't look convinced.

A little later, their carriage pulled up next to a massive white stone building, its wide front lined with tall white pillars. In the centre of the quadrant before it stood a pale marble sculpture of the serious-faced young queen.

'The British Museum,' said Devaynes proudly as they stood by the forbidding black iron gates. 'It houses all our nation's treasures.'

'Treasures your nation has acquired from others, without paying for them,' said Mohsin bravely, and then flushed.

Devaynes looked at Mohsin for a long moment. Chompa swivelled her eyes between them both, holding her breath. But then Devaynes laughed, and waved a manicured hand in the air, dismissing the point.

'Is the thing you want me to transform inside?' said Chompa impatiently. 'And once I've transformed it, we can leave?'

'Not quite, my dear. You are looking at the "thing" I wish transformed.'

Mohsin frowned. 'I don't quite understand, Sir Clive. What are we looking at? The sculpture? It's large, but I imagine Chompa could manage it if she rested afterwards.'

Devaynes smiled. 'The sculpture, *and* the building.'

'Sir Clive – one young girl cannot do all this! It's impossible. The sculpture will have to suffice.' The colour in Mohsin's cheeks was reaching his ears.

Devaynes glanced at him, his expression mild. 'Your concern is touching, Professor, but I do believe you underestimate your ward.' He turned to Chompa. 'The principle is the same as with the rose, is it not? And I'm quite sure you're strong enough.'

Mohsin snorted in disgust, but Chompa laid a hand on his arm to quieten him.

'Why?' she said, looking at Devaynes shrewdly.

Devaynes met her gaze. 'I want to inspire awe. Back in India, djinn-magic is tolerated at most. In England, it is mocked. But I wish to change that.

'As we speak, my staff are filling this magnificent structure with objects for a Great Exhibition of Magic. It will be a Palace of Wonder, if you will, where examples of the potential of magic from India and all over the world will be collected and celebrated.'

Chompa thought of the children tied up below deck on the *Albion*, on Devaynes' orders: all djinnborn and djinnspeakers. She knew every word he spoke was a lie.

'If we can persuade the powers that be that djinnborn magic is important and valuable, they'll wish to protect those who wield it. The powers that be include the dock authorities, customs officials, the police. Among them are friends of mine –' Devaynes looked meaningfully at Chompa – 'but others are more sceptical. Take Lady Inglis, for example. You could change their minds, Miss Begum.'

Chompa's stomach lurched in revulsion.

'In a week's time, I want you to turn this building to silver in front of our illustrious audience, right before their eyes. If you do this, Miss Begum, I will consider our deal fulfilled, and you'll be free to go – though perhaps this could be the start of a special friendship between us.'

Mohsin, silently seething with rage, could no longer restrain himself.

'It's too much! Sir Clive, I will pay for our passage once Chompa and I have returned to Dacca – it will take some time, but I can't allow this to go on any longer. She's a *child*.'

'Professor Kabir, you stood by and watched as this *child* offered to pay for her passage with magic. She offered to turn the fort to silver, in fact! No, no, this is the payment I want. And my friends are in high places across the city, should either of you try to renege on this.' His face drained of all warmth. 'But I do hope it won't come to that. I trust Miss Begum is a young woman of her word. Or,' he said, cocking his head to one side and looking at Chompa, 'are all your promises lies?'

*Like yours?* Chompa wanted to retort as rage blazed within her. But she restrained herself. Devaynes had just told her that he had eyes everywhere. She had to be careful. They were in enough trouble as it was.

215

She gave a curt nod. 'I can do it.'

'Wonderful,' cried Devaynes, clapping his hands together in glee. 'Why not try one of the pillars to begin with, and see how you feel?'

She stood a little straighter, held both her taviz firmly, took a deep breath in, and began with the column closest to her. The grey-white stone began to smooth and brighten, as if an invisible hand was polishing it.

Even the guards stared for a moment as the small girl with the wild hair stood with her pointed finger and turned the immense pillar to pure, glowing silver.

Devaynes remained at the museum. Mohsin was terse in the carriage back to the house. Chompa had turned the pillar back, and assured him that she still felt fine, but Mohsin looked unconvinced.

'I'm going to ask Ismail to come with me to look for a laboratory space I can use. I need to find a way to help you with this piece of magic. I can't just sit back and watch you take all this on your young shoulders. And Ismail won't be able to supervise me all the time – so, whenever I can slip away, I'll start making enquiries about Amina.'

Chompa nodded. What was *she* to do? She couldn't just stay cooped up inside, with Devaynes' staff spying on her all the time.

As they neared the house, she felt like she was being suffocated. Then suddenly her eyes lit up. Mohsin's words rang like a bell in her mind. Whatever Devaynes' instructions, his staff couldn't supervise them *all the time*. Yes! She just had to seem bored and lazy to them – and they'd get tired of watching her. She grinned. She could do that!

Chompa pretended to flump upstairs, yawning, saying loudly in Mrs Illsley's hearing that she needed to rest. When safely in her room, door closed, Chompa threw herself on the rug in front of Leeza.

'The study key – have you found out where it is?' she said, eyes utterly focused.

Leeza nodded but puffed her cheeks. It wasn't going to be good news.

'One is in Devaynes' pocket. And the other one's in the housekeeper's room. She gives it to the maid to open up to dust and light the fires in the morning, then she takes it back after. And the only key to Mrs Illsley's room is in Mrs Illsley's pocket.'

Chompa frowned, deep in thought, looking for a chink of light with which to create a plan. After a while, with Leeza staring at her, she gave a businesslike nod.

'I've got it. I know how we can get in.'

'But the housemaid!' objected Leeza. 'She'll call Mrs Illsley.'

'Arré, we just need to get the housemaid on our side.' Chompa fiddled with the double taviz in her pocket, then grinned. 'And I know just how to do that.'

Several days later, Mohsin came and sat down opposite Chompa in the library, twitching with a strange energy. He leaned over and spoke to her quietly.

'Chompa, I have been working on something today, but I'm in need of some assistance, if you don't mind?'

Chompa raised her brows at the idea that she could help with any of Mohsin's scientific research. He smiled and placed a small silver object in her palm. It looked like a thimble, but with a tiny lid.

'I want to do some further research on what's happening to the silver when you turn it. So I made this, to see if you could actually put your magic *in* the silver, and see if it can, in fact, remain there. If it does, then we might be able to siphon off and store your magic in silver.'

'Like a taviz,' Chompa said, mystified, turning it over.

Mohsin grinned, his face animated with excitement. 'Very good – very good. I actually got the idea from them!'

Chompa nodded, still staring down at the little round capsule. Mohsin plucked it from Chompa's palm, unscrewed it, and placed it upon her index finger.

'What is it you want me to do?'

'Could you focus on the silver, and think of the word "absorb"?'

She concentrated on her now silver fingertip. She could feel her finger buzzing slightly as soon as she trained her mind on the word 'absorb', and then a strange flowing sensation from her wrist, through her finger and into the silver. What was happening?

Mohsin put his hand on Chompa's shoulder. 'Now "end".'

She did as he asked.

'And now "store".'

Again, she focused on the word.

Mohsin removed the silver cap from her finger and placed it on the table. Then he raised his finger. The silver cap moved.

Mohsin smiled broadly, but Chompa looked astonished.

'I thought you said you can't do anything with metal? That only I can?'

'And that's still true for now. I couldn't have moved the cap if you hadn't imbued the silver itself with some of your magic.'

'What does this mean?' Chompa asked, still shaking her head in disbelief.

'I've been worrying about the toll that this huge piece of magic could have on you. I wondered if there might be a way of making little stores of magic, to set by, to allow you time to recover. I hate this deal with Devaynes, Chompa. I feel so powerless, and I wanted to do something to help.'

They then worked on storing a little of Chompa's magic in each of a dozen capsules.

'And what have you found out about Ammi?' said Chompa when Mohsin was packing them away.

Mohsin looked deflated. 'The truth is, I haven't been able to get very far. Ismail never leaves me alone, despite my hopes. We really need to get out of this house, away from Devaynes, Chompa, as soon as we can.' He tapped the box of capsules. 'So I think this is the best way forward. I'm aiming to devise a way that I can use my own magic to magnify yours, so that just a little magic can turn all the silver we need. If the two of us are able to work together, we should be released from this deal sooner, and start searching for Amina properly.'

Chompa understood, but couldn't also help feeling a little disappointed in him for not finding out anything about Ammi. But then sneaking around wasn't Mohsin's strength. It was hers.

She'd have to take matters into her own hands.

But taking matters into her own hands wasn't as simple as she'd thought. The housemaid, Millie, kept darting away from Chompa and Leeza every time they tried to corner her, clearly terrified of the 'exotic' new inhabitants now in residence. Chompa had thought that some pieces of silver might impress and tempt her, so, when they were alone in her room, she went round waving her finger dramatically and changing vases and lacquered boxes to silver with great flourish and pomp, while Millie was dusting or lighting fires. But if anything it made Millie even warier.

It was Leeza who found the way to gain Millie's trust.

Mohsin had arranged for several boxes of Indian treats to be packed in their luggage when they left Dacca, and as Millie swept the grate in Chompa's room one afternoon Leeza opened a box of diamond-shaped almond sweets decorated with silver leaf. She sighed sadly.

'Our last box. Either I'll have to get the cook to let me in the kitchen or we'll have to make do with *rock cakes*.'

Chompa and Leeza shared a shiver. The cook's rock cakes were horrible, dry, teeth-breaking things with only a hint of sweetness. Nothing like mishti, which could almost be *too* sweet. If such a thing was even possible.

As Chompa savoured each nibble, she noticed Leeza watching Millie, whose gaze was fixed avidly on the box. Then Leeza smiled at Millie. A big, toothy, un-Leeza-like smile. Millie shrank back, but Leeza quickly pushed the box towards her with a nod of her head. Chompa could tell that Leeza was trying not to roll her eyes, but she kept her face sweet and encouraging. It was like trying to tempt a timid kitten.

Finally, Millie's sweet tooth got the better of her. She snatched at the box and then sampled one of the sweets, nibbling off a point. Then she grinned in delight, her whole face lighting up, and swallowed the whole thing.

Leeza pulled the box back and patted the rug next to her.

'Come,' she said.

A moment later, Millie was sitting close to Leeza, tucking into the mishti. Chompa's eyes widened in surprise, and then she grinned at Leeza in relief.

'Nice work,' she whispered.

Leeza harrumphed, but Chompa noticed her cheeks glowing.

They seized their chance that very afternoon, with the help of the last mishti.

Millie nudged them into the study and pretended to be polishing the door handle to keep an eye out for Mrs Illsley.

Chompa stood for a moment, taking in the study, assessing where to start. It was a darker version of the one at the fort, with a large desk, and panels of bookshelves. There, the furniture had been of light wood and royal blue silk, but here the wood was dark, almost black, the upholstery velvet in Devaynes' distinctive shade of deep indigo. It made the study feel ominous and cold.

'What are we looking for?' Leeza whispered.

'Anything that can help us find out what he's doing with Ammi and the others, or where he's keeping them. So –' Chompa began turning over papers on the desk carefully, so that they could be kept in place – 'I'll start with these. You look through the drawers to see if there are any more taviz, keys, or other things that might help us.'

She skimmed the papers. The first: documents relating to the sale of some of Devaynes' ships. The second: an early draft of the bill to ban writing-magic. Underneath it, a speech to persuade people to vote for it. She growled and turned over the next paper.

And there it was.

A table with two columns. One listing magical abilities. The other listing prices.

*Djinnspeaker. Rose-affinity. Power: weak. Limited use, but of decorative value.*

*Auction guide price for five years' free labour (renewable): £10.*

*Djinnspeaker. Limestone-affinity. Power: of average strength. Useful for industry.*

*Auction guide price for five years' free labour (renewable): £20.*

Chompa's heart thudded in her chest. It was one thing to have met Layli and the children in the boat. It was another to see it all laid out, cold and precise like this.

She ran a finger down the far-left column. And then froze.

There.

There it was.

*Djinnborn. Water-affinity as well as djinn-fire. Powerful.*

*Many potential uses. Auction or retain?*

Ammi.

Chompa was sombre through dinner, pressure mounting inside her head. All she could see were those neat, awful columns, and the words that she had read.

Before bed, Leeza yanked at her hair with the brush, causing the throbbing to turn into a hammering pain.

'I just want to sleep . . .' wailed Chompa faintly.

'These knots will get worse if you sleep on them – and then there'll be no hope for your hair. It'll be –' Leeza scissored her fingers together in a way that made Chompa stop complaining at once.

The combing became soothing after a while. Chompa closed her eyes and for a moment remembered those quiet rituals by the river with Ammi. Then she realized Leeza had stopped.

Chompa sat up and looked into Leeza's frowning face in the mirror.

'What is it? Have you found a grey hair or something? Ammi said I had one somewhere. I was born with it.'

Leeza hurriedly pushed her hand into a pocket. 'No, no, it's just dry. This terrible cold – not good for skin or hair. I will make some oil.'

She started combing again, but more gently, still frowning.

A couple of hours later, Chompa lay in the dark, twisting from side to side in the throes of the dream.

*Mohsin! Mohsin!* screamed Ammi.

Her mother's face blazed in front of Chompa's closed eyes, a beacon of despair.

*Mohsin!*

Each scream was like a knife that drove deep into the soft core of Chompa's brain.

Last time, it had been so unexpected, Chompa had experienced the entire event in a blur of helplessness, paralysed with shock. She had almost been too terrified to relive the vision, pushing it to the back of her mind, allowing so many frivolous concerns to crowd over it.

And then Chompa woke, and it was gone, like a candle being snuffed out, the blackness and the quietness seeming ten times more intense than they had been before.

The cries had been so agonized that they stabbed at Chompa's heart and made her catch her breath. What was Ammi suffering? What was happening to her to cause her such grief and pain? She sat up, absolutely straight, and tried frantically to remember everything she could from the vision, her heart racing.

Her ammi had been thinner, paler, and there were strands of silver, Chompa could have sworn, in her once jet-black hair.

Stripes of shadow had crossed Ammi's face. She'd been twisting her face from side to side in a way that made Chompa feel that she was seated and bound. It made her breathe in sharply to think of her mother like that, to think that she could have been like that all this time, while Chompa had been having adventures, growing – living.

The rest of Ammi had been in the darkness, and, frustratingly, Chompa had not been able to make out anything in the background that might tell her where her mother was.

Except . . . she'd heard something – a ringing in a strangely discordant, tinny pattern.

Bells.

# Chapter Twenty-four

The memory of Ammi's voice echoed round Chompa's skull early the next morning. Chompa's brain felt too small to contain the sound. She lolled listlessly on the bed, trying to piece together anything else from what she'd seen.

None of the papers she'd found in the study had listed any addresses. But Ammi was near. Chompa knew it somehow.

Mohsin. As soon as she'd woken, she knew she had to tell Mohsin. Ammi was calling for him, after all. But Leeza had said he had left already for the laboratory, where he'd been working all hours. No, it would have to wait.

But Chompa needed help. Who could roam London in a search for stripes of shadow and bells?

She sat up.

She knew exactly who.

'Come, put this on,' ordered Chompa, holding out Leeza's coat and waving to her boots. 'I need some fresh air.'

Leeza snorted, her arms firmly crossed.

'Air? Fresh? In London? You'll die from either cold or the green poison in the air. I just don't know which will be first.'

Chompa groaned. 'Fine. Stay. I'll go on my own. Then, if something happens to me, you can explain to Master Mohsin why you were at home all cosy with a cup of tea while I was murdered on the street.'

Leeza huffed and grabbed the coat from Chompa mutinously.

'She would have me die, too, nah. So good she is. She wants to go for a walk, in this city of murderers and thieves, she says. Fresh air, she says.'

Millie let them out of the front door, eyes darting around nervously like a frightened mongoose. Chompa breathed in deeply, feeling a huge weight lifting from her shoulders. She was free temporarily.

Mile End Road was a bustling, busy street with carriages rolling along in both directions. It was lined with beggars and urchins, sitting defeated and dirty on the ground, trying to catch the attention of those fortunate enough to have work and change in their pockets. They noted Chompa's good coat and boots, recent gifts from Devaynes, and started reaching their hands towards her. She walked on. Leeza followed her, clucking her tongue in pity and wonder.

'Memsahib! My daughter!' cried a voice in Hindustani.

Chompa turned round sharply. The sound of an Indian language ringing clearly in the London air made her feel dizzy. She looked about her for the speaker of the words. But there were only the urchins, and the English people walking quickly with their eyes straight ahead, as if the poor were invisible.

Then she looked more closely at the beggars. One was ever so slightly darker. His hair and beard were long and wispy, and his clothes were rags upon his thin, wrinkled body.

'My daughter,' he croaked again.

Chompa kneeled before him, searching for her bag of coins. Leeza uttered a moan of disapproval, but Chompa ignored her.

'Uncle. Chacha-ji,' she spoke softly in Hindustani. 'Where have you come from?'

The man seized Chompa's wrist, but his grasp was weak. 'Bombay, meri beti,' he croaked.

'Can you not go home?' she asked sadly. 'To your family?'

The man's eyes clouded for a moment. 'No food, no family, only famine.'

He prodded her and cupped his hand. Chompa nodded and pulled a clutch of coins from her bag.

'Uncle-ji, where do lascars hide in London when they jump ship?' Chompa leaned in, ignoring the stink emanating from him.

The man reached over his head and pointed a shaking, withered finger at one end of the broad street, then waggled his finger right.

'Brick Lane. Ask for Sal. Lascar Sal.'

Chompa looked down at the dull silver alloy poisha, stamped *Indian Company Rupee*. They would be of no worth here. She grasped her two taviz and turned them to pure silver. The man blinked, unable to believe his eyes. Chompa dropped the shining circles into the man's cupped hands. She put a hand on his shoulder, to try to find out his name. But his attention was lost to her now, as he started to count the discs over and over, like a child at lessons.

She stood up and looked triumphantly at Leeza.

'I don't yet know how to find Ammi. But I do know how to find Tipu and Laurie.'

Brick Lane reminded Chompa of the Chowk Bazaar. And it thrilled her almost as much. The street seethed with life: food sellers hauled their carts and bellowed their wares, groups of scruffy children played complicated-looking games, men with bulging pockets accosted people to try to sell and steal things at the same time.

Chompa started walking faster. She hadn't realized until now how lonely she felt, how much she missed the camaraderie of the ship, the sense of belonging. She rapped on the creaking, single-hinged door that a local woman pointed out to her, her body twitching with impatience and hope. The sign above said The Pickled Egg. In English *and* Hindi.

Chompa grinned. This was the place.

A man's voice, muted at first, then louder, grumbled its way towards them. He didn't open the door, but called from behind it. 'What you want, huh?'

He spoke with an Indian accent.

She replied in Hindustani. 'I'm looking for two lascar boys, Uncle. One African, one Indian. My friends from the ship *Kohinoor*.'

The door squealed open, and a man peered out. His eyes widened at Chompa's coat, and Leeza standing behind. He directed them inside, towards one of the booths. Leeza wrinkled her nose at the smell of stale alcohol mixed with wood polish, and surveyed the blackened windows with distaste.

As they sat, he yelled hard at the ceiling.

'Arré, salahs! You never told me you had wives! They're here to drag you home!'

# Chapter Twenty-five

There was a thundering of footsteps down the stairs.

'What do you mean, Yasser, huh? Wives?'

Chompa stood up at the sound of Tipu's voice – but speaking in English.

'Just come down, yaar. I think you'll want to see.'

Then Yasser melted away into the back of the pub.

Tipu tumbled down the stairs and stopped at the sight of Chompa. Laurie crashed into his back and started swearing with gusto.

Chompa found she was unexpectedly nervous and lost for words. So much had happened since they had landed in England. Was this a foolish thing to have done, to come here? But Tipu leaped over the gate into the bar, beaming.

'Chompa! Leeza! You found us!'

She smiled.

Tipu sat down across from the two girls. But no one seemed to know what to say. Tipu stared at the table; Chompa chewed at her hair; Leeza looked at the bottles, sniffing disapprovingly. Laurie suddenly cried, 'Ah!' and then went in the back. He reappeared carrying cups and a saucepan of tea.

'Talk needs tea. Tea needs talk,' he said as he poured.

'The talk will be about this miracle here. Of you actually making it for once,' smiled Tipu as he put the cup to his lips.

Laurie shoved Tipu to move up. 'So, Madam Witch Princess, Lady Leeza,' he began, leaning in, 'how have you been? How do you find this land of Britishers so far?'

Chompa told them about Devaynes keeping her prisoner until she'd completed the huge piece of metal magic he had set out for her. Tipu whistled softly as she described the enormous pillars of the British Museum.

'What about your uncle? Can't he do anything?' asked Laurie.

'My uncle is looking for a way to help me complete the spell, and he's searching for Ammi whenever he can get away from Devaynes' manager.'

Laurie raised an eyebrow. 'Where's he been looking? We haven't seen him round these parts.'

Chompa shook her head. 'I'm not sure exactly. I've hardly seen him recently. What about you two? What are you doing here?'

The boys shared a conspiratorial grin, and the conversation began to flow, aided by the plentiful pan of tea. Leeza widened her eyes at Tipu and Laurie's transformation into magical pickpockets.

'But how are you doing magic, Tipu? I don't see any trees around here!'

Tipu brought out the green glass bottle containing the tiny half-sprouted date seed.

'She doesn't like it much, but I let her roam the city in exchange for the magic she does.'

The seed pinged against the glass.

'That's – that's Aaliya?' Leeza was astounded and Chompa leaned over, fascinated.

Tipu nodded. 'Yup. It was the only way I could find to bring her. Krishna knows there aren't any lush palms she could inhabit. The trees here are all dry-looking and half dead.'

Leeza and Chompa gazed at the bottle in wonder. Then Chompa shook herself from her reverie and looked at Tipu. She cleared her throat.

'It's lovely to see you both, really. But I also came because I need your help. Again.' She flushed.

Then she told them about the nightmares.

'They're real, I know it. I don't know how, but we've got a connection. Ammi's calling to Mohsin for help, somewhere, and she's tied up – and she's close by. I need you to help me work out where.'

'Could you make out anything about where she could be?' said Tipu thoughtfully.

Chompa shook her head sadly. 'It was very dark, but there were stripes of light across her face. The only thing I could hear beyond her screams were bells. Tinny ones ringing in an odd pattern.'

Laurie rolled his eyes. 'Church bells, you mean?'

Chompa gasped. 'Church bells! Yes!'

Something else was nagging at her brain now. 'On the *Kohinoor*, Ismail said that a church had bought one of Devaynes' boats. He mentioned a "Father" with a church mission . . . and now church bells! That's *got* to be a connection!'

Laurie looked uneasy at Chompa's excitement.

'Er, Chompa, this is England. Every other building is a church. That's not really going to narrow it down much.'

'I know, but they sounded strange somehow. Not quite right.'

'OK. So let's think about it. Where on earth has stripy light? Windows with bars. We can ask around about any building that has those next to a church,' mused Laurie, scratching his chin.

Chompa nodded eagerly.

'It's a start.' Tipu shrugged. 'We'll put the word out, too – we know a lot of the street kids now.'

Chompa felt like she could breathe again. She hadn't realized how caged she'd felt in Devaynes' house, how much she feared she was in over her head. Now she could act, and she had friends to help her. They would find Ammi together.

After they'd drunk their tea, Tipu and Laurie showed Chompa and Leeza around Brick Lane. Tipu pointed out the houses of the Indian, Jewish, and Chinese magicians, the doors marked respectively with hexagons in circles, tiny little palm shapes with an eye at the centre, or overlapping spiky little Chinese characters. Then he showed them the stalls he'd seen on his first day in Brick Lane. Miss Weisz, the magician he'd come across writing the charm on the old man's hand, waved to them. Tipu and Laurie waved back.

'Miss Weisz and the others, they do stuff like potions, spells for people in trouble. The authorities don't like them and are always trying to arrest them as cheats. But they help people.'

Leeza nudged Chompa.

'Look at her headscarf. So pretty! So many colours! We should ask her how she wrapped it.'

But Chompa wasn't listening. 'Charms for the desperate,' she murmured, suddenly far away: back in the village, back with Ammi, writing spells at her desk. Her chest tightened painfully.

Laurie glanced worriedly at Chompa in case she started crying, and ushered them onwards hastily, only for Leeza to stop abruptly by a set of posters with children's faces drawn on them. Some were Indian, others white, African, or Chinese.

'Arré, what are these?' she cried, disturbed.

Tipu and Laurie looked at each other, suddenly solemn.

'They're missing posters. For magical children.'

Chompa came back to the present with a jolt. 'Magical children are being taken *here*?'

The boys nodded.

'It *has* to be Devaynes, then,' she breathed.

'Chompa, we think so, too. I wish you weren't mixed up with him – he's too dangerous,' Tipu began, stretching an arm out towards her.

But Chompa turned away. 'I don't have a choice. I need to find Ammi.'

Tipu fell silent and then nodded.

They stopped by a Jewish bakery, and Tipu took out some

coins for four beigels. Chompa hurried to bring out her coins, but Tipu shook his head.

'No, this is our patch. Our treat.'

They walked and talked and chewed, and came upon a straggly, thin Indian man standing on the corner of the street, selling Christian pamphlets.

Laurie slapped him on the back. 'Bhai, bhai, what are you doing selling these? Come see Sal, nah? Don't mix with these people – they're not your friends.'

The man swivelled his head towards Laurie and blinked before he truly registered his presence.

'That place is the devil's place. Father Saltsworth can save you,' he uttered in a monotone.

Leeza clucked uneasily, pulling at Chompa's sleeve. 'Come, he's not good. We need to go home.'

But Chompa shrugged her off. Father Saltsworth? Wasn't that the name of the churchman Ismail had talked about? Her heart was beating fast as she came closer to him.

Laurie put a hand on the man's bony shoulder. 'Come, bhai, you don't really believe this stuff, do you? I get it – I did some pamphlet-selling myself. But you're among friends now, and we can help you.'

'You'll help me get to Hell! I can sense it on you, the stench,' cried the pamphleteer.

Laurie sniffed his armpits. 'I washed on Sunday, brother. There's no stench yet.'

Leeza clucked in disgust.

'It is so strong – strongest on you!' the man cried, thrusting a thin finger at Chompa, so close she sprang backwards. Out of the corner of her eye, she saw Tipu put his hand in his pocket to draw out his bottle – just in case. But then the man shrieked, threw a pamphlet at them, and ran.

For a moment, the four of them just watched him run down Brick Lane. They all shivered.

The pamphlet fluttered into a muddy puddle on the ground. Chompa picked it up and shook the filthy water off it as best she could. She tried to decipher the print, which was now running in rivulets on to her hands.

'Witches,' read Chompa, 'save your souls and theirs . . . bring them to Father Saltsworth – at the Church of the Right-eee-ous Dom-in-ee-on,' she read slowly.

'I think we've found your bells, Chompa,' said Laurie, shaking his head incredulously.

'Where is it?' breathed Chompa, hardly able to speak.

Laurie took the dripping pamphlet from her, turning it this way and that. 'Limehouse? Or Leamouth? I can't tell.'

Suddenly bells rang the hour. Leeza stood, counting them, and then cried out, pulling at Chompa's shoulder. 'Hai Allah! We've been gone hours. Mohsin Saheb will be frantic with worry! He must think you've been taken! He might do something reckless! We have to go back.'

Chompa looked wildly between Tipu and Laurie.

'Can you find this church? Ammi will be nearby; I just know it! Send a note to Millie at Malplaquet House, Mile End Road. It's not far. Do NOT give it to any of the other servants, all right?'

The boys nodded. Chompa thrust the leaflet back into Tipu's hand, and then she and Leeza fled.

# Chapter Twenty-six

The next day, Tipu and Laurie were out of the door before anyone else was up.

They had hot pudding for breakfast from Sal's sister, Ma Sheeran, who regaled Laurie with the tale of Tipu trying to steal from her that first day in Spittlefields.

Then they got to work.

Once they'd collected enough coins to keep Sal happy, they started with the real work: looking for this mysterious Church of the Righteous Dominion. They trekked to Leamouth first and found that 'Bog Island' didn't even have a church, that people there worshipped in the open air. So they trekked back to Limehouse, where they were met with the opposite and yet equally hopeless situation: there were so many churches active in the East End, all with long, stern-sounding names, that people just shrugged and looked confused. And if they started asking about magic, people cast dark looks at them and hurried away.

They'd started out feeling like intrepid detectives, but

trudging back to Brick Lane after their ten-mile round trip they just felt foolish. Tipu glanced at one of the missing posters up on a door. It was faded; it might have been there for a few months or more. He frowned.

'These kids have been going missing for a while . . . but we know Devaynes has been in India. Is this church working for him here, stealing the kids?'

Laurie shrugged. 'Maybe the families could tell us more. Maybe this Saltsworth visited them first. We can only ask.'

Laurie knocked on the door. It was opened by an old, wary-looking Chinese man. When his granddaughter joined him in the doorway and began to translate for him, he told the boys that Shao Ying, her brother, his grandson, had gone missing three months ago. But they hadn't seen anything – Shao Ying had just said he was going out with his friends. His face crumpling, the old man took off his glasses and wiped them. Her brother had been a djinnspeaker, the granddaughter added a little nervously, until Tipu smiled and told her that they were, too.

Tipu and Laurie knocked on each door they found with a poster on it. They spoke to a Jewish woman, her hair in a headscarf, who took Tipu's hands in her own. 'Please, find my Chava. She is only nine. Sage – her magic is sage. Please. One minute she was playing outside with some friends. Then, gone.' She mimed a puff of smoke, and then brought her hand to her mouth as tears overwhelmed her.

'Have you ever met someone called Father Saltsworth?' asked Laurie gently. She shook her head. Tipu frowned. Laurie assured her they would keep looking.

Then they visited an Indian family. They'd arrived a couple of months ago. The parents looked thin and drawn, like they'd been wrung out of all joy.

'We had to leave. We were told to change our crop from wheat to indigo. The men said we'd be paid, but the money never came. We had no food, no money to buy food. I was glad when Sushant said he was going to play. He'd been missing India so much, and I thought he was making friends, settling. We came here for a new life, but now Sushant has gone I wonder if we should just have stayed to starve there instead. At least we would all be together.'

Sushant's mother started weeping and clutched her baby close to her, while her toddler played at her feet.

'Did you ever hear the name Sir Clive Devaynes mentioned?' enquired Tipu.

The woman paled, but Sushant's father came over and put a hand on his wife's shoulder.

'Priya, don't say more. We know we can't trust anyone here.'

Tipu frowned. The parents weren't just sad – they were frightened.

'My friend's mother has gone missing, and we've met others whose children had magic and have been taken. We're trying to find out who's behind it all, trying to find them and get them back.' Tipu reached a hand out to try and reassure him.

But the man shook his head. 'Sorry. I have to think of my other children.'

Tipu and Laurie nodded, and they left quietly, not pushing further, leaving the family to their despair.

'The pedlars talked about famines, too. Look – it's even

made the British newspapers.' Laurie pointed to a handbill that was posted up on the wall.

'"SEND THEM BACK: India's famine must not result in ours." How lovely. There's that British generosity, right there.' Laurie's voice dripped with sarcasm. 'So *they* destroy *our* crops, and then refuse to accept that they're to blame.'

'And tying it all together is Devaynes: *he's* connected to the church, *he's* behind the indigo famines and *he's* behind the missing children, too,' said Tipu, jabbing a finger at the poster. 'That settles it. We need to find and follow Devaynes. He'll lead us to the kids, that's for sure.'

Chompa readied herself for bed that night, her mind still whirring about the church. They were getting closer to finding Ammi; she could just feel it. And to her intense relief, when she and Leeza had arrived back at Malplaquet House the previous afternoon, they learned from a whispering Millie that both Devaynes and Mohsin had been out all day, and their absence had gone unnoticed.

She picked up the wooden comb, her fingers twitching with that old reticence. She shook it off, looking at herself sternly in the mirror.

She raised the comb and drew it firmly through the knots and tangles of her tresses, gritting her teeth as she felt strands stretch and snap. Some of the knots gave way and unravelled under the pressure of the comb, while others tightened obstinately. She extricated the comb from the clumped ends, readying herself for another assault.

She stopped. The teak of the comb was almost entirely concealed by clouds of black strands that had remained in the teeth.

Chompa was confused. She'd run the comb through only once. This was too much – too much hair to lose with one combing.

Perhaps she was being silly. She picked out the hair from the comb, wadding it into a bundle on the dressing table, and began again.

She combed.

This time, the second time, was always slightly easier going than the first. Perhaps it had just been extra tangled. But as the comb reached the ends of her hair, she felt it. She felt the strands let go of their connection to her scalp slowly, reluctantly, like fingers slipping from a grasp.

And she knew what she would see.

The comb was black with hair.

She wanted to scream.

Putting the comb upon the soft bed of hair on the dressing table, Chompa began to run her fingers through her hair and felt it again. The loosening, the giving way, the giving up of the hair, her wild hair that her mother had washed and combed and cared for. It came away in clouds in her hands.

She looked down at her hands. It seemed like they didn't even belong to her.

Ammi had warned her that her magic would come at a price.

Was this what djinn-magic would do to her?

# Chapter Twenty-seven

Tipu and Laurie headed to Mile End down the Whitechapel Road, looking for the house.

'Mam's Pocket House?' Tipu tried out on a man with an umbrella walking past. He looked horrified and clutched his umbrella like a weapon as he backed away from them. He checked his pockets as he hurried on.

'Why, thank you, kind sir, you've been very helpful!' called Laurie with a mocking bow, pulling Tipu away.

'So not Mam's Pocket House, then. But it was something like that – a peculiar word.'

'It's definitely on Mile End Road, though, right? Not Mile Street or Miles Place or something? This isn't the fanciest part of London – hardly Lalbagh Fort, the British edition.' Laurie looked about sceptically.

Tipu shook his head. 'Definitely Mile End Road. She said it wasn't far, remember? Let's keep looking – I think we might know it when we see it.'

And Tipu was right. They stopped in front of some black

railings and looked up to see a black lion on top of each of the gates.

'Think this might be it. Dunno what gives it away,' Laurie said, grinning with a shrug.

'*Malplaquet* House, not Mam's Pocket House,' said Tipu, pointing to a gold plaque bearing the name of the house and slapping his forehead at his own forgetfulness.

They hopped over the railings and crouched behind some bushes in the front garden.

'And now what, Mr Boss Sir?' whispered Laurie.

'Let's just wait and see for a bit.'

Soon after, Devaynes' gleaming blue carriage pulled up in front of the gates. The black doors of Malplaquet House opened, and Devaynes climbed into his carriage.

'Come on,' whispered Tipu urgently. 'If he's going somewhere, we need to follow him.'

Tipu and Laurie sprang out from behind the bushes just as the carriage pulled away and jumped on to the back. They clung on as the carriage drove away from Spittlefields. As it travelled, the streets got cleaner and emptied of people. Soon they were in the heart of the City: the part of London so important it was given its own capital letter, Yasser had explained to Tipu with a snort.

The carriage slowed next to some dark railings, a gold plaque upon which read EASTERN MERCHANT COMPANY CLUB. The boys jumped off, tumbling into the street and dusting their grazed elbows and knees as they gazed up at the building in front of them. The club was a cream stone building with a sleek blue door guarded by a smart doorman in indigo uniform. Tipu and Laurie dived behind a hedge and waited for Devaynes to step out of the carriage and enter the building.

Laurie groaned as the door slammed shut behind Devaynes, and the doorman stepped neatly in front of it. 'We'll never get inside. What are we going to learn all the way out here?'

Tipu shook his head. 'Let's just see what happens.'

Laurie snoozed while Tipu watched the door avidly. When even he started to rub his eyes and doubt the point of the exercise, there was a sudden commotion. The doorman was protesting loudly at someone trying to enter. The boys craned over the hedge to see who it was, and Tipu nearly cried out.

It was Mohsin.

The stammering doorman was refusing him entry. Mohsin then began shouting through the door.

'I told you something would happen!' whispered Tipu excitedly.

'He doesn't look happy, that's for certain,' said Laurie.

It was only when Devaynes himself came to the door that Mohsin was admitted.

'Laurie, we need to get in! We need to hear what they're saying! Maybe he's going to force Devaynes to reveal where Chompa's mother is. If something happens to him, he might need our help!'

Laurie frowned. 'Can't Aaliya do something? Muyaka could tell us when it'll rain, but that's not going to help us right now.'

Tipu smacked his forehead. Aaliya! Of course!

He said the release words, and opened the bottle. There was a flicker in the air around the doorman, as Aaliya sprang into action. A glazed look came over the man's face as he pulled the front door open wide.

Moments later, the boys were hidden behind a coat stand, peering through the gap in the door to the drawing room, where Devaynes was now reclining on a plush leather sofa.

'Ah – Mohsin! Apologies, my boy. A new member of staff, I'm afraid. Hasn't had much experience of the East. Do sit. I've been looking forward to hearing how your little experiment is going.'

'I would rather stand, Clive.'

The boys glanced at one another. *Clive?*

Devaynes tipped his head to one side in a gesture of elegant acquiescence. It was an oddly Indian gesture in someone who looked otherwise entirely the English gentleman.

'The famines, Clive.'

'I've been reading about them. A terrible business.'

Mohsin slammed his hand down on the desk. 'A "terrible business"?' he repeated incredulously.

'Yes, my boy. Most unfortunate.'

'Since arriving in London, I have met countless Indians who've fled here. According to them, there are far more who are still in India, unable to afford to feed their families, let alone the price of a passage to England. I had heard rumours in India, but I'd no idea how serious things actually were. You should have compensated them! You left them with nothing!'

'It's not exactly that simple, my boy. I wish you'd sit.

246

All this pacing is making me quite exhausted.'

Mohsin continued to stand.

'Please do explain it to me, Clive. Please do explain how the blood of thousands – maybe millions – is not on your hands.'

'I think we should have some tea.' Devaynes rang a bell and instructed a waiter to bring refreshments. 'And you will sit, I hope. I've schooled the chaps in the kitchen on how to prepare an excellent chai, in the style we have back home.'

Devaynes poured tea from a blue-and-white china pot into two delicate-looking cups.

'This isn't necessary,' Mohsin said, irritated as he finally sank into a chair.

'When an English gentleman entertains guests,' Devaynes said crisply, 'tea is always a necessity.'

There was a pause as they both sipped from their cups.

'Now, I hope you're calmer, my boy. I thought you were above the baser characteristics of your race.'

Mohsin made a strange growling noise in the back of his throat. Devaynes continued blithely. 'The compensation will be paid when indigo revenues come in. I doubt those proud farmers want us to patronize them with charity! It was simply bad luck that the region's rice crops also failed this year. Bad luck, but I – as you rather crudely put it – have no blood on my hands.'

Mohsin slammed his cup down on the table. 'I have tried, for too long, to control myself. It will no longer do. I'm a spirit of fire, and I will do what fire does. Things are going to change. No more compromises, no more politeness, no more waiting. My tests are nearly finished, and, without my knowledge, you have nothing. We will proceed on my terms. No more glib words of yours. And Clive – this tea? There's far too much cinnamon.'

Mohsin swept from the room.

'What was all that about?' hissed Tipu. The boys held their breath as Mohsin stepped out on to the street and marched away angrily.

'Oof, there are dark things going on, bhai. Big things. Things bigger than two lascar kids can take on.'

Tipu was frowning. 'We need to tell Chompa . . . She needs to know what we've heard. I think . . . I don't know what's going on, Laurie, but something's not right here.'

As they headed back towards Whitechapel, Tipu heard the seed bottle ringing. Aaliya was bored, Tipu thought, and he shoved it deeper into his pocket.

They began to analyse the little scraps of information they'd gleaned as they took a short cut back to The Pickled Egg.

They were so preoccupied and tired that neither of them noticed the two boys in caps steal into the alley, followed by a group of much bigger boys.

Until it was too late, and the gang was upon them.

# PART FIVE
# THE SILVER PALACE

# Chapter Twenty-eight

Leeza bustled in, as always, heading to the wardrobe to pick out a frock for Chompa to wear the next day.

'Arré, you're still awake! You need to rest!' she said from behind the wooden doors.

'I can't sleep,' Chompa muttered. Her jaw was clenched so hard that she had to spit the words out.

'Oho. And what is on madam's mind, hnnh? Are you worried about where your next meal will come from? Whether your job will still be there today?' Leeza gave a merry little chortle.

Chompa raised a finger. The doors of the wardrobe slammed shut. Leeza stood, open-mouthed, bewildered.

'You didn't tell me,' Chompa hissed, her eyes dangerously narrowed.

Leeza shook her head, puzzled. 'Tell you what?'

Chompa jabbed a finger at the comb on the quilt.

'This. You didn't tell me *this*.'

Leeza looked down at the little wooden comb. She tipped

her head in a tiny nod as she understood.

Chompa howled, throwing herself down on the bed, tucking herself into a knot of pain. Leeza stepped forward and placed a warm hand on Chompa's shoulder.

'I'm sorry. I hoped to find a way to stop it. I didn't know how to say it.' Her voice was soft.

'You should have found a way,' mumbled Chompa.

'Yes.'

There was silence for what felt to both girls to be a long time. Chompa's shoulders rose and fell, and so did Leeza's hand upon them, as waves of tears came and went. Then they slowly eddied away, and Chompa was still.

'How long?' she whispered, her throat parched, her back still turned.

'I noticed two days ago. But it wasn't as bad then.'

Chompa sat up. 'Two days! That means it's falling out so quickly.'

'I know. I'm sorry. This hibiscus oil we've been trying – Millie got it from a Chinese magician, but it hasn't worked.'

Chompa went to sit down at her mirror. She took a deep breath. Slowly, with slightly trembling fingers, she began to lift up sections of her hair again, to count all the circles. Her scalp was like the fur of a wildcat, a dark base colour spotted all over with patches of creamy brown.

Leeza walked over to her, putting her hands on Chompa's and prising them very gently from the strands of hair.

'Arré, what good will this do, nah?' she said softly. 'Come, let me try something.'

Leeza pulled a broad length of violet cotton from one of

the drawers and draped the fabric over Chompa's head. After a couple of minutes of deft twisting and tucking, Chompa's hair was covered with an elegant wrap.

'There.' Leeza smiled, gently pulling Chompa's shoulders upward. 'That looks really nice. Much neater than your crazy hair!'

Chompa looked in the mirror. The image that faced her was nice, but it wasn't her. She wasn't like Ammi – she didn't have the grace or elegance that would set off such a style, a style that forced you to hold your head up, to hide behind nothing. Chompa was clumsy, fidgety, short of temper and of stature: her hair had been her pride, her comfort, and her most beautiful thing. And she was losing it.

Ammi, her home, and now her hair. What else did she have that meant anything? What else could she possibly lose?

# Chapter Twenty-nine

'Good morning, and welcome, my children. Welcome to God's home, where your souls and bodies will be saved. Hallelujah!'

The plump man strode up and down the viewing gallery by the iron cages in which Tipu and Laurie crouched, his hands behind his back. He had orange whiskers and a receding hairline.

'You are here not for my sake, dear children, but for your own! Magic! Superstition! Evil! The path you have chosen until now leads to only one place, children! It is the path to Hell!' He gesticulated at the ground with a pink finger.

'But, you poor heathen children, I am Reverend Saltsworth, of the Church of the Righteous Dominion. I am your new, loving Father, and you will call me that. Father. I will teach you, enlighten you, set you on the path to the best place.'

The finger now jabbed upward.

'Here, at the Home for Strange Children.'

Tipu and Laurie looked at each other, their eyes filled with a mixture of dread and incredulity.

'This is where the magical children are,' murmured Tipu almost silently, but he saw Laurie's face and knew he had realized the same.

'Now you may join the others.'

The reverend unlocked the cage doors and ushered the two boys out and towards a long, narrow hall, where a sour-looking pair of women in starched white caps ladled greyish slop into bowls. Benches and tables ran the length of the room, and crammed along them were children: dazed, silent children.

Tipu glanced down the tables, taking it all in. There were about fifty children. The djinnborn children had iron caps on their fingers, while the djinnspeaker children's djinn, like Tipu's Aaliya, must have been confiscated. Tipu reached instinctively for his empty pocket and thought of the date-seed bottle, locked away in the iron box he had glimpsed in Saltsworth's office, just like Laurie's little vial of sand.

'Come up, children, one by one, please. Come and be sustained by the Lord, with the nutritious, plain food of the Lord. None of this spiced nonsense that enrages the blood and pollutes the body here, no!'

'Oof,' muttered Laurie to Tipu, pained. 'Plain food.'

Tipu shrugged. They hadn't eaten since they arrived, blindfolded and shackled, the night before. Anything would do. But the porridge – made with water – was scarcely edible.

Laurie gulped a spoonful with a grimace. 'Some molasses would make this all right. Or fresh dates from Aaliya, chopped up . . . Ah, dates . . . I never thought I'd see the day when I'd miss the ship,' he sighed. He pushed the half-eaten porridge away. 'Oof, I just can't.'

Saltsworth was walking up and down the rows of benches, still with his hands behind his back.

'What's the matter, lad? Why are you not finishing what God has provided for you? Do you scorn His bounty?'

Laurie raised his eyebrows. 'It's burnt, sir. If it's God's bounty, surely your cooks should take some care with it?' he said.

Tipu nearly choked.

He had always wondered at the ways in which pale skin could change colour. It could be pink at one time, peach at another, sometimes even green. Saltsworth's face was now a deep shade of purple, as if he'd been scalded, and his mouth worked hard to make a sound. Then he seemed to recover himself, and the colour faded away.

'My boy, you're new here. You are not yet familiar with our ways. But at any other time, children, how would such ingratitude be punished? Hmm?'

The dead-eyed children on the other tables immediately sat straighter as they replied. 'The straight, firm rod of the Lord,' they chorused in flat tones.

Saltsworth slapped Laurie hard on the back, hard enough to make him wince.

'Now eat up, my boy.'

Laurie took up the bowl and spoon again and started swallowing the – now cold – porridge. 'Bhai,' he muttered grimly, 'we have got to get out of here as soon as possible.'

Tipu nodded, but couldn't see how. Since they arrived, their every movement had been observed and scrutinized. They had been thoroughly searched, and everything they owned, including the date-seed bottle, had been confiscated. And they had slept in a locked room. God's house, Tipu thought darkly, resembled nothing more than a prison.

After breakfast, they were subjected to Bible study in a cold, dim classroom, supervised by an elderly, whiskered tutor, who promptly fell asleep. Most of the children had clearly been so terrified into submission that they dutifully kept reading. The boy sitting next to Tipu, though, had his arm curved round his slate, meticulously writing out columns of tiny Chinese characters, and then rubbing them out and starting again.

'What are you doing?' Tipu whispered.

The boy didn't reply. Looking at the characters more closely, Tipu noticed they overlapped and were squashed together. They looked very different to the characters on the boards outside the Limehouse eating shops and lodging houses. He recognized the style from the engraving on the corner of the door he had knocked on, just yesterday.

'Is your name Shao Ying?' Tipu whispered eagerly.

The boy looked up, gripping his chalk tight. 'How did you know my name?'

'I met your grandfather and your sister. Just before we got taken. Your family's very worried about you.'

The boy stared. 'They are? I thought they'd have given up by now. It's the East End. Children go missing all the time.'

'They don't know who to tell, who to trust. But they haven't given up.' Tipu nodded at the slate. 'Is that writing-magic? I thought we were all djinnspeakers or djinnborn here?'

'I can do both. But look at all the bars on the windows. Iron.' Shao Ying gave a little dark laugh. 'To make sure we don't use djinn-magic to escape.' He frowned for a moment. 'So I'm practising my writing-magic. They don't know it's magic – they just think I'm studious. But it won't work as a spell without my yellow paper or paintbrush.'

'Where are all the kids from?' whispered Tipu.

'From all across the oceans: Indian, Czech, Irish, Russian, Yemeni, Malay, African, Chinese like me.'

'Any Siddi kids, Africans who were born in India, like me?' asked Laurie hopefully.

Shao Ying nodded over his shoulder. 'Ashwini, over there.'

Eyes bright, Laurie thew a piece of chalk in her direction, grinning when she looked up and nodded at him.

'Have you ever seen a woman here? A Bengali woman with magic?' Tipu asked.

Shao Ying looked taken aback. 'There are no women kept in this place – just children. Only children.'

The tutor stirred and mumbled, startling the boys. Shao Ying started wiping his slate, and Tipu sat back and pretended to read.

✳

It was a long day, but at night, in his new dormitory, Tipu found he couldn't sleep. Something tiny and persistent in its viciousness kept nipping at his skin. Did England have mosquitoes? he wondered dully as he lay in the dark, listening to the other children sleep. It made sense, given the permanent state of monsoon, he reflected grimly as he scratched at one place on his body, then another.

Tipu tried to doze. Muffled voices outside the room made him snap his eyes open. He rose from his lumpy mattress and edged towards the door to hear better.

'It is going well, sir. Just take a look at them. Almost angels when they sleep, are they not? Hard to believe the Devil is hard at work in them!' Saltsworth gave a short, trembling laugh, and then stopped. 'But, sir, I must say – it goes against all our values to encourage them to practise magic. We wish them to be rid of the foul habit!'

'They must continue to practise magic.' The other voice was male: deep, clipped, commanding. Familiar.

There was a pause. 'But – but it's an aberration against God, sir – it comes from their idol-worshipping ways!' said Saltsworth.

'You may civilize them and teach them to be good Christian children, as we agreed. But the magic must remain strong in them, else they're worthless. Don't worry, they may one day be rid of it – but not yet.'

'Sir, magic –'

'Do not question me again, John. Recall that you and I have no formal association with one another. I can inform the police about the whereabouts of these missing children and walk away utterly unscathed. And where will you be then, hmm?'

There was a long pause.

'Very well, sir,' replied Saltsworth in a far meeker tone. 'But do come and observe our most recent arrivals.'

Tipu raced back to bed and flung himself flat, just as two heads appeared at the small square window at the top of the door. He peered at the window under his long lashes.

There was Saltsworth's orange head.

To its left, higher up in the square window frame, was the balding head of Sir Clive Devaynes.

When they left, Tipu woke Laurie and told him about Devaynes.

'We've finally got proof it's him. But we don't know anything about what he's planning.'

Shao Ying's voice came out of the darkness. 'It's not the first time he's been here. For months, we were told that magic is bad, that we mustn't do magic,' he confided in the quietest of whispers. 'Then, a week ago, *he* came, with a slim Indian man.'

'Ismail,' said Laurie.

'And suddenly we were told to practise our magic again, in the quadrangle outside. Saltsworth hates magic. It doesn't make any sense. I think something's going to happen. Something big.'

# Chapter Thirty

'Arré,' Leeza said in an unusually perky voice as she wrapped Chompa's head in cloth the next morning, 'Tipu and Laurie haven't come by yet, have they? Maybe we should go and visit them, see what they've found out.'

Chompa sighed heavily. 'You bring back a message from them. I don't want them to see me looking so – different. I don't want to have to explain.'

'Hnnh, hnnh, I know,' Leeza said softly. 'But what if they have more information about Ammi, and need your help?'

'They would have sent a note to Millie, like I asked. But I was sure they'd have come by now.' She rallied. 'No, you're right. When Uncle and Devaynes go out, we'll set off.'

That afternoon, they hurried down Whitechapel Road, towards Brick Lane and Sal's establishment. Chompa was twitchy, fiddling with her headwrap all the way, eyes down, afraid of stares.

'Oof, in this part of London, every other woman is wearing a headscarf. Factory workers, Jewish women, Muslim women. Look!' Leeza nudged Chompa's elbow cheerfully as she pointed them out.

Chompa felt brighter for being out, she had to admit. Even though the closer they got to the lodging house, the more a twisting, nervous feeling came over her at the prospect of seeing Tipu and Laurie again. If Laurie mocked her, she wouldn't be strong enough to just rebuff him with insults. She might even cry. She took a deep breath to steady herself, and then they went in.

It was busy. The pedlars were preparing to leave. Chompa left Leeza waiting just inside the door and pushed her way through the tangle of chairs and bags to the back of the bar and Sal. She had to yell to catch her attention over the high counter.

Sal looked down. 'Girl – I've been meanin' to come round an' 'ave a word with you! Wot you done with me boys?'

Sal's cheeks were flushed, and not just with the drink and the warmth. With something like indignation.

'I 'ave no problem with 'em doin' their detectin' for yer, love. I know it's your ma they're lookin' for, but I can't keep 'em if they don't earn their way. Lord knows Laurie eats enough for four. In their own time, gal. They can 'elp you in their own time.'

Chompa was puzzled. 'What do you mean?'

Sal crossed her arms. 'I mean they en't been back 'ere in two days! TWO DAYS!'

Chompa took a step backwards. 'What? Where are they?'

''Aven't been with you?'

Chompa shook her head.

*No. Not more loss. No.*

'Last thing I know they was askin' Yasser about . . . somethin' called Mam's Pocket House, an' then they 'ightailed it out of 'ere! I thought they went to see you!'

'Malplaquet House. That's where I'm staying – but I haven't seen them!'

The heat and noise in the bar made Chompa feel dizzy. Tipu and Laurie were missing. And it was all her fault – again.

'Where can those bleeders be?'

'I don't know. I thought they'd be here.'

Sal chewed at her lip, looking pale and serious now.

'They're good boys. Arré, I've been so busy with this lot, I didn't stop to think they 'adn't gone off on their own. They're my boys now. If anything 'appens to 'em – Yasser! YASSER! Get the lads out to look for me boys!'

Chompa wound her way back to Leeza while Sal gestured and gabbled urgently to Yasser. The old man stroked his beard, his eyes without their usual sparkle. Then he started gathering the pedlars together.

'They're not here?' Leeza said, watching Sal and Yasser closely.

Chompa shook her head, her eyes filling with tears again.

'No, Leeza – they're gone! They've gone missing, too!'

Chompa rushed back to Malplaquet House, her heart beating fast in her chest. It was getting too much. Tipu and Laurie had been taken; she just knew it. She packed her things, ready to run when Mohsin got back. She no longer cared about the deal – Devaynes was too dangerous and too clever, always one step ahead.

But Mohsin didn't come back until very late that evening. Chompa hovered near the hall until Mrs Illsley forced her upstairs to bed and locked the door behind her. But Chompa couldn't settle and sleep came fitfully as she planned her next steps in her head.

The next morning, as Chompa was readying herself for her mission, Leeza came bustling in with a new pearl-grey silk frock with silver embroidery. Chompa looked at it in surprise, and Leeza shrugged apologetically.

'I've been given instructions. You're to be dressed smartly and go down for breakfast.'

In the dining room, Devaynes was sporting a crisp suit, but Mohsin was nowhere to be seen.

'Ah, Miss Begum. The scarf – the scarf is very well done.'

He beamed at her. Chompa tried to smile back, forcing her cheek muscles to pull her mouth upward. She had to be careful. If Devaynes realized she was thinking of going back on their deal, then he'd keep her *and* Mohsin locked up.

Where was Mohsin, anyway?

Before she had a chance to ask, Devaynes clapped his hands together in childlike delight.

'You may be wondering why we're dressed so lavishly today. Well, my child, I have some news! The Palace of Wonder is nearly complete! As we speak, the final objects are being transported to the British Museum. We'll travel there after lunch. Your uncle is already there, testing a device he's been working on that should help you. He was up very late last night working on it. Your magic and his science – together they'll build something spectacular. It's the beginning of our great new enterprise. The beginning of our shared, modern future.'

Chompa felt a surge of relief. Mohsin was waiting for her. They could escape straight after the magic, and head to Sal's. She smiled.

'I need to get my maid to adjust my scarf – it's loose. Please excuse me.'

She hurried up to her room. Closing the door behind her, she grabbed the bag she'd brought from the village, and began to stuff Ammi's spellbook into it.

Leeza looked up from her reading. 'Arré, what's this? Where are you going?'

'*We* are going to Sal's – straight after I do the magic at the museum. So hurry – you need to pack, too.'

'What about Mohsin Saheb, though?'

'He's not here – he's at the museum already. Go and pack some of his things – just his books – and we'll hide them somewhere and collect them tomorrow. Anything else we can get hold of when we're at Sal's. We can't come back here.'

For once, Leeza didn't question or complain, but sprang into action.

Chompa felt lighter than she had for weeks. Soon she would be free of Devaynes, free to find the source of the strange bells and, finally, Ammi.

# Chapter Thirty-one

Guests sat on fine silver chairs arranged in rows in the square of the grand fluted columns of the museum. Women clutched parasols and intricate fans they had been gifted from their Company husbands' travels, because it was an uncharacteristically warm afternoon for England. Lady Inglis was in the front row, looking sceptical. Devaynes, Mohsin, and Chompa stood at the front, on a platform, all eyes upon them.

Chompa was calm. She could spot a wisp of Leeza's sari, behind a tree across the road, where she was waiting with her bag.

Devaynes bowed his head. 'I confess, I am truly humbled. We are honoured to have with us today so many illustrious figures from government, from industry, from banking. Welcome, esteemed guests. This is but a little of what we shall achieve in the very near future, with your kind support.

'Consider a world in which ocean journeys are halved, where buildings like this will be made not from humble stone but from the finest, most precious of metals, as beacons of culture shining their light across the world. To show you what is possible, we will transform this great structure, before your very eyes, from stone to purest silver. From a museum of the old to a palace of the future.'

There were gasps of disbelief in the audience, and a couple of scoffs. But Devaynes ignored them.

'We shall do it using a resource – consider it, if you will, a form of precious energy, like gas or oil – that can be mined from all corners of our great empire, but whose potential we alone have the imagination to realize. *Magic*. This demonstration will prove what could be done if only this resource is wielded by the right hands. *Our* hands.'

Devaynes paused, and raised his hands. 'Ladies and gentlemen, if you join with our Company and what we have planned, together we stand on the threshold of a new, *magical* age.'

Devaynes gestured towards Chompa, and she felt all eyes swivel and focus on her. Suddenly she couldn't breathe.

'Dear friends, may I present Miss Chompa Begum.'

Chompa swallowed, her mouth like a desert, but Mohsin opened his palm out, and she laid her hand in it. They turned their backs to their audience and towards the site. She felt calmer again, even though she knew not a single pair of eyes had looked away. They were all still fixed on her. So she concentrated instead on what was in front of her.

She searched for any sign of Mohsin's finger-capsules.

'I'm sorry, Chompa, I couldn't get them to work,' he whispered. 'Not in time. I've been working all hours trying to, but they just wouldn't absorb my magic.'

Chompa shrugged. 'It's fine. I can manage.'

'Miss Begum will begin with our most gracious sovereign, our noble young queen.'

Devaynes stretched his arm out towards the ivory marble statue depicting the slim figure of Queen Victoria sitting on her throne. *Her face looks so sour*, thought Chompa. It'd be satisfying to change her into a lemon to match, and see what the esteemed guests made of *that*.

But she raised her index finger and focused, starting with the footstool the queen's stone feet were propped on.

Slowly, the marble began to transform: first the footstool, then the little feet, then the folds of her dress, up, up, up, until finally all that was left was to turn the crown to silver. Chompa paused for effect, and then, with a flourish, it was done.

The stone queen had only been in place a year, when the museum had opened, but had already started to turn grey in the sooty London air. It had made her seem grave, serious, but also already a little fragile, ageing despite her youth. Now that she was gleaming pure metal, she looked terrifying. Invincible. Chompa hated what she'd done.

But the audience swooned. Thunderous applause met Chompa's ears. She ignored it, and raised her finger again, this time up and down each fluted column, and then along the building itself.

Within a few minutes, the entire museum was dazzling: made of pure bright silver.

The applause this time was deafening. But it hurt

Chompa's head. She needed to get away from it – she needed to get to Leeza. Her part was done now, and they had to get away. She extricated herself from Devaynes on the platform, and walked down the steps.

Or she tried to.

Her legs gave way under her.

'Chompa!' cried Mohsin, catching her by the elbow before she fell. 'I knew this would be too much!' he snapped angrily at Devaynes.

Devaynes looked uncomfortable, glancing at the audience who were craning their necks to see what was happening.

'The child simply needs a little rest and refreshment.' He positioned himself in front of Chompa, trying to conceal her from the audience while he summoned his housekeeper, who had been hovering at the back of the platform. 'Mrs Illsley,' he muttered through his smile, 'please take her into the museum and tend to her.'

It all seemed to be happening somewhere else, as if Chompa was underwater and everyone else was on a ship above her. She felt Mrs Illsley's cold hand grip her shoulder and found she didn't have the strength to resist. Panic started to rise in Chompa, despite her exhaustion, as she tried to catch Leeza's eye, to tell her to wait. But when she looked across the road, Leeza was gone.

'Mrs Illsley, I'm honestly feeling much better,' insisted Chompa, trying to wriggle out of her painful grip.

'Sir Clive has tasked me to care for you and care for you I will,' said the woman grimly.

She plonked Chompa down roughly on a bench and

pulled a brown bottle from her bag. Opening it, she wafted it under Chompa's nose.

Chompa sprang back from the powerful chemical smell, eyes watering. Mrs Illsley yanked Chompa's head into the crook of her arm and waved the bottle under her nose again.

'Never known a child to make such a fuss, really I haven't. *English* children are rarely seen and never heard. You ought to learn from your betters, young lady.'

Chompa choked and spluttered, fighting her instinct to bite and run. She knew she wouldn't get far. So instead she went limp, glazed her eyes over and put on a sweet, simpering smile.

'Sorry, I've never smelled –'

'Smelling salts.'

'Smelling salts.'

*More like smell-y salts*, she thought with an inner eye-roll.

'They've done wonders, really. I'll just sit here quietly for a while.'

Mrs Illsley made no attempt to move from her side. Chompa wanted to scream. She needed a diversion, anything, so she could get away and find Leeza. She thought furiously. Millie had once said that Mrs Illsley was obsessed with the queen and Devaynes' royal connections. It was a long shot, but it would have to do.

She craned her neck as if noticing something in the distance, and gasped.

'No! Surely not! Oh, Mrs Illsley!' she cried, clapping her hand over her mouth in apparent delight.

Mrs Illsley turned her head in the direction of Chompa's adoring gaze.

'It's just too wonderful! I think I . . . Did I – did I just see the queen herself arriving?' Chompa breathed, pointing to the crowds clustering in the doorway.

Mrs Illsley frowned. 'I don't see anything –'

'The crowd's in the way, but I'm *sure* of it. Oh, I feel so weak! I can't believe we're going to miss an audience with her! Uncle Clive said we might *meet* her!' Chompa let out a sob.

Mrs Illsley looked at Chompa, then back towards the crowd, clearly conflicted.

Chompa made her eyes huge. 'It's been such a dream of mine,' she sniffed. 'Mrs Illsley, would you mind, would you mind going to see her for me? I'm just too weak to move. I'm simply desperate to know what she looks like in real life, her jewels, *everything*. Do make sure you remember every tiny detail! And tell her I was the one who made her statue shine!'

Mrs Illsley didn't have to be told twice. 'Oh, very well. But stay *put*.'

With that, the housekeeper made off towards the crowd, adjusting her hat and smoothing her dress.

There was no time to waste. Chompa rose from the bench and hurried in the opposite direction, searching for another exit. She glanced down each corridor, looking for a chink of light indicating a doorway, only to stumble into the back of someone. She sprang away, ready to run, in case it was Lady Inglis or Devaynes himself. But the figure was small and dressed in soft bright cotton, and was carrying two big cloth bags on her back. Heart bursting with relief, Chompa realized it was Leeza.

'Oh, thank the stars!' she gasped as she hugged her hard. She pulled her own bag off Leeza's shoulder and slung it across her body.

The colour drained from Chompa's face when she realized Leeza hadn't said anything. Chompa couldn't remember Leeza *ever* being so silent.

'What's the matter?' Chompa said.

Leeza said nothing, and just pulled her by the hand into a huge circular room.

'What on earth?' muttered Chompa, bewildered.

The room was filled with two large enclosures fitted with gleaming silver bars.

'Look, Chompa! Oh, it's terrible! We have to help them!' Leeza whispered, pointing a trembling finger at the cage in front of them. A guard glanced in their direction, frowning. Then he took in Chompa's fine frock, and turned away, bored.

Chompa looked at the cage. And her heart plummeted.

Inside, dressed in neat white smocks, were five children of different ages training fingers on objects that kept changing. A girl of about nine had her finger directed at a pearl in an oyster shell, which grew larger and smaller as she moved her finger. Another child of about five had a chubby finger pointed at a bowl of little orange fish. They leaped into the air, making graceful patterns, and then dropped into the water again.

Finger-magic.

*Djinnborn* magic.

All five were djinnborn, like her!

Maybe Ammi was in the second cage, with other adults? Chompa's heart thumped wildly. She hurried forward.

But she wasn't. The second cage contained children, too, and only children. The difference was that they each clutched a little bottle or box. *Djinnspeakers.*

Chompa swallowed hard, tears of disappointment threatening to overwhelm her. Then she shook herself. They were all still children, caged. She had to free them even if Ammi wasn't there. She had to do what she'd failed to do for the children on the *Albion.*

She walked up to the bars, touching the cool silver with quivering fingers, puzzled. How had these come to be? She hadn't transformed anything like that. She noticed there was a plaque on both cages. She kneeled to read one.

FIVE YEARS' FREE LABOUR FOR SALE BY PUBLIC AUCTION. FOR DETAILS OF EACH PROPERTY CONTACT AGENT EASTERN MERCHANT COMPANY.

Chompa's blood boiled. They were children! Not things to be sold, and owned!

'Bechara,' Leeza breathed. 'Poor mites. We have to help them.' She clicked her tongue softly in pity.

But Chompa wasn't listening. She pressed her face against the bars to get a better look and whispered, 'Tipu! Laurie!'

The boys glanced warily at the guard before inching forward to the front. Tipu was clutching the seed bottle containing Aaliya in one hand, while Laurie wore his glass vial of sand round his neck.

'Chompa!' Tipu whispered. 'What are you doing here?'

'And what happened to your –' A sharp elbow from Tipu brought Laurie's question to an abrupt end.

The other children started plucking and prodding at Laurie and Tipu to explain what was happening. The sudden noise in the otherwise still room attracted the attention of the guard, who walked over towards the cage. Chompa whispered to Tipu and Laurie and the other children to go back to their work. Turning from them, she squared her shoulders imperiously, even though she was still shaking inside.

'Can I help you, miss? Are they causing trouble? They do that sometimes.' The doorman darted a suspicious, slightly frightened look at the cage.

Chompa tossed her head haughtily. 'Oh, they were, but only because my maid was teasing them.' Chompa glared at Leeza, who looked at her feet with appropriate humility. 'I'll keep her under control. But – but I'm feeling a little faint after helping Sir Clive this afternoon. Would you mind fetching me a glass of water? I'm terribly sorry – I know it's not your job.' She smiled winningly and fanned herself with fluttering, delicate hands.

The young man glanced at the cage, where all appeared to be as it was before. He bowed wordlessly and left the room.

Chompa whipped round. 'We don't have much time. Tell me everything. Quickly.'

Tipu and Laurie took turns to describe being kidnapped and the Home for Strange Children. Chompa's eyes darkened.

'People keep coming in and gawping at us and pointing. I think we're going to be sold, like magical cattle. They gave all us djinnspeakers our djinn back this morning, and the only explanation I can think of is that they need to sell us along with our djinn.' Tipu's tone was bitter, and there were dark blue crescents below his eyes. 'But, Chompa, I need to tell you something –'

Tipu reached out to Chompa, but she wasn't listening, her eyes focused on the bars. 'Later. We haven't got much time.'

'Can't any of you use your magic to escape?' asked Leeza.

Laurie shook his head.

'We tried that at the Home, and then here. None of us can use magic on these silver bars. It's only Chompa who can work with metals.'

'Chompa, listen! It's important!' Tipu grabbed Chompa's arm through the bars.

'Not now!'

'Yes, *now*.'

Tipu put as much force into his voice as he could, and Chompa's mouth fell open in surprise. Tipu spoke quickly.

'Chompa – just before we got taken, we were following Devaynes. Your uncle went to see him at his club. Something about the conversation wasn't right. Like they were *working* together.'

Chompa stamped her foot impatiently. 'Of course they are – all three of us were. We made this whole Palace of Wonder together!'

'No – this was something else. It sounded like your uncle was talking about a *deal*.'

Chompa shook her head. 'There *is* a deal, remember? To get to London? Argh! We don't have time for this!'

'Chompa, trust me – something's wrong,' pleaded Tipu desperately.

Chompa touched the bars once more and closed her eyes. Her voice was level and her face calm when she spoke again.

'What's wrong is what Devaynes is doing. So I'm going to end all this. Right now.'

# Chapter Thirty-two

Chompa and Leeza hurried into the empty corridor. Devaynes' voice echoed through the hallways; he was giving yet another speech. Chompa talked quickly.

'You need to get that guard away through that door there. Pretend something's happened.' She pointed at a door that led to the refreshment tent.

'You mean, like *acting*?' Leeza said, eyes wide.

'Yes. I know you can do it,' said Chompa encouragingly.

To her surprise, Leeza puffed herself up with indignation.

'*I* know I can! I've watched every drama that came to the campus. Yes! Let's see . . .' She began to pace, plotting out the scene. 'You fainted; I panic. That needs lots of arrés and hai Allahs – like this.' She stretched her eyes as wide open as they would go, clutched the end of her scarf to her mouth, the other hand pressed to her forehead.

Chompa rolled her eyes. 'Maybe . . . turn it down a notch? I fainted. I wasn't struck dead by lightning.'

'Oho, now she's a drama expert,' sniffed Leeza. '*Fine.*'

She dropped the end of her scarf and settled her face into a more natural expression of worry.

'Better. Good. I'll wait here. You rush in and make a commotion, saying I took a walk and fainted. Draw the guard through the door into the grounds, as far from here as you can. OK?'

Leeza nodded eagerly and was gone.

Chompa had to remain calm. But there were too many thoughts racing around her head, not least that Tipu suspected Mohsin of something. She'd dismissed it, but now it came back again. Mohsin hadn't said anything about visiting Devaynes at his club. But there had been so much going on . . .

Chompa's skull pulsed with a terrible pressure. She scrabbled at her headscarf. Suddenly it felt like it was suffocating her, and she couldn't focus.

She put her hands up to the scarf and tugged. It came away in a pile of fabric. She ran her fingers over her head and found that it was surprisingly smooth. The short spikes of hair must have fallen out over the last few days. She hadn't even noticed.

Hair was what princesses worried about, but in real life it got in your eyes and mouth and always had to be tied up or done something with. Chompa threw the scarf aside. She was never going to be a princess. And she didn't want to be one, either.

She was something far more powerful.

She was a witch.

The guard hurried behind Leeza, who was repeating, 'Help, please,' and jabbing her finger at the door. Chompa could see the man trying to talk to Leeza, but she shook her head wildly, saying, 'No Engrish, no Engrish!'

Chompa smiled. Leeza was doing a great job. Now it was her turn.

She knew the children might find her appearance alarming. But she needed to focus fully on the magic. They'd get used to it.

She crept up to the large cage containing the djinnspeakers. She thrummed quietly on the bars. The vibrations made the children stand up and turn round. Tipu nodded silently. Some of them started to point at Chompa and whisper to each other, which made her wince.

'Can you tell them to be quiet? Otherwise the guard will come back!'

Laurie went round lowering pointing fingers, explaining who Chompa was and what she was about to do. The children settled, but their eyes remained wary.

'Good.' Chompa took a deep breath and wrapped her fingers round the silver of the bars. It was cool and smooth, as close to silk as a hard metal could be. She raised her finger and thought, *Melt. Melt.*

The silver columns began to soften and lose shape like molten wax. Within a minute, there was a large gap in the cage, and a glimmering pool on the slate floor.

Tipu clapped Chompa gently on the back and then released Aaliya to go ahead and act as a lookout.

'Shabbash, Madam Witch, excellent work!' chuckled Laurie.

Chompa melted some more of the bars, and the children began to squeeze out. She turned and started to walk towards the other cage when her knees gave way beneath her. Tipu caught her under the arm on one side, Laurie on the other before she fell, and she leaned heavily against them.

'Rest for a minute,' Tipu whispered. 'You've done a lot of magic today.'

Chompa looked down at the ground, bewildered. She hadn't had enough time to recover her strength from transforming the building. But it didn't matter. She had to finish this.

'Help me,' she muttered to Tipu and Laurie through clenched teeth. 'Help me get there.'

Tipu and Laurie exchanged worried glances, but wordlessly supported her over to the cage. She trained her finger on it, but nothing happened.

And then Chompa thought she heard voices. She turned to the boys in dismay.

'I can't melt this one – my magic's run out. I . . . I didn't even know that could happen. I'll try again, but there's no time. You have to go – take the djinnspeakers. I'll follow with the djinnborn.'

The three of them looked at the djinnborn cage. The children inside were now copying Chompa, training their fingers on the bars. But they didn't have Chompa's affinity, and nothing happened. Chompa put her fingers to the bars and tried again, but then shook her head furiously.

The voices got louder. Chompa turned round. 'It's no good – you'll have to go.'

'You've got to come with us. Devaynes will know it was you. We can't leave you,' said Laurie, frowning.

Chompa straightened her back and stuck her chin in the air. She had lost her mane of hair, but she looked more powerful than she ever had: she was defiant, haughty, magnificent.

'I'll be fine. I just need a little bit more time for my magic to replenish, and then I can melt this one.'

'But Devaynes –'

'I'm finished with Devaynes! I've done what he wanted, and now I'm going to go and find Ammi on my own.'

'We'll head back to Sal's. She'll know where to hide the kids until this all dies down. Meet us there.' Tipu cast an eye over Chompa, worried. 'Do you want us to take your bag? It looks heavy, and you're tired.'

Chompa ran a hand over her throbbing eyes and shook her head. 'No, no, I might need it.'

Tipu hesitated as Laurie peeked out to check if the hallway was clear. Chompa gazed at him. 'If you don't leave now, it'll all be for nothing. Don't let it be for nothing, Tipu.'

Tipu allowed himself to be tugged away by Laurie, who had hurried back for him. 'We'll see you, Chompa. Back at Sal's.'

She nodded, waving them away as if they were flies, and trained her finger again on the silver bars. The children within looked at her, eyes huge with hope. As she waited for her magic to return, she felt a strange serenity.

She had acted on her own. She'd done a piece of magic for

a reason that was right and true. Come what may, she would have no regrets this time. And she wouldn't leave until every last child was free.

Mohsin appeared at the door moments later.

'Chompa!' he cried, aghast, seeing her sitting on the floor, surrounded by pools of shimmering silver. 'Devaynes has been alerted – his guards are coming! Can you walk?'

'I'm fine, Uncle. But I can't go anywhere – I've got to open the cage! We have to set those children free!'

'There's no time – if he captures us, how will we ever find Amina?'

Chompa shook her head. 'Ammi would want me to save them.'

'And we will, but we can't if we're caught – come *on!*' Mohsin's voice was urgent as he pulled her to her feet, and then away from the cage, away from the djinnborn children, and out of the museum.

Tipu and Laurie stumbled through the doors of The Pickled Egg, the djinnspeaker children trailing in after them. Sal was polishing the pint glasses.

'Hai Allah! Look wot the cat's dragged in! Yasser, Yasser, come right now!' she bellowed, slapping the rag and the glass down on to the bar and hurrying round. 'Who you got 'ere?'

Tipu explained everything. 'And Chompa's on her way with five more.'

'And they're all magic?'

Laurie nodded. Sal and Yasser looked at each other.

'We need to split 'em up, get 'em scattered and 'idden about Spittlefields, Limehouse an' Wapping. Not the lascar lodgin' 'ouses or the magic shops – they'll search those first.'

Yasser stroked his beard sceptically. 'No one who isn't magic is going to take these kids in.'

'We 'ave to try.'

'Tipu,' Laurie interrupted, 'we all need a feed first. These kids have been barely surviving on Saltsworth's generous Christian rations. They'll drop if we try to drag them round East London right now.'

Tipu frowned. Time was of the essence. But the younger ones had already started to squirrel into the booths, curling up and falling asleep on the floor under the benches. Yasser hurried away, and the familiar scent of frying spices spooled from the kitchen. Tipu's stomach clenched painfully. He had to ignore it.

'I'll go and talk to the magicians. We know some of them now, and we're going to need their help in getting these kids somewhere safe – we can't take them all in one group like this, anyway.' He glanced at Laurie. 'I could do with you, Laurie – but it's up to you if food's more important.'

Laurie groaned. 'Arré, salah . . . You'll be the death of me.' He rubbed his stomach, and then sighed as he looked at the sleeping children. 'Fine. Come on.'

Tipu glanced at Shao Ying. 'I can at least reunite one with his family,' he said.

The three boys began heading towards the door.

'One sec, lads!'

Sal emerged from the kitchen, wrapping some ghee-slathered parathas in a cloth. She knotted the cloth up into a bundle and handed it over, along with a bag of coins.

'Savoury for you, sweeteners for the magicians. Tell 'em Sal will owe 'em one.'

Tipu and Laurie nodded, and Sal slapped them on their backs, pushing the three of them through the door.

Shao Ying's parents had already left for work, but his grandfather and sister were home. The old man wept and hugged Tipu and Laurie as if he had lost them, too.

Shao Ying shook the boys' hands solemnly.

'Bring us some of the children. We'll look after them. If you need anything else from us, you know where we are.'

Tipu grasped his hand warmly.

'We will need you. Have no worry about that.'

There was a black hackney carriage waiting outside the museum. Mohsin bundled Chompa inside.

'Quickly!' he called urgently to the driver. The horses picked up the pace.

Chompa turned round, expecting to see Leeza in the carriage. But it was just the two of them.

'Leeza, where's Leeza?' she said, her voice trembling.

Mohsin wiped his forehead and tried to catch his breath.

'I . . . I thought Leeza was at the house,' he said, looking utterly confused.

Chompa sat down, horrified.

'Uncle! We have to go back, NOW! Argh – I thought you'd found her and told her to wait in the carriage!'

'Chompa, we can't go back! We'd be captured immediately! No, we have to hide, regroup, and then find her.'

Chompa shook her head and tried to pull open the door. Mohsin put a hand over hers to stop her. 'If you try to jump, you'll break your neck,' he said more calmly, now his breathing had steadied. He took off his glasses and looked at her, his green eyes serious.

'Please listen to me – we're in terrible danger. Devaynes has such powerful friends, and now all of them know your value. We still haven't found Amina. We can't take any more risks. We've got to find your mother first, then Devaynes won't have any leverage over you. *Then* we free the children, and *then* we go home.'

Chompa opened her mouth to argue, and Mohsin's eyes flashed. 'No arguments. We're in enough trouble as it is.'

Chompa pursed her lips and glared out of the window, too angry to speak or ask where they were headed. She knew he was right, and yet leaving those children felt so, so wrong.

She wondered where the others would hide. She wanted to tell him about Sal's place, but he didn't seem in the mood to talk to her. She hugged her bag closely – at least she still had Ammi's book and taviz-making things, thanks to Leeza. *Leeza*. Her pulse quickened again with worry for her friend, left all alone. She glared at Mohsin, who was staring out of the window, ignoring her entirely.

The carriage rolled through the streets towards the docks, slowing to a stop outside a warehouse at some remove from all the others.

'Come, Chompa.'

Mohsin stepped out of the carriage, and Chompa's nerves thrummed: Mohsin was so quiet, so strangely stiff.

He drew a large key from his pocket, placed it in the lock, and pushed open the door.

It was dark inside the warehouse. There was one solitary street lamp outside on the street. Its yellow-orange light seeped through the gaps between the planks of the walls, casting stripes in the darkness.

Then church bells began to ring, horribly out of tune.

# Chapter Thirty-three

As she became used to the darkness and the silence, Chompa could make out a scuffling sound. Rats? She kept shaking her head.

Stripes. Bells.

It couldn't be.

When Mohsin spoke, his voice sliced through the silence and the dark; cold, hard, and razor-sharp.

'I'm sadder than you will ever know about today. I had hoped I'd done enough to earn your trust, for us to work together. But I always suspected that it wouldn't be so easy, that I wouldn't be able to tame your wildness. That I'd need something else, something that would ensure your obedience to me. To the work.'

Suddenly light flooded the space, so bright that Chompa's eyes clamped shut in pain.

'Open your eyes. See.'

Instinctively, she squeezed her eyes closed even harder. She did not want to see, whatever it was.

But Chompa felt her eyelids being pulled upward even as she tried to force them down. It was such an invasive, horrifying thing, to have your eyelids peeled open forcibly, but she found she couldn't scream. Terror or magic? It was impossible to know when the two were the same.

And the worst of it was that this wasn't a surprise, or a shock. She knew what she would see now – now that her eyes were truly open.

In the centre of the room, gagged and tied to a chair, but twisting and rocking, fighting the restraints – always fighting – she was just as she'd appeared in Chompa's dreams. Her nightmares.

Ammi.

Chompa tried to scream again. Her mouth was open, but there was no sound. She emitted a soundless, wordless, heaving croak that came from deep, deep within. *No. No. No. Not like this.* She'd dreamed about finding her mother so many times. But not like this.

It had to be another nightmare. If she closed her eyes, then she'd wake up, perhaps. But Ammi's eyes were wide, only looking at Chompa. As Chompa tried to move, she shook her head almost madly in warning.

*It couldn't be him.*

Chompa felt like she was falling. She wanted to be sick. She'd been duped from the very beginning. From the night Ammi had been taken, she'd been caught, too, and she hadn't even realized it. All her investigations, her deal with Devaynes – and she'd never once worked out she was a creature in a trap, being toyed with. How clever, how brave she'd thought she was. How stupid she'd been.

Then a little thing like hope flared in her chest, something to work with.

'Is Devaynes forcing you to do this? If so, we can work together – we can defeat him; I know we can.'

But Mohsin stood, cool and impassive, and did something that horrified Chompa more than all the horrors she'd seen so far.

He smiled.

'No, Chompa, Devaynes isn't behind this particular part of the plan. The Company may help with some of the details – especially now we have the full backing of the British government, thanks to your exertions at the museum – but the vision for *this*? Chompa, that's all mine.'

Mohsin turned away, busying himself in an unlit corner.

Chompa seized the moment and tried to creep towards her mother. She nearly tripped. She looked down, and saw that little roots and tendrils had pushed through the earth and wrapped themselves round her shoes.

'Ah, Chompa,' said Mohsin, without turning round, 'you can't trick me the way you tried to do with Devaynes. I'll be taking every precaution. And here's one instance where my affinity comes in particularly useful.'

There was a rumbling noise, and Chompa gasped as Mohsin wheeled over a large machine – a machine that looked just like the one she'd seen in his glasshouse at the university. A large canister, on wheels, with a pipe attached. But that had been made of clay. *This* one was made of silver.

'How did you –?' she asked before she could help herself.

Mohsin smiled. A horrid, knowing smile. 'I didn't, really.'

He put a hand in his pocket and drew out one of the silver capsules.

'*You* made all of this possible.'

Mohsin clipped the capsule on to the pipe, and then clipped one end of the capsule to Ammi's finger. Ammi glared at him, and tried to shake the capsule off.

'Like mother, like daughter,' said Mohsin drily. 'Amina, unless you wish Chompa to be connected to this machine, I suggest you stop fighting.'

Chompa swivelled her head round towards Mohsin. His coolness, the mocking tone, made fire blaze in her veins. 'Get away from her!' she bellowed. 'My magic's more powerful than yours – you have to do what I say!'

Mohsin bowed his head in mock assent. 'Then please do demonstrate that.'

She tried to summon fire. She tried to search for materials around her to transform into something she could use against him. But her mind was a blur of rage, betrayal, and deep exhaustion, and she couldn't focus.

'Chompa, your difficulty is your emotion. I feared that twice the djinn blood would also make for twice the will, the stubbornness, the defiance. Hence I took precautions.'

'Twice? Twice?' Chompa whispered hoarsely. 'You mean . . . my father was djinnborn, too? You knew my father?'

Mohsin gave a short laugh, tilting his head to where Ammi sat behind him. She had stopped fighting and was completely still, her eyes fixed on Mohsin with a cold black hatred.

Mohsin flicked a switch. Chompa watched in horror,

rooted to the ground. There was a kind of whirring, and Ammi looked paler and paler.

'Stop! You're hurting her!'

'Come now, Chompa, did it hurt when we tried this out on you? No, it was utterly painless. I'm just taking a little magic from your mother. To show you what's at stake if you disobey.'

Chompa watched Ammi's body getting limper. She couldn't bear it.

'Stop, stop! Please, I'll do whatever you want, I promise. She's not well. If you need magic, take mine. Just leave her alone.'

'If you insist.' Mohsin smiled and Chompa thought she'd be sick. Within a few moments, he'd wheeled over the machine and connected her up to it instead.

'Did you make those cages? The ones for the children?'

'I did. Oh, if you'd only left them alone, Chompa! I wouldn't have to do this right now.'

'I don't understand – you don't have a silver-affinity.'

'When you placed the capsules on your finger and channelled some of your magic into them, you changed the properties of the silver itself – just as I'd hoped, just as my research had suggested. That allowed me to be able to work with it in new ways. When I connected those capsules to other silver objects, I discovered that I could make the silver change shape, expand, and grow. Hence the cages! Your tiny, thoughtless act of magic has opened a gateway of possibilities. But one capsule can only be used for one piece of silver – at the moment, at least. So, right now, I still need you to fill them.'

Chompa shivered. The words *right now* suggested he was coming close to a breakthrough that would mean he wouldn't need her, or Ammi, soon. They were on borrowed time.

'And the children *in* the cages? They're djinnborn and djinnspeakers!'

'The djinnspeakers –' he spoke the word as if it was nothing – 'were to be split between Devaynes and me. He was to have the stronger ones, to sell. I was to have the weaker ones, to extract their magic using this machine, to create a concentrated pool. Once the capsules are activated by your magic, all we have to do is clip them to any djinnspeaker, and their magic will be absorbed into the capsule, too. And then a djinnborn just has to clip it on their own finger, and absorb the magic from the capsule. It will help us to grow stronger, to break past our limitations, to avoid the exhaustion you're feeling at this moment, to prevent the other . . . costs.'

His eyes lingered on her head. Scorn burned in Chompa's chest. She didn't want this kind of help from anyone.

'And the djinnborn? Were you going to extract their magic, too?'

Mohsin looked grave, as if she'd said something terrible. 'Chompa, have you not been listening? When we first met, did I not tell you that djinnborn are exceptionally rare, exceptionally special? I would not take djinnborn magic. Quite the opposite! This is the key to a new, stronger djinnborn future! As I've explained, once the djinnspeaker magic has been extracted, it's us, the djinnborn, who are to have full use of it. We are a higher form of being, Chompa.

Consider: it'll be a service to the djinnspeakers, in a way. Some have such paltry powers – predicting the weather! Changing the colour of flowers! And for what? A few coins? For being an outcast? No, it's better for them to be rid of their powers, and for *us* to use them instead.'

Chompa knew she had to remain neutral, calm, even though rage screamed in her ears, and her cheeks were hot. Tipu, Laurie, devoid of magic! Tipu, unable to connect with the djinn who for so long had been his only friend? Laurie, without his sand-djinn, his confidence? Magic was part of them; it made them all who they were. How dare Mohsin take it from any of them, just because he thought they weren't strong enough, because he thought they didn't deserve it!

'But *I'm* djinnborn, and so is Ammi! If we're so special, why are you draining *our* magic? You're making us weaker!'

'It was necessary, I'm afraid,' Mohsin said, gesturing at the machine. 'As I said, your little rescue mission at the museum today forced my hand. Had I had the djinnspeaker children as planned, I would not have had to resort to this, Chompa. It pains me to use a djinnborn in this way.'

'So why were those other djinnborn children in a cage?' Chompa demanded.

'I knew that other djinnborn existed, but I didn't have the resources to find them – and I wanted to find them, Chompa. I wanted that very much. Once I heard that Devaynes had acquired Suleiman's silver trace-box, and had been using it to track down magical children for his own schemes, I confess I saw an opportunity. I approached him and suggested a . . . partnership, if you will.'

*Suleiman's trace-box.* Was that how she and Ammi had been discovered? The ancient device that had been meant to help djinnborn?

Mohsin smiled, seeming to understand what she was thinking. 'Yes, the trace-box – and a certain letter addressed to an old friend, though I will admit that wasn't intended for me. Devaynes' guards have been intercepting the correspondence of the most influential writing-magic campaigners in India for several months. I had to replace Amina's original envelope with one addressed to me, and do a little forgery of your mother's writing. I needn't have worried; you scarcely looked at it, so eager were you to be on your way to Dacca. It was all beautifully timed, I have to say.'

The letter. The letter Ammi had sent before she was taken. Mohsin had arrived in the village with it, and had used it to gain Chompa's trust. It hadn't been meant for him at all. Then who . . .

'*Farhana*,' Chompa said quietly. 'Ammi wrote that letter to Farhana. *She* was supposed to help me, to teach me writing-magic. Not you. Never you.'

She stared in horror at Mohsin. He spoke so calmly of kidnap, lies, terror, as if it was a business deal. Something within Chompa shattered.

'But the djinnborn were never meant to be there in the museum. Devaynes lied to me about that. They were supposed to be given to me, to start my community. But I'll get them back,' Mohsin muttered darkly.

Chompa stored all this information away carefully – there was a conflict there that might come in useful at some point.

Careful not to let Mohsin show she'd registered it, she burst forth with more emotion.

'You lied to me from the very beginning! You pretended you were our friend when it was you all along who stole my mother away! For what?'

Mohsin looked angry. 'For us, of course! Do you not see? All of this is for us, for you, Chompa! For all djinnborn! To restore us to our rightful position – to give us the powers we once had, and then the respect and influence we deserve, have deserved for centuries! If only you'd been a little more patient and less nosy, we could have worked together. It doesn't matter now. Because I will always be able to make you obey in the end.'

Chompa looked up and glared fiercely at Mohsin. 'My magic is stronger than yours. I'll get my strength back, and then –'

'It makes no difference. You won't use it. Your mother's life now depends on what you do.'

'Life?' she whispered.

Mohsin gave the slightest nod. Chompa's mouth was suddenly dry, her tongue sandpaper.

'I hope it won't come to that. You'll be making magic capsules for me from now on. If you obey me, she'll be safe. *If* you do what I say.'

Chompa's mind was racing, searching for a solution, searching for some way she could free herself and Ammi. But Mohsin was one step ahead. He always had been. She nodded.

'Don't try anything, Chompa. I warn you now; I'm

coming close to a point when I won't need you, either. From now on, I will not tolerate the slightest resistance. If you continue to be an obstacle, I'll remove you, both of you – djinnborn or no.'

All thoughts, all animation drained from her. She was trapped, Ammi was trapped, and there was no way out.

'Now look at your mother. Keep her image within your mind. Remember what's at stake, and think carefully about how you wish to proceed.'

Mohsin stepped to the side so that Chompa and her mother were face to face once again.

There were more grey streaks in her hair, and she was thin, so thin. But Ammi's eyes were as dark and bright as ever, light dancing within them – lights, Chompa thought, that were trying to tell her something. But, just as with her mother's spellbook, she couldn't decipher the language. She shook her head from side to side, tears coming now, finally, as she tried to speak to her mother without words.

She was shaken out of her misery by movement in the corner of her vision. Mohsin, pacing and avoiding looking at either of them. Chompa swallowed her tears and observed him from under her lashes.

He was agitated. Possibly even feeling *guilty*. *Interesting*, she thought. Another detail to file away for later.

'Enough,' he said after a few moments in a dry voice. 'Let us begin.'

Mohsin tapped the capsule on Chompa's finger. She did the spell as she had before, back when she'd thought Mohsin was trying to help her, thinking of the word 'absorb'. She felt the flutter of magic leaving her body, and then placed the capsule back in Mohsin's upturned palm. Mohsin trained his index finger on it. It twitched, now transformed by Chompa's magic. With a quick nod, he put it in his pocket, and clipped another on her finger.

By the fifth capsule, Chompa couldn't feel the flutter. And, sure enough, when Mohsin tested the capsule, it didn't move. He looked at her intently. Chompa found her heart was pounding – she was frightened. She was failing, failing at what he wanted. What would he do to Ammi?

'I'll do more tomorrow, I promise, but I can't do any more today,' she said. 'It was the museum – I've not had time to recover. Please don't do anything to my ammi,' she said in a small voice, looking up at him.

Mohsin paused, and then nodded tersely, placing the completed capsules in his pocket. As Chompa turned to gaze at Ammi, Mohsin looked away abruptly.

She sank to the floor. She didn't mind the tendrils fixing her there now: she *wanted* to remain there. If she couldn't touch her ammi, if she couldn't speak to her, if she couldn't free her, then she just wanted to stay here forever.

But the tendrils unfurled, and when Mohsin called for her to leave, she had to follow.

In the carriage, Chompa was numb, unable to speak. She looked out of the window, but saw nothing except her mother, chained and gagged in the warehouse behind them.

She looked out of the window, too, because she couldn't bear to look at Mohsin, who sat opposite her calmly. Part of Chompa wanted to scream, shake him, magic him into doing her bidding. But the other part was terrified, terrified of what he might do if she did. Truly, the last few hours had shown that he was capable of anything.

When they entered Devaynes' house, it was silent. It was late, she thought, her brain dull and heavy in her head. They'd been gone many hours.

Mohsin went into his room and shut the door behind him without uttering a single word to her, without calling for Mrs Illsley to lock the doors. It wasn't necessary any more. Now, it dawned on Chompa, she really *was* a prisoner. Even if the doors were unlocked and wide open, she couldn't, wouldn't, leave. If she attempted to escape, to rescue Ammi, and Mohsin caught her, Ammi would die.

She trudged up the stairs to her room. Each step was an effort for her sluggish, exhausted limbs. Leeza's bedding roll was still gone. Where was she? Where would she go without much English? But then Chompa's stomach spasmed. She couldn't help Leeza. She couldn't help anyone. Her magic had run out, and whenever it came back she'd need it for the capsules.

She paused. Her *finger*-magic had run out. But that wasn't the only magic she had.

Chompa pulled her mother's spellbook from the bag. There was no reason she'd be able to control the floating, shifting letters any more than she had every time she'd tried to read the spellbook before, but she had to do something to see if she could understand it.

She began to unfasten the bulky silver clasp. Then she paused again.

There was a single deep groove in the clasp, worked into the centre of the ornate carved patterns. She pressed her fingers into it. It was lozenge-shaped, flat, and deliberately smoothed out at the bottom. As if . . . as if something was supposed to sit there.

A lozenge-shaped something.

It was almost muscle memory, then, sensing the positive shape that would fit the negative space. Chompa's hand went straight to her pocket. The two nestled there were close to identical, but she knew she was looking for her own, the one Ammi had made especially for her. Her fingers closed round it.

Cool, smooth, cylindrical.

Her taviz.

It clipped into place perfectly, but nothing happened. Chompa sighed in frustration, but then she had an idea. Rummaging in Ammi's writing-charm box, she found a length of purple thread. She tied the taviz on to her wrist, and then placed her wrist over the clasp, pushing the taviz into the hollow.

It clicked. She held her breath.

The words on the pages began to twist and dance. The letters unfurled themselves in front of her, opening their meanings like jasmine petals at dusk, coming to rest finally as Bangla characters.

Chompa traced the letters with her finger in wonder.

Her taviz was not a distraction, a deception, or a superstition.

Her taviz was a key.

She turned page after page. Spells for healing wounds. Spells for river sickness. For crops. Chompa groaned with frustration. She would learn them all – in time. But none would help her now. *Study the spellbook*, her mother had said. There had to be something in these pages, so carefully concealed, that could help her. That could help them both.

She scanned through the book and then looked at the central fold. Two pages were stuck together. She'd never noticed it before. She slit the pages open with a pair of scissors.

Then she cried out.

There was a single neat little blue envelope addressed to her. Her hands shook as she peeled the pages from the envelope.

*My dearest Chompa,*

*If you are reading this, then what I have feared for so long has come to pass. Please understand, my heart. You are my shona, my shining golden one, and I wanted to keep you so, innocent, untarnished, for as long as I could.*

Chompa's breath had stopped in her mouth.

*There are terrible things happening in the world. I always told you that you were special, Chompa. You refused to believe it. But you are – and perhaps unique, as the child of two djinnborn. Your power is twice that of either of your parents. You are more djinn than perhaps anyone else in the world. I had to hide you away from those who sought you, those who would use you, use your unique power.*

*If you are reading this, then I must have failed. I am gone, and you are alone – or worse.*

Here the letters were smudged and blurred. Chompa had to peer closely to make out the words.

*You always asked me to teach you finger-magic. But I feared that this would only bring him closer, that he would sense your magic, which is partly of him and partly of me – and find us. As you grew, my beautiful, stubborn, strong-willed inferno of a girl, I confess I also feared, just a little, how you might take to magic.*

There was a sharp pain somewhere deep inside Chompa.

*Your father was good once. Good, and true, and brave. I loved him, and I believed – I still believe – he loved me. We had dreams, a vision of the world we wanted to create: a fair, just one. We worked together to bring it into being. We were happy, and, when I knew I would have you, we were the happiest we had ever been.*

*But that was when he started to change. He became almost obsessed with the idea of you, even though you were not even born yet. A darkness crept into him, and I became increasingly afraid.*

*He began to scorn the work we had done to spread writing-magic among the people. He scorned the spellwork I loved, saying it was old-fashioned, that it was superstition. He made new friends – friends I distrusted, even disliked. He started to talk of djinnborn as superior to djinnspeakers and charm-writers. He designed new plans, new experiments that at first he shared with me. Then he hid them from me when he realized that they disturbed me.*

*What those experiments were, I never quite understood. But the idea that obsessed him was how to find and make djinnborn more powerful – and how to remove the cost of that magic, so that only power would remain.*

*The day you were born, I saw his eyes, his entire being, alter. And I knew I had to run away with you that very night. I had to hide you from him forever. If he ever found you, you would be lost, and so would the whole world.*

Chompa put down the letter in a daze. Words rang in her memory from the warehouse.

Twice. Twice the djinn blood.

Ammi had not named him in her letter.

But it didn't matter because Chompa knew.

He had found her. He'd found them both, deep in that jungle, despite all her mother's efforts to hide them away.

Mohsin had found them.

He was her father, and the world was lost.

She went downstairs and knocked on the door of the room Mohsin had been using as an office.

'Come in, Chompa.'

He was making marks on one of his plans. Chompa recognized it as a map of the docks.

'I'm your daughter.'

Mohsin put his pencil down on the table and looked up. His eyes were rimmed with red again, shot through with scarlet and blue veins. She observed it, noted that he was tired. *Good.*

'You are.'

'Ammi was your wife.'

He stood, his face impassive. 'She's still my wife.'

For a moment, the whole world shifted off its axis. But Chompa forced herself to remain composed, to ground her body into the floor.

'Then how can you do this? How can you do this to us, your own wife and your own daughter?'

Mohsin turned away, looking out at the street lamps through the windows behind.

'I thought I told you that I wouldn't brook any more questions. It's because of this questioning – this inability to obey – that both of you are in this predicament.'

He smiled a little sadly. 'But you did, you did so unquestioningly at the beginning. You should have asked questions of me then, but you didn't.'

Chompa's cheeks burned in shame at the truth in Mohsin's words.

'You lied, from the very beginning.'

'Yes, I lied. But, Chompa, lying is the way of the world. Devaynes lied to me about the djinnborn he had located. Even your mother, in never telling you about me, in never telling you who you truly were, lied. A lie of omission. Everyone lies. It is the way of the world. They say djinn are treacherous, but they're the truest beings in the universe for not pretending to be otherwise. We're special, Chompa, and anyone who pretends otherwise lies.'

Chompa's mind raced. There was still a possibility here – the faint glimmer of a possibility. She had to seize upon it. 'We – we could still work together. If you free her, we could work together, the three of us. Djinnborn.'

Mohsin spun round. His eyes were the colour of the sky before a storm. Terror thrilled through Chompa like an ice-cold breeze.

'And you're lying now. But no matter. It's too late. Go to bed. You have work to do tomorrow. You'll need all your strength and focus.'

Chompa returned to her room, but she couldn't rest. She had magic to do. Magic that mattered. Something to help Ammi. But what?

Ammi's spellbook had an index she used to scribble in. Chompa looked down the page – many healing spells for illnesses, for failing crops: the usual village problems. She scanned them impatiently. Then the spells became more interesting: spells to hide and reveal messages; silent alarms;

and then, finally, one Chompa knew she could use: 'Communication (unspoken)'. Yes. *Yes*.

As she wrote the beautiful looping Farsi script out seven times, Chompa mouthed the letters, allowing them to roll into one another. *Sohbat. Converse. Basda. Silent.*

From barely being able to decipher the characters, she was now able to click the sound together with a meaning almost straight away, like a key fitting a lock, one that opened a whole new world. Another kind of magic. One Mohsin had discarded, had completely forgotten.

She drew a seven-pointed star, and wrote out sohbat on one side, and basda on the other, as her mother had instructed. Then Chompa hesitated. She still had Ammi's taviz in her pocket, the one she'd taken from Devaynes' study. She could open it, take out the spell and use that. But the idea of reaching into her pocket and not finding it there any more made her feel unmoored somehow. And she needed it for the silver-magic. She opened Ammi's box, and pulled out a new silver locket instead.

She rolled the piece of paper and placed it within the small silver tube, threaded it, then wrapped the thread round her wrist. It sat just above Chompa's spellbook taviz, and she almost smiled, remembering Farhana's jangling wristful of charms. Her own wrist would soon be the same, at this rate. Chompa waited, scared even to breathe for a few seconds in case she missed whatever it was she was supposed to listen out for.

Suddenly a huge amount of noise poured into her brain – the scratchings of animals outside, the clanging of pots in the kitchen of the house next door, a man muttering over and over in a study across the square. She clapped her left hand upon her taviz, and the sound was muffled.

Heart thumping, Chompa thought furiously. She needed to focus in on the one sound she wanted to hear. What was that sound? The one person whose voice she wanted to hear – of course.

Of course.

This time, she remembered her mother telling her stories, singing her to sleep. She remembered the deep, warm, honey-mango tones of Ammi's voice, and raised the taviz to her ear.

For a moment, she thought it was silence again. But then she listened harder, and overlapping the sound of her own breathing there were other breaths. Short, ragged breaths. Her mother's breaths.

Chompa focused on just one word.

*Ammi.*

Chompa heard Ammi's breath turn to a brief gasp. She had heard!

*My shona.*

It was almost her undoing. She nearly cried out as her mother's pet name for her reverberated in her heart, her throat, her chest. How long it had been since she'd heard her mother call her that!

*Ammi, I learned how to make a taviz.*

*Yes, I can hear. How clever you are, my love.*

*I am sorry, Ammi –*

*Shona. You have nothing to be sorry for. My love, I'm not very strong right now. Nor is my magic. I'm not sure how long I can speak, even now. I have been trying, trying so hard to speak to you, to warn you away from him. But you couldn't hear me. I don't think you were wearing your taviz, so I could only speak to you when you were sleeping, and then only when he took off the iron cuffs for me to give my magic to the machine.*

Chompa nearly gasped. *Mohsin!* She had heard Ammi calling his name, but she hadn't understood. If only she'd understood!

*Shona – you must do one thing for me. It will set us free. Can you do it?*

*Anything, Ammi. I'll do anything. What do you want me to do?*

*That's my blaze of a girl. Good. You must bring me a taviz.*

*What kind?*

*Just an empty one.*

*An empty one? Why?*

*You have to trust me. I have a plan. Chompa?*

*Yes, Ammi.*

*Can you bring it and find a way to tie it on me without him noticing? It's very important.*

*I'll find a way. Don't worry, Ammi.*

*That's good . . . I'm feeling very tired now, my shona. I can't speak for much –*

Ammi's voice faded away. Chompa felt hollow, bereft, and tears started to fall on the spellbook, leaving dark spots.

Then she scrubbed at her face. Ammi had a plan – a plan to set them both free. And Chompa needed to play her part.

# Chapter Thirty-four

Tipu and Laurie spent all the next morning in the docks, searching for Saltsworth's Home, and the djinnborn children who had been left behind at the museum, with no luck. It was evening when a blue carriage nearly shoved them into the gutter.

Tipu looked at Laurie. Laurie looked at Tipu. They spoke at the same time.

'Isn't that –?'

'Wasn't that –?'

They didn't need to finish, having mutually confirmed their thoughts. They raced behind the carriage as it wound its way deeper into the docklands, away from Spittlefields.

Tipu jumped as he ran, craning his neck to see into the carriage. Was Chompa there? It took a few jumps, but yes – yes, she was. He could make out her scarf-wrapped head. Tipu's heart was pounding – after the magic in the museum, she was supposed to escape. She hadn't turned up at Sal's, but he assumed she'd found somewhere else to hide, maybe at Millie's. But he'd been wrong. Devaynes must have caught her!

The road narrowed suddenly, and a massive pothole opened up in front of them. A food cart pulled by an elderly donkey, which had been slowly approaching from the opposite direction, stopped, and a man started selling food out of the cart. The way was entirely blocked.

A figure – Chompa's uncle, Tipu realized – jumped out of the carriage and started shouting at the food seller who had now crossed his arms obstinately. It was their chance.

Tipu tapped quietly on the window.

Chompa didn't hear at first, but kept looking – not quite ahead, and not out of the windows, but somewhere else. When he tapped on the window again, she turned, and he stepped back in shock.

She was so pale and worn-looking. And she didn't look happy to see him *at all*.

Chompa's heart leaped, and then plummeted when she saw Tipu and Laurie. Seeing them right now was the worst thing that could possibly happen. She couldn't let them know; she couldn't risk them interfering when they had no idea what was at stake.

She opened the window carefully while Mohsin and the food seller bickered.

Tipu was the first to speak. 'Chompa!'

'Shh! Shh!' she hissed, glaring pointedly at Mohsin.

'Are you all right? You look ill.'

'I'm fine. It was a lot of magic yesterday; it's taking me a while to recover.'

'Is everything all right? Why are you in Devaynes' carriage? I thought you were leaving.'

'No – no, it's fine. We reached an agreement. It's all sorted out,' she said impatiently, trying not to make eye contact with either of them. She needed to get them away from Mohsin as quickly as possible – before they became fodder for his machine.

'Why are you going to the docks?' asked Laurie, his eyes gleaming shrewdly.

Chompa tried to summon her old haughtiness, straightening her back and shaking her head in what she hoped was an imperious manner. 'Listen – you should go. Devaynes has agreed that djinnborn like us can be free, because we're powerful. But it's just not safe for all you djinnspeakers now.' She tried to close the window.

Tipu put a hand on the ledge to stop her. 'So you're all right?' he demanded.

She turned to him now, with a bright smile and bright eyes.

'I'm fine. I'm really fine. My uncle made me promise I wouldn't fraternize with you because you're so far below my station now. You're lascars, and djinnspeakers, and I'm – well, I'm Madam Witch Princess, aren't I?' she said with a twisted smile. Laurie hung his head. 'So we can't be friends any more. And that's fine by me. Being friends with you both has just got me into even more trouble. So leave me alone. All right?'

Tipu let go of the ledge. Chompa looked back out at them, once, before she closed the window, and the carriage was gone.

'Well, that's that, then.' Laurie sighed, patting Tipu consolingly on the shoulder.

Tipu turned round sharply. 'What's what?'

Laurie stepped back, confused. 'Well, she doesn't want anything to do with us, does she?'

Tipu flicked Laurie hard on the shoulder, so that Laurie yelped.

'Arré, she was lying. Couldn't you see? She was lying, and she was frightened. Frightened of her *uncle*. Something's going on. There's no way she'd sit in Devaynes' carriage, happily working for him, after all he's done. We need to help her. We have to follow that carriage.'

Ammi's taviz was cool and smooth against Chompa's throat. She had wrapped her scarf carefully so it was fully concealed, but easy to unloop, so she would be able to place the taviz quickly over Ammi's head when the time came.

She still wasn't sure when that time would come. But Mohsin's guilt, his inability to meet her eyes, played upon her mind again and again. It was a weakness, and weaknesses, Chompa knew, were important.

She looked back through the carriage window. They were gone, Tipu and Laurie. Her words had done the trick, but how could emptiness feel so solid? she wondered.

In the warehouse, Mohsin presented Chompa with her capsules – a whole box of them. Ammi was nowhere to be seen.

'You will transform all of these tonight. You've had plenty of rest now, Chompa. I don't want to hear any more excuses.'

Two men stepped through the warehouse door.

'It's ready. Take it and prepare it for departure,' Mohsin said, his voice commanding in a way Chompa had never heard before, and the men began to roll the machine out of the warehouse.

Chompa's heart beat fast in her chest. Departure? Where was he sending it? India? When it arrived, no djinnspeaker would be safe. They could be taken from their families, their magic extracted from them, and no one in power would even notice or care. All over the world.

'When you showed me the capsules, you said you wanted to help me,' she said quietly, once they were alone again.

'And I did. All of this was to help you. Help us. But I knew you wouldn't see it that way.'

Chompa sensed something in him, a wall, crumbling. She seized her chance.

'I want to speak to Ammi *now*, before I start. Otherwise how will I know she's still alive? How can I trust you're not lying to me again?'

Mohsin looked amused, the wall back up. 'You think you're in a position to barter with me? But I'm not the brute you think I am, so very well.'

In the room at the back of the warehouse, Ammi was wan and unmoving, the gag still round her mouth, her skin sallow under the harsh light of the bright mantle lamps. Chompa's eyes fell immediately on the restraints about her wrists and ankles, which were, of course, iron.

Chompa took off her scarf, and the taviz hidden in its folds, transferring it to her pocket. Ammi just looked at Chompa as if she was the most beautiful thing she had ever seen, her eyes shining. For a time, Chompa and her mother simply gazed at one another, dry- and clear-eyed, noting every beloved feature, every changed aspect, in the other's face. It was as if they were back by the stilled river; and, for a moment, it was enough.

And then it wasn't, and words and tears welled in both of them, the cruelty of it all too much to contain.

Mohsin turned away suddenly, agitated. The suddenness of the movement made Chompa look over at him. Today he didn't seem to revel in his actions, as a villain in a story would, but started to pace up and down, as if he wished to be anywhere else.

Briskly, Mohsin turned back to her and looked at his watch. There wasn't much time.

'Tonight will be your last meeting for some time. Once

you've transformed the capsules, I will be taking you, Chompa, back to India, to work with me and the machine. Amina, you're not strong enough to travel so you will remain here to recuperate until you can join us. If either of you plots to escape or disobeys me, though, you will endanger the other.'

Chompa staggered backwards. She'd be separated from her mother – again! After two brief, tortuous meetings? He couldn't be so cruel!

'How could you? How can I go with you and trust that you won't kill her? How will I ever trust you?' Chompa's voice shook with horror and rage.

Mohsin looked up, almost surprised. He walked a little closer to Ammi. 'Do you really have any choice?' he replied mildly. 'You may say your goodbyes now. This one time, you may embrace your mother.'

Suddenly it was as if a little candle had been lit in the dark. A chance. Chompa remembered what Leeza had done at the palace, and she let rip with her own performance.

She stamped her foot.

'I will not go with you! I won't do anything – anything! Kill me if you want – I have had enough! I want to die!' She screamed and stamped and screamed again, her fists balled in rage, tears flowing freely down her cheeks. Ammi shook her head from side to side, pleading silently with her wide, liquid eyes for Chompa to be calm.

Mohsin ran his hands through his hair, looking at the door. 'Chompa, enough of this silly show of emotion!'

She had unsettled him.

'I do! I do want to die! You've made it intolerable to live! I can't bear to be in the same room with you!' She began to cry harder.

Mohsin looked agonized now, and Chompa felt a thrill of satisfaction go through her and took care to conceal it under another wave of tears.

'Look – nothing will happen if you and your mother obey me. You've both put me in a terrible situation. This – none of this was what I wanted.'

Chompa started to cry more quietly, but she continued to hiccup and shudder with each breath in a distressingly childlike way as she shuffled towards him. Mohsin stepped back, almost at the door.

'I just wanted a family. I wanted a father, a mother, to love me. Why couldn't you love me?' she screamed as she stepped forward again, stretching out her arms as if demanding his embrace.

Mohsin looked genuinely startled as he backed away again.

Across the threshold.

Chompa had one second, just one, to give Mohsin her most contemptuous, scornful, hate-filled smile before she slammed the heavy wooden door shut and locked it behind her.

She pushed some boxes against the door. Then she raised her finger and turned the door to silver.

Chompa ran to her mother as Mohsin slammed his fists against the door, bellowing for her to open it.

She flung her arms round Ammi, sobbing with relief. They were close, so close to being free. She twisted off the cloth gag, sodden and filthy, and flung it to the floor. She took a file from her pocket and started working at the chain connecting the iron bracelets. It was difficult: the chain was thick, and the file was flimsy, and her fingers started to blister with the effort. But she managed to prise one link apart. Pulling hard, she freed her mother's wrists. But the ankle bracelets, connected to a heavy iron ball, were thicker.

'Ammi – Ammi – I can't break them!' Chompa cried in frustration.

'My darling, you've done so well. My shona.' Ammi's voice was calm, and her body was very still. She wasn't fighting to free herself.

It made Chompa stop what she was doing. It made Mohsin's rage and hammering fade away into silence. Looking at her mother, so peaceful, so serene, Chompa started to feel uneasy.

'Chompa.'

'Ammi?' It came out as a tiny, shaky sound, the sound of a young child.

'Chompa, give me the taviz.'

Chompa stepped backwards, giving a slight shake of her head.

'No . . . tell me why you want it – tell me what you're going to do.'

Ammi now became a little agitated, her gaze flicking towards the door, over and over.

'Chompa, my shona, there's no time. You must trust me. I've asked only that one thing of you, Chompa, in your whole life. Please, my shona, do not refuse me the taviz.'

'Ammi – I'm scared. You're scaring me.'

'Don't be scared. You're so brave! You have been so, so brave! My love – we have little time. If Mohsin finds something to break through the other side, which he will, we'll be lost. We'll all be lost. He will show no mercy now. You must give it to me and trust me.'

'I – I've always trusted you, Ammi. Ever since that day, with the cooking hut. I know, I know this is all my fault. But I promised to stay hidden – I let them take you. It was the hardest thing I've ever done, but I did it.'

She stepped forward and placed the taviz round her mother's neck.

Ammi breathed a sigh of relief.

'It wasn't your fault, my shona. None of this is. He was waiting for me to do my finger-magic so he could trace us – he's been waiting ever since I left him. I should have trusted *you* – I should have seen you were old enough to know the truth. Look at you now. So much stronger than I could ever have imagined.'

Ammi stroked Chompa's cheek with her hand. It was trembling ever so slightly.

There was the sharp snap of wood breaking behind Chompa, just as Ammi had predicted. She looked over her shoulder to see a splintering crack in the timber wall. She turned back towards Ammi. If there was more time, she could find some magic to do . . . something else. But Mohsin was coming, and Chompa couldn't think.

'Come, put your arms round me once more, Chompa. I've missed those arms so much.'

Chompa didn't hesitate. She wrapped herself tight about her mother. She would never let go.

Ammi spoke softly into Chompa's ear, pressed against her face.

'Chompa, I'm going to set you free. You must trust me. And, when you're free, you must do everything you can to share writing-magic as widely as possible – that's the only way to stop the British, to stop those like Mohsin who want to use djinn-magic for their own gains. Do you promise?'

Chompa stared into her mother's face. It was tear-stained, but Ammi wasn't crying now. Again, that terrible, terrifying serenity.

Another crash, revealing a hole in the wood. Mohsin would not be long now. There was no time. No time at all.

'Swear it, Chompa. On my life.' Ammi's voice was urgent, almost in pain.

'I swear,' said Chompa, her voice hoarse. More timbers fell, and Chompa knew Mohsin was nearly through.

'I will always love you, my shona. Love doesn't die – it's the fire that burns forever, within everything.'

Chompa didn't like these words. She'd wanted to hear them for so long – but not this way. There was something wrong about them . . .

Ammi held her even closer, almost too tight. Chompa felt a pressure on her wrist, and looked down to see Ammi's finger on Chompa's spellbook taviz. Chompa felt briefly dizzy, and then her eyes grew wide as she realized what had happened. Ammi had taken some of her magic. Before she could ask why,

Ammi spoke again in a trembling, urgent whisper.

'Let go of me now, shona. You vowed to obey me. Now do so. RUN.'

Suddenly Chompa was thrown from Ammi by a huge repelling force. She landed on her back just as Mohsin burst through and ran towards Ammi with a roar.

Ammi closed her eyes, put one hand to her neck and raised her finger.

The taviz exploded in a single, terrible, gigantic burst of pale red flame. The flames seethed and surged, surrounding her mother as if she was haloed, and then engulfed her. Mohsin kept running towards Ammi, ripping off his own jacket, racing towards the flames that now billowed and caught at the huge, high ceiling, that spread and surged towards Chompa.

Chompa screamed and screamed, but could not move. She could not run.

She could not obey her mother's final wish.

# Chapter Thirty-five

Tipu and Laurie jumped out from behind the crates. They'd seen Chompa and Mohsin go into the warehouse; they'd heard Chompa screaming at Mohsin. Tipu had wanted to charge in, but Laurie had held him back, urging him to wait – and then they'd seen the bizarre sight of Mohsin being shoved out of the warehouse, locked out, the door turning silver behind him, and then breaking his way back in through the timber walls with an old piece of iron pipe. And then they'd felt, rather than seen, the explosion.

That was when Laurie released Tipu, and the two of them had run into the warehouse together.

The fire had caught so fast in the wooden structure, helped by the gas lamps, which were bursting into flames one by one above their heads, sending fine fragments of glass down upon them. Smoke made it hard to see as both boys ripped off their shirts and wrapped them round their heads and covered their mouths. They dared not split up in case one of them got lost or went down. They clung together as they searched for Chompa and for Mohsin.

They almost tripped over Chompa's unconscious body before they saw her. She lay on the floor, curled into a ball. Tipu shook her, but they couldn't wake her. The boys looked at each other, and lifted her by her arms and legs, hauling her out into the sharp, cold, fresh dock air that hit their lungs like a fist. Tipu and Laurie started coughing, while the cold, damp gravel next to her face made Chompa stir beneath them.

Now that Tipu and Laurie knew she wasn't dead, it was time to act again. They nodded to one another, knowing what they had to do. They had to go back in for Mohsin. They wrapped their shirts about their mouths again and dived into the flames, coming out within minutes with his unconscious form. There were burns to his arms and face and chest. Tipu had to lean in close to hear if he was alive.

'Just about, I think,' he croaked to Laurie.

Laurie looked behind him. The flames leaped out of the windows and had started to lick through the great wide doors.

'Tipu, brother, we have to move. Now.'

Chompa sat up groggily. Her throat was hoarse from screaming and the smoke. She began to cough and splutter, before being violently sick on the gravel. Then she found her voice and began to scream again.

Tipu jumped to her side. He couldn't make out what she was saying; the smoke had ravaged her throat, and she was like a crazed animal, screaming and throwing her hands out towards the warehouse. Tipu had to grab her, contain her arms, and drag her away as the flames danced towards them, threatening to engulf the way out towards the quay. She was fighting, spitting, kicking, screaming all the way.

Laurie followed, dragging Mohsin unceremoniously by his ankles.

Chompa was screaming, if anything louder, the further she got from the warehouse. 'Aammm! Aammm!' she cried in a terrible, hoarse croak as she wept and beat at Tipu. She didn't seem to recognize him, or Laurie, or understand anything, just kept screaming and pointing.

Tipu grabbed her hands in his and brought his face close to hers.

'Chompa, it's Tipu. Tipu. You're all right – you're going to be all right, Chompa,' he said in soft, steady tones.

She crumpled in a weeping, exhausted, defeated heap. Then she saw Mohsin's body and began to scream again.

Tipu and Laurie exchanged worried glances.

'I don't know what's happened here, but we need to get her away from him, get her water, and get her to rest. Oof, I need a rest, too,' Laurie said, grimacing as he wiped away the sweat that was pouring into his eyes from the heat of the blaze. He looked down at Mohsin and grimaced again. 'We can't carry him. Arré, we've saved his life. Leave him; it's Chompa we need to be worrying about.'

Tipu nodded, wiping his brow. Chompa was still and silent now, her eyes fixed only on the fire. He crouched by her, lifting her limp right arm about his neck, Laurie doing the same with the left, supporting and raising her carefully. The three of them limped and hobbled slowly, painfully away from the inferno, leaving Mohsin's body on the timber planks of the quay.

✳

It took them a long time to get to Spittlefields. By the time they arrived, the silver line of the coming sunrise could be seen.

Tipu hammered on the door of the lodging house three times before anyone came, and it was Yasser in his dreadful nightcap who opened the door, using all the foul language a multilingual sailor had at his disposal. The curses died on his lips when he saw them, covered in soot and dark red burns. His eyes settled upon the almost immobile, mute form of Chompa.

He opened the door wide for them to come in, shut it carefully, and then yelled hard for Sal.

The boys settled Chompa in a booth, but didn't move from her side. She had still not said a word since they'd left the docks, and that worried them most of all.

'Wot the bleedin' 'eck is going on?' Sal grumbled as she hobbled down the stairs. Then she saw Chompa and fell silent.

Tipu and Laurie explained what they knew.

'She's in shock, she is,' said Sal with a firmness that spoke of experience. 'She needs hot sweet chai, even sweeter than you boys like, an' bed.'

She pushed Tipu and Laurie out of the way and started examining Chompa's burns and bruises with her rough, kind hands. 'Leeza, Leeza, oop, oop, me gal!'

Leeza skittered down the stairs. Tipu's eyes widened.

'What are you doing here?'

'I lost Chompa and Mohsin Saheb at the museum. I didn't know where else to go. I got lost, but I arrived here yesterday, after you'd both left – Sal's got me looking after the little djinnspeakers –' She paused, catching sight of Chompa. Her face drained of all colour. 'Hai Allah!' she cried, running over to her.

Tipu heard the kettle whistling on the stove and knew chai was on its way. His shoulders sagged with tiredness and relief and something else. The ease of heart that comes with being at home. This was home.

Yasser hurried out with the tea things and the sugar pot on a tray. He pushed the boys' cups towards them, and heaped spoonful after spoonful into Chompa's.

Leeza took the cup from Yasser, and gently spooned some tea into Chompa's cracked blueish lips.

At first, she didn't even swallow, and it dribbled down her chin. It was painful to see, and Tipu found himself looking away.

But Sal scrubbed at Chompa's face with the edge of her skirt, stroking Chompa's head and cheeks, while Leeza stood on the other side and tried again, the two of them a protective huddle of care.

Several minutes later, Chompa blinked, and opened her mouth slightly, and then swallowed some tea three or four times. Then she blinked again, twice, and her eyes opened wide, and the light behind her dark pupils returned. Tears began to pour from her eyes, hard, as she shakily took the cup from Leeza and sipped it herself.

Yasser, Tipu, Laurie, and Sal sat in hushed, pensive silence.

Once she'd finished the tea, Chompa's tears stopped. She set down the cup carefully.

'Thank you, thank you, everyone,' she said in a hoarse whisper. 'You have always been my friends.'

She turned slowly, stiffly towards Tipu and Laurie.

'You saved me. I half wish you hadn't. You saved him, too. I wish with all of me that you hadn't, that you'd let him burn. But my mother was in there as well. My ammi. She started the fire, and she's gone now, I know it. I thought I would always know if she was gone, and I do, and she is. She's gone.' Chompa forced the words out, to try to make it real. But she just couldn't believe it – she couldn't allow herself to. If she did, she thought she might crumble to ashes. And she didn't have the time for that, not yet.

Tipu and Laurie looked at Chompa in shared, unspeakable horror. Her mother had been in there – they'd left her mother in there . . . They hadn't even looked for anyone else –

She seemed to hear their guilt, the rush of awful leaden thoughts in their heads, and she interrupted them. 'There was nothing you could do. She was gone before I passed out. Before you got there . . .'

Chompa's calm was almost unnerving. If they'd seen her mother in the warehouse, they would have been stunned at how similar Chompa was to her now, in her serenity, her dignity, the power of purpose in her eyes and the firm set of her mouth.

Leeza put a hand gently upon Chompa's shoulder, sensing the plan that was brewing.

'Chompa, whatever it is can wait. Now you must rest,' she said.

Chompa shook her head. 'No. It's not over. There are things that have to be done –'

Tipu stopped her. 'Then tell us! Me and Laurie – we'll do it!'

Chompa shook her head again. 'You can help – I'll need everyone's help. But you'll need me, too. There are things that need undoing that only I can undo.'

Chompa turned back to Sal, her eyes wide, almost pleading, because again she sensed Sal inwardly preparing to take charge, to march her off to bed.

'It has to be this morning. It can't wait – really it can't.'

Sal gazed at Chompa thoughtfully. She took her hands off her hips and pressed her temples, suddenly looking weary and sad. Then she wheeled about to the three of them, the old fire returning.

'Mornin', you said? Well, it en't mornin' yet. Get a couple of hours' sleep or you three won't even make it through the day. I'll wake you all at dawn.'

# Chapter Thirty-six

Tipu thought the sleep actually made him feel worse. On waking, his head spun and his mouth was like a desert. But he hauled himself off his mat, even though his blanket was warm, and the room was cold, and his body screamed in protest. He wondered if Chompa had slept at all.

She had. She didn't think she would when Leeza had led her to her room, a tiny, sloping attic space with a little canvas cot in it, but she did, dreamlessly. She woke refreshed, calm, purposeful. Vengeance had brought her djinn-fire back.

By her bed, Leeza had left a clean dress, trousers, and a fresh strip of cloth for her headscarf. Chompa picked up the kameez and the trousers, but left the scarf. She would not hide her true self any more.

There were pans of hot water outside each of their rooms. When they got downstairs, after sorely needed, wonderfully hot washes, the three of them saw breakfast ready on the table: parathas, spiced scrambled eggs, a fresh pan of chai. They looked at each other and smiled.

This was what home meant.

Chompa called Leeza, Yasser, and Sal from the kitchens. They sat quietly round the table with the boys, both of whom were slightly awed by this formidable girl with her straight back, her smooth, graceful head, her huge eyes that were dark and bright at the same time.

'It doesn't matter if Mohsin's dead or not. And he isn't – I know that just as much as I know –' Chompa's voice cracked, and for a moment she couldn't speak. She clutched at the table and breathed before continuing. 'But it doesn't matter because he's made this machine, to take our powers, and the machine survived. Devaynes will learn about it. He might even already have it – and he'll work out how to use it. All he'll need is a djinnspeaker – or a djinnborn, because Devaynes won't care about the difference, not in the way Mohsin did. And Devaynes has plenty to choose from. So first we must free the other children, right away.

'While we're rescuing them, someone has to find the machine – we need people who know the docks and can break into the warehouses and locate it. We'll bring the children back here and wait behind the Customs House for a message.'

Yasser coughed. 'I can take care of that; I'll get our pedlars on the case.'

Chompa nodded. 'Then I need to destroy the machine before it gets sent to India. Only I can do that because I helped make it.' She swallowed as the guilt threatened to overwhelm her. 'The Company – and Mohsin, if he's still alive – they'll be looking for me. They know I'll try this, and they'll be planning to stop me in any way they can, with magic, with weapons, everything. We also have to stop the Company guards, Mohsin, and Devaynes from getting back to India for as long as possible. That means taking down their ships – all except the *Kohinoor*, which we need. That must be towed carefully elsewhere.'

Yasser and Laurie looked at each other.

'We can deal with that.'

'It's going to be like war. So I'll need help – an army almost – to fight them, while I destroy them all.'

Tipu spoke now. 'Aaliya can sink the ships. We can get the East End magicians to come and help as well. Their magic might be different, but this affects all magical people. This is their fight, too.' He smiled wryly. 'Plus, they all love making things that explode.'

Chompa nodded again.

Laurie chewed at his lips. 'We need to tell people about this fast, and we don't have much time. There are only six of us here, and we can't go everywhere and do everything we need to do.'

There was silence. Then Leeza gave a little gasp, ran upstairs, and back down again, carrying Ammi's silver box.

Chompa's eyes widened.

'I thought it was at Devaynes' house? How?' she said, emotion choking her throat.

'Gal called Millie brought yer bag here this morning, while you were asleep,' said Sal.

Out of breath, Leeza handed Chompa the box.

'The pedlars – I heard them, last night, talking about how

some of the villagers back home were passing warnings about the Company coming their way. I don't know if it'll really work, but . . . Yasser, we have lots of rotis, right?' she asked, her eyes sparkling.

Yasser nodded, while Chompa looked confused.

'Bring them here, please.'

Leeza grinned as Yasser fetched a stack of rotis from the kitchen and set them on the table. She leaned over to Chompa and whispered in her ear. Then Chompa gave a small smile, too. She opened the box and pulled out a taviz and some thread. They all watched in silence as Chompa wrote out letters large and clear on paper, and Leeza copied them on to a tiny scroll – Chompa swiftly and fluently, Leeza sweating with concentration on every curl and flick. When Leeza finished, she glanced at Chompa, who nodded at her work, and placed the scroll in the locket. Chompa tied the taviz on Leeza's wrist.

Then she and Leeza placed their fingers on the silver taviz on Leeza's wrist and their other hands on the topmost roti.

The charred parts clustered together in a pool of black in the centre of the bread, and then flowed out in tiny rivulets again, leaving a message, written in charcoal black, imprinted on to each chapatti, before they rearranged themselves back into splodges.

Tipu picked one up, puzzled for a moment, then, in front of his eyes, the splodges rearranged themselves into Gujarati. The message spoke, too, when he put the bread to his mouth. Chompa's words, in Chompa's voice: '*Please help.*

*The Company are coming for us all. Come to Sal's at noon. We will defeat them together.'*

He dropped it on to the table, astounded.

Leeza and Chompa shared a satisfied grin. Writing-magic – with just a dash of djinn-magic. Within minutes, they'd enchanted the whole stack.

Chompa handed the stack to Sal. 'Ask the pedlars to give these out to the sailors, the magicians, anyone who could help. And Sal – I never thought I'd say this, but I need a frock. Do you have anything I could use?'

Leeza blushed, ran upstairs, and brought down a dark green frock Chompa had worn a few days ago.

'You weren't going to wear it, and Dacca muslin is so fine, I thought I could sell it or make it into a kameez,' she said.

Chompa smiled. 'It'll suit you much more than me. I just need to borrow it for a bit.'

Soon, they were all at work. Tipu had the date-seed bottle out on the table and was talking to Aaliya, explaining everything she'd need to do. Leeza sang as she rolled more rotis in the kitchen. Sal, Laurie, and Yasser conspired in a corner.

Chompa felt a new energy thrum in her limbs, in her chest cavity, in her heart. She could see everything in front of her – everything that would happen – clearly, as if lit with the brightest, purest spring light.

An hour later, Chompa, clad in her frock, strode down Brick Lane with Tipu, Leeza, and Laurie, a bulky saddlebag swinging by her left hip. As they hurried along, Tipu breathlessly described the layout of the Church of the Righteous Dominion Home for Strange Children.

They reached West India Dock Road as the Bow bells rang seven times. The Customs House's yellow-gold bricks gleamed in the early-morning light, plump with power among the grubby wooden warehouses.

The four of them crouched behind a crate and watched. Tipu said he'd heard that Saltsworth always came for the morning call-on, when dock managers ran a lottery to choose their workers for the day, as those who didn't get work were more likely to listen to the pastor. Lean, shabbily dressed men thronged by the dock gates, waiting to see if they'd be lucky that day. There were small groups of Chinese and Indian sailors among them, but they were glared at, and kept their heads down.

And sure enough, as the crowds grew thicker, a black-clad, plump figure popped up on the wharf, scurrying around like an oversized pigeon, a stack of books and pamphlets in the crook of one arm. As Saltsworth turned his back, his head glistened in the light, sweaty from his exertions.

He waddled up to groups, bellowing, 'Hello there! Nei ho! Salaams!' The men all gave a slight nod while Saltsworth began rattling away earnestly in English, Cantonese, and Hindustani, and passed round pamphlets and books. As soon as he moved on to another group, the dockers, more often than not, quietly dropped the pamphlets into the water.

'Honestly, why don't they just refuse the pamphlets and

tell him to go away?' Leeza clucked as this happened for the fourth time.

Laurie shrugged with a world-weary sigh. 'He runs soup kitchens, a sailors' home for African and Asian sailors, and you can sell pamphlets for him if you're in a bad way. They need to keep him onside just in case.'

Tipu's toes tingled at the memory of his first cold night in London, not far from where they were crouching.

Chompa let out air from her cheeks, tapping her foot.

'He's only got a couple of tracts left. He's nearly done,' observed Laurie.

They stole closer to the pastor and kept him in sight as they wound their way through Limehouse, hiding themselves in doorways when he stopped to post one of the last remaining pamphlets through any door with a magical symbol over it, sometimes crossing himself and muttering a prayer while shaking his head sadly.

'He really hates magic, doesn't he?' said Chompa, and Tipu nodded.

They kept following until Saltsworth stopped at a large brick building with a drinking fountain at the front. It looked like a paupers' school. He patted his pockets, found a large key, and slipped in through the heavy iron doors.

'So. This must be it, then.' Laurie shook his head. 'Funny, we arrived bundled under a blanket and left for the museum the same way. I'd never have known it was this building.'

'I don't know how we'll free them . . .' Tipu whispered uncertainly. 'There's so many staff, always watching and recording everything.'

'Leave that to me.' Chompa grinned, tapping the saddlebag. Then, remembering herself, the playfulness vanished, and she was serious again. 'Do you know where the keys to the sleeping quarters are kept?'

Tipu nodded. 'In the office. There's always staff in there, and Saltsworth's study is next to it . . .' Tipu trailed off doubtfully. 'That's where all our djinn and magical equipment were kept while we were here, too.'

'We need a distraction to get them away from there, then.'

'How are we even going to break in, though?'

'We're civilized people, Tipu. We're going to knock like civilized people.'

Chompa bent down to mutter in Laurie's ear and passed him the heavy bag. Tipu looked wary as Laurie slunk into the shadows. Chompa prodded him. 'Tipu, focus. Work on looking hungry and dirty.' She raised an eyebrow. 'Actually, you're good. Leeza, grab his arm.'

With one hand, she twisted Tipu's ear painfully, while with the other she rapped smartly on the door.

'Hello, *hellooo*!' Chompa called in a much higher than usual voice, with a crisp English accent. 'Is Father in, please? Do hurry – I think he'll get away otherwise!'

Tipu squirmed, his ear burning. There was a tinkling of keys, and the door creaked open again to reveal a dour old housekeeper.

'Father has only just come in from his rounds. What do you want?' Her tone was suspicious.

Chompa shoved Tipu forward, her fingers still firmly clamped to his ear.

'My maid and I found this child on the streets, and Sir Clive asked me to bring him to you at once!'

The housekeeper nodded with satisfied respect at Chompa's cruelty as she peered at Tipu. 'Ah, the little blighter! Come in, miss. I'll fetch Father right away.'

She scurried off. Without, Tipu noticed, locking the heavy iron doors behind them.

Leeza, Chompa, and Tipu were ushered in through the office, towards the study, the housekeeper emitting a stream of complaints about the 'scandal' of Tipu and the other ungrateful children having escaped her good master at the museum. Tipu did his best to look stupid and contrite, which amounted to pretty much the same expression. The housekeeper became silent only as they approached the study door. Then her back straightened, and she coughed to clear her throat before knocking.

They could see him through the glass. Saltsworth was at his desk, absorbed in writing up his docklands exploits in his journal. Everything was recorded in minute detail, as if writing it was to control it. Shao Ying had explained to Tipu that Saltsworth was an obsessive journal-keeper. He would visit their classes, watching them closely and scribbling away. Once, during an energetic sermon, it had fallen out of his pocket. Shao Ying had been rewarded with sugar on his gruel the next day for returning it, but not before he'd had a good look through. Tipu knew that he and Laurie were in there, as was every one of the magical children, not by name, but by an intimate physical description that pinned them down to the very shade of whiteness of their teeth.

The housekeeper tapped timidly on the door.

'Sir, I'm awfully sorry. It's important, this one, but I hate to disturb you,' she said, shifting from foot to foot.

Saltsworth put down his pen slowly. He looked up.

'It's all right, Margery. I was just finishing, as the Lord would have it! Now, what is the problem?' Saltsworth's eyes fell upon Leeza and Chompa with Tipu between them, Tipu's ear still in Chompa's fist. 'Ah.'

Saltsworth rose from his chair, extending a fleshy pink hand towards Chompa. He didn't even look at Leeza. Chompa took it calmly, shaking it with a firmness that seemed to surprise and impress the pastor, who switched easily out of English into Hindustani.

'An excellent British handshake, my dear!'

He nodded eagerly, pointing at a chair.

'Do sit, do sit. Margery, please bring refreshments for the young lady. Miss Begum, I have heard a great deal about you, of course, from our patron, Sir Clive. In fact, I hear from Sir Clive that neither you nor your uncle returned home last night. I do hope all is well?'

Chompa smiled serenely. 'Oh yes. We've both been very busy, trying to round up the runaways.'

'Of course, of course! And speaking of runaways – pray, do tell me how you came across this . . . unfortunate soul.'

Chompa sat, fingers laced over pressed-together knees, a picture of ladylike propriety, while Leeza stood behind her, still grasping Tipu's arm.

'Father, I recognized this young man attempting to enchant some coins from a purse on Mile End Road. I heard him speaking some words to a little bottle. Luckily, my maid and I caught him. I knew he had to be one of yours.'

Saltsworth steepled his fingers together, his face creased in sympathy and seriousness.

'Like you, I have been searching all over London for these children. I was terribly worried about them! There are all kinds of nefarious types who would want to exploit them, make them stray down the path to darkness.'

Chompa clucked her tongue in disgust. 'How awful!'

'Yes, quite. I'm very glad to see this boy again. Perhaps he'll lead the way to the other children.'

'I do hope so, for your sake and theirs, Father. Actually, Father, Sir Clive asked me to do something while I was here. Might I put some extra protections in place? We wouldn't want anything like what happened at the museum to occur again.'

Saltsworth looked pale for a moment. Tipu held his breath. But then Saltsworth shook his head rapidly and bowed his head low.

'Of course, of course. Do come with me. Can your maid stay here, ensure the boy doesn't move? I will deal with him presently.'

Tipu kept his head down, staring at the floor for as long as he could hear their voices. It looked like repentance. But he was concentrating.

The seed bottle in his pocket started to jangle.

They sprang to work as soon as the door closed. Tipu pulled out the bottle, popping the cork stopper. There was a faint flicker of pale red flame as Aaliya left her prison and drifted unseen into the air. Leeza let out a whispered cry of triumph as she located the keys in a tiny cupboard on the wall. Tipu nodded, and whispered to Aaliya to create an illusion of the keys in the cupboard as Leeza pocketed the real ones. Aaliya grumbled at even mimicking metal, but did it nevertheless.

Then they crept out. It was a dangerous business. Tipu had to hope that Chompa would stall Saltsworth long enough in the hall so that he could get to the bunk rooms.

He jumped up to have a look through the square glass window of the first room, the key primed between his fingers. He uttered a little curse – the children were fast asleep. They would have to wake them, and then they'd be groggy and slow and confused. And noisy. He could whisper to Aaliya to silence them, but that would just get them kicking and thumping with excitement at the prospect of being reunited with their own djinn.

He unlocked the door.

'Arré, get up, get up,' Leeza whispered, shaking each child by the shoulder before moving on to the next, while Tipu scrambled up the ladder to wake the children on the upper bunks. Then they both froze as they heard the door creak behind them.

Tipu flattened himself on a bunk and froze. The child he was basically lying on opened his eyes wide in alarm. Tipu put his finger to his mouth again, grasping the child's hand.

'Tipu, Leeza,' whispered a familiar voice in the dark.

Tipu hauled the boy down the ladder.

'Hai Ram, Laurie. I thought we'd had it.'

'I've done my bit. We need to get out now.'

Leeza narrowed her eyes. 'And what exactly was it that she asked you to do?'

'My skills are not just magical, you know.' Laurie grinned, showed Leeza his half-empty bag, now full of bottles, tools, and amulets. Then he bundled his fists together and splayed them wide, fingers waggling upward, mouthing *boom*.

There was a new urgency to their efforts now. Aaliya floated ahead, looking for dangers, while Tipu and Leeza gathered and moved the children onwards. They could smell smoke as they approached the office and study area. No one had discovered Laurie's diversion yet, and Chompa and Saltsworth were nowhere to be heard or seen. They crept forward, one great clump of magical child bodies. Tipu and Laurie hauled the great iron doors – still, happily, unlocked – open, and the children scurried through into the street.

'Where is Chompa? I thought she'd be back by now.' Leeza was troubled, looking down the street back towards the Home.

Tipu could make out fine plumes of smoke beginning to wind out from under the doors. Laurie pushed the children onwards, down an alley, and pulled at Tipu and Leeza to leave, too.

At that moment, Chompa slipped out from the Home, coughing and breathless.

'Saltsworth rushed straight for his office as soon he smelled the smoke,' she said once she'd recovered a little. 'Nice work, Laurie. You've started quite the blaze there.'

They fell silent as they watched the doors open and the four or five staff pour out, accompanied by spools of smoke, coughing, spluttering, and shouting. Saltsworth was still nowhere to be seen.

'Do you think he's going back for the children?' asked Leeza, eyes wide in alarm. 'What will he do when he finds them gone?'

But a moment later a spluttering, scorched Saltsworth tumbled out. In his arms were his leather notebooks.

'Ah. Not the children. Those,' said Tipu. 'Much more precious.'

The children began to shift restlessly.

'We should go, before he catches us,' Chompa said.

'You three go. I'm off to the docks, see if I can't find this machine you're talking about,' said Laurie. 'Meet you back at Sal's, achaa?'

Tipu, Leeza, and Chompa nodded, and, herding the children, they turned on their heels and ran, as fast as they could, from Limehouse, from the fire, from the Home for Strange Children.

Back at Sal's, the three of them crouched by the children. The eldest and most confident was Dan, the boy with a small clay golem doll. Chompa explained to him that it was important they stay upstairs, and that Sal would look after them. Dan nodded importantly, and he and the golem began to shunt the children to their rooms.

'No mischief,' Tipu said with surprising sternness, and the children nodded.

Tipu, Leeza, and Chompa had a quick cup of chai. The Bow bells rang ten times just before Laurie pushed the doors open, a crowbar slung jauntily over his shoulder. Chompa's heart leaped to see him.

'Did you find the warehouse where the machine's being stored?'

Laurie shrugged. 'Arré, it wasn't difficult. Ask the right questions of the right people, get the right answers. The *Kohinoor* has also been, um, acquired, and it'll be moored on the Lea for us when this is all over.' He grinned. 'The lascars were only too happy to oblige when I explained what was going on.'

Chompa flung her arms about him in a hug that made Tipu raise his eyebrows. 'I was so worried it would be difficult!'

Laurie shrugged Chompa off hastily. 'Ah, Madam Witch, that was always going to be the easy part. The next one, unfortunately, will not be. Devaynes has found the machine. It's just on the edge of the wharf, right near his fleet, and it's guarded all about like the queen's own palace.'

Laurie explained how the soldiers had muskets and cannons. Chompa's heart sank a little.

'He knows about Mohsin. He's expecting me,' she said quietly.

But she forced her spirits to rise again. 'And we were expecting that,' she said lightly. 'We just need Spittlefields on our side.'

# Chapter Thirty-seven

'I must say, I'm impressed. I've rarely seen writing-magic being used so creatively. Rotis. Clever.'

Farhana walked through the door, carrying a heavy bag on her back, scrolls of paper under one arm, and a roti in her hand. Chompa leaped from her seat.

'Farhana! I – I don't understand! How are you here?'

She rushed towards her and hugged her tight about the waist. Farhana hugged back hard. Then Chompa stepped away, holding Farhana's arms fast in her hands, looked into her eyes, and shook her head. Farhana closed her eyes.

It was done. They both knew that Ammi was gone.

'I used to live and work in London,' said Farhana after a while. 'After the raid on the printing press – there have been many such on writing-magic establishments in India – it wasn't safe to stay, so I paid the lascars to stow me away on that djinn ship, in one of the crates of provisions, and bring me food and water. I heard voices at one point, but thought I was dreaming.'

'That was us! We were on the same ship!' gasped Chompa.

'When we were listening in to Devaynes' conversation – Leeza thought she heard rats . . . that must have been you!'

Farhana's eyes widened with incredulity. Then she sighed heavily. 'I had no idea you were on that ship. I had no idea you were with *him*. Chompa, there's so much – so much – I wish I'd done and said differently. If I'd trusted you back when you came to see me –' Farhana broke off, looking at her hands as tears fell and made dark spots on the wooden table.

Chompa shook her head gently. 'And there's so much I want to ask you, too, so much I need to know. But not now. We haven't got much time.'

Farhana wiped her eyes. 'Tell me what you need,' she said.

Chompa explained everything as quickly as she could. It wasn't long before magicians and sailors began to crowd the room, well before the noon hour. For once, Spittlefields was punctual because Spittlefields was curious.

Laurie and Tipu shook hands with as many people as they could, patting some of the men on the back and engaging in friendly banter. Chompa was pleased to see women there, too – among them, a serious-eyed Russian woman and a studious-looking African girl, with books of magic under their arms. They had all come to hear what she had to say.

The saloon filled with bodies, as if it was back to its heyday and a Friday night. As she looked about, Chompa felt nervous for the first time. Why should these people help her? They didn't even know her.

If Sal's was now her home – and really where else did she have? – then these were her people. She'd have to make them take her in, whether they wanted to or not. Tipu came to stand by her, and placed a firm hand on her shoulder, as if he knew exactly how she was feeling. Laurie stood on her other side, giving some of the sailors lip. Every now and again, she caught someone staring at her bald, smooth head. It rankled, but she shook it off. It was important that they saw her as she was.

Then the Bow bells chimed again, pure and clear. It was noon.

She raised Ammi's taviz in her fist. The crowd hushed. Then Chompa began to speak slowly, in English, pausing after each sentence so Laurie could translate into Hindustani, Miss Weisz into Yiddish, and Shao Ying into Chinese.

'I know many of you have cause to dislike or distrust me. Some of you might have heard about me helping Sir Clive Devaynes and his Company to build the Palace of Wonder. And my magic helped to build the cages they kept your children in.'

There were grumbles and mutters in the crowd, but Chompa continued.

'But what I did, I did because they took my mother. They took her to get to me. I thought I could trick them. And now I've also lost my mother, and my home, and a father I didn't know I even had. The Company, Devaynes, my father – they're my enemies, just as much as they're yours.'

There were more grumbles and even the odd distinct curse word thrown in her direction. She started to feel fearful, but knew she had to stay in control. Chompa had to raise her voice above the din as the room grew louder and louder.

'I asked you here for help to do that because something terrible is about to be set in motion. Once it does, as magical people, as poor people, as the ones who don't have power – we're all going to be in danger, and it will be almost impossible to turn it back. They say they want to protect and empower us. But they only want us to extract our magic. Bleed it out of us. And use that magic to rule the whole world as they wish.'

Gasps of shock rippled round the room.

'But if we take a stand together, today, we can ruin the Company, destroy its terrible plans, and stay safe and free. And it will be dangerous, I must warn you. So you're free to leave. But I ask you all: will you join me? WILL YOU JOIN ME?'

There was a moment of silence, as everyone made their decision.

Then the crowd roared back. It was the pure animal sound of a herd, an army, ready to protect its young, its family, its patch, its home. Spittlefields was one; fierce, proud, ready to be led into battle by a small, strange Indian girl.

Chompa, Leeza, Tipu, and Laurie split the crowd into groups and delegated tasks and leaders. Even Sal's sister, Ma Sheeran, and her boy Sam were there, feeding everyone pudding. Sam plonked himself down by Leeza, who was sitting with some younger kids.

'You teachin' 'em magic, then? Can I learn?' he said eagerly in Hindustani.

'No, not yet. We're learning letters. English letters,' she said with a grimace. Then she looked at the rotis stacked up on the table and smiled. 'But . . . words are magic, too. Powerful. Dangerous. That is why they don't want us to learn.'

'Learnin' letters – dangerous? Wish someone 'ad told me that earlier! I want in. Shove up,' said Sam, elbowing a little boy to move and share his slate.

Farhana and Tipu taught the djinnspeaker children the binding and rebinding spells that Farhana had shown Tipu on the *Kohinoor*. Chompa taught djinnborn and non-djinnborn writing-charms, rows of East End folk sitting on the floor, bent over tiny pieces of paper and silver lockets.

Some magicians hurried back to their quarters and brought back carts full of unusual and somewhat terrifying-looking objects. Others started flicking through books and scrolls, preparing writing-charms in all seven of the magical languages.

By three o'clock, they were ready to go.

Leeza stayed behind at The Pickled Egg with the younger children. Chompa, Tipu, and Laurie led at the front, and the people of Spittlefields flowed, like a river, through its half-deserted streets.

By the time they got to the docks, the sun was getting low in the sky and everything was tinged with red.

Chompa and Laurie climbed on a wall to look out ahead. Tipu and the djinnspeakers stood in front with their little bottles clasped in their hands, by the rails, directly opposite the Company ships, the first line of attack. Laurie pointed out the warehouse across the rectangle of dark water that made up the Company export dock, each of the four platforms around it guarded by a chain of soldiers with muskets. At the front of each platform was a line of massive, brutal-looking cannons.

The low sun was behind them, mercifully. Chompa could make out much more than they could, on their side of the dock. She could even, she realized with a rush of fear and immediate, curdling hate, see Sir Clive standing there, lazy and tall in his gentleman's suit. No armour, no helmet for him. She shrugged. That would make it easier for her.

The Company was defending. Chompa had to attack. It was strange looking around her, seeing this motley group of adults, children, magicians, and non-magicians awaiting her orders, as if she was a general and not just a twelve-year-old girl. But she was their general, if anyone was, and there would be no fight unless she started it.

She looked down at Tipu and nodded.

Then she screamed, as loud as she could, 'NOW!'

Many things happened all at once. Tipu and the djinnspeakers unbound their spirits from their vessels, and Tipu released Aaliya to corral them. Sensing movement, the soldiers opposite began to fire their muskets right at the people of Spittlefields.

They didn't have guns, but what they did have was magic, rage, and each other.

Some of the East End magicians focused on the air currents around the bullets, causing many to bend away and hit the water with satisfying splashes. The Jewish magicians chanted Hebrew adjurations to make birds swoop down in flocks over the soldiers, pecking at them, making them drop their weapons. The Chinese magicians worked in pairs, one painting red symbols frantically on yellow paper lanterns while the other set them alight using djinn-fire and sent them flying towards the Company men. And others – those without charm or djinn-magic, but filled with the power of a shared purpose – just ran about, throwing fireworks or rocks or shoes, causing havoc.

Devaynes had underestimated the power of ordinary, extraordinary people working together.

Chompa clambered off the wall, and Laurie took over the direction of operations. He patted Chompa on the back as a message of good luck. Tipu waved at her, his attention trained on Aaliya.

A whispering part of Chompa wondered if she'd ever see them again.

Chompa raced round the back of the quay, taking care to stay unnoticed. She approached the warehouse, and found it was fully guarded, on all sides.

But where was Mohsin?

She couldn't worry about that now. She had to get on. She had to get in.

Suddenly there was breathing behind her. Chompa swung round, ready to scratch, bite, summon her djinn-fire.

It was Tipu. She shoved at his chest, stamping her foot, furious.

He shrugged with a rueful smile.

'Sorry, I knew you wouldn't have let me come if I'd asked. But you need a distraction now, don't you? You can't just run at them.'

She knew he was right.

'I'm just going to stay here and cause them some problems.'

He clambered up a street lamp effortlessly.

She remembered him trying to teach her to climb, and smiled.

Tipu began to whisper to Aaliya. She swirled and twisted, just visible in the red light of the sun, a transparent, delicate tornado of flames. Looking up at the sheer power, beauty, and freedom of Aaliya, Chompa found herself desperately wanting to join her: to cast off her body, free herself of all ties to this human world, its pain, its cruelty, and just be the fire she was.

But she had things to do.

Chompa watched as Aaliya raised one of Devaynes' smaller ships, a sleek blue sloop, in the air. The curious shadows it created caught the attention of some of the now unarmed soldiers. They ran from their posts, pointing and calling out in alarm. But they had no time, and no weapons that could stop the djinn. The sloop flew at force through the air, towards the warehouse, as if thrown by a massive fist of flame. The side of the warehouse crumpled like a cardboard box.

Moments later, Chompa crept through the splintered wound in the wall.

The walls muffled the sounds outside. It was dark in the warehouse, and the glow of the dusk light came through in deep red and burgundy stripes. She shivered, recalling the stripes of light from her nightmares, from the warehouse close by where Ammi had been held. Her eyes became used to the light, and she looked around, hoping she wouldn't have to retrieve the machine from the rubble of wood.

Her stomach clenched.

She shook her head. It couldn't be.

The warehouse was empty.

A trap.

Chompa ran. She found her feet choosing particular streets, as if they had their own purpose. She was pulled by a part of her will that was almost separate from her, towards one place, one place she didn't want to go, but had to.

Her feet slowed as she came to it.

The docks were crammed with closely clustered warehouses, as if the whole area was one giant warehouse itself, and the buildings just crates stacked against one another. There was no room, no sky, just skinny dark alleys and box after box after box.

That was why the gap, the open space, was so jarring when Chompa saw it. It was a gaping wound.

A massive piece of flattened, blackened, smoking ground. The place where her mother had died.

# Chapter Thirty-eight

And Mohsin was there. As she had expected, she realized with surprise. As she'd known all along.

He stood in front of the machine, brought back to this place where he knew she'd return to, waiting for her. His kurta was immaculate, even now. But he looked tired, and there were burns upon his brow and arm.

'You tried to save her,' said Chompa quietly.

'I did.'

'Why? If it wasn't for you, she would never have needed to do – that. Why then try to save her, after everything you put her through?'

Mohsin raked his hands through his hair. It was such a young, unsure gesture that suddenly a wave of something like pity came over Chompa. It revolted her, and she pushed it away.

'I loved her.'

Chompa uttered a hollow laugh. 'Was it worth it? You have destroyed so much. Did you really think we'd be free this way?'

'Who deserves to be free? Those ragged, filthy beggars you brought here to fight? Those charm-writers hopelessly scribbling away? Those djinnspeakers with their pathetic powers? We, the djinnborn, are marked with exceptional, extraordinary powers for a reason, Chompa. Our magic strengthened, freedom and power would be ours to take.'

She was tired now of talking, of being near him. Him. She could not, would not, think of him as that. As her father. The thought, the word, made her feel ill.

Mohsin stepped towards her, and Chompa's senses suddenly sprang awake.

It was a trap. She had to think, summon energy, before he could catch her. He walked closer, his eyes focused almost hungrily on her. She retreated.

She noticed he wasn't using magic yet as he came for her. He was saving it, she thought with dread. Saving it.

She stepped backwards, further, and further, tripping over a beam that crumbled away under her feet. And still Mohsin advanced.

Chompa scrabbled in the dirt, grasping at the soot and ashes.

A crunching sound broke the stillness around them. Soldiers' boots, getting louder. Devaynes was coming. The Company was coming.

Mohsin looked at Chompa. He rubbed his temples, and his shoulders slumped.

Then in one sure, swift movement he shoved Chompa behind a blackened warehouse beam. Chompa fought to push him away, but he forced her down again. She got ready to fight, grabbing a handful of soot and ash to fling into his eyes. But he released her, and stood in front of the beam, whispering to her to hush.

She was confused. Instead of pulling her up, restraining her, showing her to the Company, he was concealing her.

*Chompa*, he uttered soundlessly.

Behind the beam, Chompa started. His voice was in her head. Mohsin was using the same piece of magic that Chompa had done to communicate with Ammi, only yesterday. Somewhere, concealed from view, Mohsin was wearing a taviz. Chompa felt sick, dizzy, completely disorientated.

*Chompa, Devaynes must not find you. Whatever happens, Devaynes cannot get you, your power. Do you understand? Chompa, tell me you understand.*

*You're helping me? Why?* she responded shakily, as the first soldiers came into view. Mohsin sighed heavily.

*I thought we could only survive as djinnborn by strengthening our strongest. I've gone about everything in the wrong way. And most of it I can never put right. Just this.*

*Devaynes knows about the machine, as I'm sure you've realized. He has the plans, and took some of the capsules. He's seen how strong your power is, and he wants it for himself, for the Company. Whatever happens, you can't allow him to have it. You have no cause to trust me, Chompa, but you must – help me to help you get away.*

Chompa's hands grabbed and scrabbled at the soot. Part of her still wanted to throw it in his eyes and run. But his green eyes were wide, desperate, a storm of feeling. For the first time, she realized he was being genuine.

The regular tick-tock crunching got louder. The soldiers would be upon them soon.

*Quick, we need to bind them with something. But there's nothing! Nothing – no roots or tendrils I can use – the fire has burned everything away!* Mohsin was agitated in a way she'd never seen.

Chompa, however, was calm. She thought back to her lessons, all the different types of transformation they'd tried in the effort to find her affinity. She'd turned rain to ice, seawater into salt, sand into glass.

There was no sand around, but there was soot.

Ash.

She knew what soot could be turned into. And there was so much of it here.

*Ash. We can transform the ash.*

*Ash – into . . . ah! Chompa. You outdo me, not just in power.*

There was a light in Mohsin's eyes, but Chompa turned away. His pride in her didn't make her feel anything any more.

*Come, together. Remember, Chompa, that you must also bind me.*

*But I need to destroy the machine, too!*

*There's no time. Come now – we must hurry.*

He passed his hand behind his back. She could see columns of dark blue shapes in the distance. They were coming.

With a flutter of nausea, Chompa took Mohsin's hand. She looked at him out of the corner of her eye, and it almost hurt physically. Her father. She couldn't even begin to forgive him for what he'd done. But there was a bigger enemy coming their way.

Together, they raised their index fingers and lifted the ashes from the ground, swirling them in the air. As they swirled, Chompa focused on the word 'compress' and turned the ash into the other thing that soot was, its other self.

The cloud became a softer grey, then paler and paler until it sparkled like light itself.

Chompa kept focusing on the word 'compress', even as her own brain began to feel compressed. The brightness coalesced into hard, shimmering shards. Then she lowered her finger, and the shards rained down upon the soldiers: fragments of the hardest, sharpest diamond. They cried out, shielding their faces and eyes.

Then she collected clusters of the gems to form restraints. They locked about the men's arms, wrists, ankles and slammed together, as if pulled magnetically. The soldiers fell to the floor, wriggling like helpless beetles.

*Now bind me, Chompa. Hurry. When Devaynes gets here, I still need to pretend I'm on their side.*

She nodded. The diamonds clicked into place. Mohsin gazed down at the glittering bracelets on his wrists, and spoke aloud.

'We are all three of us djinnborn, Chompa. But your magic is beautiful. And good. Just like your mother's.'

Chompa heard footsteps.

'More men will come once Devaynes sees what has happened. Go. Make the most of your head start.'

Chompa looked up at Mohsin. His eyes were no longer storm-coloured. The storm had died. They were a sad, pale green.

She turned and ran.

When she'd raced round the first corner, she paused. She didn't quite trust him.

She saw Devaynes arrive with Ismail, and Saltsworth huffing and puffing behind them. They were flanked by burly men. She had a sharp shock of recognition when she saw their dark livery and plate-like hands. The pale men.

They tried to prise the restraints from Mohsin, and, when they failed, kicked him liberally with their heavy brown boots.

'Enough, enough, gentlemen,' came the smooth, oily voice of the Eastern Merchant Company's director. 'We need him to speak, at least.'

He kneeled next to Mohsin. 'Now. Where is the girl?' he growled.

Chompa strained to hear Mohsin's reply, holding her breath. He could give her away, or he could lie for her. Which would he choose?

'She and her friends have arranged a rendezvous point in Southampton. The Gateway to the World, is it not? Clive – I think you'll find there's a ship of yours missing, apart from those that were sunk. Your flagship, the *Kohinoor*?'

Southampton. The ship was on the Lea. Mohsin was sending them off on a wild goose chase to the furthest port he could. He had lied for her.

Devaynes looked at Ismail for verification, who gave an apologetic nod as he began to wheel away the machine. Devaynes snarled in frustration and began to issue orders to his men.

Chompa had to leave. She had to leave the machine. She had to leave Mohsin. He might go back on his word later – in which case, there was no time to spare. But she didn't think he would. He'd protected her; he'd lied for her. Perhaps it should have brought her comfort as she ran through the alleys of the docklands, back towards Brick Lane. But she felt nothing. Just hollow.

Spittlefields was strangely still when she arrived: dark windows, empty streets. Though it was late at night, the city didn't usually sleep at all. Chompa felt a mounting unease as she walked – where was everyone? Arrested? Hurt? Or . . . worse? She walked faster.

It was surreal, the peace. And false. Because Chompa knew that violence didn't die – it only slept. The silence was only the silence of darkness, and with the light, the dawn, the Company would come for her, Tipu, the other children. They weren't safe in Spittlefields, their home wasn't safe, until the Company itself was gone. The famines Devaynes' indigo project had caused had to be put right. The smashing of printing presses and the banning of schools, books, everything that would spread the magic of writing among ordinary people – that all had to be reversed. No matter what they'd done today, the Company was still more powerful than any other force India had faced.

Yes, the work was back in India now.

Chompa had thought she'd return with her mother, and

they might start afresh in Dacca together. But now she'd be going alone, and there was no starting afresh: just undoing the terrible things her father had done. The knowledge weighed heavy, her sadness and regret many-layered.

Only Sal's windows were glowing with light when she got to the pub. Chompa breathed a sigh of relief.

She was home.

## Chapter Thirty-nine

When she walked into The Pickled Egg, a pile of bodies descended upon her. But these bodies laughed and hugged her; they wrapped soft arms about her; they nudged and patted her with love and affection. She crumpled to the floor, and they fell, too, still hugging, still laughing, not even realizing that she was crying, crying, crying.

It was Leeza who established order and broke apart the scrum.

'Arré, let the girl breathe!' she bellowed, forcing herself through the crowd. Chompa clung to Leeza, who put her arms gently round her as she cried until there were no more tears in her.

The room was hushed by the time she had recovered a little and let Leeza release her. The saloon was full to the brim. No one had gone home. There were lascars, magicians, Farhana, Tipu, Laurie, Sal. Lots of the kids from the Home were there, too, all looking at their feet, embarrassed. Chompa smiled awkwardly, embarrassed, too, wiping her face with her filthy, blackened hands.

Then Yasser hurried in, always, it seemed, armed with chai when it was most needed.

'What's this, what's this? She's back! Our Witch Queen of Spittlefields, dressed in her finest!' he chortled.

And there was merry laughter in the saloon at this notion, but then someone with a flute, and another with a tabla, picked up the line in song.

Sal ushered Chompa to a table and Tipu and Laurie came and sat opposite her, Leeza by her side for the moment, not saying anything. Yasser set a mug of chai before her. The scent of ginger, cinnamon, clove, and cardamom wafted upward. Mingling, pungent, and perfectly balanced, just like Spittlefields itself.

Saying goodbye the following morning was not easy for any of them. They had sung and drunk tea late into the night, and the morning after they were as stiff as the decks of the hidden ship they needed to head towards. The saloon was like the scene of the children in the cages at the British Museum, when they were performing their magic: but now in colour, tinted with the joy of freedom. One child was enchanting droplets of water into shimmering baubles that were suspended, glowing, round the lamps; another was enchanting a pocketful of seeds to grow into tiny fruit-laden trees in a row by the bar; two others played games of noughts and crosses in the air with shells and pebbles.

Chompa looked about, trying to preserve each and every part of it in her mind. She saw Tipu and Laurie doing the same.

It all went too quickly that morning. Packing, breakfast, cases in the hackney carriage. Yasser made up parcels of food. Sal gave them each a hard, rough hug, a bit too long, as if by holding them she could keep them. Leeza, who had decided to stay, wept, murmuring blessings upon them.

'Are you sure you won't come with us?' said Chompa, her throat tight with emotion.

Leeza glanced back at Farhana, Sal, and Yasser.

'There's work to be done here. Not maid work – writing, reading, schooling work. Besides, you'll only be gone for a bit, nah? You'll be back here soon.' Leeza nudged her with a look that was half playful, half hopeful.

Chompa clasped her in a hug, and didn't let go for a long time.

But there was much to do back home, their other home. Chompa looked at her friends. Laurie and Muyaka would get them there safely this time, and Aaliya and Tipu would keep them fast and true. Tipu had a box of bottles he carried carefully in front of him, containing the djinn of Spittlefields children who longed for the trees of Gujarat, Bengal, Punjab. Farhana was teaching the London djinnspeakers writing-magic, and

Chompa was teaching Tipu and Laurie on the ship. Soon they would have no need for magic that imprisoned others.

Chompa looked down at the writing-charms on her wrist: the one she'd made to speak to Ammi, which would never work again, and the one to unlock the spellbook, which would. She felt a protectiveness coming over her. It wasn't djinn-magic but writing-magic, the magic her mother cherished, that could really help others. She had to save it – to save her people. Ammi's taviz was still in her pocket, and she gripped it tightly, imagining her mother's fingers curling round hers instead.

As they clambered aboard their diamond of a ship, their *Kohinoor*, stolen back, they looked at the land behind them. They could have been anywhere in the country, anywhere in the world, a sweet breeze singing upon the air, the river glittering in the sun. It was hard to believe, as they hauled up the anchor, as Tipu released Aaliya into the date tree for the very last time, that they were even still in London.

But that was London for you, Chompa marvelled.

London held the whole world.

# Author's Note

The characters, plot, and world of *City of Stolen Magic* are fictional. However, much of the inspiration for them – including for the magic – comes from real historical events, people, and objects.

I was first inspired to write *City of Stolen Magic* while working as a historian, when I began looking into the history of Muslim communities in the East End. When I first started doing my research, I thought that migrant communities of colour only arrived in London after the Second World War, to work or to study, as my own father had done. However, I discovered that Africans, Arabs, and Asians have actually been travelling between London and other global ports over hundreds of years.

Seafarers known as 'lascars', who hailed from across the world, including India, Malaysia, Indonesia, Yemen, and Oman, also worked on British merchant navy ships, such as the famous shipping line the P&O. In their work, these seafarers would come to cities like London, stay for a few weeks or months until their ships were ready to return, make friends and acquaintances, and sometimes even be tempted to 'jump ship' – which meant leaving their jobs and former lives behind, losing their wages, and trying to settle in

London. Some of these ship-jumpers ended up marrying local women and running lodging houses with cafes on the ground floors for their fellow seafarers – the first Indian restaurants – just like the one Sal runs in the story. While most seafarers were men, younger boys also used to work on the ships – just like Tipu and Laurie.

Clive Devaynes' sinister Company, with its indigo-blue livery, is meant to remind us of the real and equally sinister and exploitative East India Company. Clive Devaynes is, in fact, a name made up of the surnames of two East India Company directors – Robert Clive and William Devaynes. Between 1757 and 1857, the East India Company actually ruled India – often using violence to do so – extracting its riches, such as tea, spices, and silk, for British gain. The Company created widespread famine and suffering throughout the Indian subcontinent by forcing farmers to turn their fields over to non-food crops like indigo, among many other terrible activities. While my version of the Company in *City of Stolen Magic* is fictional, the devastation wrought by the East India Company and the British government was very real, and it is estimated that £36 trillion worth of wealth was extracted from India during Company and British rule, which has never been repaid. Even worse, it's estimated that thirty-five million Indians died as a result of the famines and oppression.

Devaynes' display of the children in his so-called 'Palace of Wonder' is disturbing, but also drawn from real events that took place during this period. Racist, exploitative human exhibitions, particularly displays of African people, were a source of dubious and dehumanizing entertainment during the whole of the nineteenth century throughout Europe. Sometimes performers in these exhibitions were brought over from their homelands (occasionally sent back afterwards, and other times abandoned), while others were recruited from London's local African, Indian, and Chinese populations, and were required to sit in cages, or in replicas of 'huts', and dress in exotic costumes that had nothing to do with their actual heritage or cultures.

Tipu and Laurie, and the other magical children in the cages, were transported to London, and are due to be sold to work, unpaid, for five-year terms of service. Poor and desperate South Asians were also exploited in this way, by a system called 'indentureship' that came into place in 1826, after the abolition of slavery, and continued, shockingly, until as late as 1917. As part of indentured servitude, over a million South Asians – often whole families, including small children – were paid a small fee in advance, which they then were expected to 'work off' without further pay, by being transported across the world to other British colonies. They would then have to earn their return passage to India. Needless to say, given the terrible conditions in which they worked, many were never able to make the journey home. However, some remained and settled after winning their hard-earned freedom; which is why there are South Asian populations in the colonies of Fiji, the Caribbean, and South Africa, among others.

Although the final standoff in East India Dock is fictional, it is also inspired by a long history of ordinary people standing up to intolerance and oppression in the East End. I was particularly thinking of the Battle of Cable Street, which took place in 1936, when Oswald Mosley's fascist Blackshirts parade through the East End was blocked by local communities from many different cultures who came together, shouting 'They shall not pass.' But I was also thinking of the dock strikes and the matchgirls' strikes of the 1800s, the many demonstrations and marches against racism that took place between the 1970s and 1990s, and then against Islamophobia in the 2000s – all situations where ordinary people from different communities rose up together to speak truth to power, with courage and determination.

Other influences on this story have come from closer to home. Amina and Farhana's printing press comes from the fact that making books runs in my blood. My nana, my maternal grandfather, started out by selling books to Dhaka University students on the street. He went on to own a bookshop, and eventually his very own printing press. I remember my grandfather taking me to see our books being printed there: the massive, dark machinery, the smell of ink and paper, the ink wet and glistening on the fresh new pages. It was such a mesmerizing experience for a child who lived through books, and I wove it into this story as another type of magic. I learned to read Bangla from primers printed by my grandfather. We still have a bookshop known as Banglabazar in the book-selling area of Dhaka (which I've renamed the Library Quarter in this book).

Chompa loses her hair and ends up wearing a headwrap, eventually removing it to be proudly and unashamedly bald.

Ten years ago, I too lost my long, thick hair – not, alas, to magic, but to alopecia universalis. Chompa experiences this as well, because I wanted children who experience hair loss, and other appearance-changing conditions, to find a fierce, proudly different-looking heroine in Chompa.

The magic that Chompa is born with is something I have imagined into reality, but stories of djinn are to be found across South Asia, and djinn, as figures who once walked the earth and lived among us, are still perceived in some places as real. There was a bamboo bush in my father's village that was said to have a djinn living in it; the story of the man Yasser remembers being enticed to the river to rescue his goats, and almost drowning, actually happened when I was visiting my family there, aged seven.

Writing-magic, again, is an invented tradition, and yet I remember older members of my family in Bangladesh wearing taviz, amulets with little metal capsules threaded upon them, containing tiny scrolls upon which verses of the Qu'ran were written, in order to protect them from the evil eye or bad spirits. In creating the magical world for this story I was profoundly influenced by these two things: the idea that magic is still real in some places, and that words have the power to protect us from harm. I believe in both.

# Leeza's Guide to Understanding the Ingrezi Language

Cigarette – **bidi** (disgusting smelly things, why do you even want to know about them?).

Penny coins – **poisha** (bidis are a definite waste of them).

Oh no – **O-ho** (our version is so much more dramatic, nah? Even better with a slap of the forehead for maximum effect). We have so many versions too – **Ai-Hai, Arré, Baap ré, Hai Allah, Hai-ré**. We're just more expressive as a people than these tight-lipped Britishers. They'll explode one day if they don't let it out.

London – this filthy scrap of a city we have found ourselves in. The Britishers call it **Larnden** (who knows why LOndOn gets pronounced with no Os whatsoever, when it was their word in the first place), Tipu and Laurie call it **Lunn-dunn** because Gujarati flattens all vowels, but me and Chompa call it **Lon-don**. You know, the way it's actually spelled. Bangla is always right, achaa?

Nonsense – Tipu and Laurie would call it **baakvaas** (and they are experts in it); we would call it **bokosh** – basically any of the stuff that comes out of Britishers' mouths.

Lad – affectionate term for a little boy – the way Laurie uses **chokro** about Tipu or I like to use **baccha** about the street children.

Nippers/babies – what we'd called **baccha**.

Dog – **kuttah** (there are as many on the streets here as in Dacca!).

Betel leaf – my beloved **paan**, which is so difficult to find here. They always help me think – not just the chewing, which Yasser bhai says makes me look like a cow, but the whole process of filling the leaf with raisins, coconut, and lime paste, wrapping it up into a tiny parcel, and then popping it in my mouth. When I tell Yasser bhai to stop smoking bidis because they're bad for him, he always says that chewing paan is just the same, but I don't stuff mine with tobacco the way the pedlar brothers do. They do stain your teeth red, though, so maybe it's a good thing I can't find them here.

Friend – I'd call them my **bondhu**, but all Hindustani speakers use **yaar** – and ALL THE TIME. Even to people who aren't friends. Bengalis are more discerning.

# Acknowledgements

This book has been ten years in the making. Over those years, I've been mentored, supported, and enabled to write it by so many beloved friends, family, colleagues, and writers. A veritable city of strength and love – all of whom I need to thank here.

Firstly, I must thank all the people who live in the home of my heart. Roshan, our light: this book would not exist were it not for you. That you'll be ten when this book comes out, the perfect age to read this, seems so ridiculously meant to be. My clever, funny bookworm/Greek philosopher/maths whiz – I do hope you'll like your story. Khushi, our joy: the next book is for you, featuring not one, but two rebellious, fierce queens that you so resemble. And Monkoo, my daemon: we fell in love over His Dark Materials and Bartimaeus, and you continue to be my book-soulmate as well as my soul-soulmate, and the critic whose opinion I most value for that reason. Thank you for shouldering so much to enable me to get this story out into the world, and not least, for encouraging my cautious self to take the risks I was so scared of. Amu: thank you for the trips to Muswell Hill Library on Fridays, and teaching me the magic and refuge of books (and libraries) that I will carry with me forever. My sister, Nasreen, but always known to me as Louise:

# ACKNOWLEDGEMENTS

thank you for being my very first reader, the person with whom I entrust all my stories, even the terrible ones. Dad: your calm and quiet support is the anchor of our family ship. Jo Forshaw: thank you for always being ready to scoop the Duchess and the Bunny away for adventures, so that I could actually write this one. And my loved ones who will not be able to hold this book in their hands, who are sleeping above, in the eaves: Baba, Ma, and Claire. Thank you for being with me always, urging me onwards.

Thank you to all my teachers, in the schoolhouse of my heart, from those at Bounds Green Primary School, to Brambletye, Dunottar, Warwick, Oxford, City Lit and Arvon. But *especially* Mrs Das Gupta, who guided and pushed me to find my voice and my mind by giving me the books I needed but didn't know existed.

My Warwick family live in this city, close by. Some of them heard the very beginnings of this story on a stormy day in Wahaca in Waterloo, ten years ago, and did not laugh. For that, and so much more, thanks to George Ttoouli, Emma Clipp, Brian McBride, Ali Hussain, Sara Hafeez, and Simon Turner – and, most of all, Georgina Holmes, who always drew me back to the path she knew was for me, writing, even when I lost sight of it. As best friends do.

My passion to give voice to silenced stories stems from growing up in a family of activists – and I need to thank them for their courage in fighting injustice. There they are, arguing in a Bangla cafe in my heart: my father, a communist warrior to his last, and my maternal grandfather, a printer and seller of books – both active in the liberation struggles that created Bangladesh in 1971. I am so proud to be your daughter and granddaughter. Others have joined the conversation as I have studied and read: Neil Lazarus, Edward Said, Priyamvada Gopal, and more. Thank you all for firing me with a rage that keeps me writing.

In the university buildings down the road are my colleagues past and present. Alana Harris, Eve Colpus, Jane Garnett, Ben Gidley, and Michael Keith: working with you all on the East London migration project gave me so much of the historical stuff that this story is made from. David Gilbert, Claire Dwyer, Laura Cuch, Natalie Hyacinth, and Katy Beinart on Making Suburban Faith at UCL, the project that spurred me towards this creative path: you are no longer colleagues, but will always, *always* be family. To my new Exeter Creative Writing family – especially Sam North, Ben Smith, Andy Brown, Wendy O'Shea Meddour, Ellen Wiles, and Aiysha Jahan – thank you for making me a home, and giving me the chance to teach and share the stories I breathe *for a living*. I simply cannot believe my luck.

In a nearby Dishoom (this is the city of my heart, after all) book people are having energetic, passionate meetings over rose and cardamom lassis. Siena Parker and Louisa Burden-Garabedian: I wouldn't be in a position to be writing this note if it were not for the WriteNow programme, to which I applied (with uncharacteristic impulsiveness) when all I had of this story was five thousand words of fragments I had written for Roshan during the first sleep-deprived months of motherhood. My fellow mentees, especially Nelson Abbey, Charlene Alcott, Katie Hale, Rebecca Pizzey, Geraldine

# ACKNOWLEDGEMENTS

Quigley, Emma Smith-Barton, and Benjamin Wilson: thank you for being my writing family through thick and thin. I am SO lucky to know and love you and have you in my corner. Louise Lamont: thank you for being an agent who shares my love of Mary's Milk Bar and *The Murderer's Ape* and with whom days in Edinburgh's Honeycomb & Co. can happily tick by. To my first amazing editor Mainga Bhima, here, but now reading a medical textbook: thank you for seeing what Spittlefields could be. To Tig Wallace, many thanks for helping me clarify the worldbuilding. And most recently, the dream-team of Natalie Doherty and India Chambers: thank you both for shaping, finessing and clarifying *City of Stolen Magic* into its current incarnation, and in the process, helping me find my feet and my voice as a writer. To everyone in Penguin Children's, and to my incredible copy-editors Shreeta Shah and Jane Tait – you have been the best, most helpful critics and advocates and I am grateful to you all for believing in me and the love and dedication you have put into making *City of Stolen Magic* come to life.

In the bookshop of my dreams next door are all the writers I've met along the way who have supported me through their words, wisdom and warmth. Sufiya Ahmed, Susmita Bhattacharya, Sita Brahmachari, Joanna Brown, Liz Flanagan, Catherine Johnson, Patrice Lawrence, Amita Murray, Rashmi Sirdeshpande, Yarrow Townsend, Katherine Woodfine: thank you for all the encouragement, friendship, and your beautiful, wonderful stories.

Upon the shelves, too, are the works of certain writers that have helped me upon my journey to becoming a writer. Jane

## ACKNOWLEDGEMENTS

Austen, Charlotte Brontë, Susanna Clarke, Roald Dahl, Judith Kerr, Toni Morrison, A. A. Milne, Sylvia Plath, Salman Rushdie, William Shakespeare: thank you for being my teachers and for expanding my idea of what kinds of stories we can tell. I have learned much of my craft from Philip Pullman's Sally Lockhart and His Dark Materials series. The former is one of my favourite renditions of Victorian London, while the latter showed me that children's writing can tell the most difficult and ambitious stories eloquently, and for all. Jonathan Stroud: your Bartimaeus trilogy taught me that djinn can have a voice and that fantasy can make us laugh, think, rage, and weep. Catherine Johnson: your vividly imagined historical stories, which give voice to those who were silenced by official history-keeping, showed me how I too could listen in to the gaps and make them speak. Finally, Rozina Visram: your pioneering, painstaking historical research on the four-hundred-year presence of South Asians in Britain, conducted before the age of Google, completely changed my idea of how I and my family belong here in the UK. Thank you. This story wouldn't exist without you.

There are countless others who have helped me along the way, and are part of this city behind the *City*. I thank you all, even if I haven't been able to name you here. I hope you'll forgive me for that.

To all of you, my dear readers, who have picked up this book and are reading these words: thank you, too. It is the greatest gift a writer could wish for, and you too live in the city of my heart.